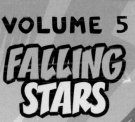

TEEN TITANS GO!™

VOLUME 5

FALLING STARS

Sholly Fisch   Ivan Cohen
Matthew K. Manning   J. Torres   Amanda Deibert
Writers

Marcelo DiChiara   Lea Hernandez
Jeremy Lawson   Erich Owen   Sandy Jarrell
Artists

Franco Riesco   Lea Hernandez
Jeremy Lawson   Erich Owen
Colorists

Wes Abbott
Letterer

Marcelo DiChiara
and Franco Riesco
Collection Cover Artists

SUPERMAN created by Jerry Siegel and Joe Shuster
By special arrangement with the Jerry Siegel family

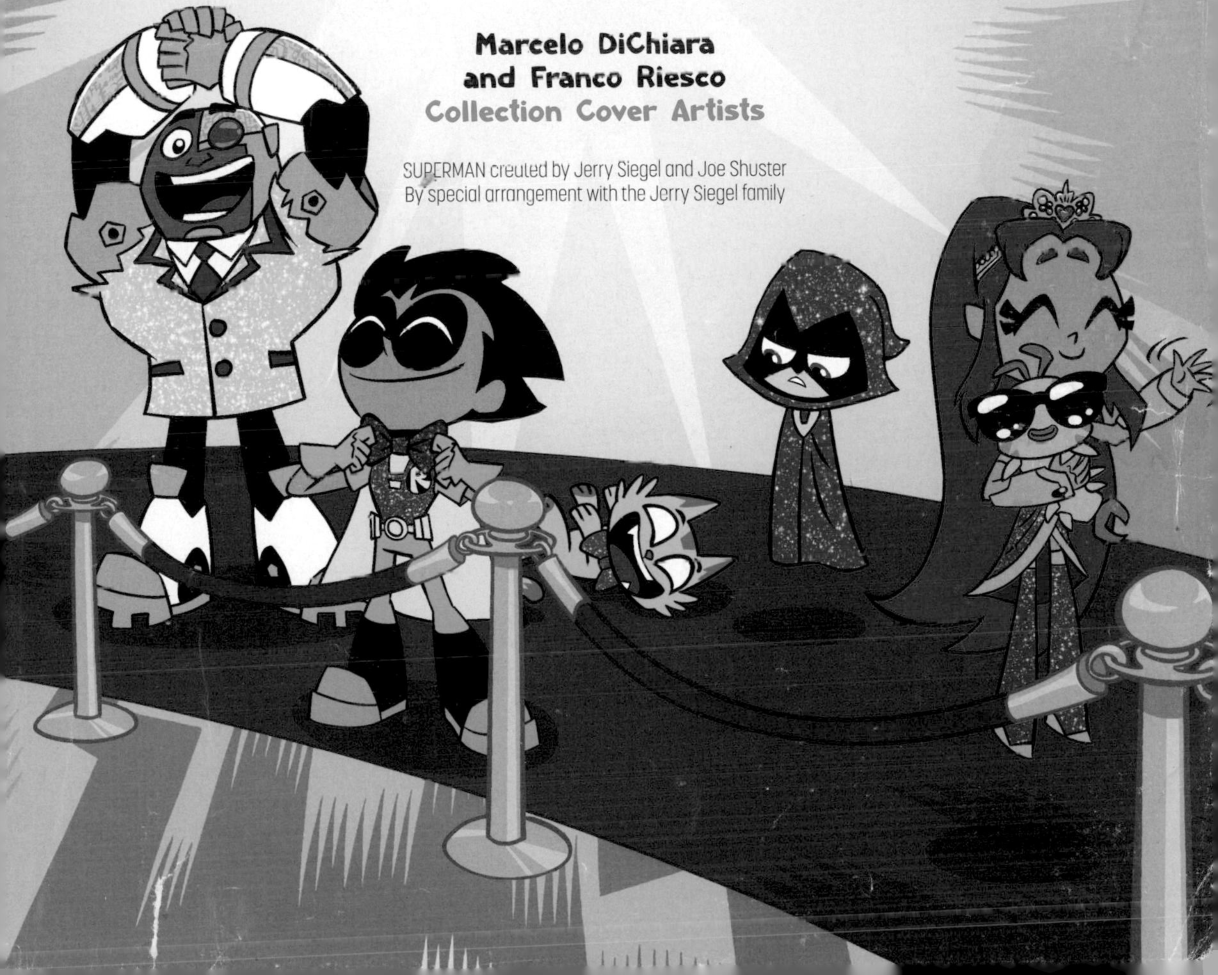

KRISTY QUINN Editor - Original Series
JEB WOODARD Group Editor - Collected Editions ERIKA ROTHBERG Editor - Collected Edition
STEVE COOK Design Director - Books LORI JACKSON Publication Design

BOB HARRAS Senior VP - Editor-in-Chief, DC Comics
PAT McCALLUM Executive Editor, DC Comics

DAN DiDIO Publisher JIM LEE Publisher
AMIT DESAI Executive VP - Business & Marketing Strategy, Direct to Consumer & Global Franchise Management
BOBBIE CHASE VP & Executive Editor, Young Reader & Talent Development
MARK CHIARELLO Senior VP - Art, Design & Collected Editions JOHN CUNNINGHAM Senior VP - Sales & Trade Marketing
BRIAR DARDEN VP - Business Affairs ANNE DePIES Senior VP - Business Strategy, Finance & Administration
DON FALLETTI VP - Manufacturing Operations LAWRENCE GANEM VP - Editorial Administration & Talent Relations
ALISON GILL Senior VP - Manufacturing & Operations JASON GREENBERG VP - Business Strategy & Finance
HANK KANALZ Senior VP - Editorial Strategy & Administration
JAY KOGAN Senior VP - Legal Affairs NICK J. NAPOLITANO VP - Manufacturing Administration
EDDIE SCANNELL VP - Consumer Marketing COURTNEY SIMMONS Senior VP - Publicity & Communications
JIM (SKI) SOKOLOWSKI VP - Comic Book Specialty Sales & Trade Marketing
NANCY SPEARS VP - Mass, Book, Digital Sales & Trade Marketing MICHELE R. WELLS VP - Content Strategy

TEEN TITANS GO! VOLUME 5: FALLING STARS

DC Comics, 2900 West Alameda Ave., Burbank, CA 91505
Printed by LSC Communications, Kendallville, IN, USA. 10/12/18. First Printing.
ISBN: 978-1-4012-7873-1

Library of Congress Cataloging-in-Publication Data is available.

PEFC Certified
This product is from sustainably managed forests and controlled sources
www.pefc.org
PEFC
PEFC/29-31-337

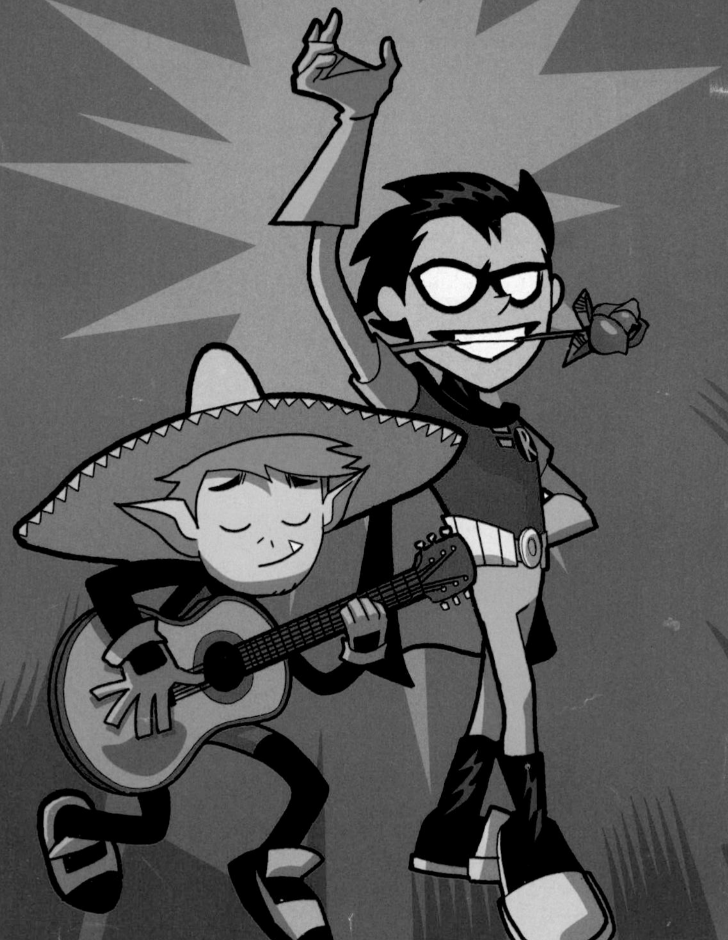

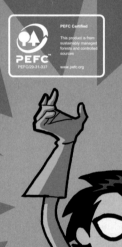

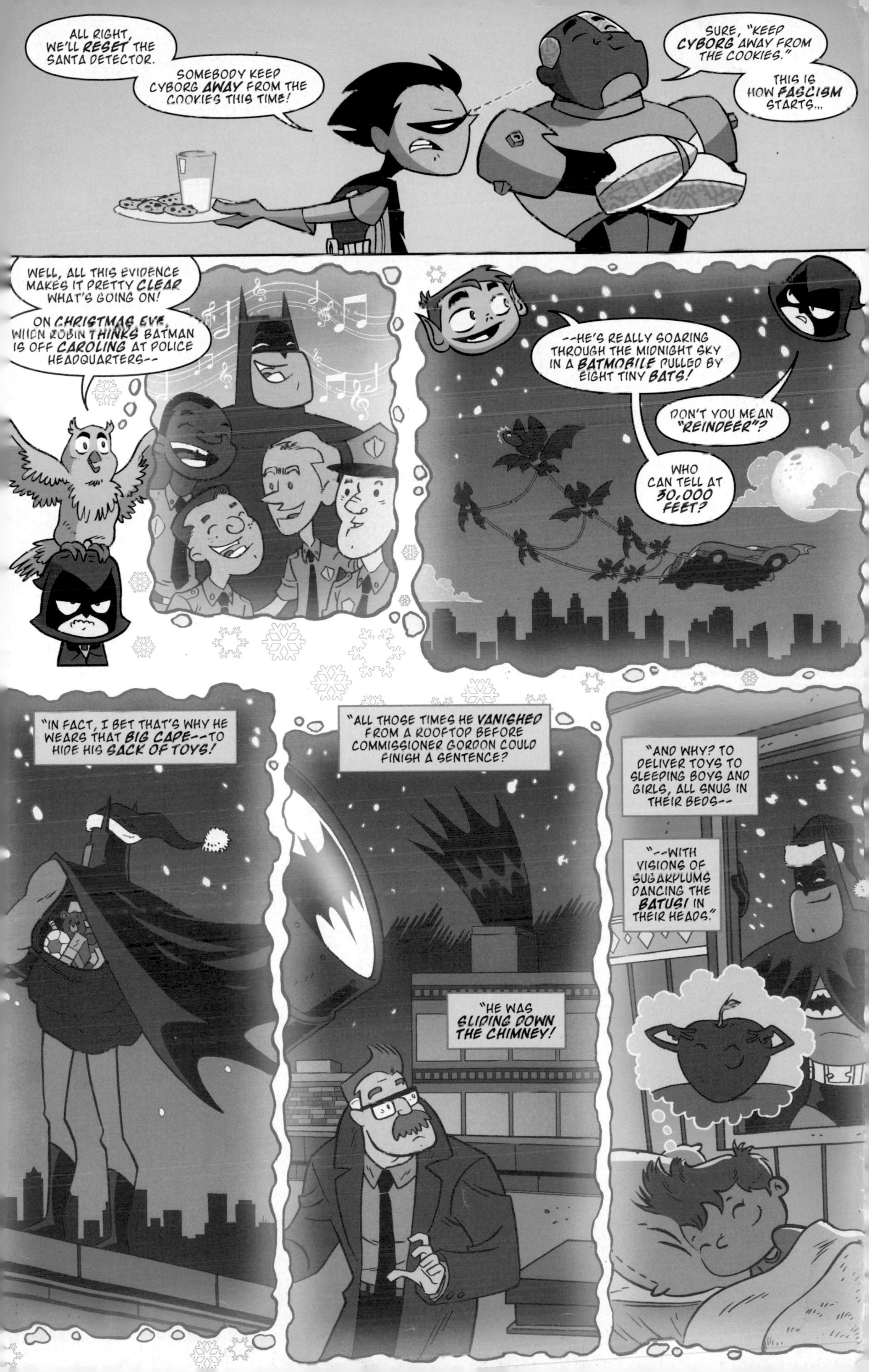
ALL RIGHT, WE'LL RESET THE SANTA DETECTOR.
SOMEBODY KEEP CYBORG AWAY FROM THE COOKIES THIS TIME!
SURE, "KEEP CYBORG AWAY FROM THE COOKIES."
THIS IS HOW FASCISM STARTS...
WELL, ALL THIS EVIDENCE MAKES IT PRETTY CLEAR WHAT'S GOING ON!
ON CHRISTMAS EVE, WHEN ROBIN THINKS BATMAN IS OFF CAROLING AT POLICE HEADQUARTERS--
--HE'S REALLY SOARING THROUGH THE MIDNIGHT SKY IN A BATMOBILE PULLED BY EIGHT TINY BATS!
DON'T YOU MEAN "REINDEER"?
WHO CAN TELL AT 30,000 FEET?
"IN FACT, I BET THAT'S WHY HE WEARS THAT BIG CAPE--TO HIDE HIS SACK OF TOYS!
"ALL THOSE TIMES HE VANISHED FROM A ROOFTOP BEFORE COMMISSIONER GORDON COULD FINISH A SENTENCE?
"HE WAS SLIDING DOWN THE CHIMNEY!
"AND WHY? TO DELIVER TOYS TO SLEEPING BOYS AND GIRLS, ALL SNUG IN THEIR BEDS--
"--WITH VISIONS OF SUGARPLUMS DANCING THE BATUSI IN THEIR HEADS."

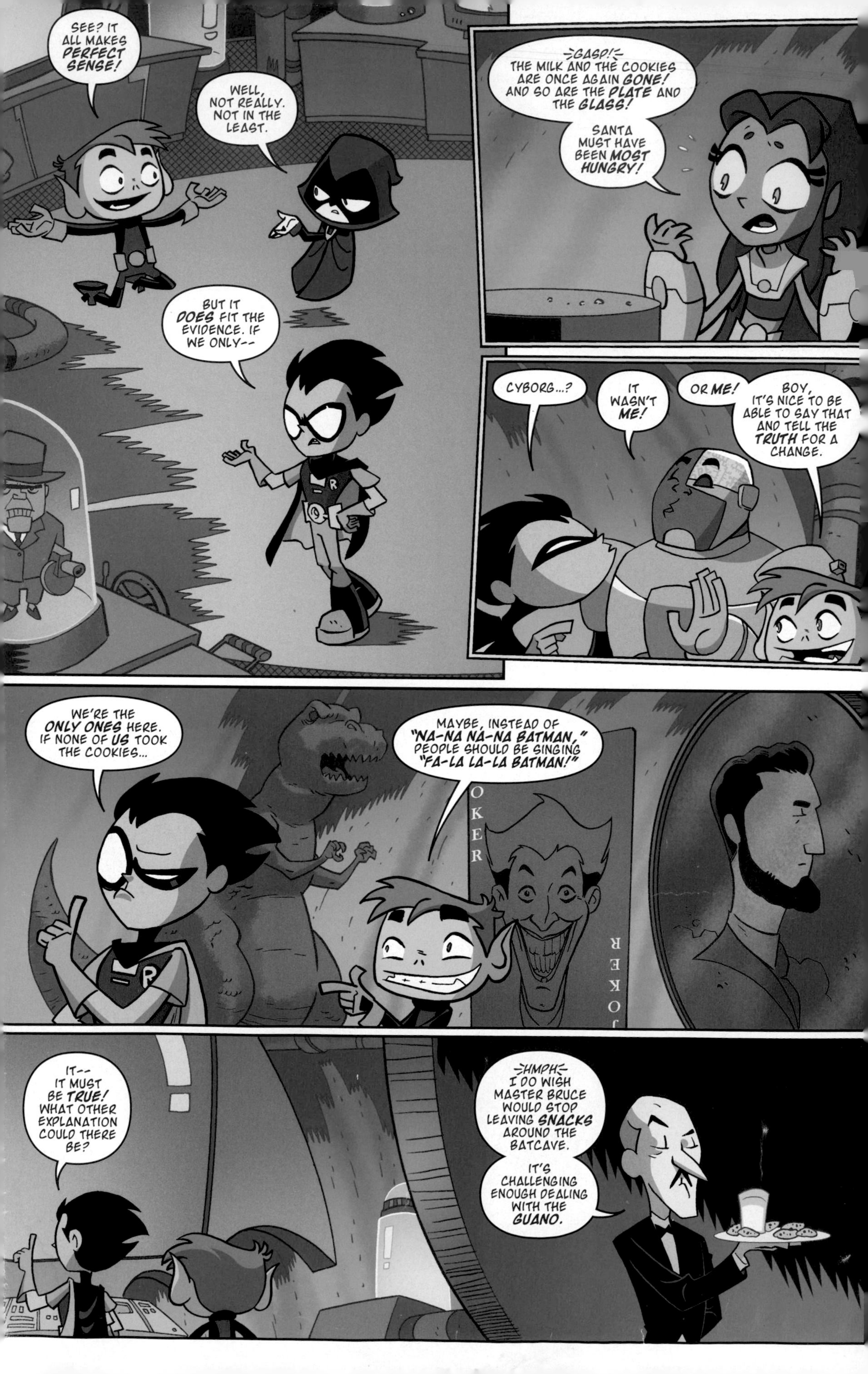
SEE? IT ALL MAKES PERFECT SENSE!
WELL, NOT REALLY. NOT IN THE LEAST.
BUT IT DOES FIT THE EVIDENCE. IF WE ONLY--
GASP! THE MILK AND THE COOKIES ARE ONCE AGAIN GONE! AND SO ARE THE PLATE AND THE GLASS!
SANTA MUST HAVE BEEN MOST HUNGRY!
CYBORG...?
IT WASN'T ME!
OR ME!
BOY, IT'S NICE TO BE ABLE TO SAY THAT AND TELL THE TRUTH FOR A CHANGE.
WE'RE THE ONLY ONES HERE. IF NONE OF US TOOK THE COOKIES...
MAYBE, INSTEAD OF "NA-NA NA-NA BATMAN," PEOPLE SHOULD BE SINGING "FA-LA LA-LA BATMAN!"
OKER
REKOJ
IT-- IT MUST BE TRUE! WHAT OTHER EXPLANATION COULD THERE BE?
HMPH! I DO WISH MASTER BRUCE WOULD STOP LEAVING SNACKS AROUND THE BATCAVE.
IT'S CHALLENGING ENOUGH DEALING WITH THE GUANO.

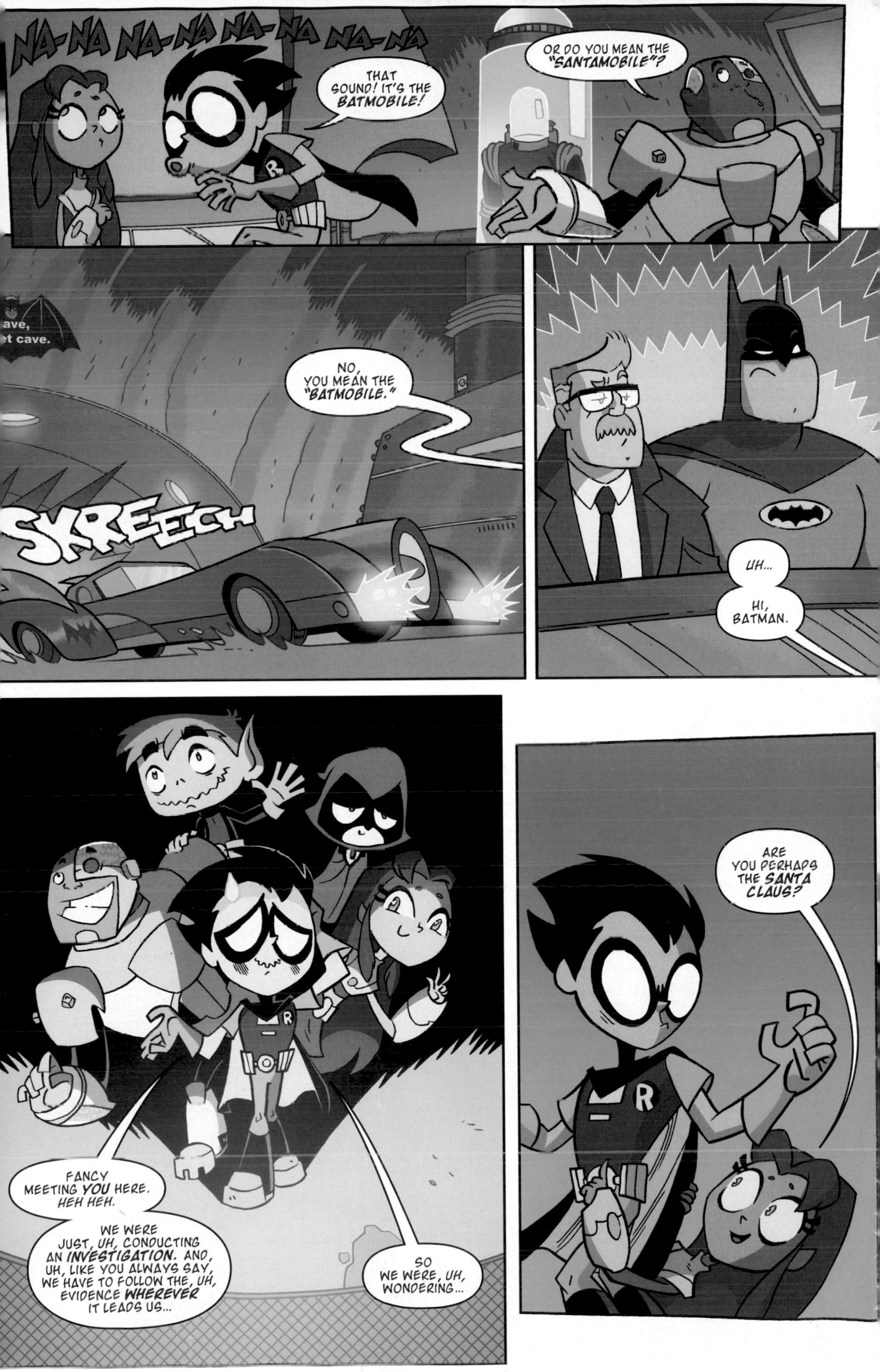
NA-NA NA-NA NA-NA NA-NA
THAT SOUND! IT'S THE *BATMOBILE!*
OR DO YOU MEAN THE *"SANTAMOBILE"?*
SKREEECH
NO, YOU MEAN THE *"BATMOBILE."*
UH...
HI, BATMAN.
FANCY MEETING *YOU* HERE. *HEH HEH.*
WE WERE JUST, UH, CONDUCTING AN *INVESTIGATION.* AND, UH, LIKE YOU ALWAYS SAY, WE HAVE TO FOLLOW THE, UH, EVIDENCE ***WHEREVER*** IT LEADS US...
SO WE WERE, UH, WONDERING...
ARE YOU PERHAPS THE *SANTA CLAUS?*

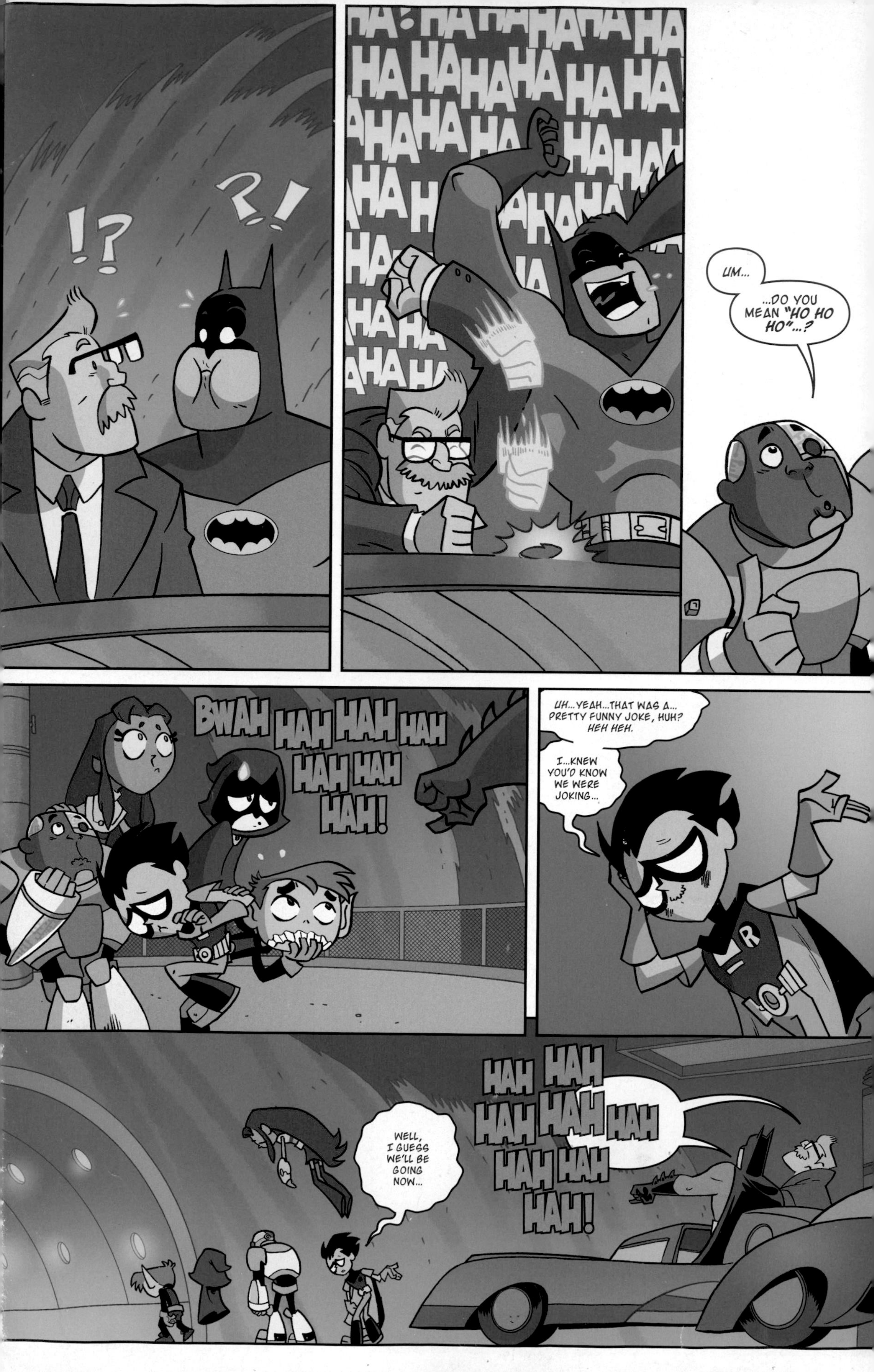
!?
?!
HA! HA HAHAHAHA HA
HA HAHAHA HA HA
UM...
...DO YOU MEAN "HO HO HO"...?
BWAH HAH HAH HAH HAH HAH HAH!
UH...YEAH...THAT WAS A... PRETTY FUNNY JOKE, HUH? HEH HEH.
I...KNEW YOU'D KNOW WE WERE JOKING...
HAH HAH HAH HAH HAH HAH HAH HAH!
WELL, I GUESS WE'LL BE GOING NOW...

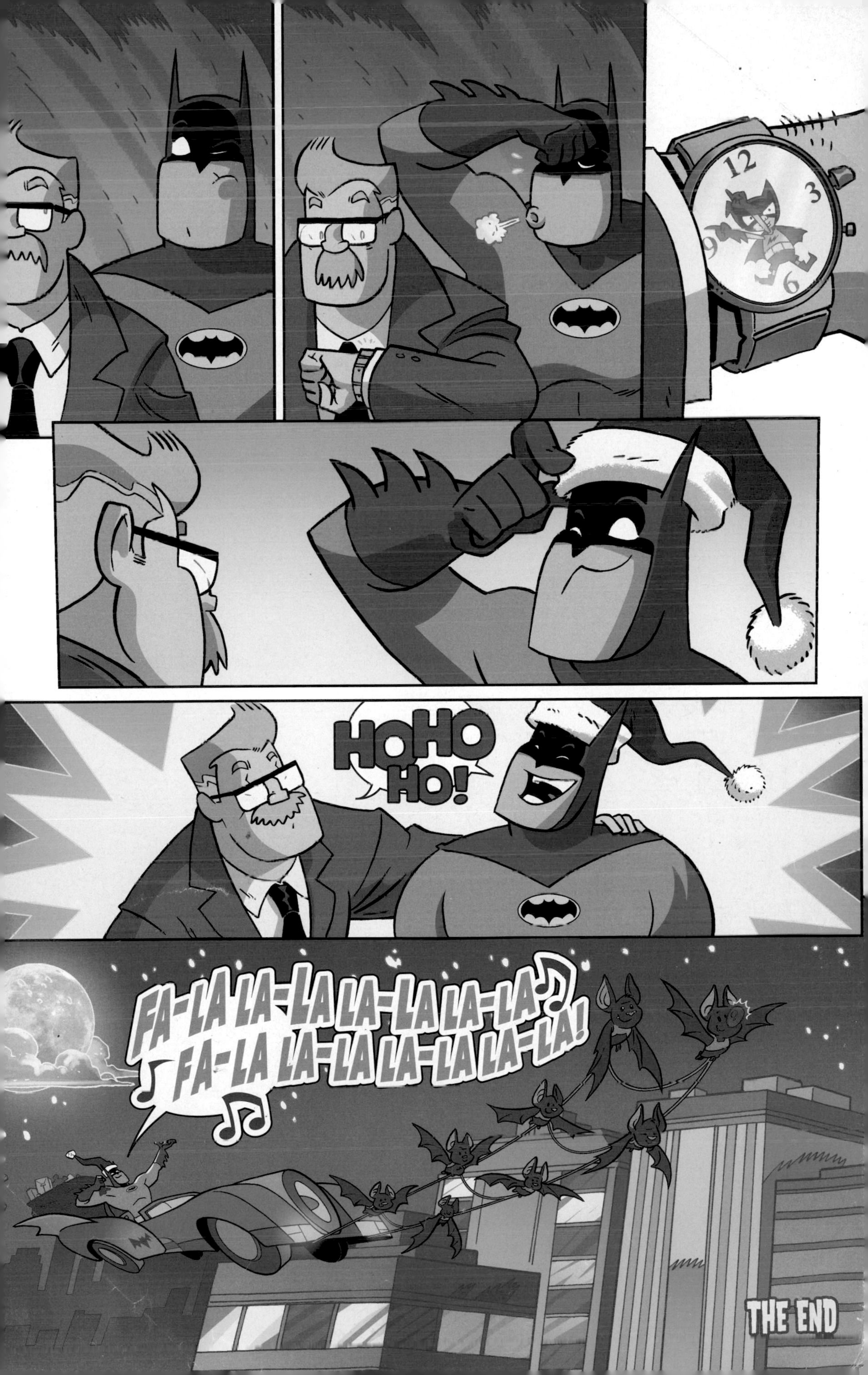

HOHO HO!
FA-LA LA-LA LA-LA LA-LA
FA-LA LA-LA LA-LA LA-LA!
THE END

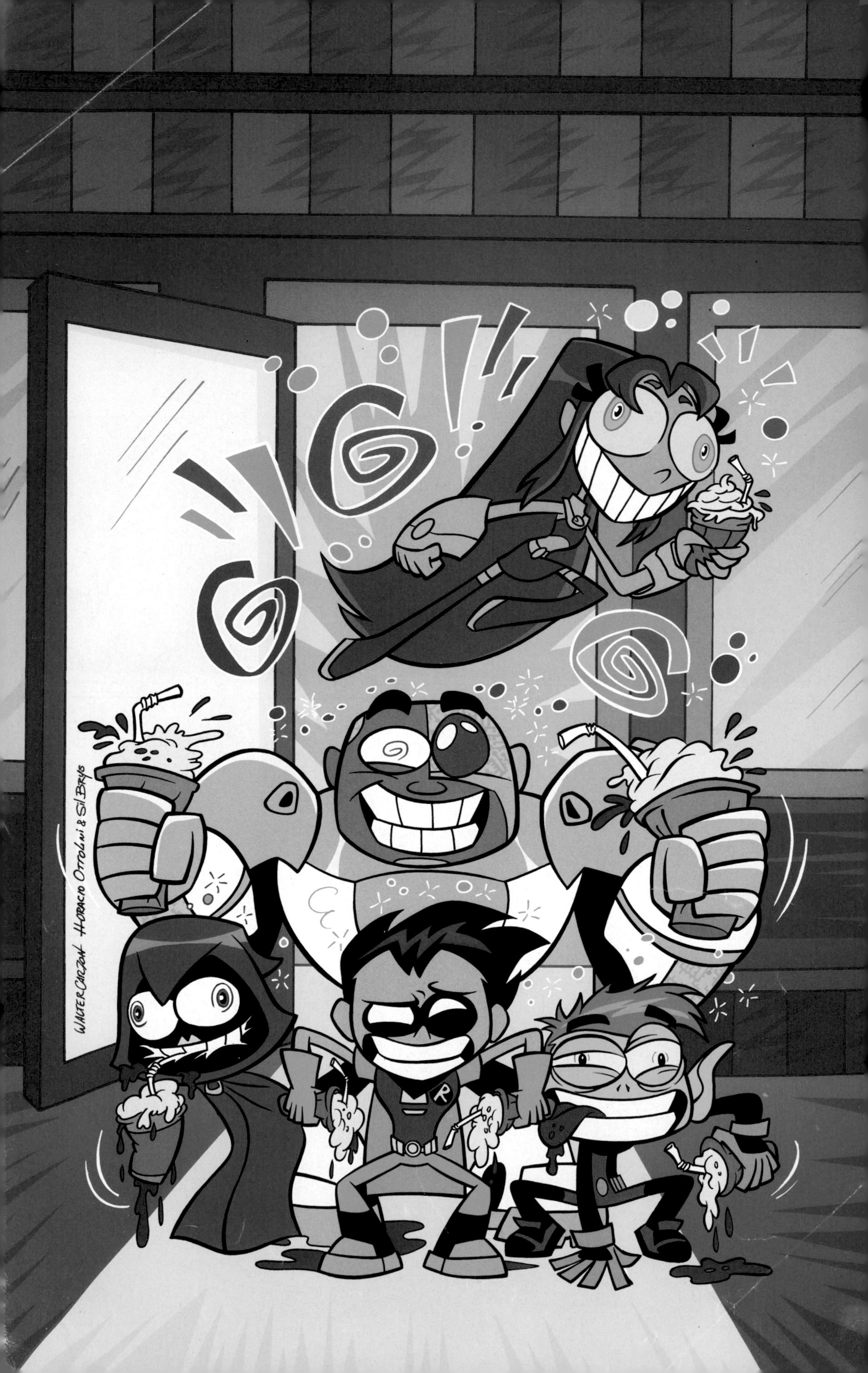
WALTER CARZON HORACIO OTTOLINI & SIL BRYS

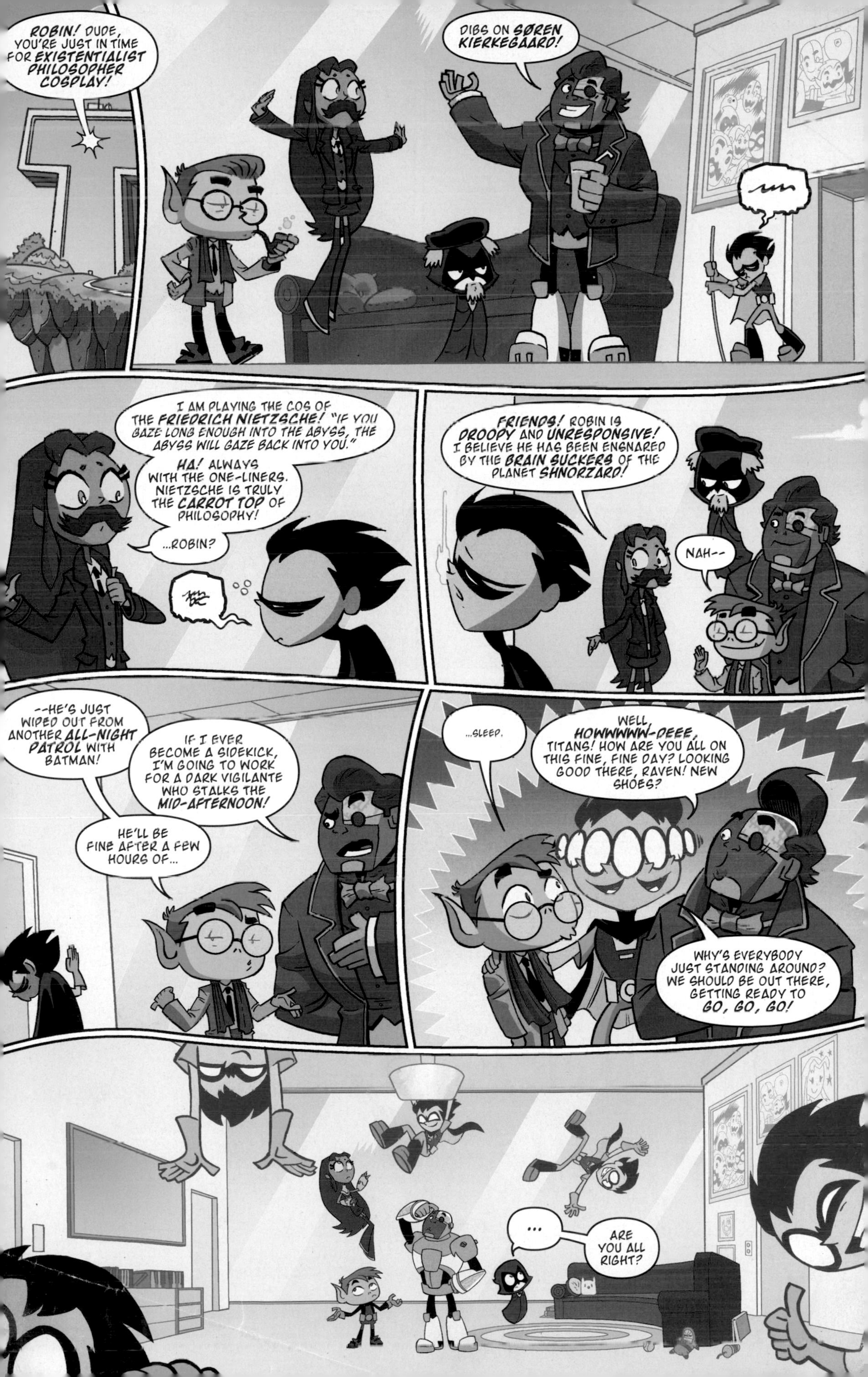
ROBIN! DUDE, YOU'RE JUST IN TIME FOR EXISTENTIALIST PHILOSOPHER COSPLAY!
DIBS ON SØREN KIERKEGAARD!
I AM PLAYING THE COS OF THE FRIEDRICH NIETZSCHE! "IF YOU GAZE LONG ENOUGH INTO THE ABYSS, THE ABYSS WILL GAZE BACK INTO YOU."
HA! ALWAYS WITH THE ONE-LINERS. NIETZSCHE IS TRULY THE CARROT TOP OF PHILOSOPHY!
...ROBIN?
FRIENDS! ROBIN IS DROOPY AND UNRESPONSIVE! I BELIEVE HE HAS BEEN ENSNARED BY THE BRAIN SUCKERS OF THE PLANET SHNORZARD!
NAH--
--HE'S JUST WIPED OUT FROM ANOTHER ALL-NIGHT PATROL WITH BATMAN!
IF I EVER BECOME A SIDEKICK, I'M GOING TO WORK FOR A DARK VIGILANTE WHO STALKS THE MID-AFTERNOON!
HE'LL BE FINE AFTER A FEW HOURS OF...
...SLEEP.
WELL, HOWWWWW-DEEE, TITANS! HOW ARE YOU ALL ON THIS FINE, FINE DAY? LOOKING GOOD THERE, RAVEN! NEW SHOES?
WHY'S EVERYBODY JUST STANDING AROUND? WE SHOULD BE OUT THERE, GETTING READY TO GO, GO, GO!
...
ARE YOU ALL RIGHT?

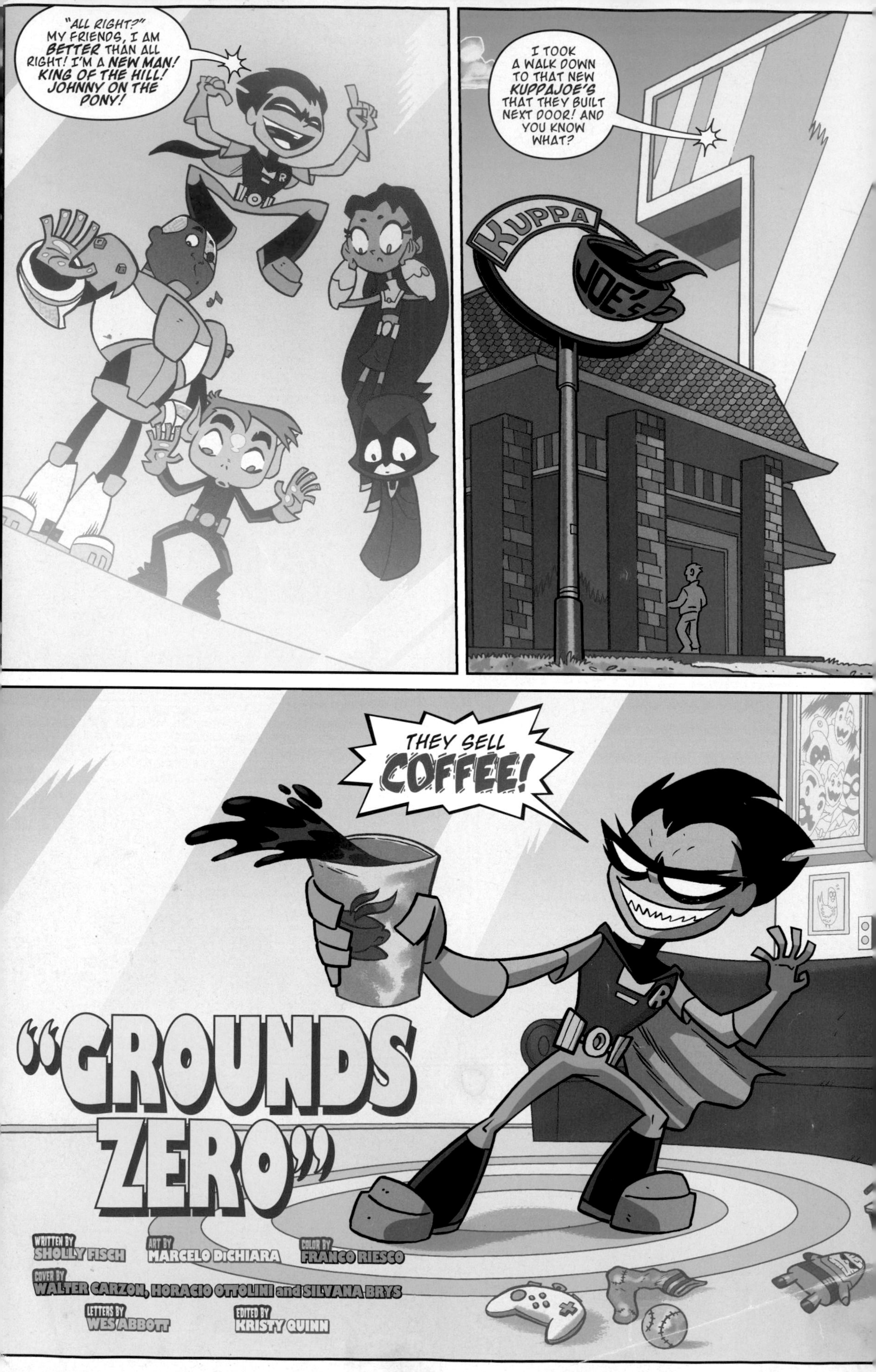

"ALL RIGHT?" MY FRIENDS, I AM BETTER THAN ALL RIGHT! I'M A NEW MAN! KING OF THE HILL! JOHNNY ON THE PONY!
I TOOK A WALK DOWN TO THAT NEW KUPPAJOE'S THAT THEY BUILT NEXT DOOR! AND YOU KNOW WHAT?
KUPPA JOE'S
THEY SELL COFFEE!
"GROUNDS ZERO"
WRITTEN BY SHOLLY FISCH
ART BY MARCELO DiCHIARA
COLOR BY FRANCO RIESCO
COVER BY WALTER CARZON, HORACIO OTTOLINI and SILVANA BRYS
LETTERS BY WES ABBOTT
EDITED BY KRISTY QUINN

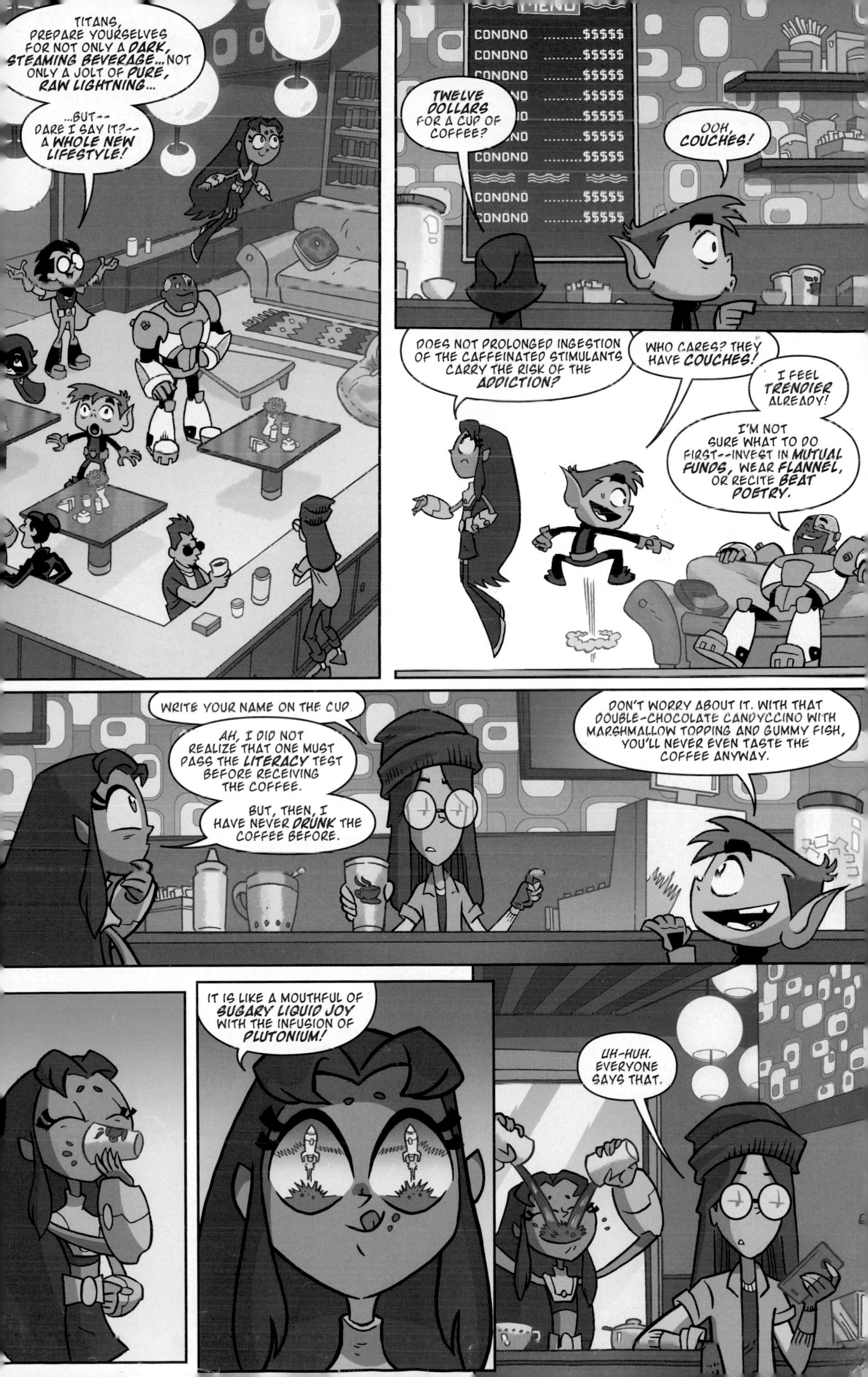

TITANS, PREPARE YOURSELVES FOR NOT ONLY A DARK, STEAMING BEVERAGE... NOT ONLY A JOLT OF PURE, RAW LIGHTNING...
...BUT-- DARE I SAY IT?-- A WHOLE NEW LIFESTYLE!
TWELVE DOLLARS FOR A CUP OF COFFEE?
OOH, COUCHES!
DOES NOT PROLONGED INGESTION OF THE CAFFEINATED STIMULANTS CARRY THE RISK OF THE ADDICTION?
WHO CARES? THEY HAVE COUCHES!
I FEEL TRENDIER ALREADY!
I'M NOT SURE WHAT TO DO FIRST--INVEST IN MUTUAL FUNDS, WEAR FLANNEL, OR RECITE BEAT POETRY.
WRITE YOUR NAME ON THE CUP.
AH, I DID NOT REALIZE THAT ONE MUST PASS THE LITERACY TEST BEFORE RECEIVING THE COFFEE.
BUT, THEN, I HAVE NEVER DRUNK THE COFFEE BEFORE.
DON'T WORRY ABOUT IT. WITH THAT DOUBLE-CHOCOLATE CANDYCCINO WITH MARSHMALLOW TOPPING AND GUMMY FISH, YOU'LL NEVER EVEN TASTE THE COFFEE ANYWAY.
IT IS LIKE A MOUTHFUL OF SUGARY LIQUID JOY WITH THE INFUSION OF PLUTONIUM!
UH-HUH. EVERYONE SAYS THAT.

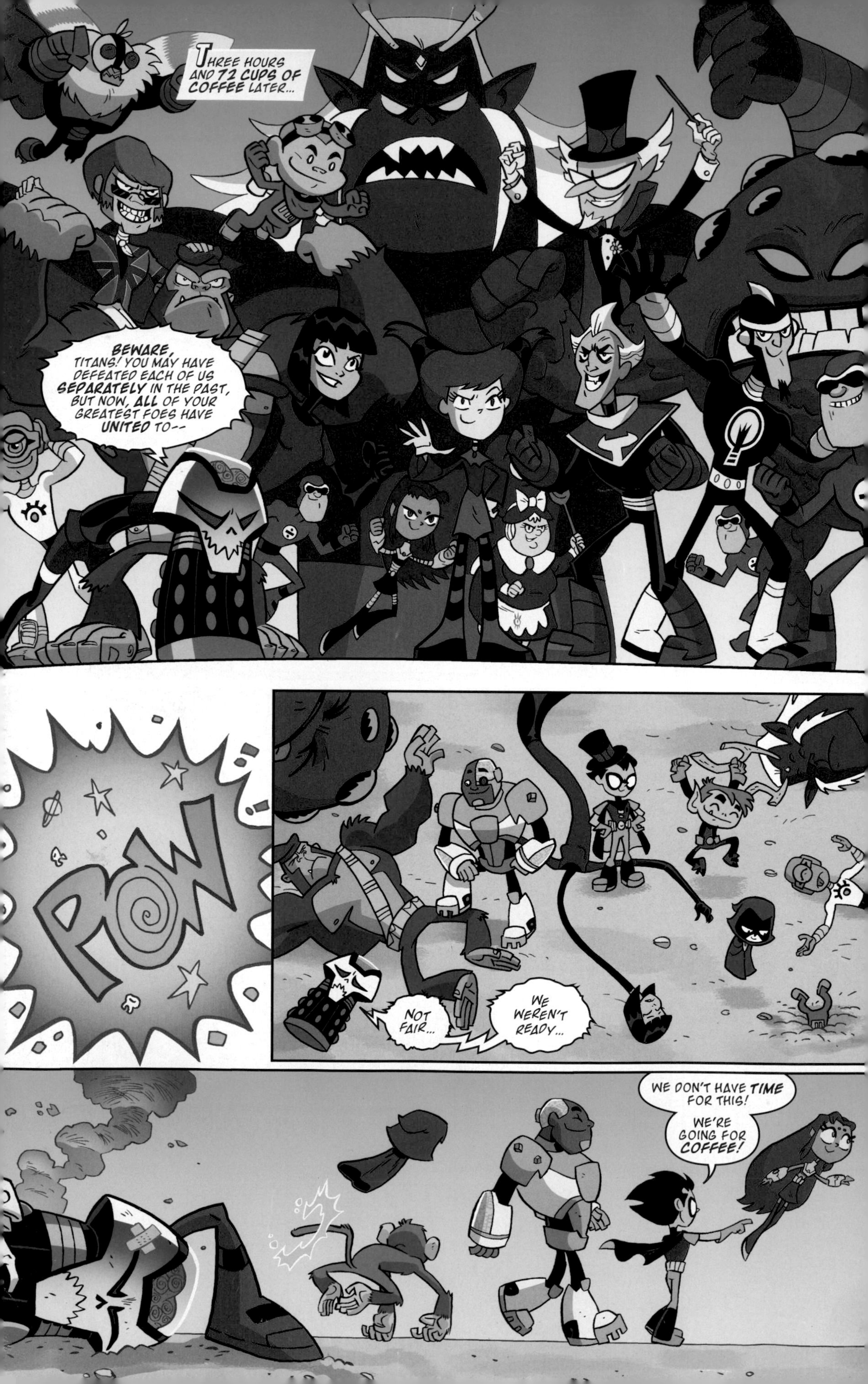
THREE HOURS AND 72 CUPS OF COFFEE LATER...
BEWARE, TITANS! YOU MAY HAVE DEFEATED EACH OF US SEPARATELY IN THE PAST, BUT NOW, ALL OF YOUR GREATEST FOES HAVE UNITED TO--
POW
NOT FAIR...
WE WEREN'T READY...
WE DON'T HAVE TIME FOR THIS!
WE'RE GOING FOR COFFEE!

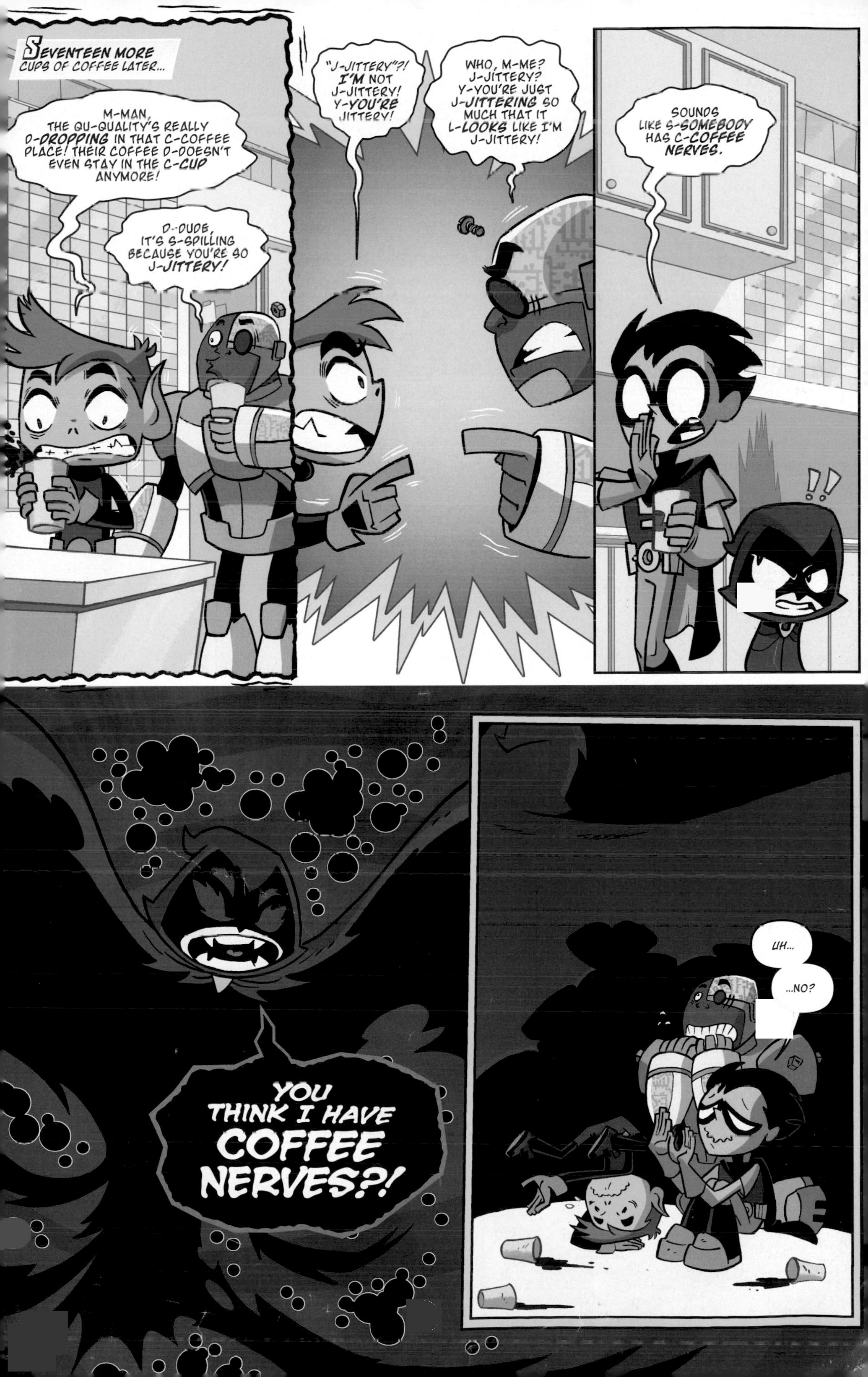
SEVENTEEN MORE CUPS OF COFFEE LATER...
M-MAN, THE QU-QUALITY'S REALLY D-DROPPING IN THAT C-COFFEE PLACE! THEIR COFFEE D-DOESN'T EVEN STAY IN THE C-CUP ANYMORE!
D--DUDE, IT'S S-SPILLING BECAUSE YOU'RE SO J-JITTERY!
"J-JITTERY"?! I'M NOT J-JITTERY! Y-YOU'RE JITTERY!
WHO, M-ME? J-JITTERY? Y-YOU'RE JUST J-JITTERING SO MUCH THAT IT L-LOOKS LIKE I'M J-JITTERY!
SOUNDS LIKE S-SOMEBODY HAS C-COFFEE NERVES.
!!
YOU THINK I HAVE COFFEE NERVES?!
UH...
...NO?

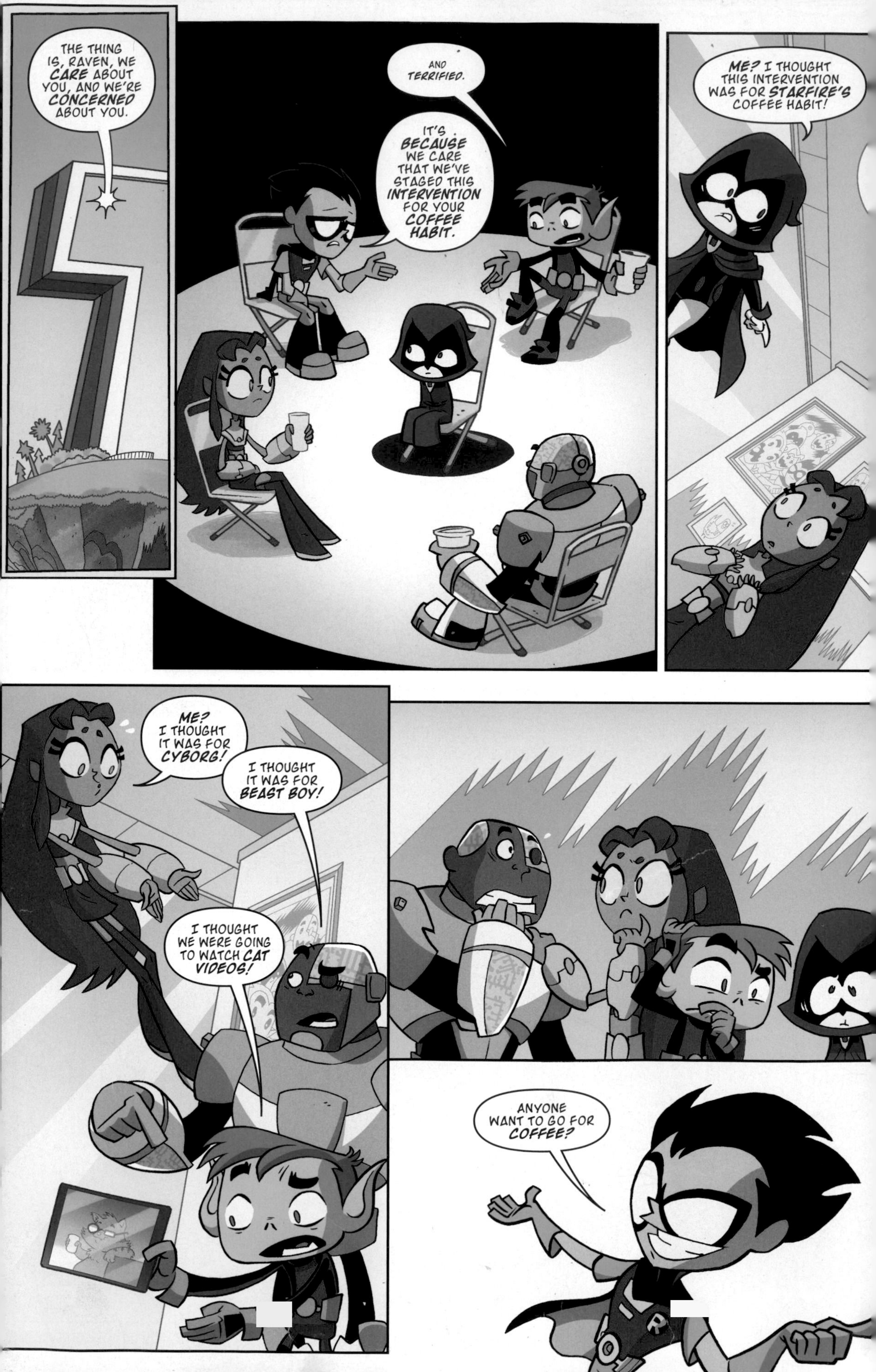
THE THING IS, RAVEN, WE CARE ABOUT YOU, AND WE'RE CONCERNED ABOUT YOU.
IT'S BECAUSE WE CARE THAT WE'VE STAGED THIS INTERVENTION FOR YOUR COFFEE HABIT.
AND TERRIFIED.
ME? I THOUGHT THIS INTERVENTION WAS FOR STARFIRE'S COFFEE HABIT!
ME? I THOUGHT IT WAS FOR CYBORG!
I THOUGHT IT WAS FOR BEAST BOY!
I THOUGHT WE WERE GOING TO WATCH CAT VIDEOS!
ANYONE WANT TO GO FOR COFFEE?

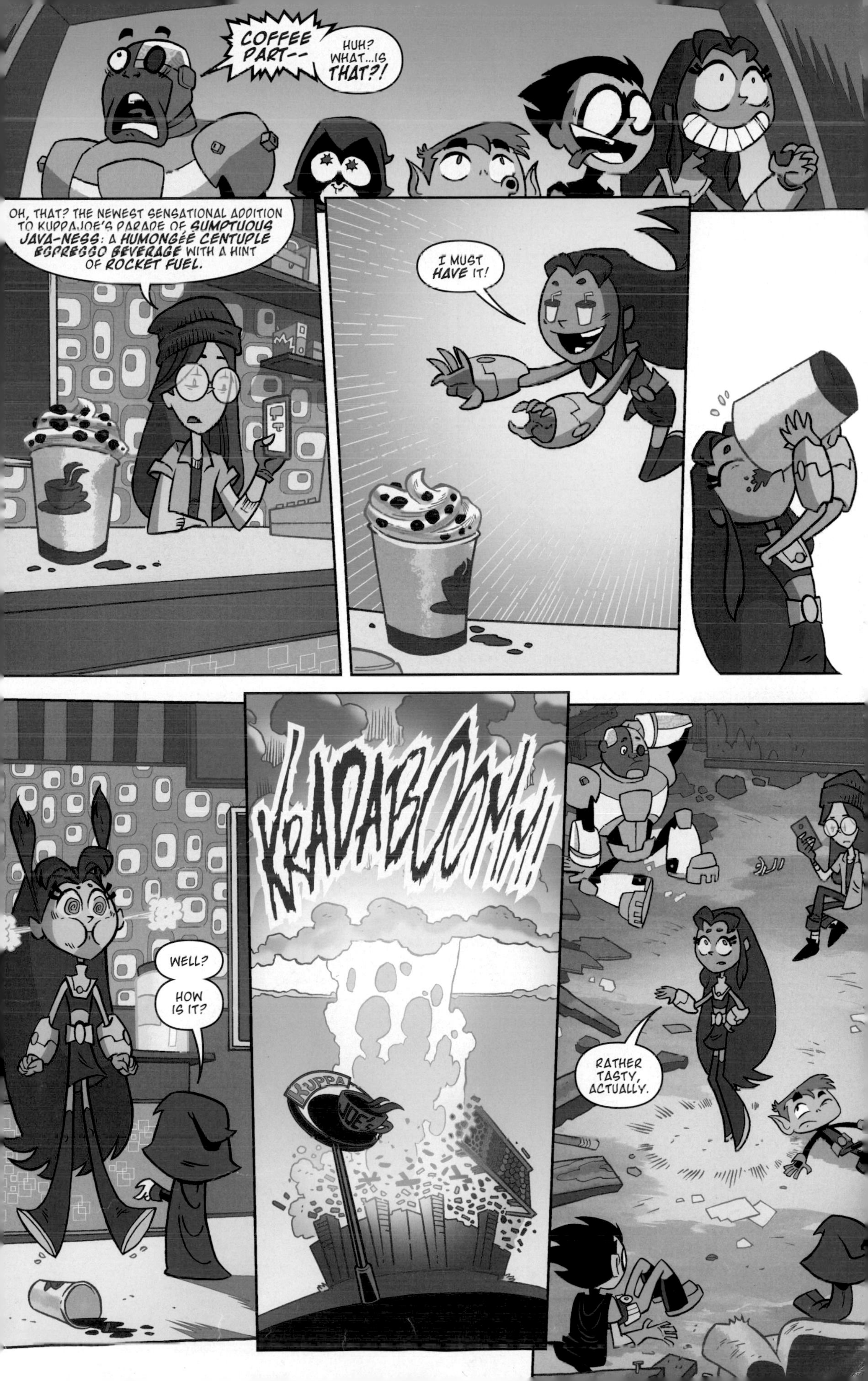

COFFEE PART--
HUH? WHAT...IS THAT?!
OH, THAT? THE NEWEST SENSATIONAL ADDITION TO KUPPAJOE'S PARADE OF SUMPTUOUS JAVA-NESS: A HUMONGÉE CENTUPLE ESPRESSO BEVERAGE WITH A HINT OF ROCKET FUEL.
I MUST HAVE IT!
WELL?
HOW IS IT?
KRADABOOM!
KUPPA JOE'S
RATHER TASTY, ACTUALLY.

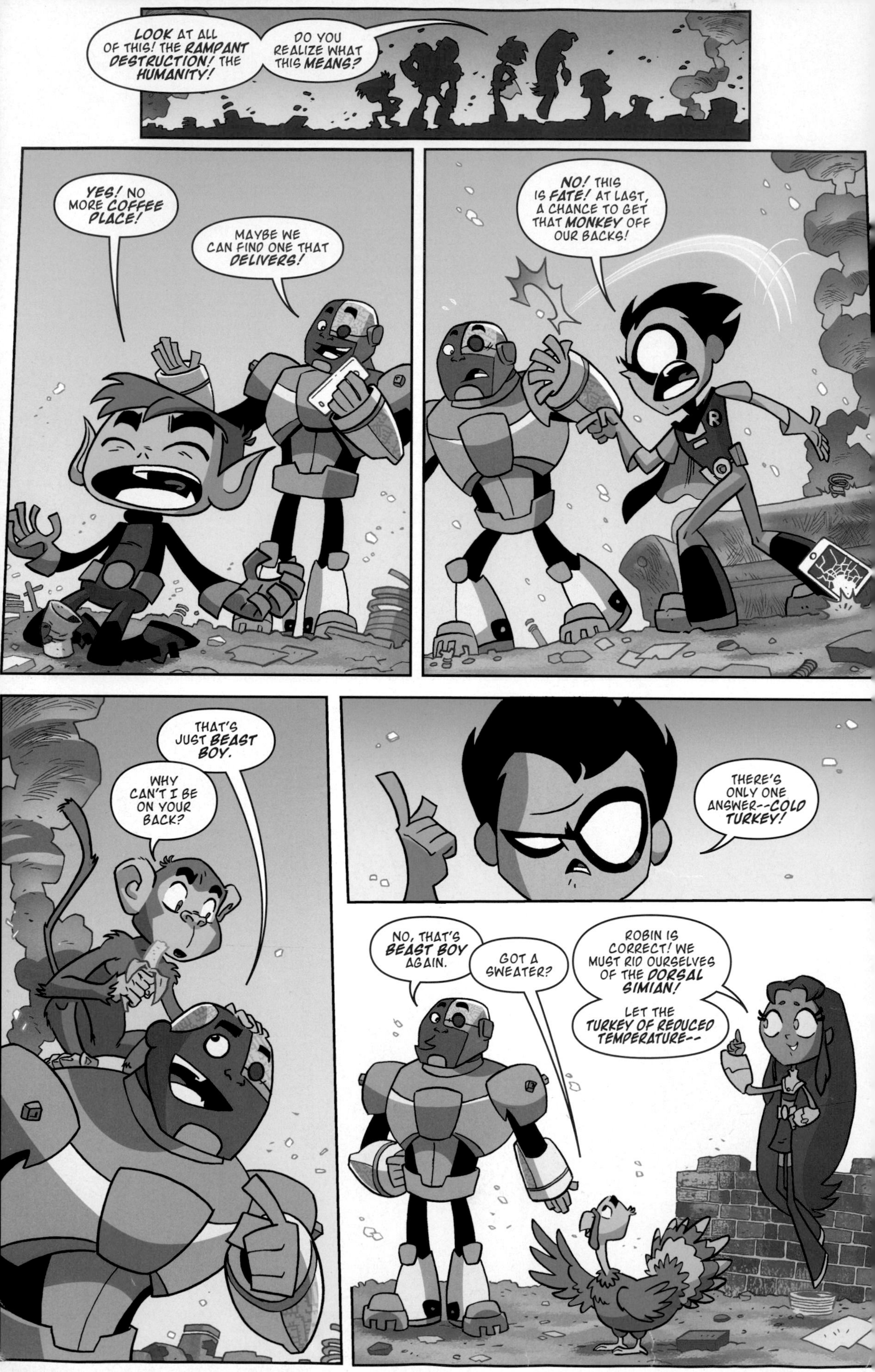
LOOK AT ALL OF THIS! THE RAMPANT DESTRUCTION! THE HUMANITY!
DO YOU REALIZE WHAT THIS MEANS?
YES! NO MORE COFFEE PLACE!
MAYBE WE CAN FIND ONE THAT DELIVERS!
NO! THIS IS FATE! AT LAST, A CHANCE TO GET THAT MONKEY OFF OUR BACKS!
THAT'S JUST BEAST BOY.
WHY CAN'T I BE ON YOUR BACK?
THERE'S ONLY ONE ANSWER--COLD TURKEY!
NO, THAT'S BEAST BOY AGAIN.
GOT A SWEATER?
ROBIN IS CORRECT! WE MUST RID OURSELVES OF THE DORSAL SIMIAN!
LET THE TURKEY OF REDUCED TEMPERATURE--

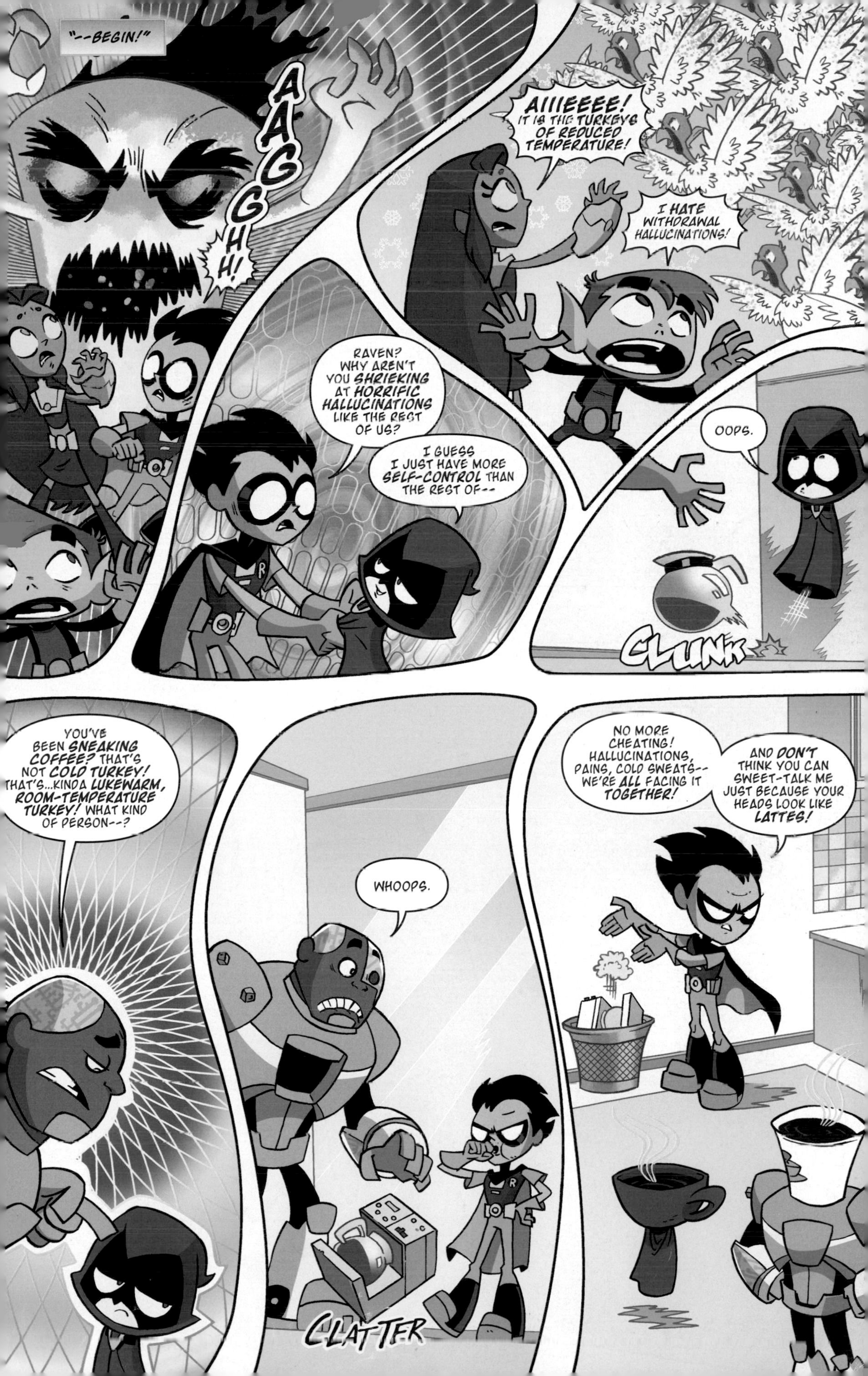
"--BEGIN!"
AAGGHH!
AIIIEEEE! IT IS THE TURKEYS OF REDUCED TEMPERATURE!
I HATE WITHDRAWAL HALLUCINATIONS!
RAVEN? WHY AREN'T YOU SHRIEKING AT HORRIFIC HALLUCINATIONS LIKE THE REST OF US?
I GUESS I JUST HAVE MORE SELF-CONTROL THAN THE REST OF--
OOPS.
CLUNK
YOU'VE BEEN SNEAKING COFFEE? THAT'S NOT COLD TURKEY! THAT'S...KINDA LUKEWARM, ROOM-TEMPERATURE TURKEY! WHAT KIND OF PERSON--?
WHOOPS.
CLATTER
NO MORE CHEATING! HALLUCINATIONS, PAINS, COLD SWEATS-- WE'RE ALL FACING IT TOGETHER!
AND DON'T THINK YOU CAN SWEET-TALK ME JUST BECAUSE YOUR HEADS LOOK LIKE LATTES!

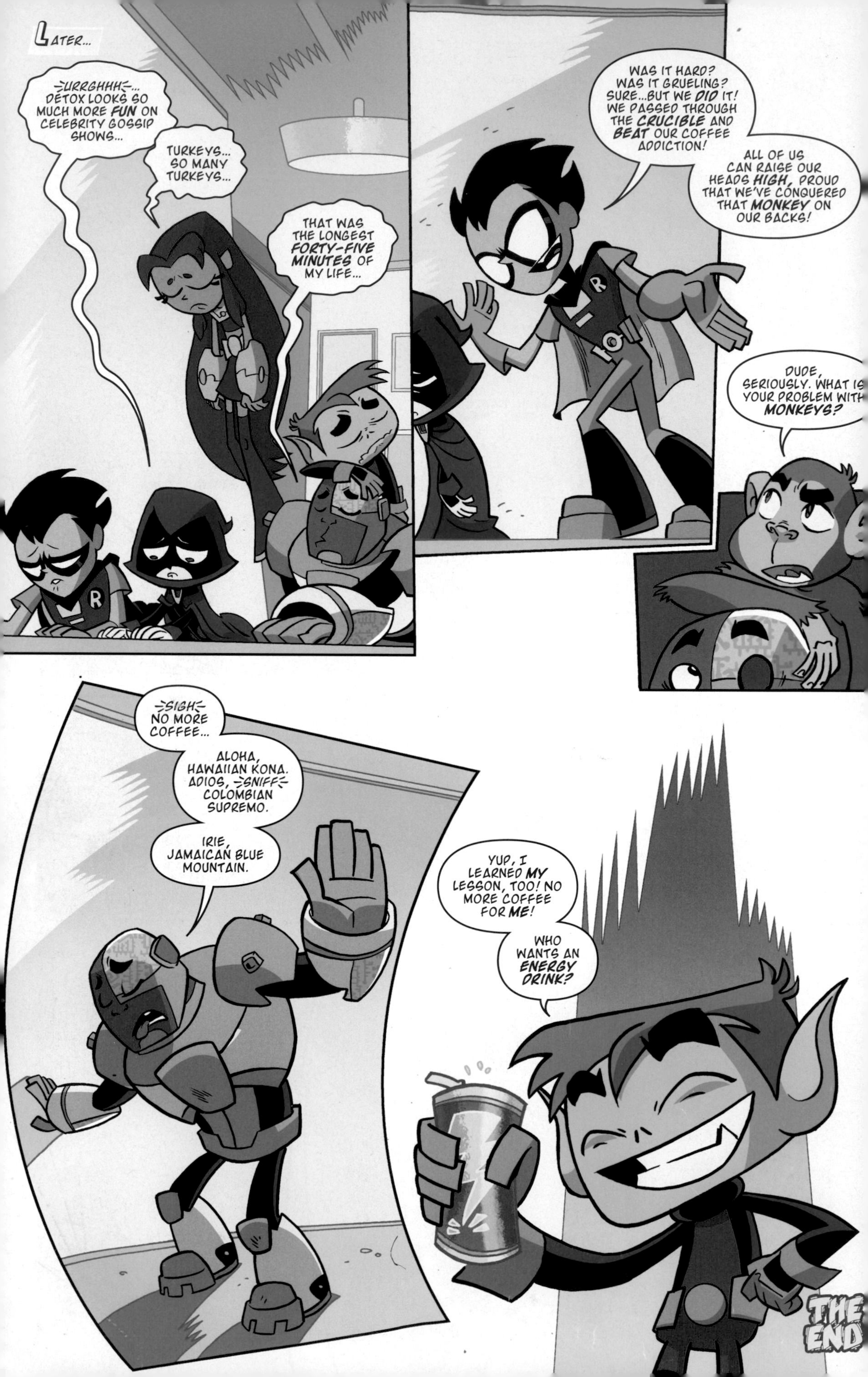
LATER...
-URRGHHH-... DETOX LOOKS SO MUCH MORE FUN ON CELEBRITY GOSSIP SHOWS...
TURKEYS... SO MANY TURKEYS...
THAT WAS THE LONGEST FORTY-FIVE MINUTES OF MY LIFE...
WAS IT HARD? WAS IT GRUELING? SURE...BUT WE DID IT! WE PASSED THROUGH THE CRUCIBLE AND BEAT OUR COFFEE ADDICTION!
ALL OF US CAN RAISE OUR HEADS HIGH, PROUD THAT WE'VE CONQUERED THAT MONKEY ON OUR BACKS!
DUDE, SERIOUSLY. WHAT IS YOUR PROBLEM WITH MONKEYS?
-SIGH- NO MORE COFFEE...
ALOHA, HAWAIIAN KONA. ADIOS, -SNIFF- COLOMBIAN SUPREMO.
IRIE, JAMAICAN BLUE MOUNTAIN.
YUP, I LEARNED MY LESSON, TOO! NO MORE COFFEE FOR ME!
WHO WANTS AN ENERGY DRINK?
THE END

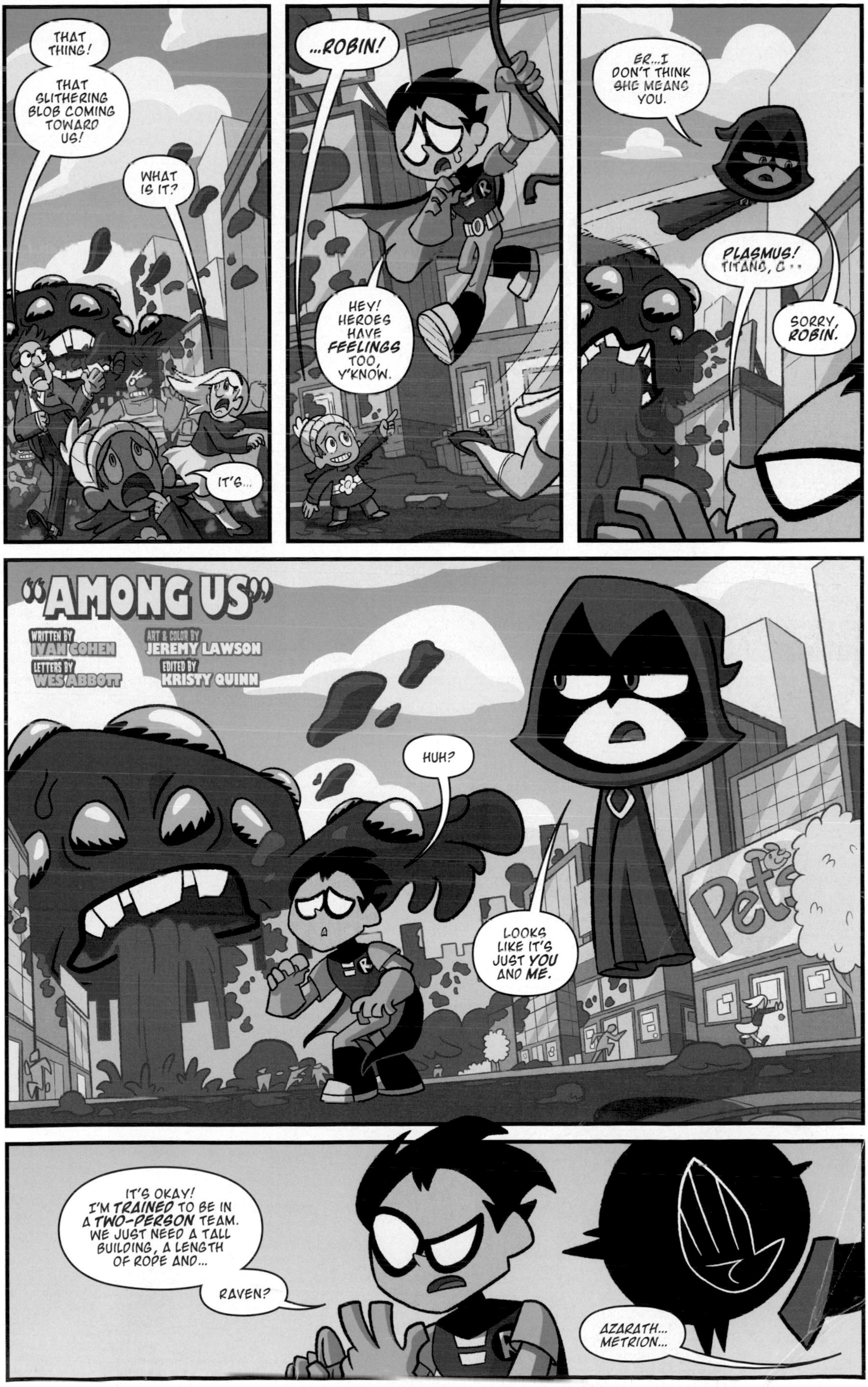
THAT THING!
THAT SLITHERING BLOB COMING TOWARD US!
WHAT IS IT?
IT'S...
...ROBIN!
HEY! HEROES HAVE FEELINGS TOO, Y'KNOW.
ER...I DON'T THINK SHE MEANS YOU.
PLASMUS! TITANS, G...
SORRY, ROBIN.
"AMONG US"
WRITTEN BY IVAN COHEN
ART & COLOR BY JEREMY LAWSON
LETTERS BY WES ABBOTT
EDITED BY KRISTY QUINN
HUH?
LOOKS LIKE IT'S JUST YOU AND ME.
Pets
IT'S OKAY! I'M TRAINED TO BE IN A TWO-PERSON TEAM. WE JUST NEED A TALL BUILDING, A LENGTH OF ROPE AND...
RAVEN?
AZARATH... METRION...

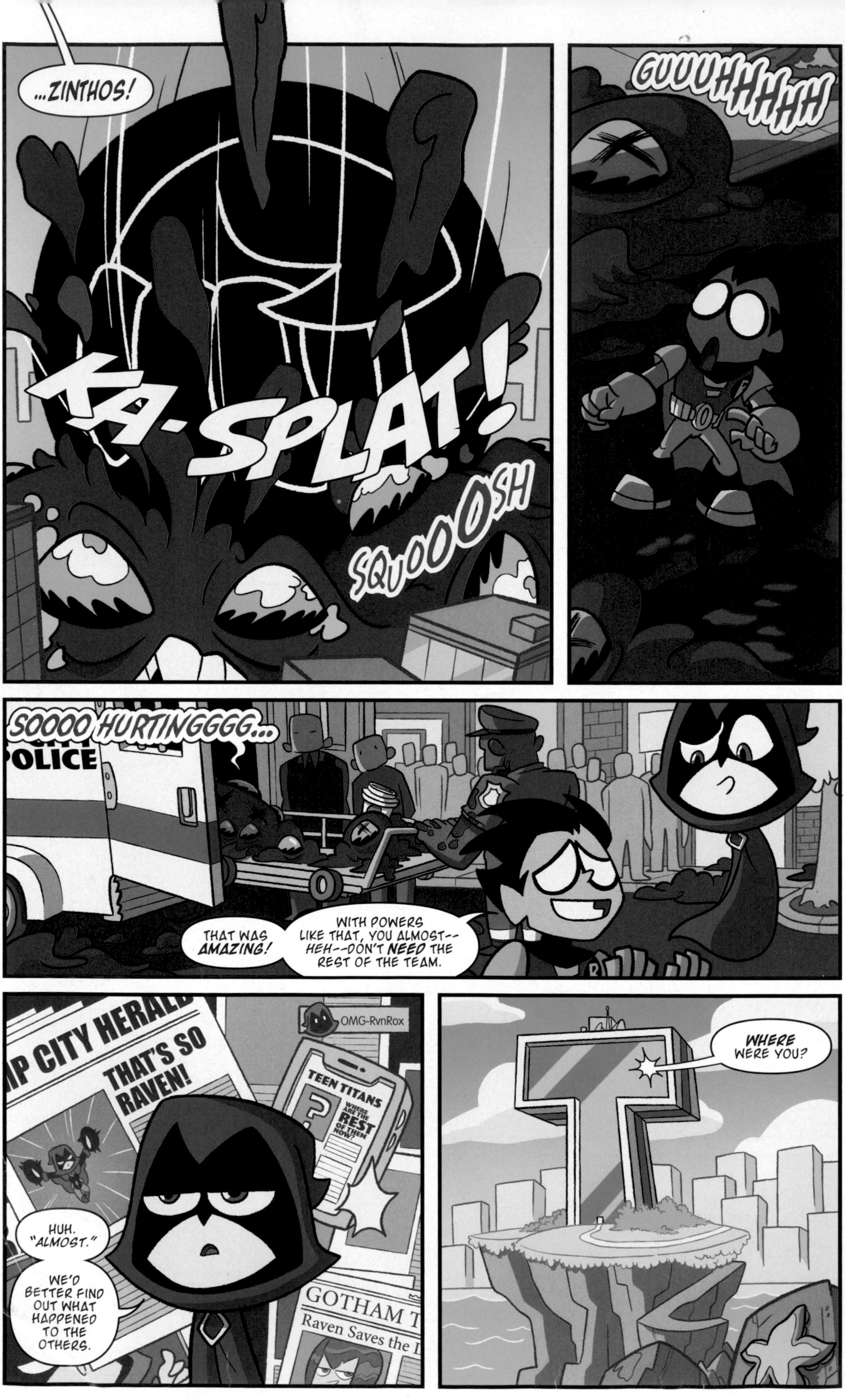
...ZINTHOS!
KA-SPLAT!
SQUOOOOSH
GUUUHHHHHH
SOOOO HURTINGGGG...
POLICE
THAT WAS AMAZING!
WITH POWERS LIKE THAT, YOU ALMOST--HEH--DON'T NEED THE REST OF THE TEAM.
P CITY HERALD
THAT'S SO RAVEN!
OMG-RvnRox
TEEN TITANS
WHERE ARE THE REST OF THEM NOW?
HUH. "ALMOST."
WE'D BETTER FIND OUT WHAT HAPPENED TO THE OTHERS.
GOTHAM T
Raven Saves the
WHERE WERE YOU?

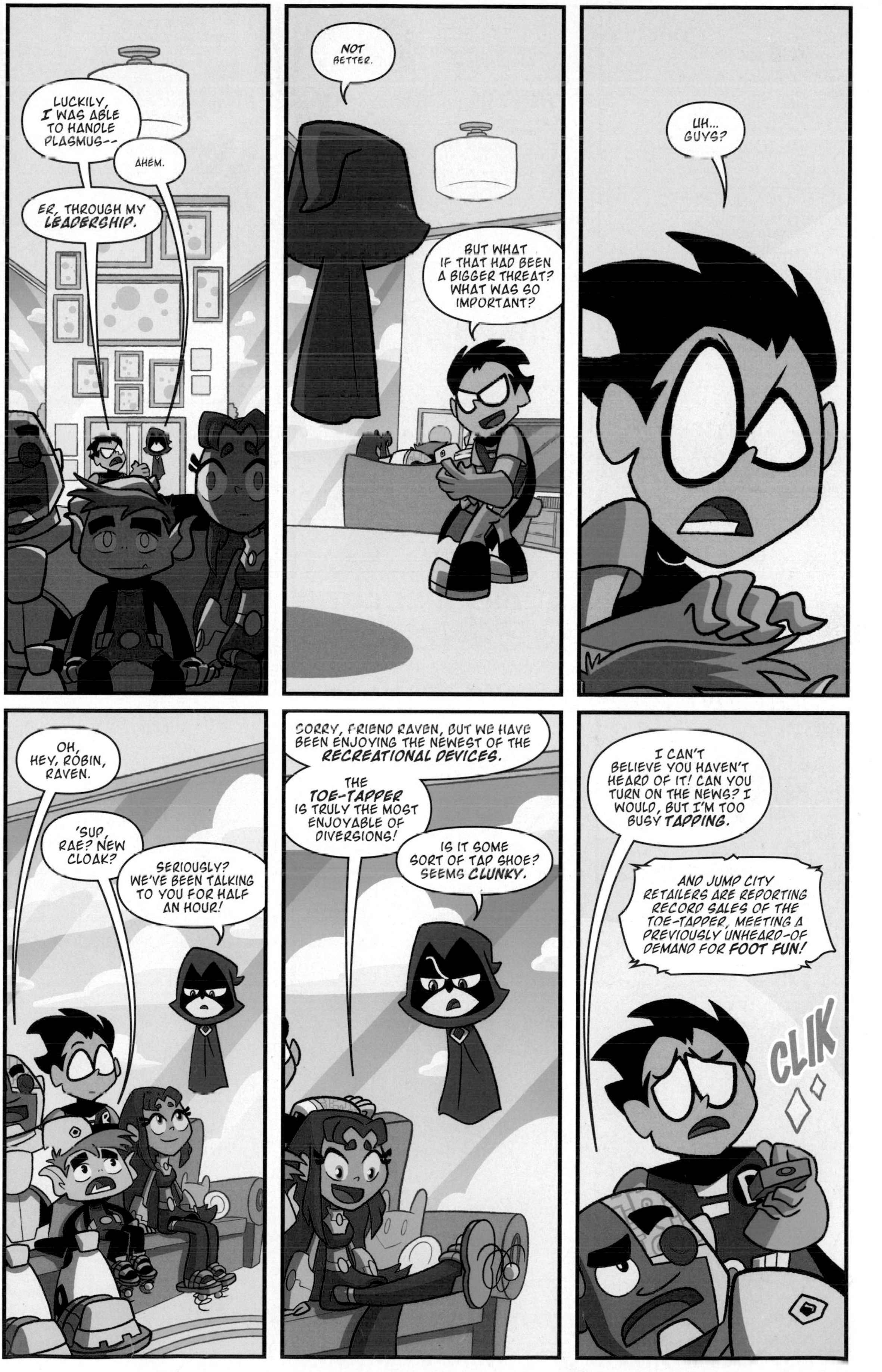
LUCKILY, I WAS ABLE TO HANDLE PLASMUS--
AHEM.
ER, THROUGH MY LEADERSHIP.
NOT BETTER.
BUT WHAT IF THAT HAD BEEN A BIGGER THREAT? WHAT WAS SO IMPORTANT?
UH... GUYS?
OH, HEY, ROBIN, RAVEN.
'SUP, RAE? NEW CLOAK?
SERIOUSLY? WE'VE BEEN TALKING TO YOU FOR HALF AN HOUR!
SORRY, FRIEND RAVEN, BUT WE HAVE BEEN ENJOYING THE NEWEST OF THE RECREATIONAL DEVICES.
THE TOE-TAPPER IS TRULY THE MOST ENJOYABLE OF DIVERSIONS!
IS IT SOME SORT OF TAP SHOE? SEEMS CLUNKY.
I CAN'T BELIEVE YOU HAVEN'T HEARD OF IT! CAN YOU TURN ON THE NEWS? I WOULD, BUT I'M TOO BUSY TAPPING.
AND JUMP CITY RETAILERS ARE REPORTING RECORD SALES OF THE TOE-TAPPER, MEETING A PREVIOUSLY UNHEARD-OF DEMAND FOR FOOT FUN!
CLIK

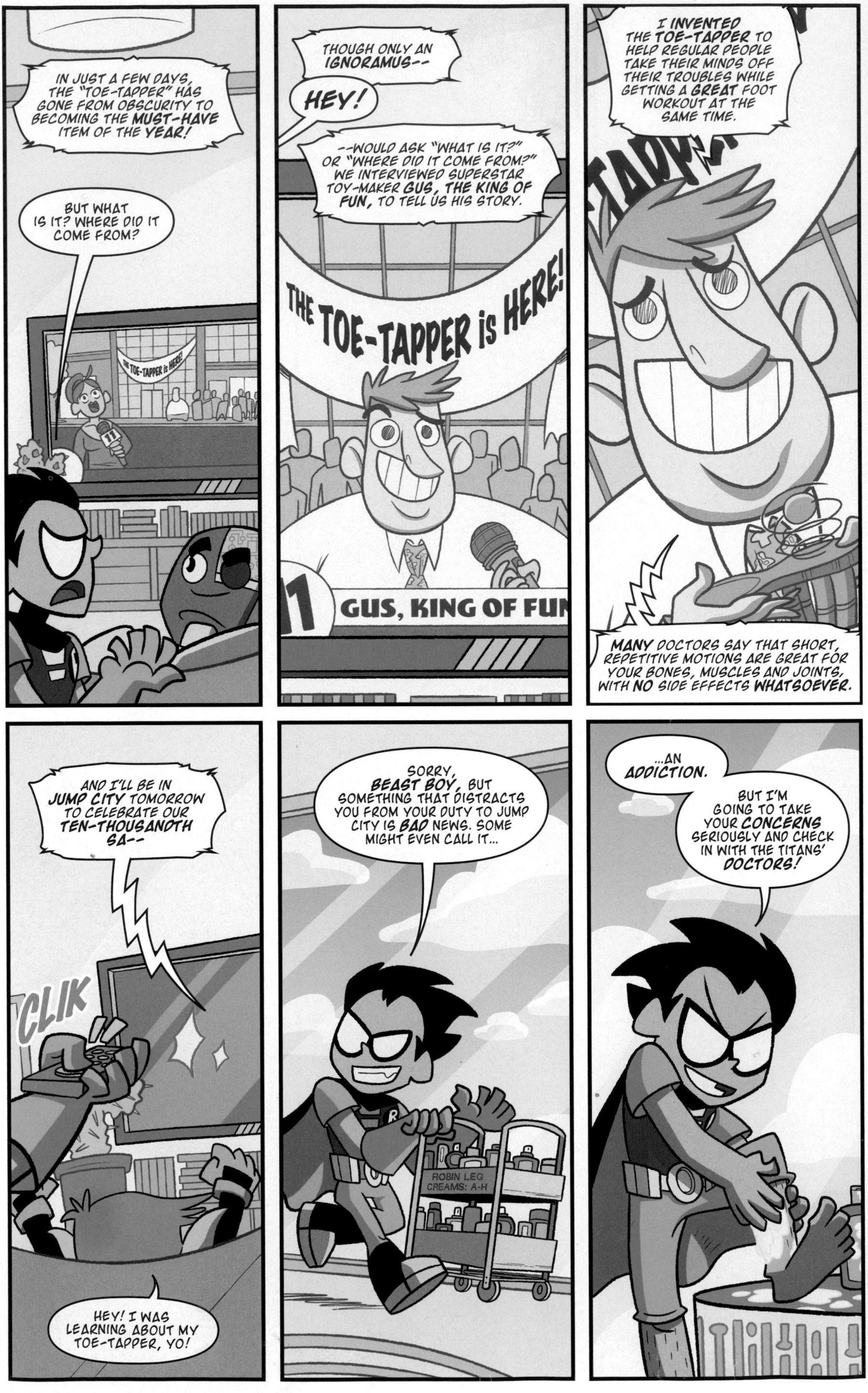
IN JUST A FEW DAYS, THE "TOE-TAPPER" HAS GONE FROM OBSCURITY TO BECOMING THE MUST-HAVE ITEM OF THE YEAR!
BUT WHAT IS IT? WHERE DID IT COME FROM?
THE TOE-TAPPER is HERE!
THOUGH ONLY AN IGNORAMUS--
HEY!
--WOULD ASK "WHAT IS IT?" OR "WHERE DID IT COME FROM?" WE INTERVIEWED SUPERSTAR TOY-MAKER GUS, THE KING OF FUN, TO TELL US HIS STORY.
THE TOE-TAPPER is HERE!
GUS, KING OF FUN
I INVENTED THE TOE-TAPPER TO HELP REGULAR PEOPLE TAKE THEIR MINDS OFF THEIR TROUBLES WHILE GETTING A GREAT FOOT WORKOUT AT THE SAME TIME.
MANY DOCTORS SAY THAT SHORT, REPETITIVE MOTIONS ARE GREAT FOR YOUR BONES, MUSCLES AND JOINTS, WITH NO SIDE EFFECTS WHATSOEVER.
AND I'LL BE IN JUMP CITY TOMORROW TO CELEBRATE OUR TEN-THOUSANDTH SA--
CLIK
HEY! I WAS LEARNING ABOUT MY TOE-TAPPER, YO!
SORRY, BEAST BOY, BUT SOMETHING THAT DISTRACTS YOU FROM YOUR DUTY TO JUMP CITY IS BAD NEWS. SOME MIGHT EVEN CALL IT...
ROBIN LEG CREAMS: A-H
...AN ADDICTION.
BUT I'M GOING TO TAKE YOUR CONCERNS SERIOUSLY AND CHECK IN WITH THE TITANS' DOCTORS!

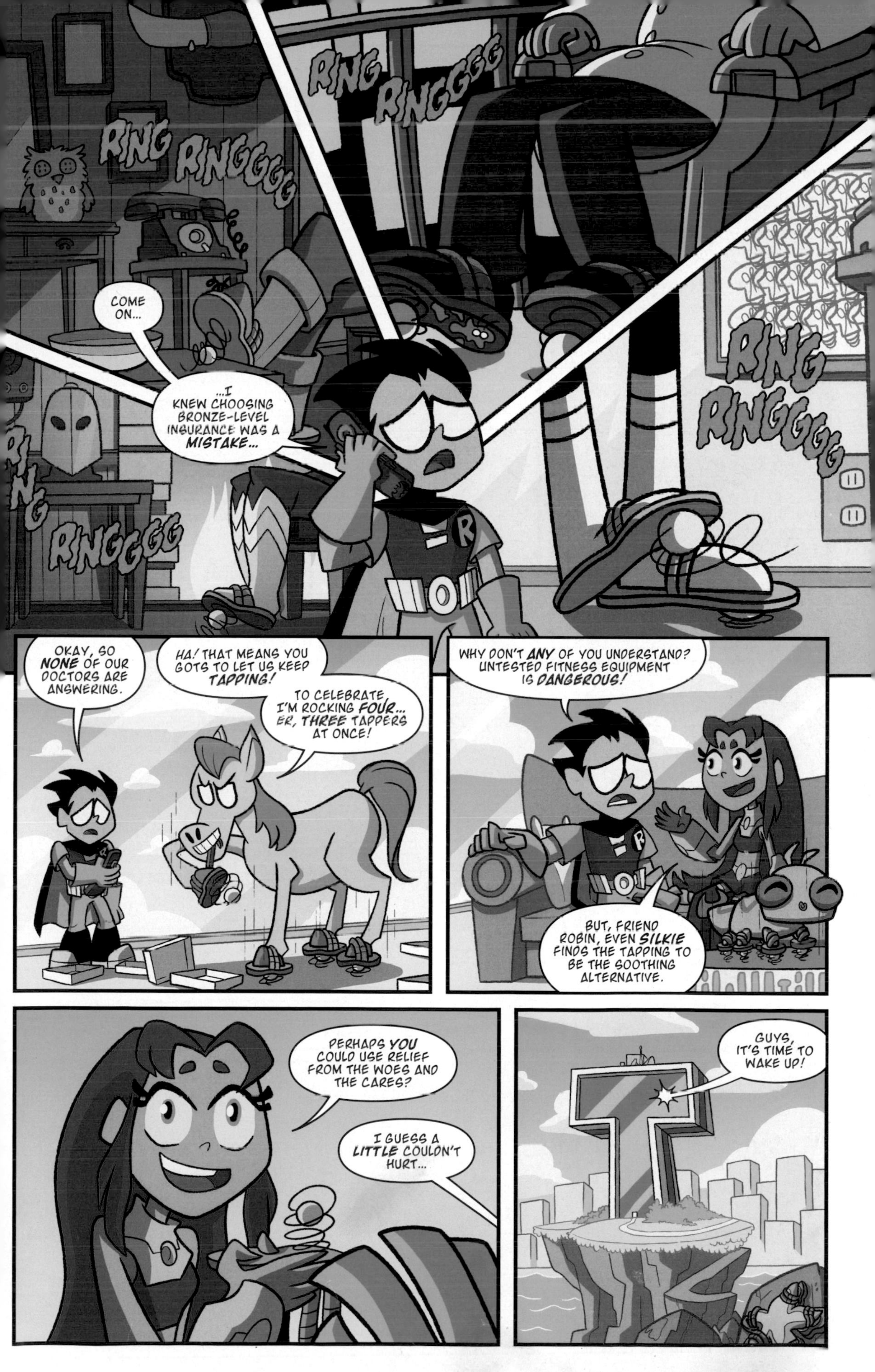
RING RINGGGGG
RING RINGGGG
COME ON...
...I KNEW CHOOSING BRONZE-LEVEL INSURANCE WAS A MISTAKE...
RING RINGGGGG
RING RINGGGG
OKAY, SO NONE OF OUR DOCTORS ARE ANSWERING.
HA! THAT MEANS YOU GOTS TO LET US KEEP TAPPING!
TO CELEBRATE, I'M ROCKING FOUR... ER, THREE TAPPERS AT ONCE!
WHY DON'T ANY OF YOU UNDERSTAND? UNTESTED FITNESS EQUIPMENT IS DANGEROUS!
BUT, FRIEND ROBIN, EVEN SILKIE FINDS THE TAPPING TO BE THE SOOTHING ALTERNATIVE.
PERHAPS YOU COULD USE RELIEF FROM THE WOES AND THE CARES?
I GUESS A LITTLE COULDN'T HURT...
GUYS, IT'S TIME TO WAKE UP!

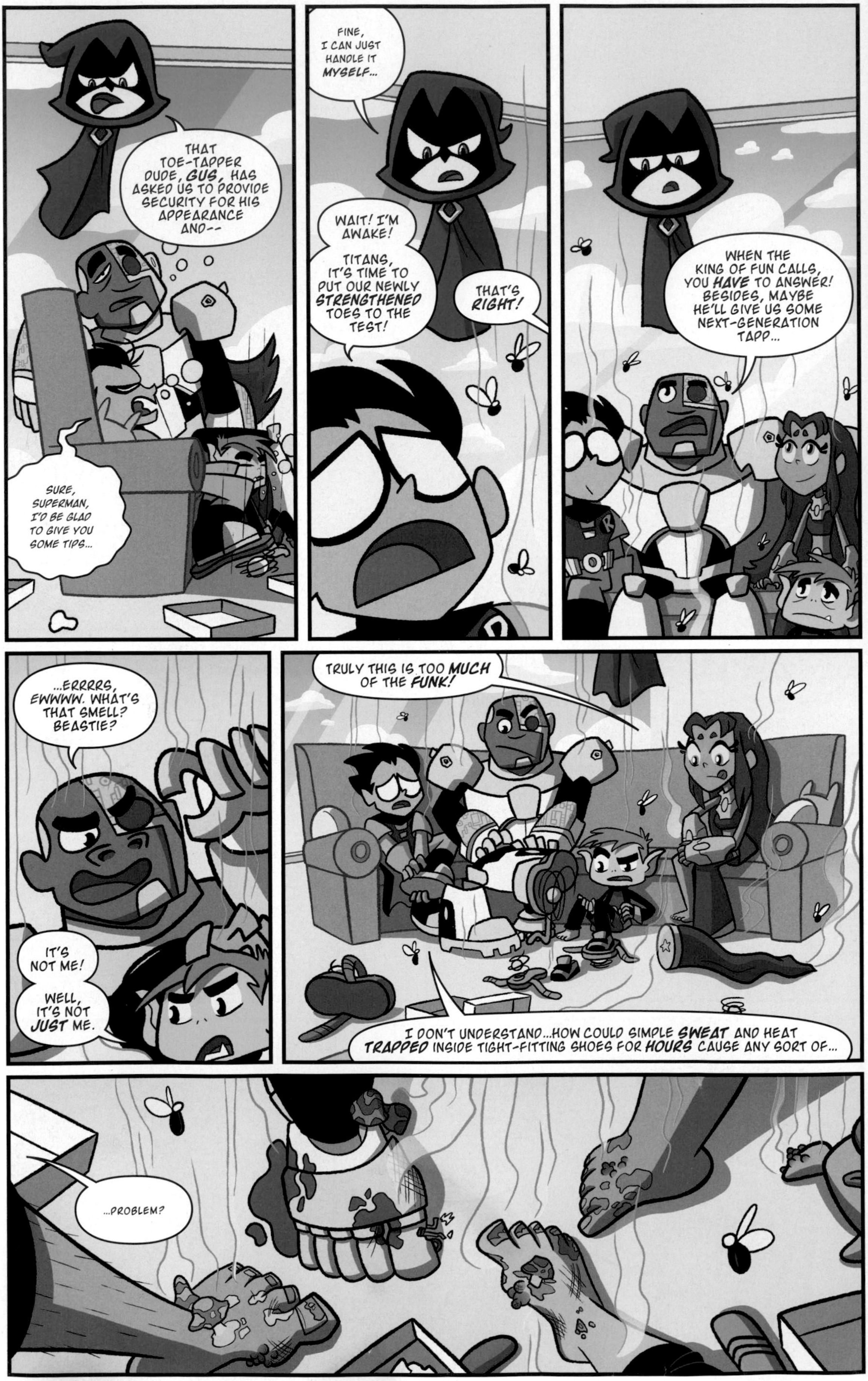
THAT TOE-TAPPER DUDE, GUS, HAS ASKED US TO PROVIDE SECURITY FOR HIS APPEARANCE AND--
SURE, SUPERMAN, I'D BE GLAD TO GIVE YOU SOME TIPS...
FINE, I CAN JUST HANDLE IT MYSELF...
WAIT! I'M AWAKE!
TITANS, IT'S TIME TO PUT OUR NEWLY STRENGTHENED TOES TO THE TEST!
THAT'S RIGHT!
WHEN THE KING OF FUN CALLS, YOU HAVE TO ANSWER! BESIDES, MAYBE HE'LL GIVE US SOME NEXT-GENERATION TAPP...
...ERRRRS, EWWWW. WHAT'S THAT SMELL? BEASTIE?
IT'S NOT ME!
WELL, IT'S NOT JUST ME.
TRULY THIS IS TOO MUCH OF THE FUNK!
I DON'T UNDERSTAND...HOW COULD SIMPLE SWEAT AND HEAT TRAPPED INSIDE TIGHT-FITTING SHOES FOR HOURS CAUSE ANY SORT OF...
...PROBLEM?

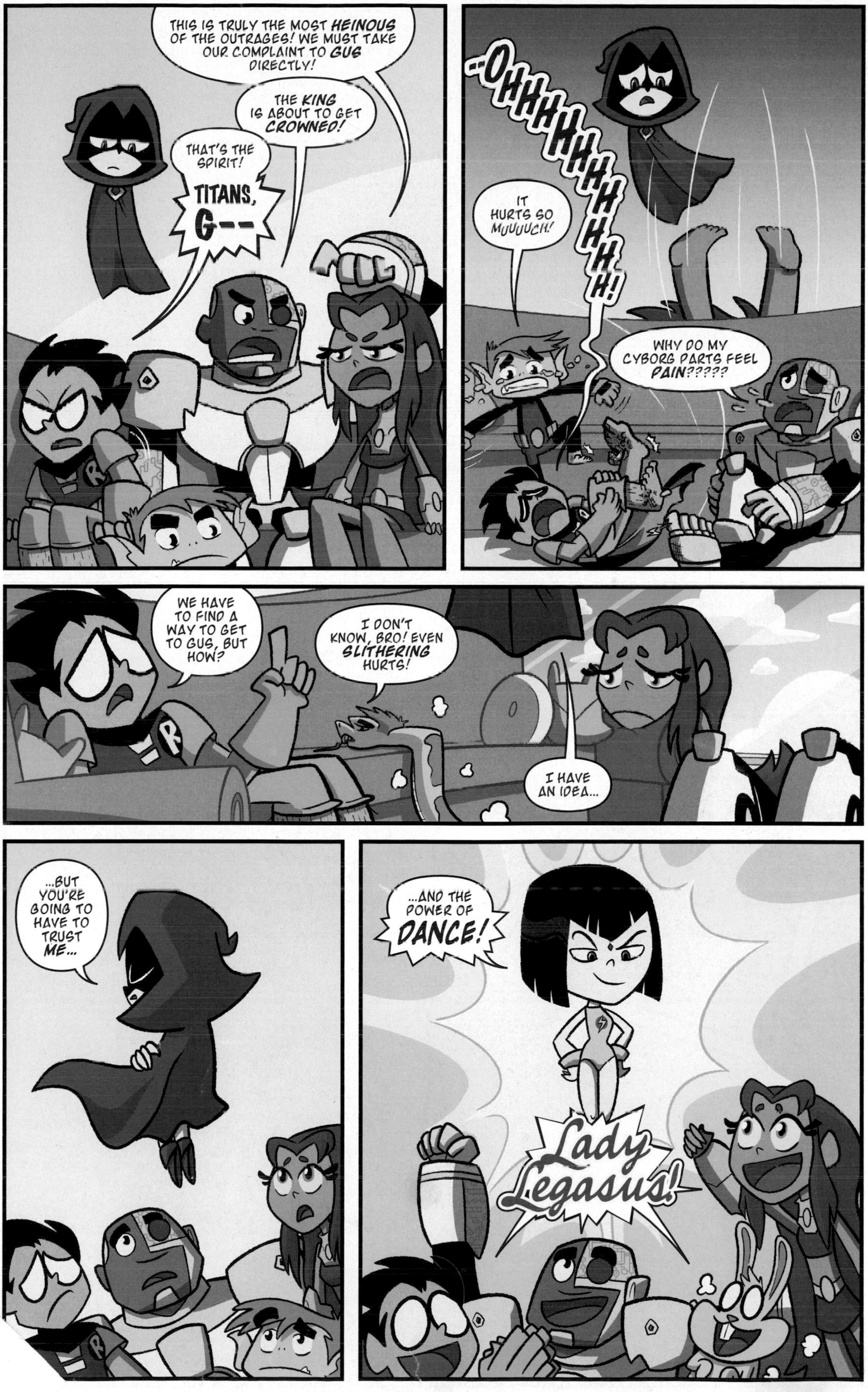
THIS IS TRULY THE MOST HEINOUS OF THE OUTRAGES! WE MUST TAKE OUR COMPLAINT TO GUS DIRECTLY!
THE KING IS ABOUT TO GET CROWNED!
THAT'S THE SPIRIT!
TITANS, G--
-OHHHHHHHHHH!
IT HURTS SO MUUUUCH!
WHY DO MY CYBORG PARTS FEEL PAIN?????
WE HAVE TO FIND A WAY TO GET TO GUS, BUT HOW?
I DON'T KNOW, BRO! EVEN SLITHERING HURTS!
I HAVE AN IDEA...
...BUT YOU'RE GOING TO HAVE TO TRUST ME...
...AND THE POWER OF DANCE!
Lady Legasus!

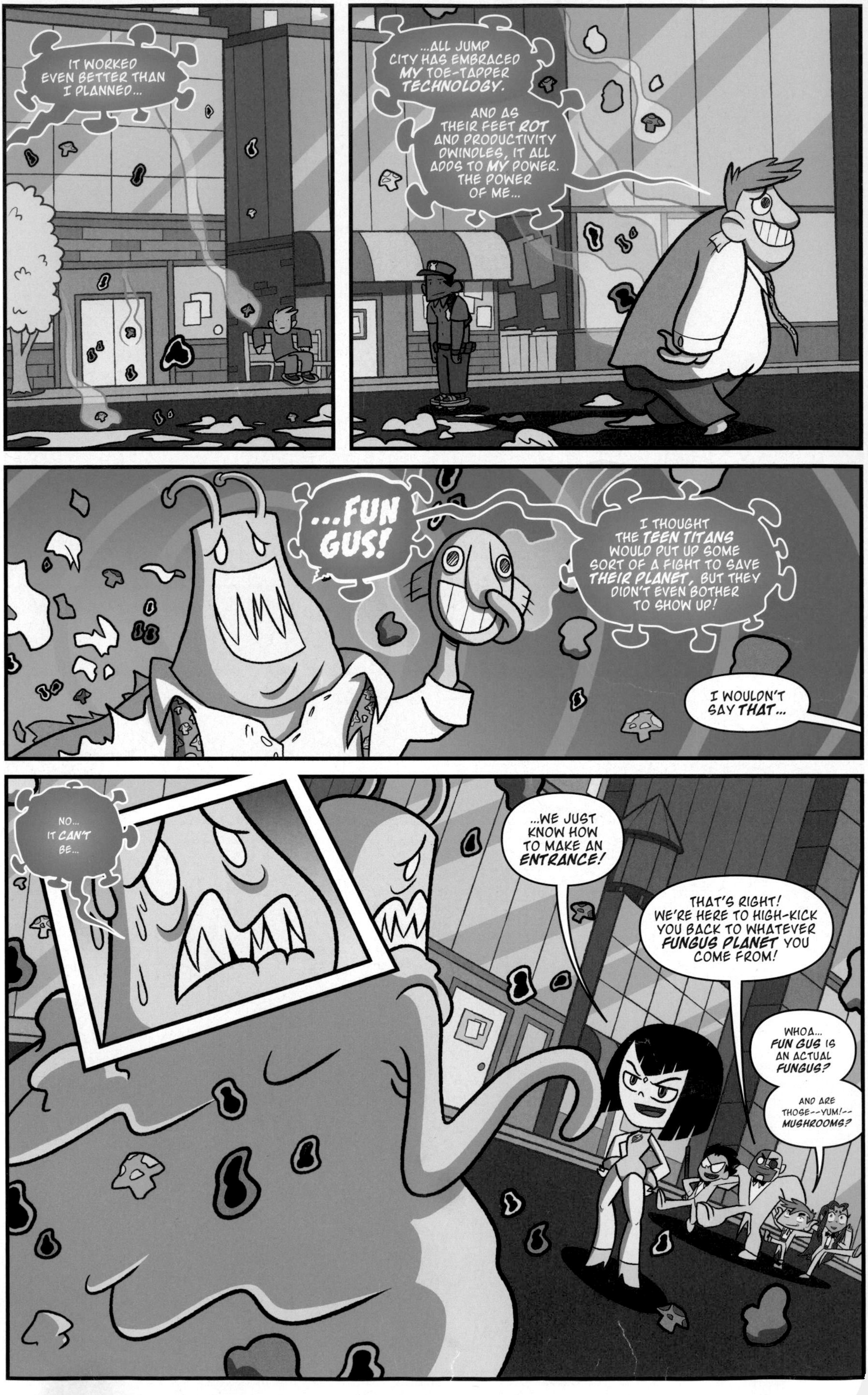
IT WORKED EVEN BETTER THAN I PLANNED...
...ALL JUMP CITY HAS EMBRACED MY TOE-TAPPER TECHNOLOGY.
AND AS THEIR FEET ROT AND PRODUCTIVITY DWINDLES, IT ALL ADDS TO MY POWER. THE POWER OF ME...
...FUN GUS!
I THOUGHT THE TEEN TITANS WOULD PUT UP SOME SORT OF A FIGHT TO SAVE THEIR PLANET, BUT THEY DIDN'T EVEN BOTHER TO SHOW UP!
I WOULDN'T SAY THAT...
NO... IT CAN'T BE...
...WE JUST KNOW HOW TO MAKE AN ENTRANCE!
THAT'S RIGHT! WE'RE HERE TO HIGH-KICK YOU BACK TO WHATEVER FUNGUS PLANET YOU COME FROM!
WHOA... FUN GUS IS AN ACTUAL FUNGUS?
AND ARE THOSE--YUM!--MUSHROOMS?

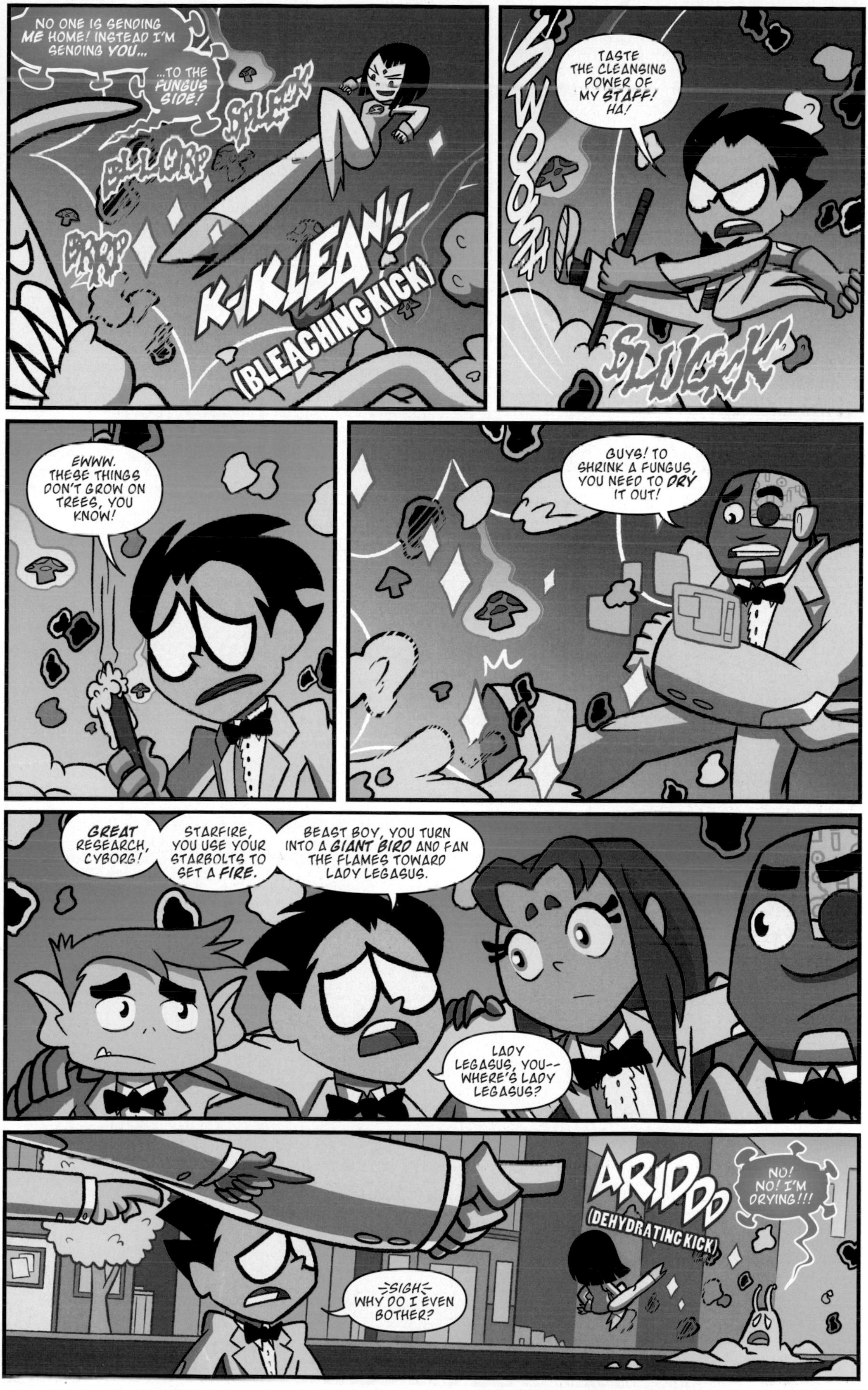
NO ONE IS SENDING ME HOME! INSTEAD I'M SENDING YOU...
...TO THE FUNGUS SIDE!
SPLEECK
BL-LORP
BRRP
K-KLEAN!
(BLEACHING KICK)
SWOOOSH
TASTE THE CLEANSING POWER OF MY STAFF! HA!
SPLUCKK
EWWW. THESE THINGS DON'T GROW ON TREES, YOU KNOW!
GUYS! TO SHRINK A FUNGUS, YOU NEED TO DRY IT OUT!
GREAT RESEARCH, CYBORG!
STARFIRE, YOU USE YOUR STARBOLTS TO SET A FIRE.
BEAST BOY, YOU TURN INTO A GIANT BIRD AND FAN THE FLAMES TOWARD LADY LEGASUS.
LADY LEGASUS, YOU-- WHERE'S LADY LEGASUS?
ARIDDD
(DEHYDRATING KICK)
NO! NO! I'M DRYING!!!
SIGH
WHY DO I EVEN BOTHER?

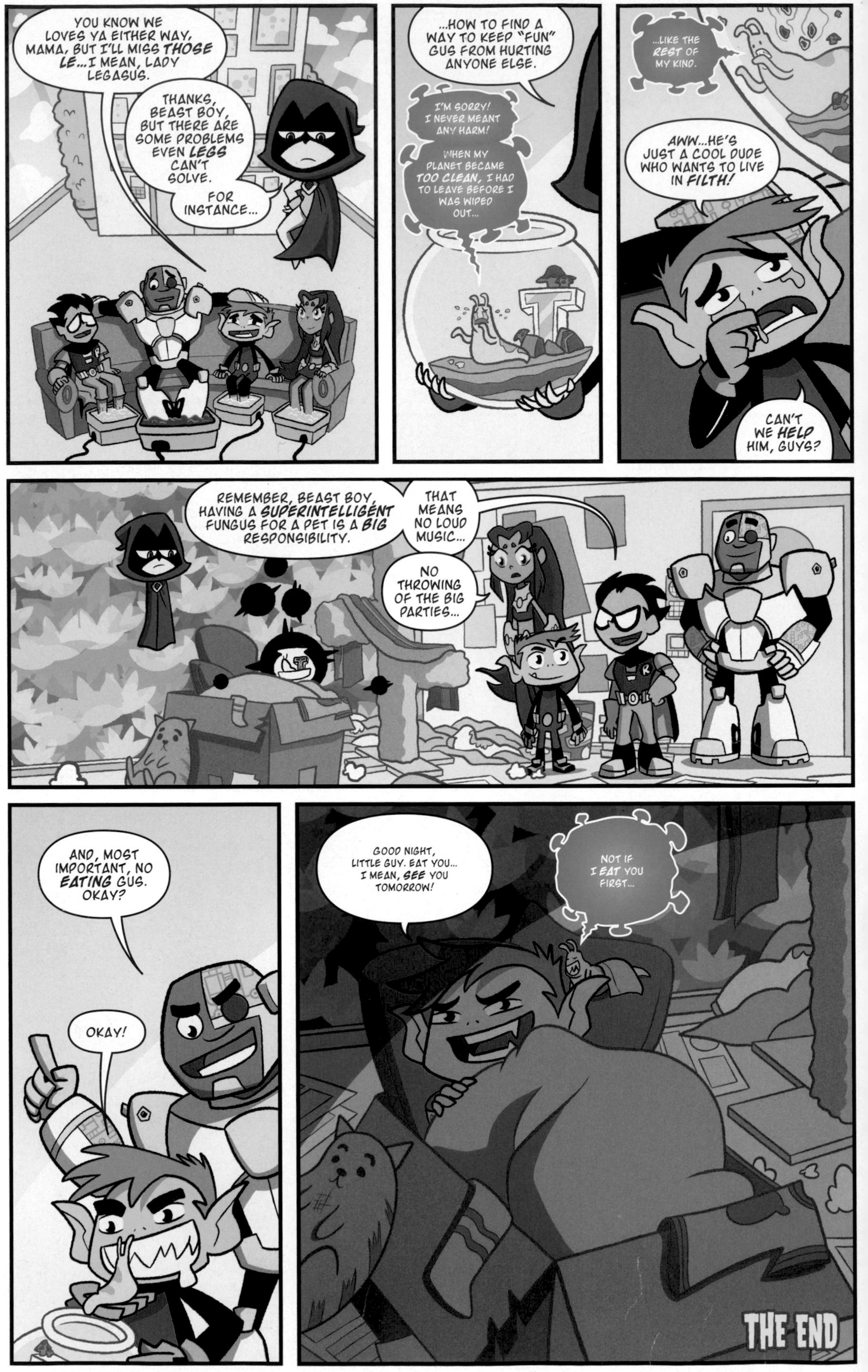

YOU KNOW WE LOVES YA EITHER WAY, MAMA, BUT I'LL MISS THOSE LE... I MEAN, LADY LEGASUS.
THANKS, BEAST BOY, BUT THERE ARE SOME PROBLEMS EVEN LEGS CAN'T SOLVE.
FOR INSTANCE...
...HOW TO FIND A WAY TO KEEP "FUN" GUS FROM HURTING ANYONE ELSE.
I'M SORRY! I NEVER MEANT ANY HARM!
WHEN MY PLANET BECAME TOO CLEAN, I HAD TO LEAVE BEFORE I WAS WIPED OUT...
...LIKE THE REST OF MY KIND.
AWW...HE'S JUST A COOL DUDE WHO WANTS TO LIVE IN FILTH!
CAN'T WE HELP HIM, GUYS?
REMEMBER, BEAST BOY, HAVING A SUPERINTELLIGENT FUNGUS FOR A PET IS A BIG RESPONSIBILITY.
THAT MEANS NO LOUD MUSIC...
NO THROWING OF THE BIG PARTIES...
AND, MOST IMPORTANT, NO EATING GUS. OKAY?
OKAY!
GOOD NIGHT, LITTLE GUY. EAT YOU... I MEAN, SEE YOU TOMORROW!
NOT IF I EAT YOU FIRST...
THE END

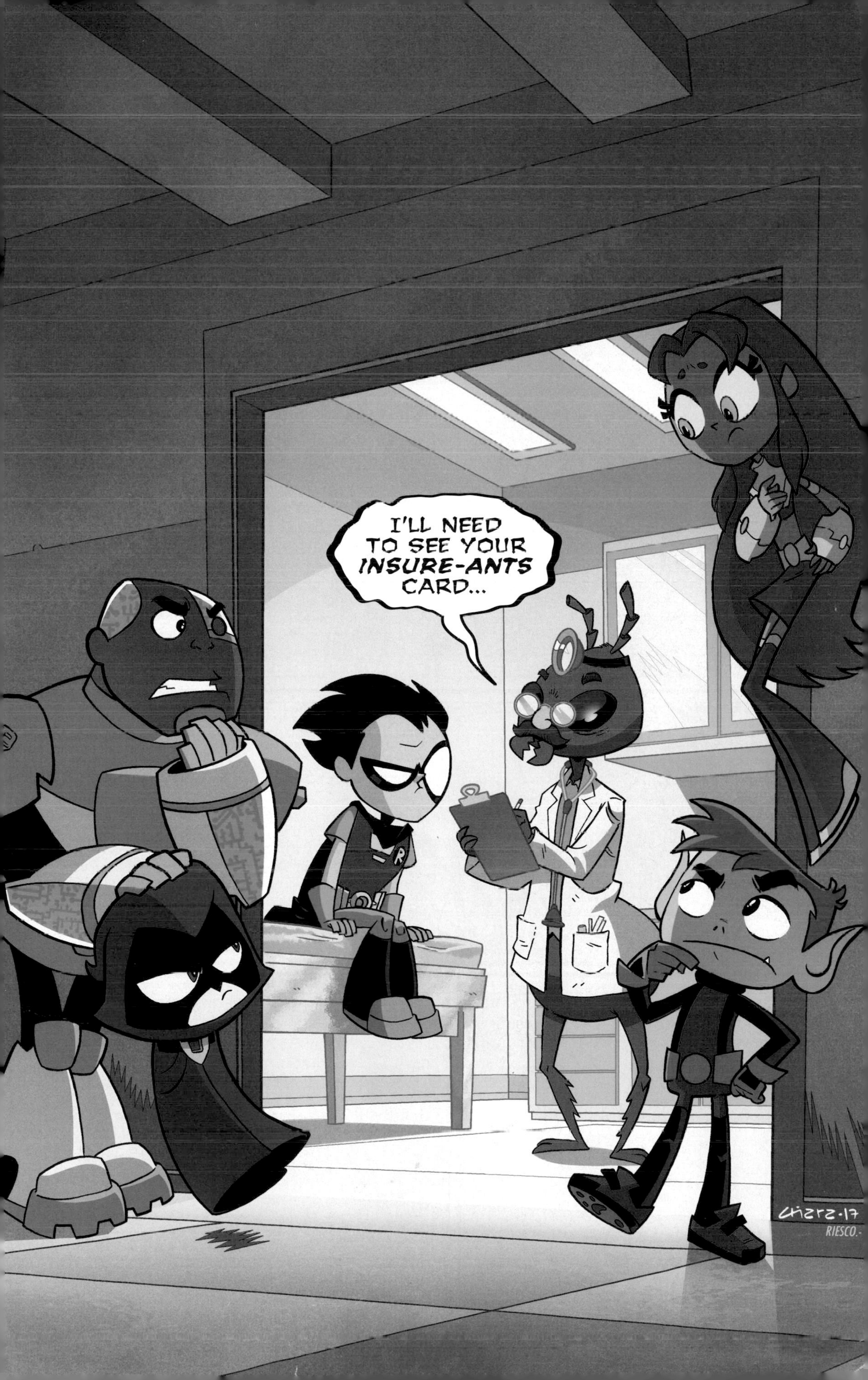
I'LL NEED TO SEE YOUR *INSURE-ANTS* CARD...
RIESCO.

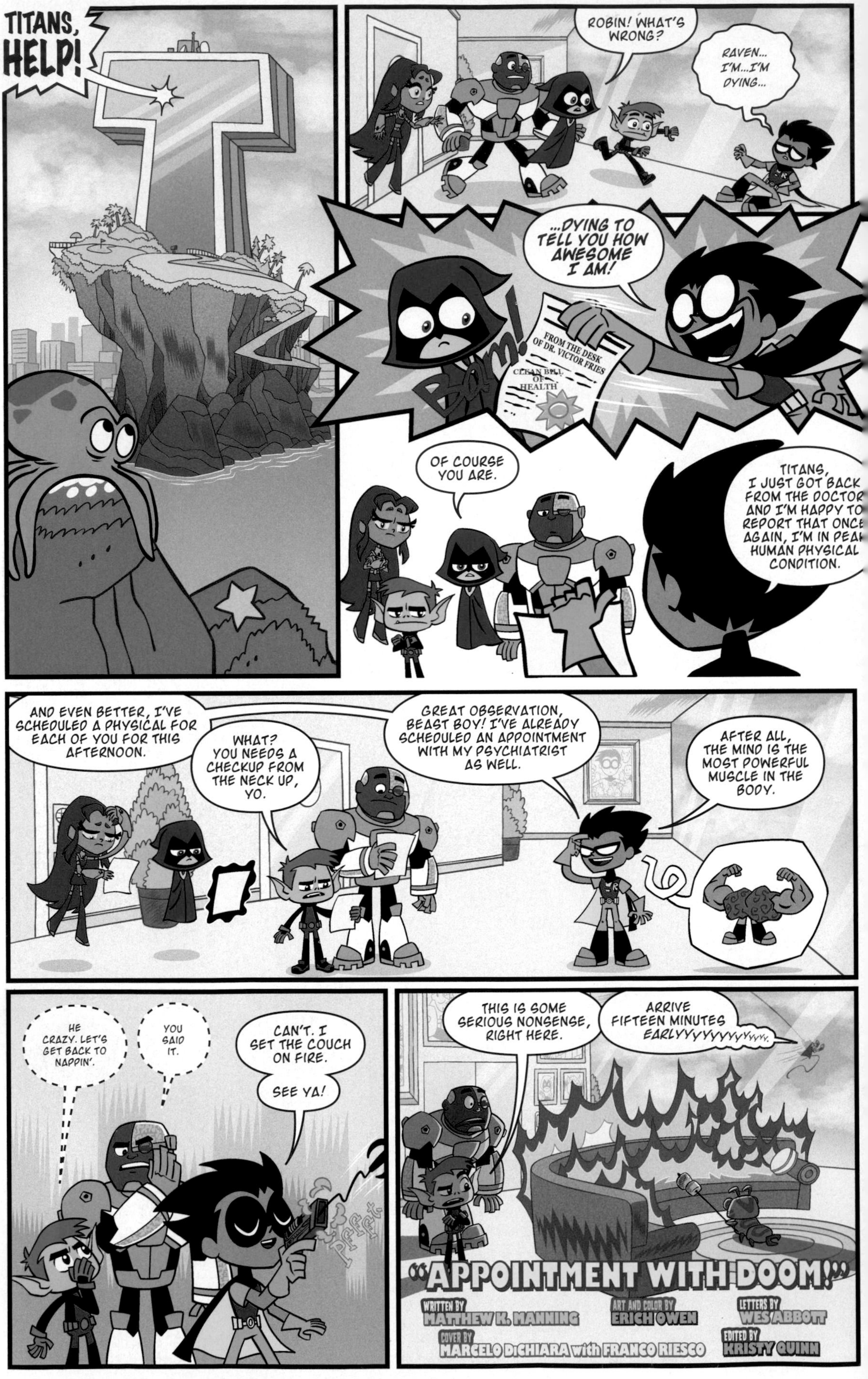
TITANS, HELP!
ROBIN! WHAT'S WRONG?
RAVEN... I'M...I'M DYING...
...DYING TO TELL YOU HOW AWESOME I AM!
BAM!
FROM THE DESK OF DR. VICTOR FRIES
CLEAN BILL OF HEALTH
TITANS, I JUST GOT BACK FROM THE DOCTOR AND I'M HAPPY TO REPORT THAT ONCE AGAIN, I'M IN PEAK HUMAN PHYSICAL CONDITION.
OF COURSE YOU ARE.
AND EVEN BETTER, I'VE SCHEDULED A PHYSICAL FOR EACH OF YOU FOR THIS AFTERNOON.
WHAT? YOU NEEDS A CHECKUP FROM THE NECK UP, YO.
GREAT OBSERVATION, BEAST BOY! I'VE ALREADY SCHEDULED AN APPOINTMENT WITH MY PSYCHIATRIST AS WELL.
AFTER ALL, THE MIND IS THE MOST POWERFUL MUSCLE IN THE BODY.
HE CRAZY. LET'S GET BACK TO NAPPIN'.
YOU SAID IT.
CAN'T. I SET THE COUCH ON FIRE.
SEE YA!
PFFT
THIS IS SOME SERIOUS NONSENSE, RIGHT HERE.
ARRIVE FIFTEEN MINUTES EARLYYYYYYYYYYyyyy.
"APPOINTMENT WITH DOOM!"
WRITTEN BY MATTHEW K. MANNING
ART AND COLOR BY ERICH OWEN
LETTERS BY WES ABBOTT
COVER BY MARCELO DiCHIARA with FRANCO RIESCO
EDITED BY KRISTY QUINN

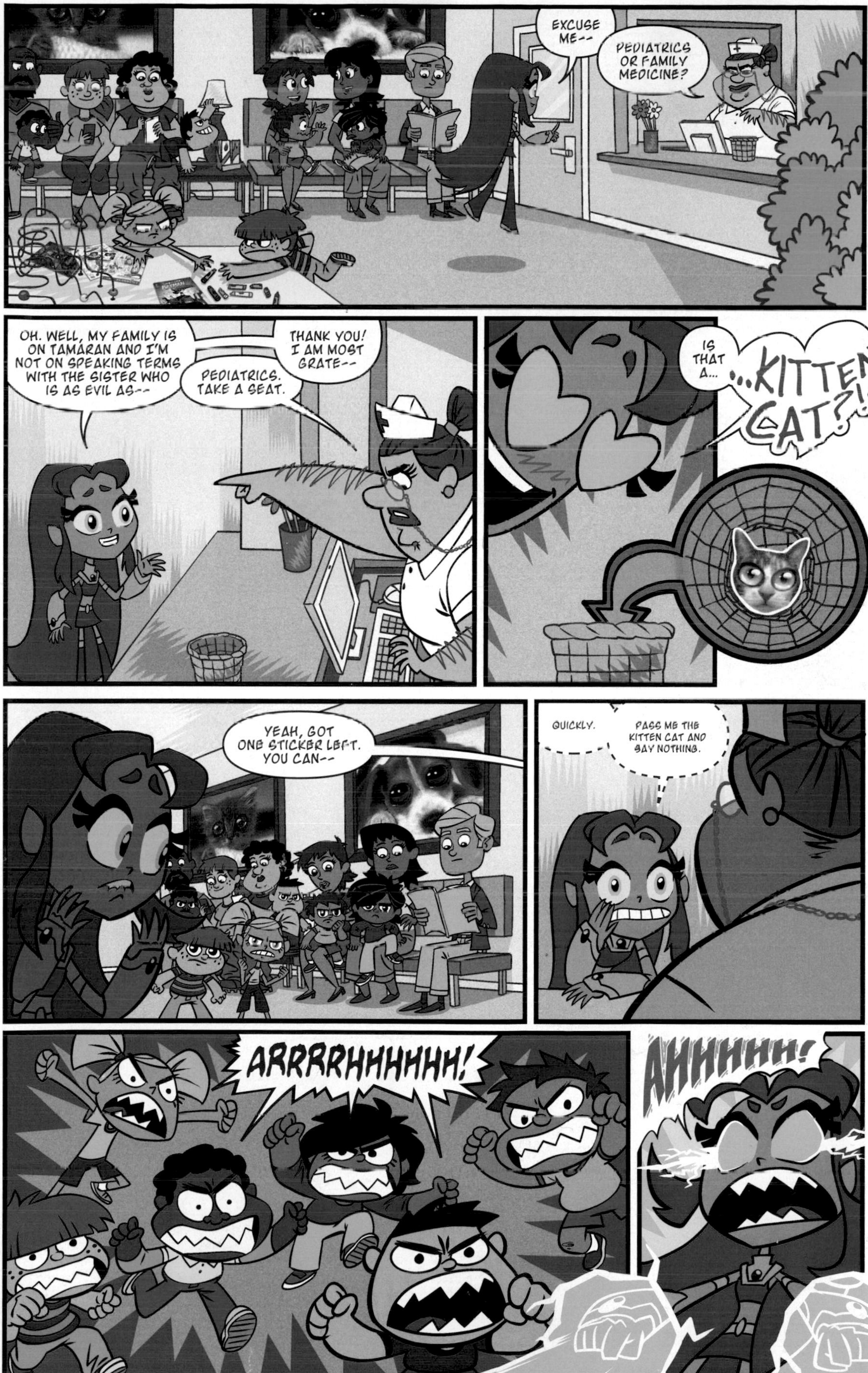
EXCUSE ME--
PEDIATRICS OR FAMILY MEDICINE?
OH. WELL, MY FAMILY IS ON TAMARAN AND I'M NOT ON SPEAKING TERMS WITH THE SISTER WHO IS AS EVIL AS--
PEDIATRICS. TAKE A SEAT.
THANK YOU! I AM MOST GRATE--
IS THAT A...
...KITTEN CAT?!
YEAH, GOT ONE STICKER LEFT. YOU CAN--
QUICKLY.
PASS ME THE KITTEN CAT AND SAY NOTHING.
ARRRRHHHHHH!
AHHHHH!

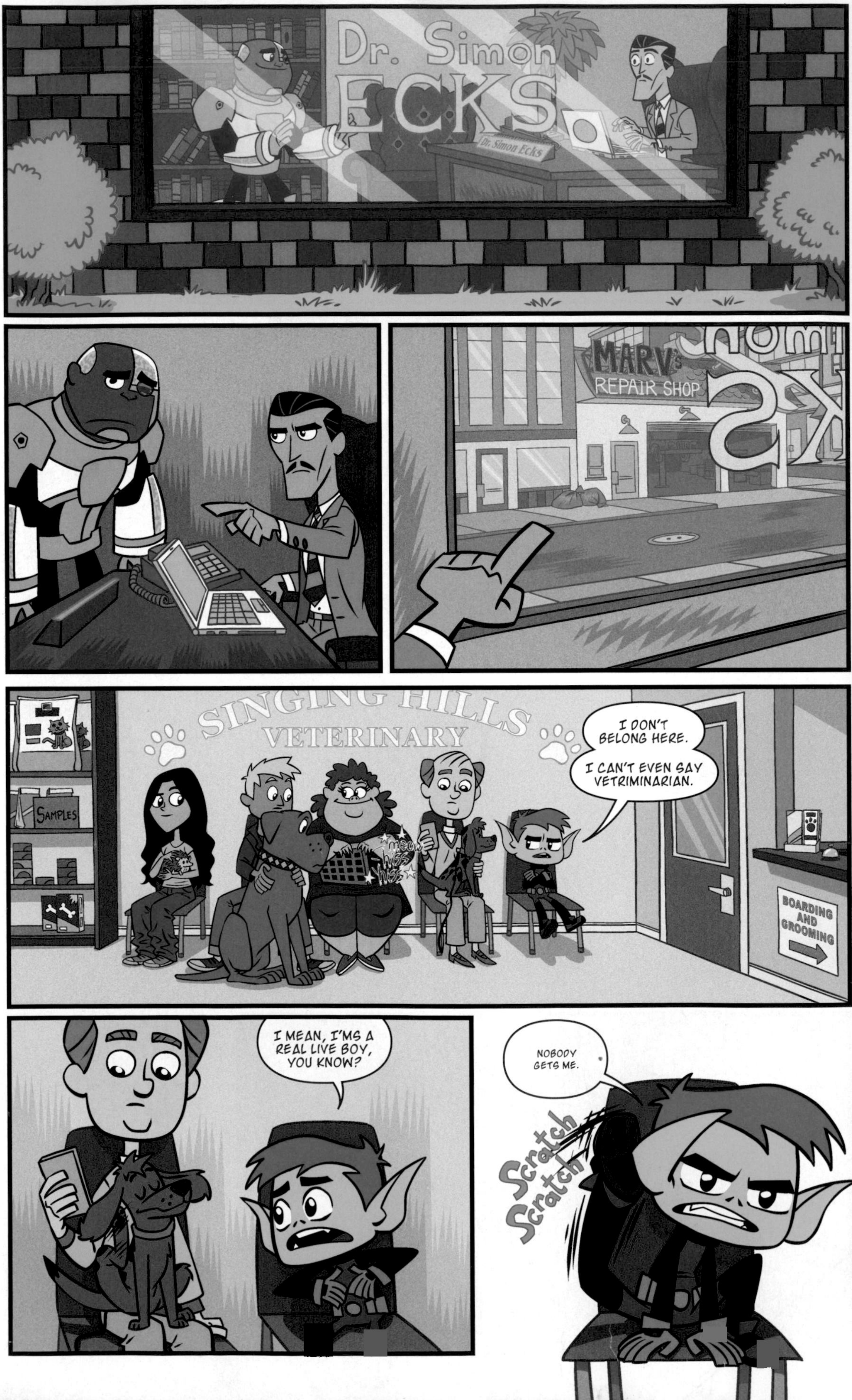
Dr. Simon ECKS
Dr. Simon Ecks
MARV's
REPAIR SHOP
SINGING HILLS
VETERINARY
SAMPLES
meow
hiss
hiss
I DON'T BELONG HERE.
I CAN'T EVEN SAY VETRIMINARIAN.
BOARDING AND GROOMING
I MEAN, I'MS A REAL LIVE BOY, YOU KNOW?
NOBODY GETS ME.
Scratch
Scratch

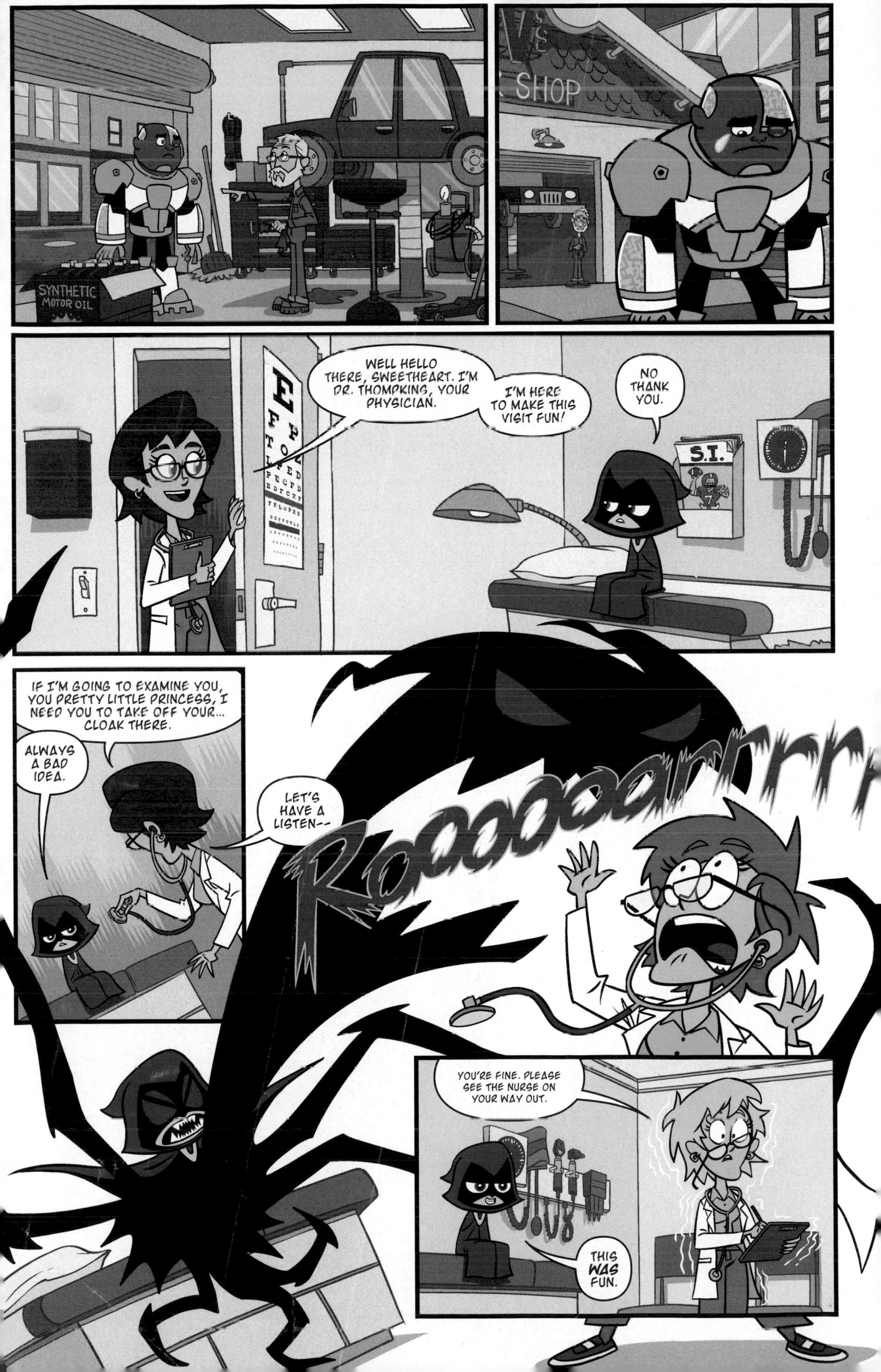
SYNTHETIC MOTOR OIL
SHOP
WELL HELLO THERE, SWEETHEART. I'M DR. THOMPKINS, YOUR PHYSICIAN.
I'M HERE TO MAKE THIS VISIT FUN!
NO THANK YOU.
S.I.
IF I'M GOING TO EXAMINE YOU, YOU PRETTY LITTLE PRINCESS, I NEED YOU TO TAKE OFF YOUR... CLOAK THERE.
ALWAYS A BAD IDEA.
LET'S HAVE A LISTEN--
Roooooaarrrr
YOU'RE FINE. PLEASE SEE THE NURSE ON YOUR WAY OUT.
THIS *WAS* FUN.

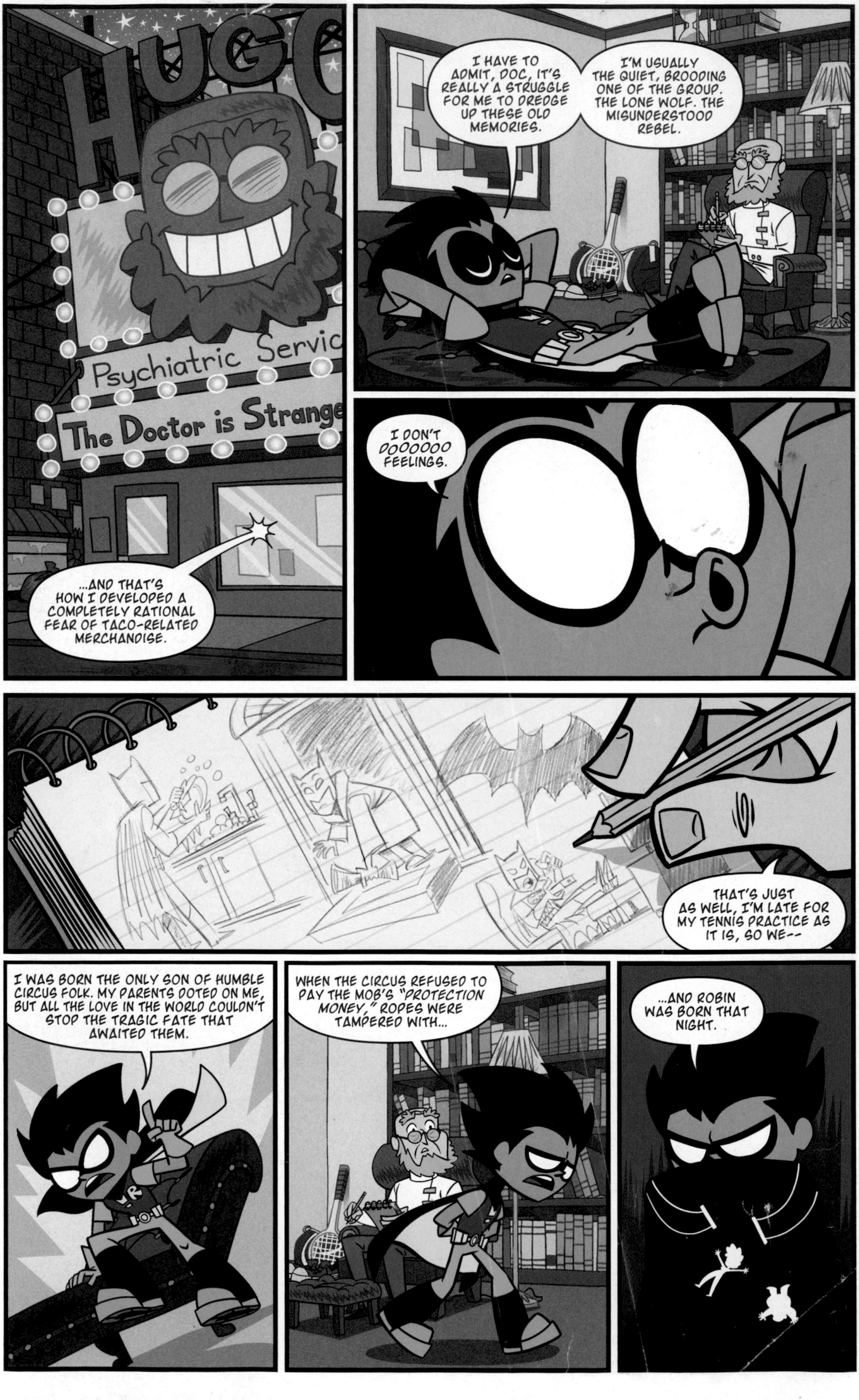
HUGO
Psychiatric Servic
The Doctor is Strange
...AND THAT'S HOW I DEVELOPED A COMPLETELY RATIONAL FEAR OF TACO-RELATED MERCHANDISE.
I HAVE TO ADMIT, DOC, IT'S REALLY A STRUGGLE FOR ME TO DREDGE UP THESE OLD MEMORIES.
I'M USUALLY THE QUIET, BROODING ONE OF THE GROUP. THE LONE WOLF. THE MISUNDERSTOOD REBEL.
I DON'T DOOOOOO FEELINGS.
THAT'S JUST AS WELL, I'M LATE FOR MY TENNIS PRACTICE AS IT IS, SO WE--
I WAS BORN THE ONLY SON OF HUMBLE CIRCUS FOLK. MY PARENTS DOTED ON ME, BUT ALL THE LOVE IN THE WORLD COULDN'T STOP THE TRAGIC FATE THAT AWAITED THEM.
WHEN THE CIRCUS REFUSED TO PAY THE MOB'S "PROTECTION MONEY," ROPES WERE TAMPERED WITH...
...AND ROBIN WAS BORN THAT NIGHT.

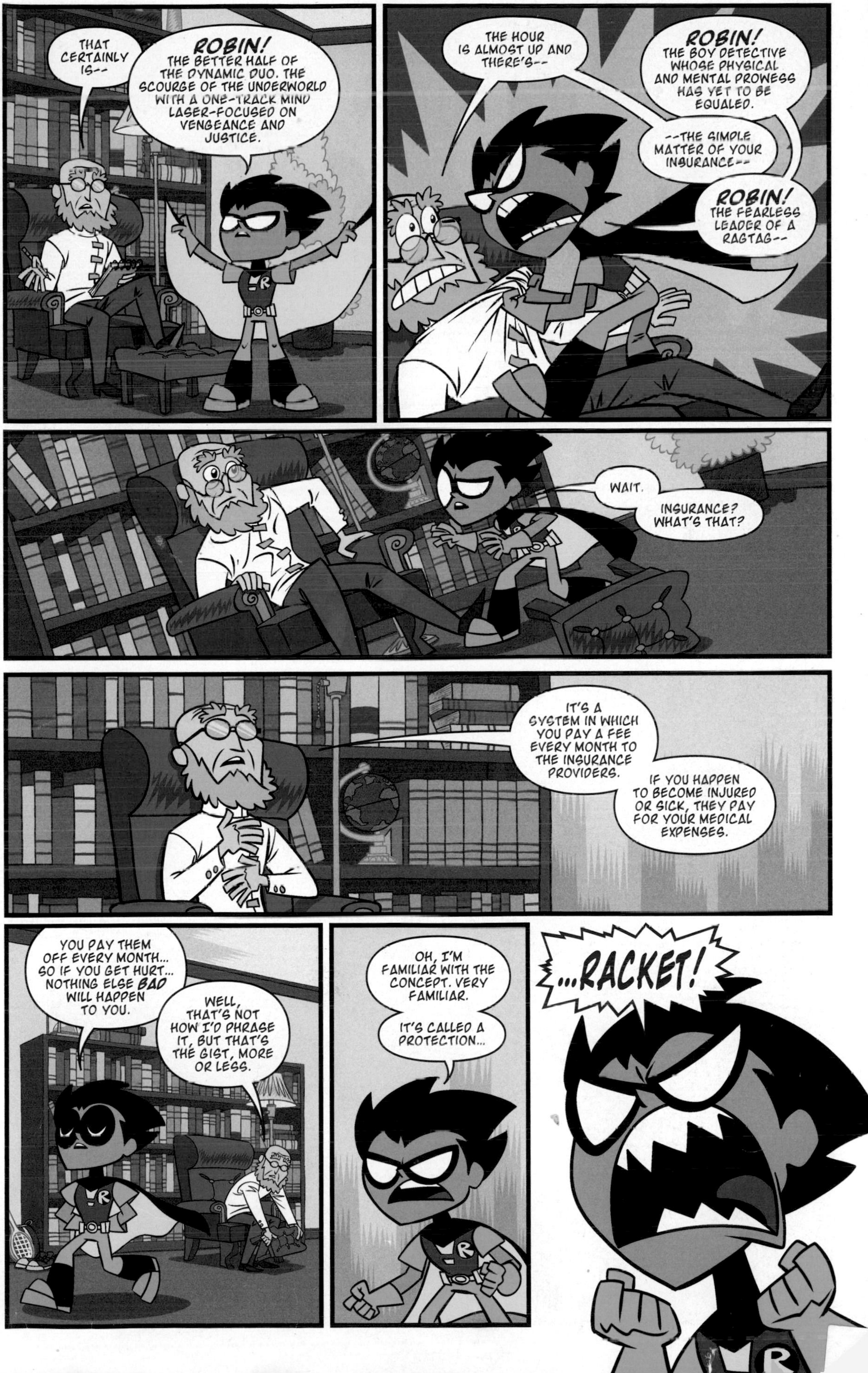
THAT CERTAINLY IS--
ROBIN! THE BETTER HALF OF THE DYNAMIC DUO. THE SCOURGE OF THE UNDERWORLD WITH A ONE-TRACK MIND LASER-FOCUSED ON VENGEANCE AND JUSTICE.
THE HOUR IS ALMOST UP AND THERE'S--
ROBIN! THE BOY DETECTIVE WHOSE PHYSICAL AND MENTAL PROWESS HAS YET TO BE EQUALED.
--THE SIMPLE MATTER OF YOUR INSURANCE--
ROBIN! THE FEARLESS LEADER OF A RAGTAG--
WAIT.
INSURANCE? WHAT'S THAT?
IT'S A SYSTEM IN WHICH YOU PAY A FEE EVERY MONTH TO THE INSURANCE PROVIDERS.
IF YOU HAPPEN TO BECOME INJURED OR SICK, THEY PAY FOR YOUR MEDICAL EXPENSES.
YOU PAY THEM OFF EVERY MONTH... SO IF YOU GET HURT... NOTHING ELSE BAD WILL HAPPEN TO YOU.
WELL, THAT'S NOT HOW I'D PHRASE IT, BUT THAT'S THE GIST, MORE OR LESS.
OH, I'M FAMILIAR WITH THE CONCEPT. VERY FAMILIAR.
IT'S CALLED A PROTECTION...
...RACKET!

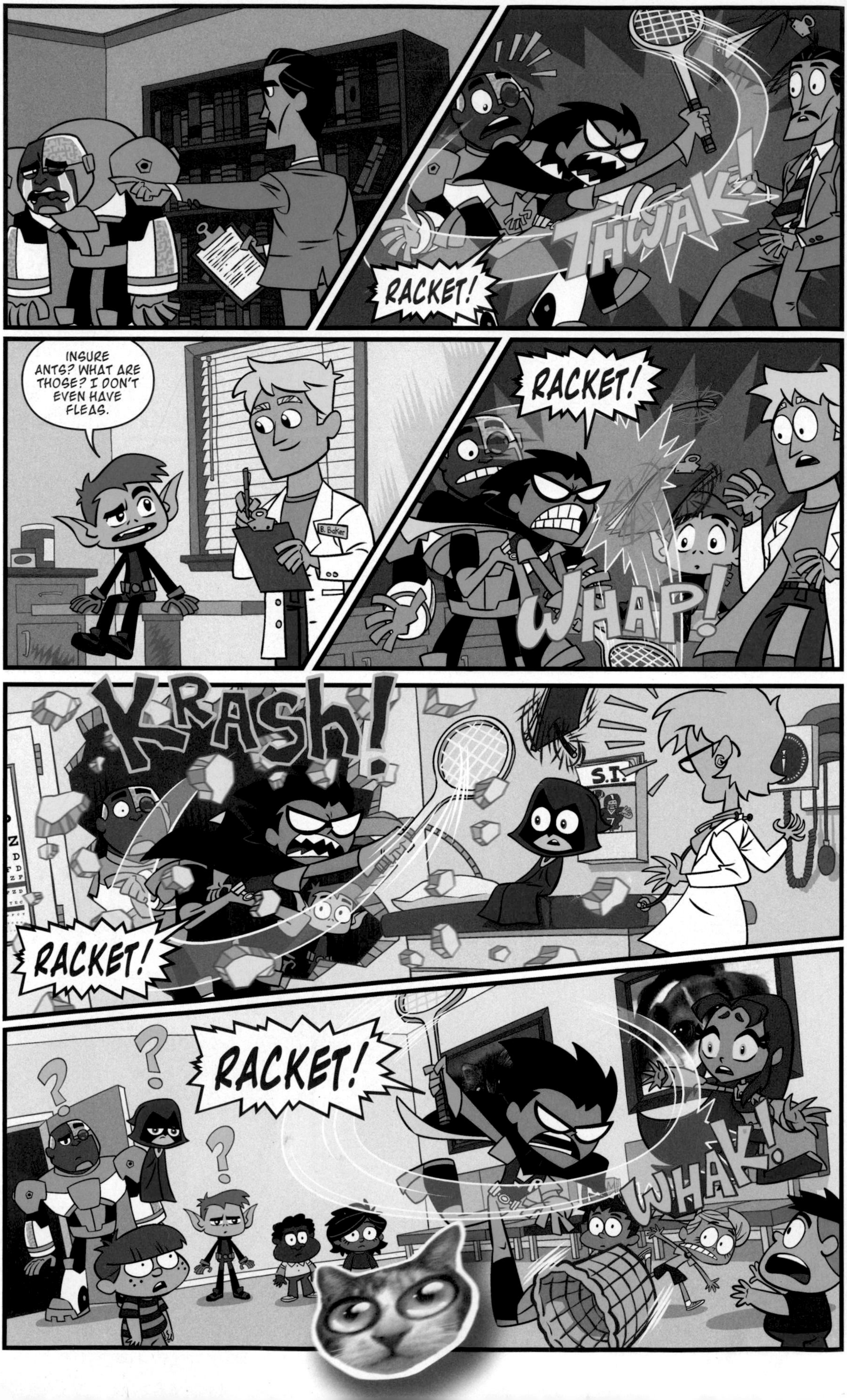

THWAK!
RACKET!
INSURE ANTS? WHAT ARE THOSE? I DON'T EVEN HAVE FLEAS.
B. BAKER
RACKET!
WHAP!
KRASH!
S.I.
RACKET!
RACKET!
WHAK!

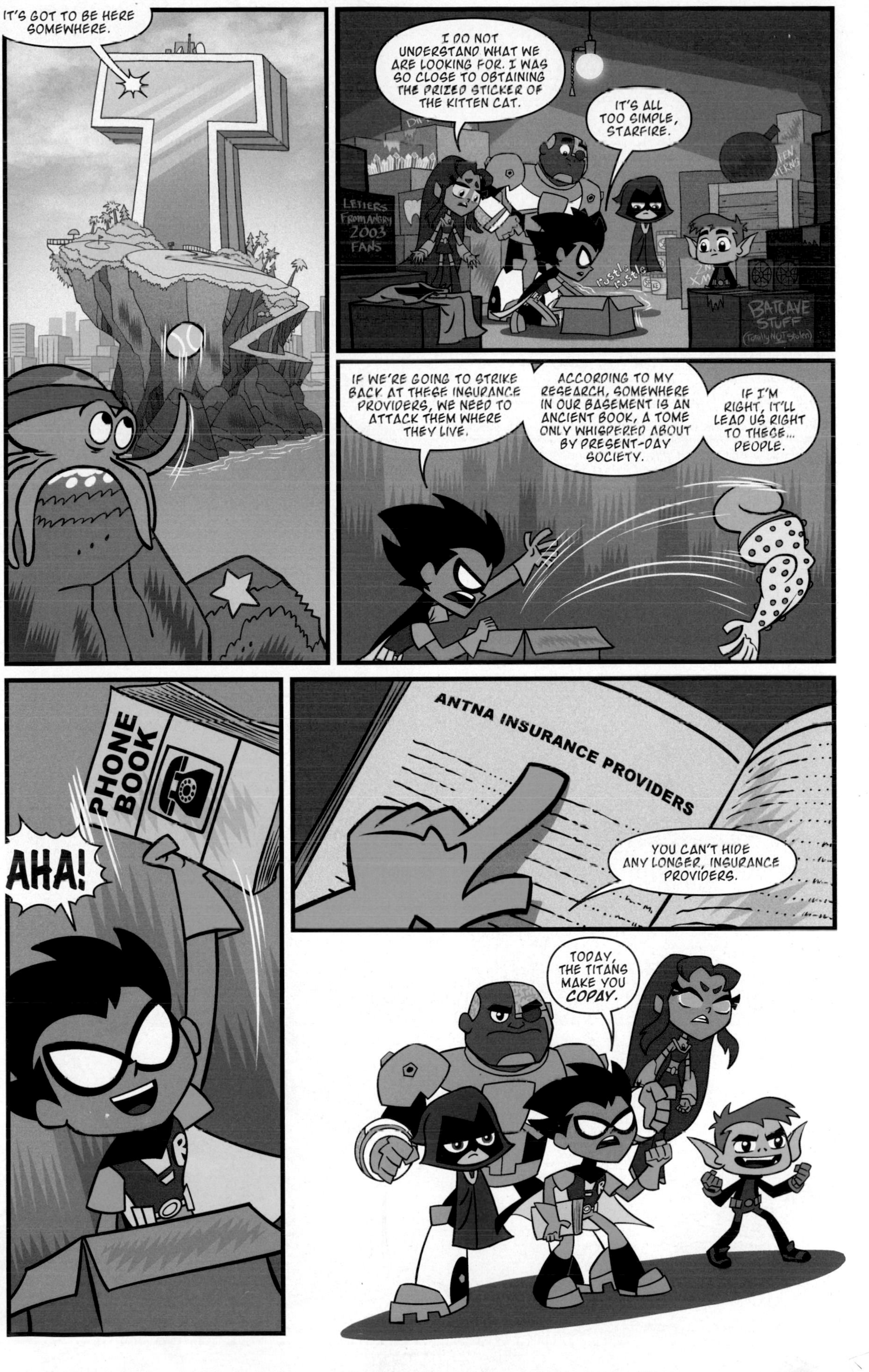
IT'S GOT TO BE HERE SOMEWHERE.
I DO NOT UNDERSTAND WHAT WE ARE LOOKING FOR. I WAS SO CLOSE TO OBTAINING THE PRIZED STICKER OF THE KITTEN CAT.
IT'S ALL TOO SIMPLE, STARFIRE.
LETTERS FROM ANGRY 2003 FANS
rustle rustle
BATCAVE STUFF (Totally NOT Stolen)
IF WE'RE GOING TO STRIKE BACK AT THESE INSURANCE PROVIDERS, WE NEED TO ATTACK THEM WHERE THEY LIVE.
ACCORDING TO MY RESEARCH, SOMEWHERE IN OUR BASEMENT IS AN ANCIENT BOOK, A TOME ONLY WHISPERED ABOUT BY PRESENT-DAY SOCIETY.
IF I'M RIGHT, IT'LL LEAD US RIGHT TO THESE... PEOPLE.
PHONE BOOK
AHA!
ANTNA INSURANCE PROVIDERS
YOU CAN'T HIDE ANY LONGER, INSURANCE PROVIDERS.
TODAY, THE TITANS MAKE YOU COPAY.

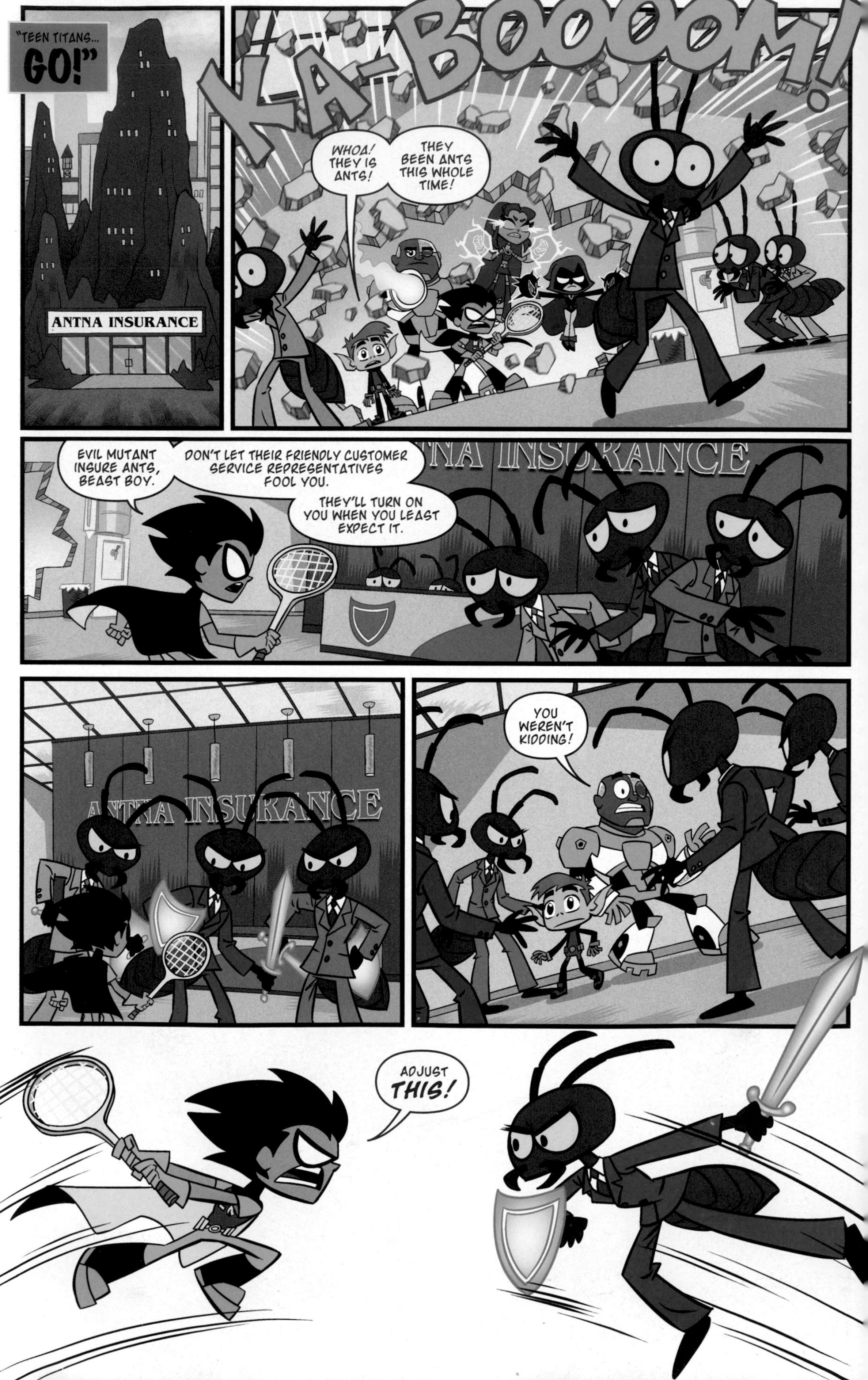
"TEEN TITANS... GO!"
ANTNA INSURANCE
KA-BOOOOM!
WHOA! THEY IS ANTS!
THEY BEEN ANTS THIS WHOLE TIME!
EVIL MUTANT INSURE ANTS, BEAST BOY.
DON'T LET THEIR FRIENDLY CUSTOMER SERVICE REPRESENTATIVES FOOL YOU.
THEY'LL TURN ON YOU WHEN YOU LEAST EXPECT IT.
ANTNA INSURANCE
YOU WEREN'T KIDDING!
ADJUST THIS!

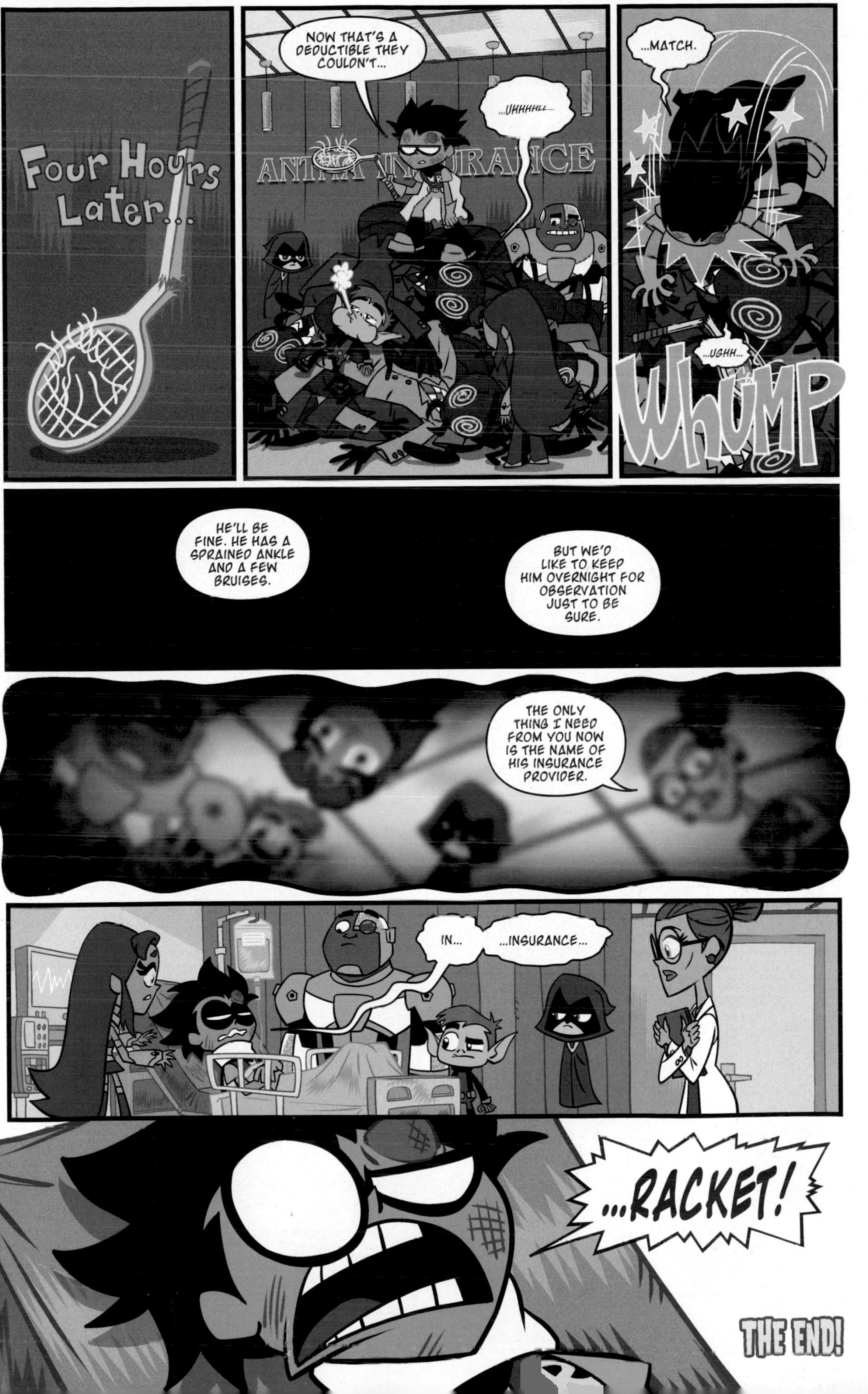
Four Hours Later...
NOW THAT'S A DEDUCTIBLE THEY COULDN'T...
...UHHHHLL...
...MATCH.
...UGHH...
WHUMP
HE'LL BE FINE. HE HAS A SPRAINED ANKLE AND A FEW BRUISES.
BUT WE'D LIKE TO KEEP HIM OVERNIGHT FOR OBSERVATION JUST TO BE SURE.
THE ONLY THING I NEED FROM YOU NOW IS THE NAME OF HIS INSURANCE PROVIDER.
IN...
...INSURANCE...
...RACKET!
THE END!

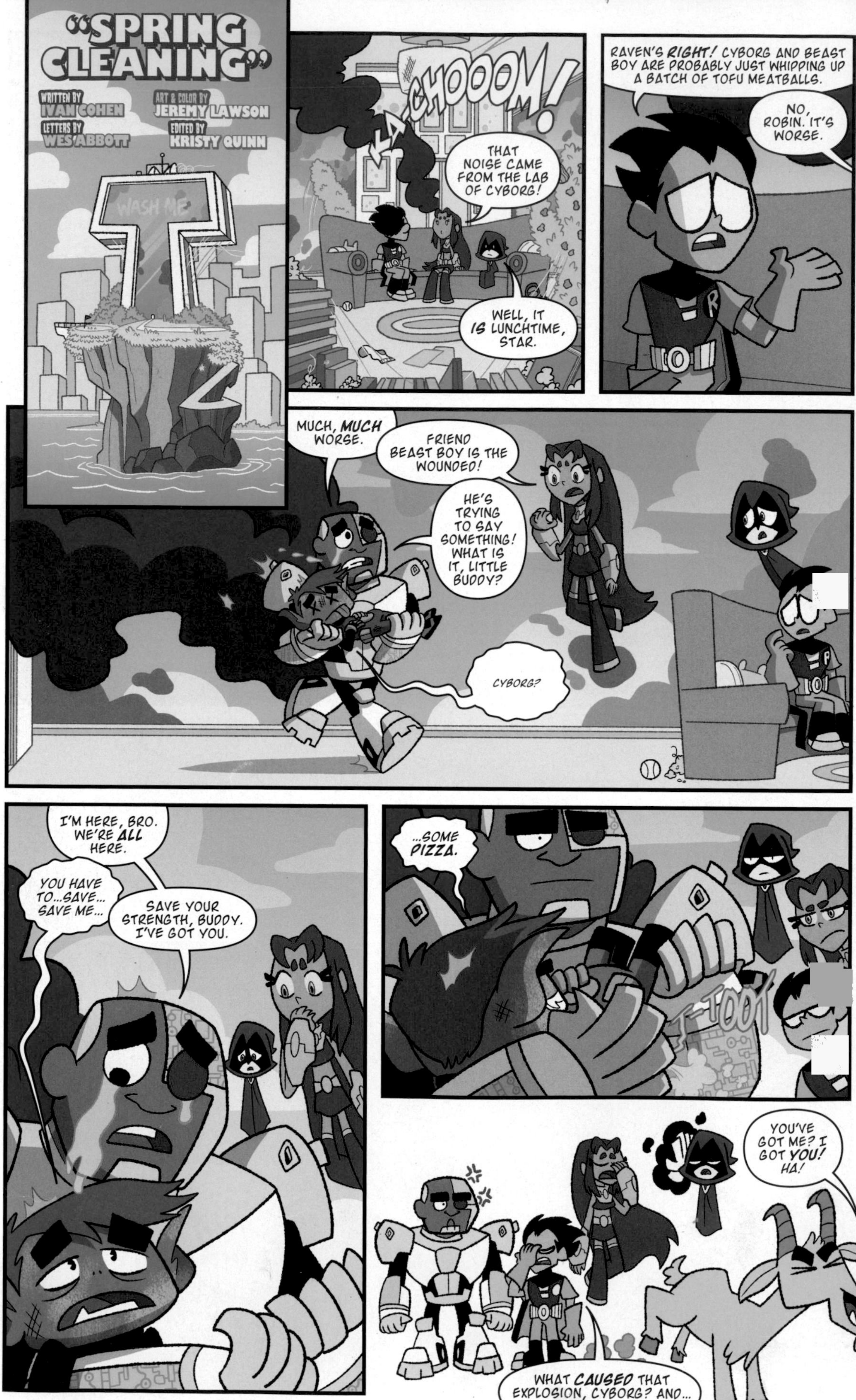
"SPRING CLEANING"
WRITTEN BY IVAN COHEN
ART & COLOR BY JEREMY LAWSON
LETTERS BY WES ABBOTT
EDITED BY KRISTY QUINN
WASH ME
CHOOOM!
THAT NOISE CAME FROM THE LAB OF CYBORG!
WELL, IT IS LUNCHTIME, STAR.
RAVEN'S RIGHT! CYBORG AND BEAST BOY ARE PROBABLY JUST WHIPPING UP A BATCH OF TOFU MEATBALLS.
NO, ROBIN. IT'S WORSE.
MUCH, MUCH WORSE.
FRIEND BEAST BOY IS THE WOUNDED!
HE'S TRYING TO SAY SOMETHING! WHAT IS IT, LITTLE BUDDY?
CYBORG?
I'M HERE, BRO. WE'RE ALL HERE.
YOU HAVE TO...SAVE... SAVE ME...
SAVE YOUR STRENGTH, BUDDY. I'VE GOT YOU.
...SOME PIZZA.
T-TOOT
YOU'VE GOT ME? I GOT YOU! HA!
WHAT CAUSED THAT EXPLOSION, CYBORG? AND... IS THERE PIZZA?

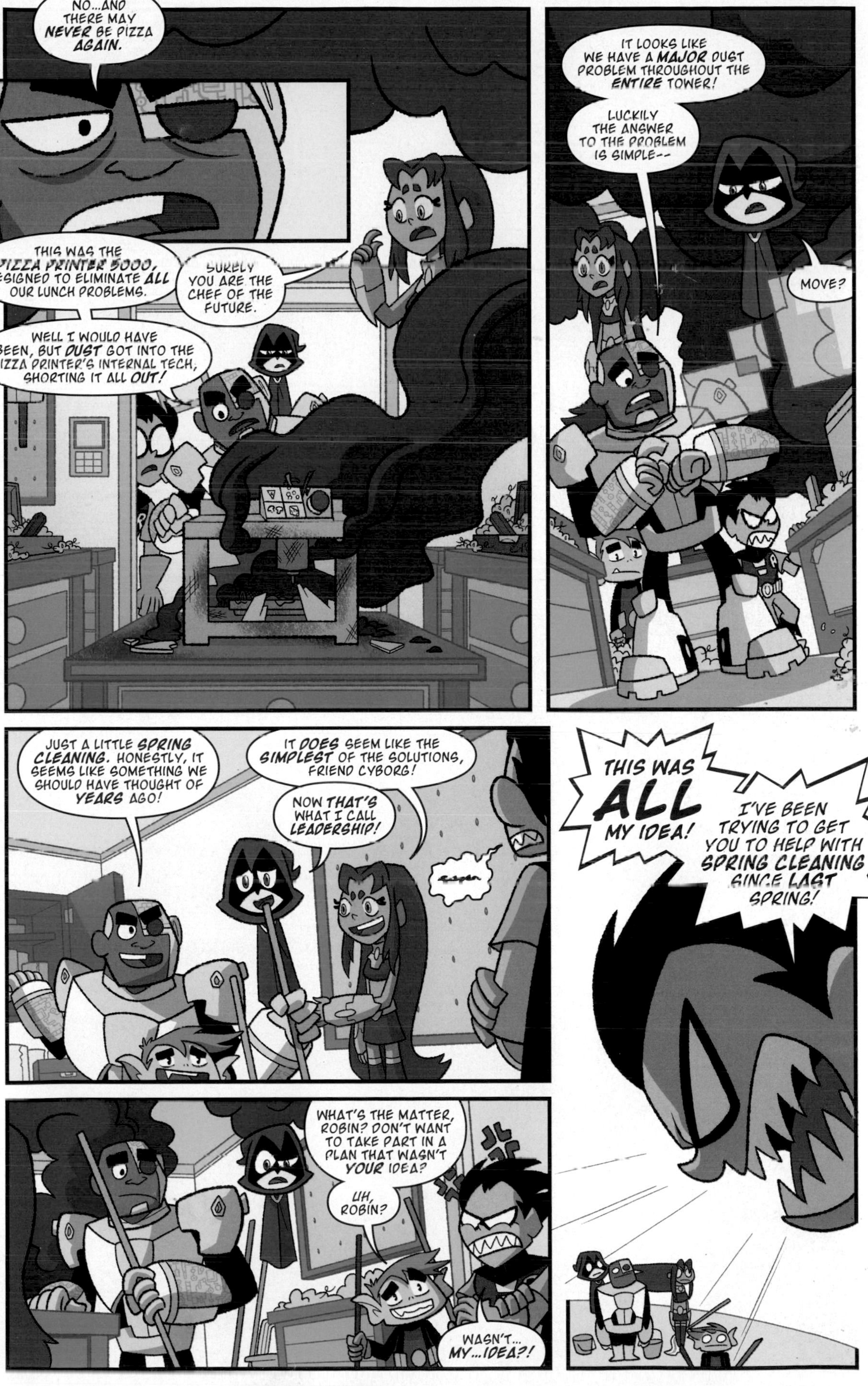
NO...AND THERE MAY NEVER BE PIZZA AGAIN.
THIS WAS THE PIZZA PRINTER 5000, DESIGNED TO ELIMINATE ALL OUR LUNCH PROBLEMS.
SURELY YOU ARE THE CHEF OF THE FUTURE.
WELL I WOULD HAVE BEEN, BUT DUST GOT INTO THE PIZZA PRINTER'S INTERNAL TECH, SHORTING IT ALL OUT!
IT LOOKS LIKE WE HAVE A MAJOR DUST PROBLEM THROUGHOUT THE ENTIRE TOWER!
LUCKILY THE ANSWER TO THE PROBLEM IS SIMPLE--
MOVE?
JUST A LITTLE SPRING CLEANING. HONESTLY, IT SEEMS LIKE SOMETHING WE SHOULD HAVE THOUGHT OF YEARS AGO!
IT DOES SEEM LIKE THE SIMPLEST OF THE SOLUTIONS, FRIEND CYBORG!
NOW THAT'S WHAT I CALL LEADERSHIP!
WHAT'S THE MATTER, ROBIN? DON'T WANT TO TAKE PART IN A PLAN THAT WASN'T YOUR IDEA?
UH, ROBIN?
WASN'T... MY...IDEA?!
THIS WAS ALL MY IDEA!
I'VE BEEN TRYING TO GET YOU TO HELP WITH SPRING CLEANING SINCE LAST SPRING!

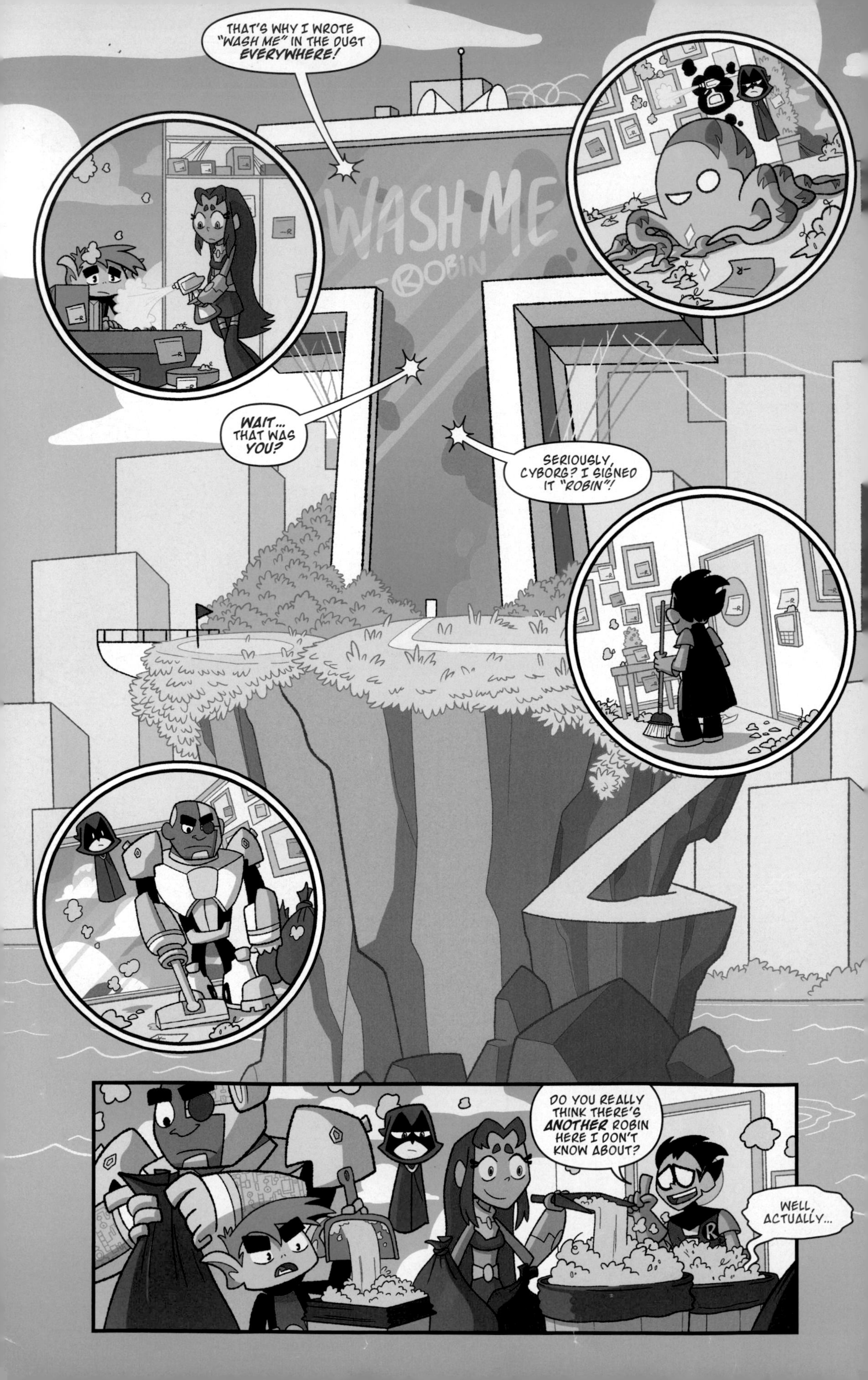
THAT'S WHY I WROTE "WASH ME" IN THE DUST EVERYWHERE!
WASH ME -ROBIN
WAIT... THAT WAS YOU?
SERIOUSLY, CYBORG? I SIGNED IT "ROBIN"!
DO YOU REALLY THINK THERE'S ANOTHER ROBIN HERE I DON'T KNOW ABOUT?
WELL, ACTUALLY...

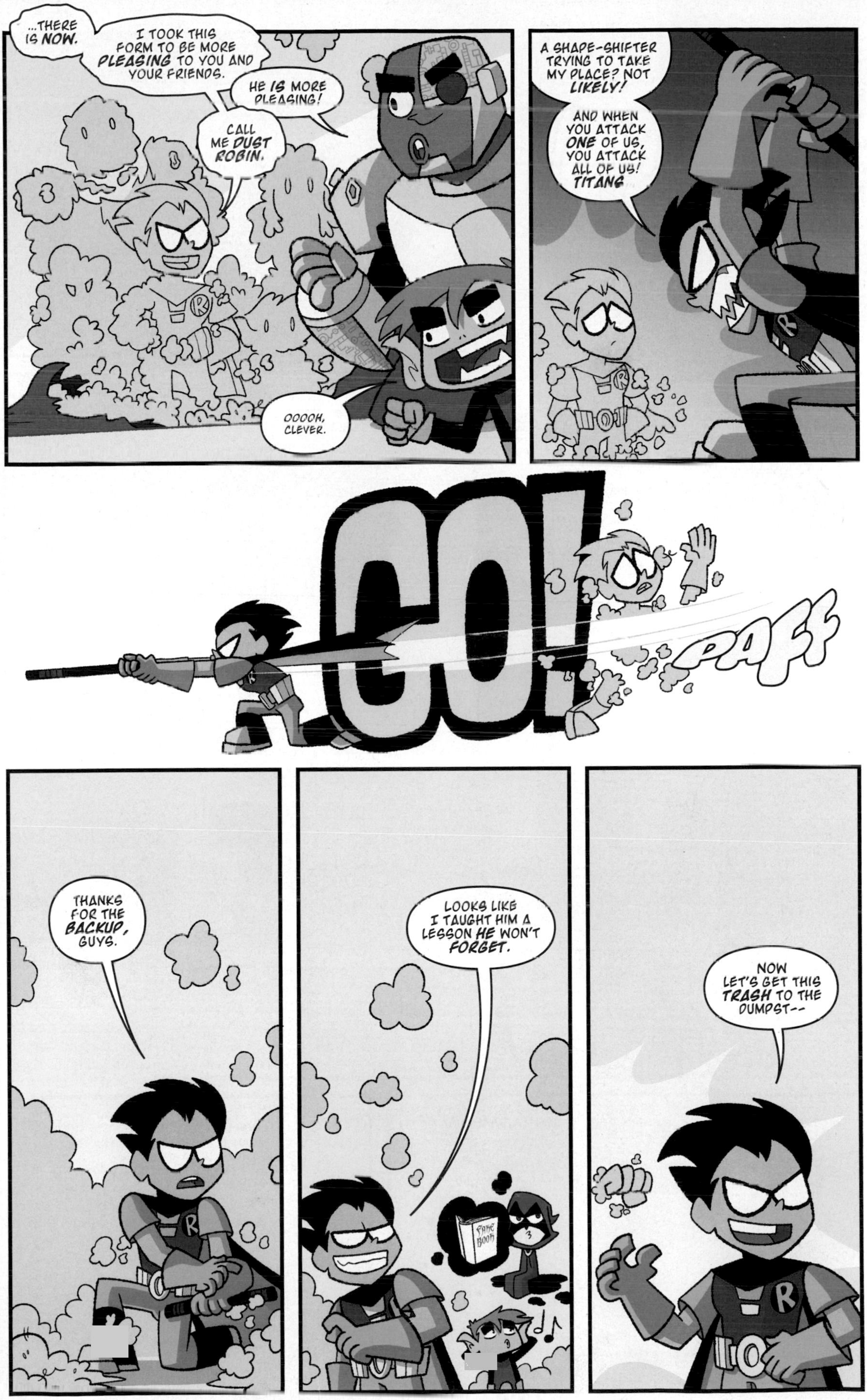
...THERE IS NOW.
I TOOK THIS FORM TO BE MORE PLEASING TO YOU AND YOUR FRIENDS.
HE IS MORE PLEASING!
CALL ME DUST ROBIN.
OOOOH, CLEVER.
A SHAPE-SHIFTER TRYING TO TAKE MY PLACE? NOT LIKELY!
AND WHEN YOU ATTACK ONE OF US, YOU ATTACK ALL OF US! TITANS
GO!
PAFF
THANKS FOR THE BACKUP, GUYS.
LOOKS LIKE I TAUGHT HIM A LESSON HE WON'T FORGET.
FAKE BOOK
NOW LET'S GET THIS TRASH TO THE DUMPST--

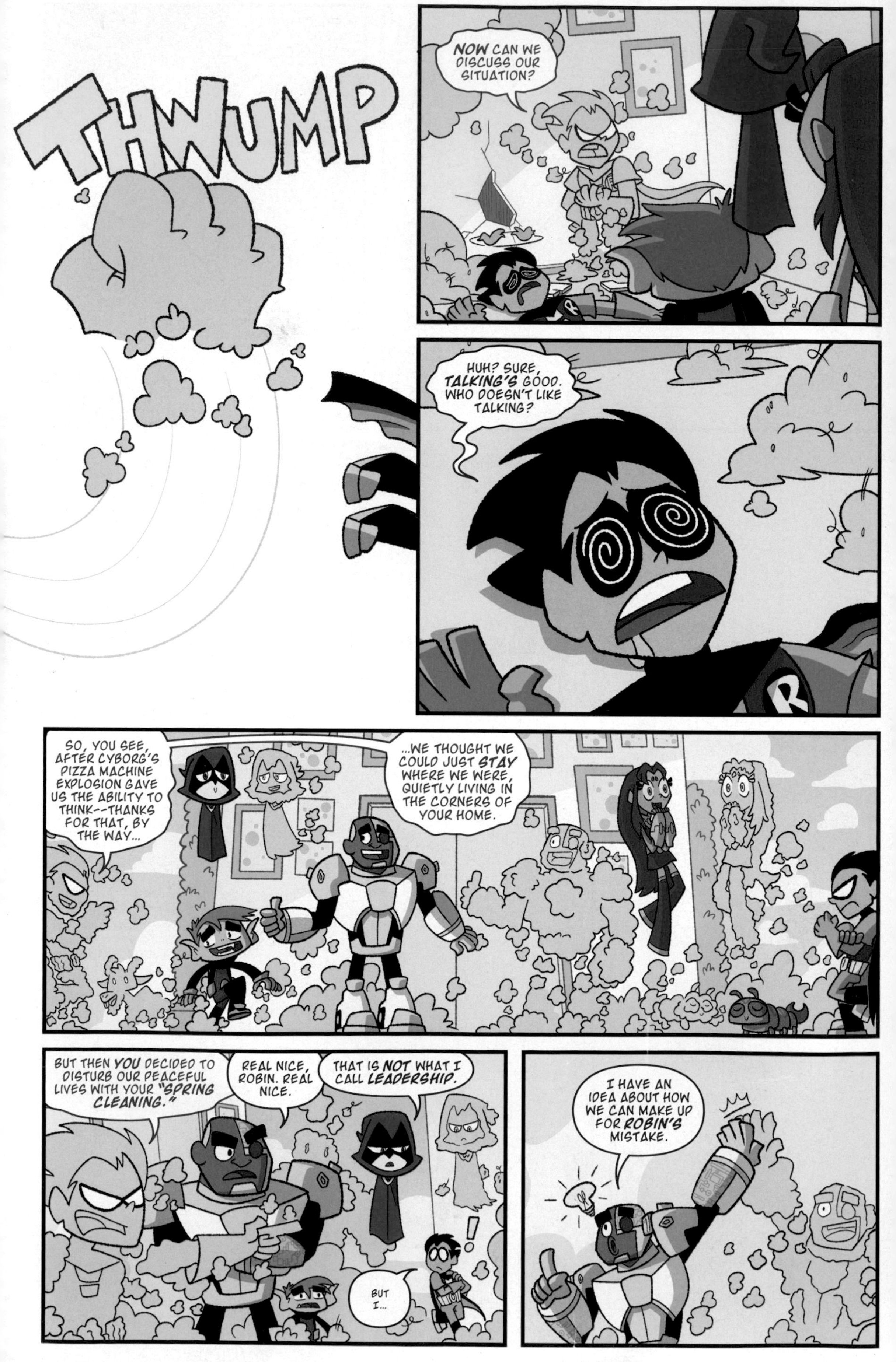
THWUMP
NOW CAN WE DISCUSS OUR SITUATION?
HUH? SURE, TALKING'S GOOD. WHO DOESN'T LIKE TALKING?
SO, YOU SEE, AFTER CYBORG'S PIZZA MACHINE EXPLOSION GAVE US THE ABILITY TO THINK--THANKS FOR THAT, BY THE WAY...
...WE THOUGHT WE COULD JUST STAY WHERE WE WERE, QUIETLY LIVING IN THE CORNERS OF YOUR HOME.
BUT THEN YOU DECIDED TO DISTURB OUR PEACEFUL LIVES WITH YOUR "SPRING CLEANING."
REAL NICE, ROBIN. REAL NICE.
THAT IS NOT WHAT I CALL LEADERSHIP.
!
BUT I...
I HAVE AN IDEA ABOUT HOW WE CAN MAKE UP FOR ROBIN'S MISTAKE.

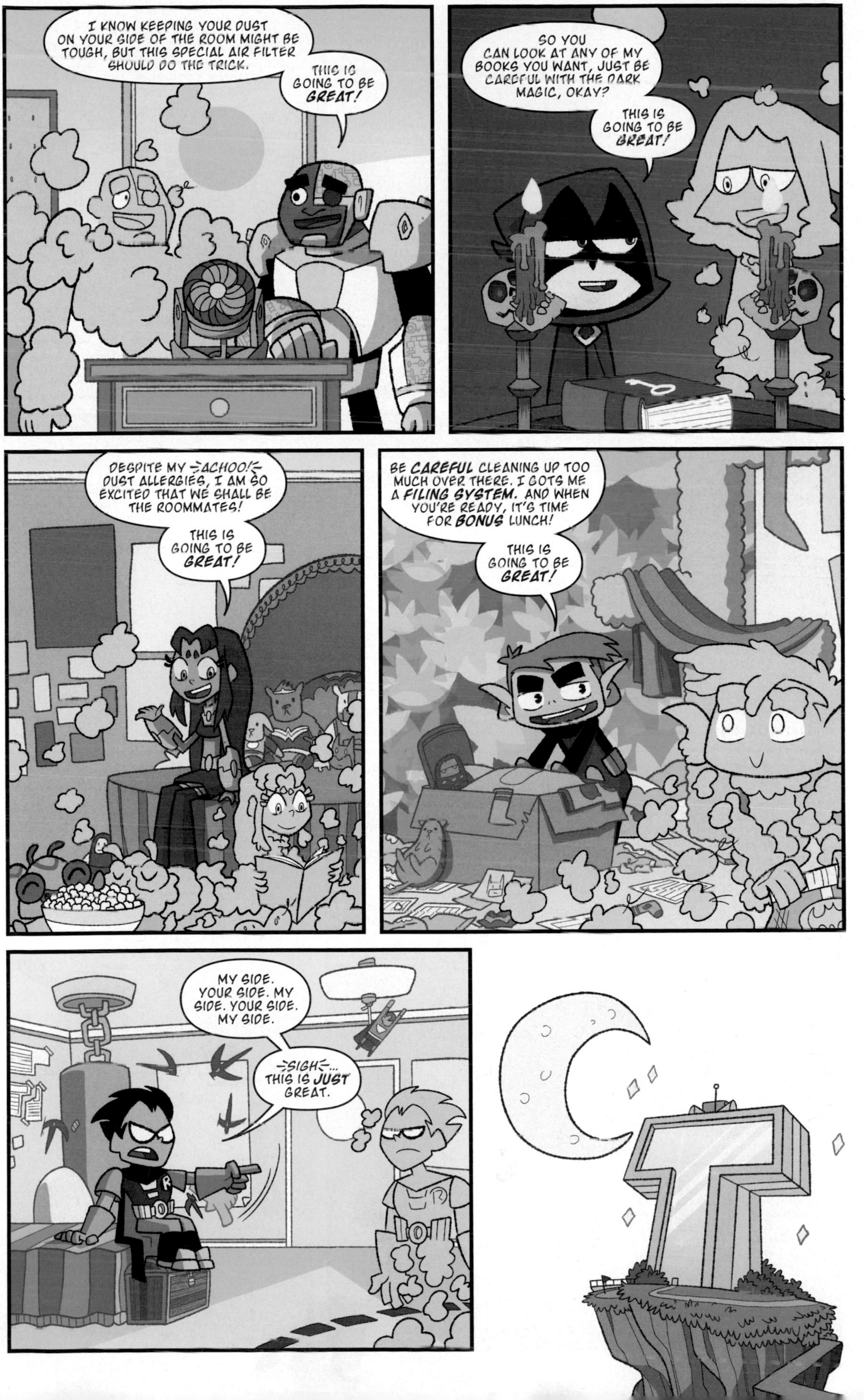
I KNOW KEEPING YOUR DUST ON YOUR SIDE OF THE ROOM MIGHT BE TOUGH, BUT THIS SPECIAL AIR FILTER SHOULD DO THE TRICK.
THIS IS GOING TO BE GREAT!
SO YOU CAN LOOK AT ANY OF MY BOOKS YOU WANT, JUST BE CAREFUL WITH THE DARK MAGIC, OKAY?
THIS IS GOING TO BE GREAT!
DESPITE MY ACHOO! DUST ALLERGIES, I AM SO EXCITED THAT WE SHALL BE THE ROOMMATES!
THIS IS GOING TO BE GREAT!
BE CAREFUL CLEANING UP TOO MUCH OVER THERE. I GOTS ME A FILING SYSTEM. AND WHEN YOU'RE READY, IT'S TIME FOR BONUS LUNCH!
THIS IS GOING TO BE GREAT!
MY SIDE. YOUR SIDE. MY SIDE. YOUR SIDE. MY SIDE.
SIGH... THIS IS JUST GREAT.

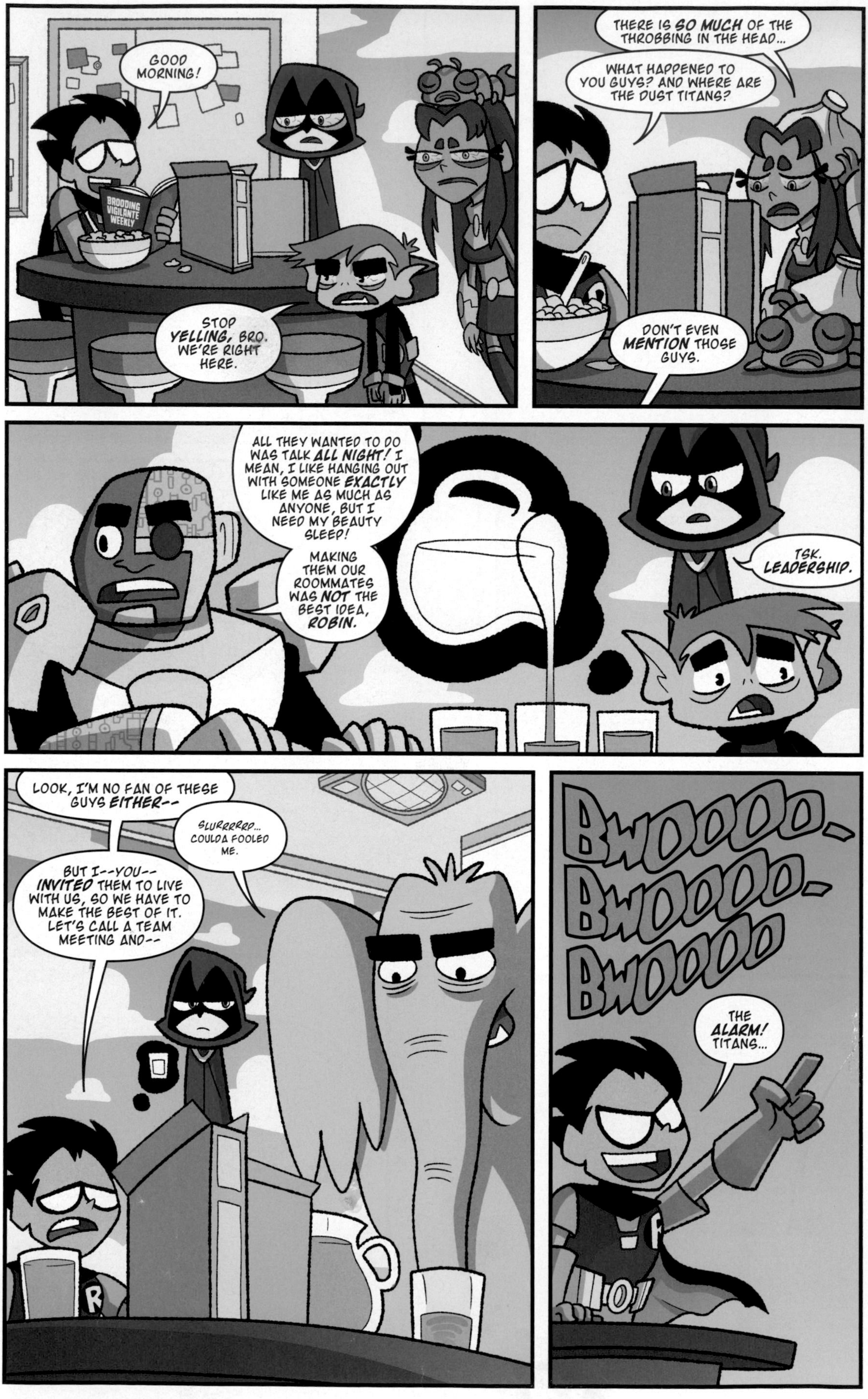
GOOD MORNING!
BROODING VIGILANTE WEEKLY
STOP YELLING, BRO. WE'RE RIGHT HERE.
THERE IS SO MUCH OF THE THROBBING IN THE HEAD...
WHAT HAPPENED TO YOU GUYS? AND WHERE ARE THE DUST TITANS?
DON'T EVEN MENTION THOSE GUYS.
ALL THEY WANTED TO DO WAS TALK ALL NIGHT! I MEAN, I LIKE HANGING OUT WITH SOMEONE EXACTLY LIKE ME AS MUCH AS ANYONE, BUT I NEED MY BEAUTY SLEEP!
MAKING THEM OUR ROOMMATES WAS NOT THE BEST IDEA, ROBIN.
TSK. LEADERSHIP.
LOOK, I'M NO FAN OF THESE GUYS EITHER--
SLURRRRRP... COULDA FOOLED ME.
BUT I--YOU--INVITED THEM TO LIVE WITH US, SO WE HAVE TO MAKE THE BEST OF IT. LET'S CALL A TEAM MEETING AND--
BWOOOO-BWOOOO-BWOOOO
THE ALARM! TITANS...

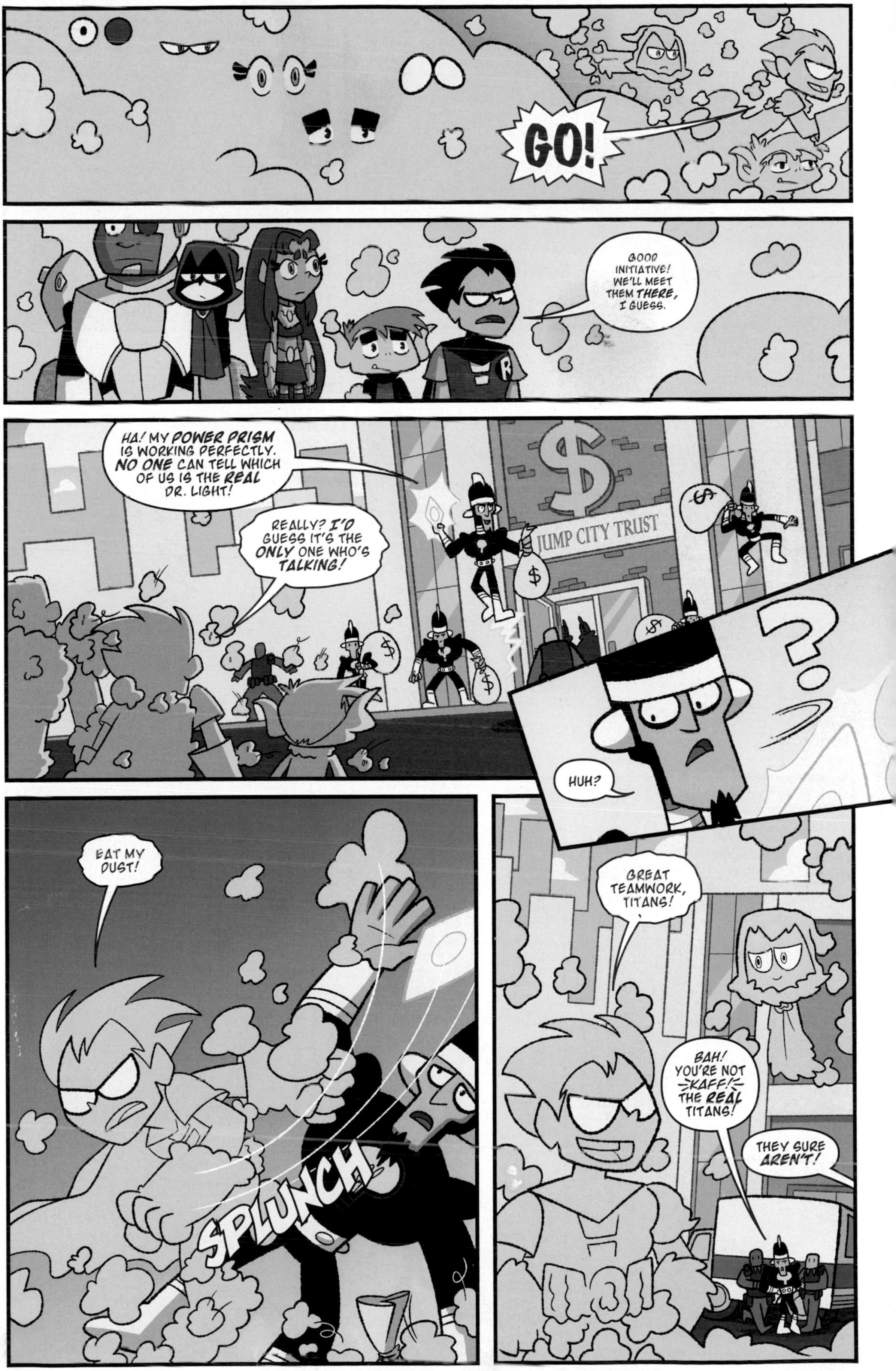
GO!
GOOD INITIATIVE! WE'LL MEET THEM THERE, I GUESS.
HA! MY POWER PRISM IS WORKING PERFECTLY. NO ONE CAN TELL WHICH OF US IS THE REAL DR. LIGHT!
REALLY? I'D GUESS IT'S THE ONLY ONE WHO'S TALKING!
JUMP CITY TRUST
HUH?
EAT MY DUST!
SPLUNCH
GREAT TEAMWORK, TITANS!
BAH! YOU'RE NOT -KAFF!- THE REAL TITANS!
THEY SURE AREN'T!

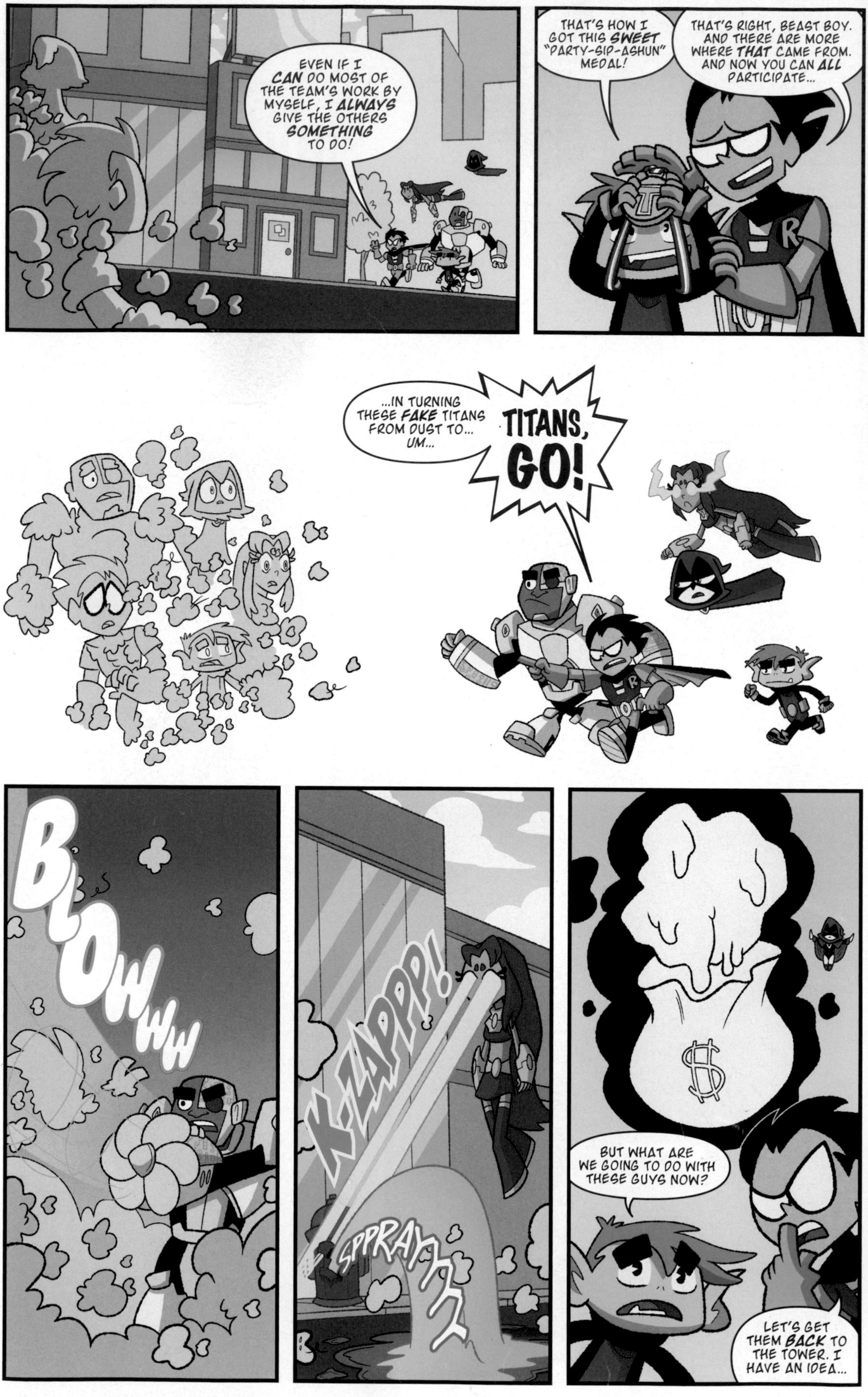
EVEN IF I CAN DO MOST OF THE TEAM'S WORK BY MYSELF, I ALWAYS GIVE THE OTHERS SOMETHING TO DO!
THAT'S HOW I GOT THIS SWEET "PARTY-SIP-ASHUN" MEDAL!
THAT'S RIGHT, BEAST BOY. AND THERE ARE MORE WHERE THAT CAME FROM. AND NOW YOU CAN ALL PARTICIPATE...
...IN TURNING THESE FAKE TITANS FROM DUST TO... UM...
TITANS, GO!
BLOWWWW
K-ZAPPP!
SPPRAYYYY
BUT WHAT ARE WE GOING TO DO WITH THESE GUYS NOW?
LET'S GET THEM BACK TO THE TOWER. I HAVE AN IDEA...

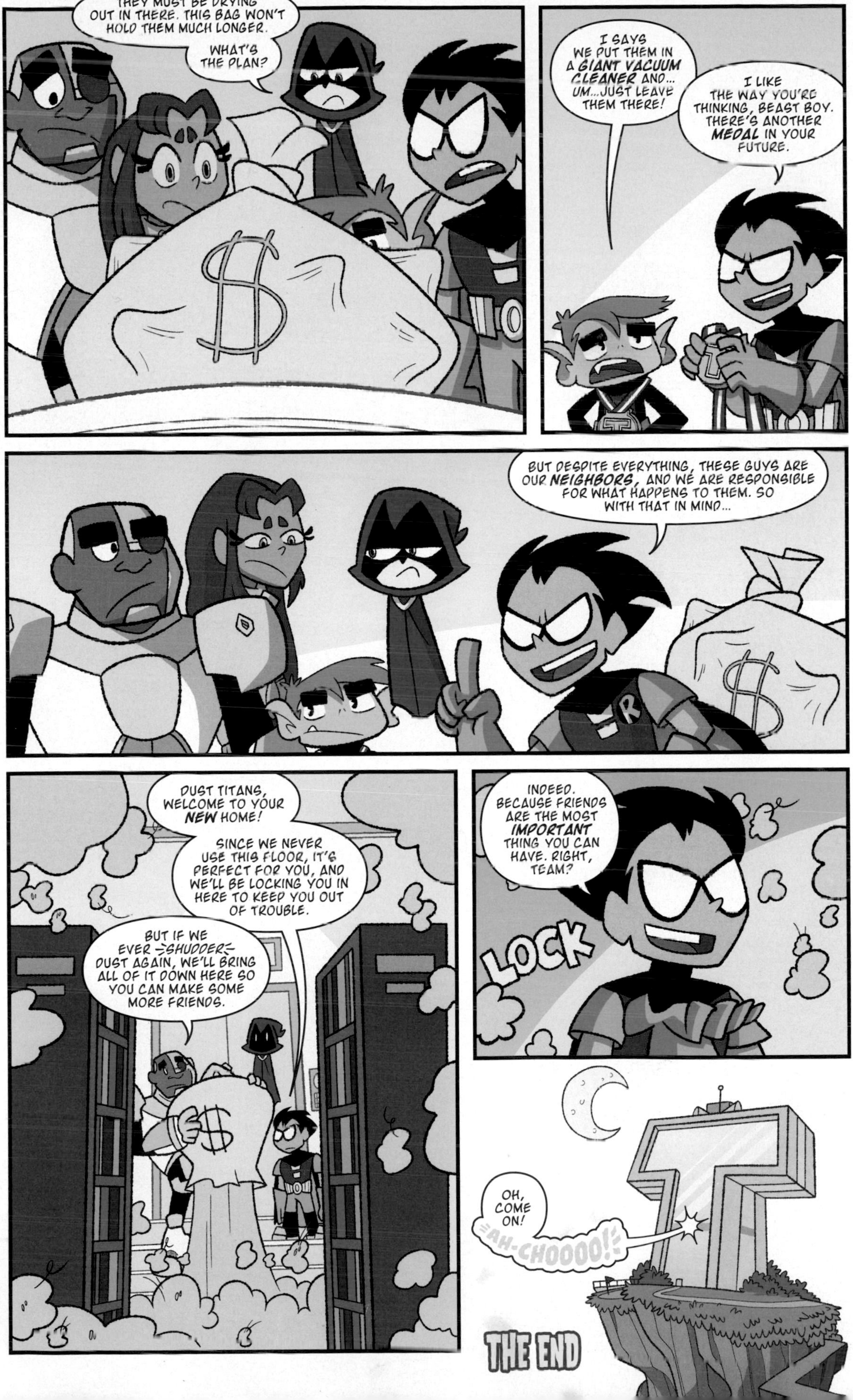
THEY MUST BE DRYING OUT IN THERE. THIS BAG WON'T HOLD THEM MUCH LONGER.
WHAT'S THE PLAN?
I SAYS WE PUT THEM IN A GIANT VACUUM CLEANER AND... UM...JUST LEAVE THEM THERE!
I LIKE THE WAY YOU'RE THINKING, BEAST BOY. THERE'S ANOTHER MEDAL IN YOUR FUTURE.
BUT DESPITE EVERYTHING, THESE GUYS ARE OUR NEIGHBORS, AND WE ARE RESPONSIBLE FOR WHAT HAPPENS TO THEM. SO WITH THAT IN MIND...
DUST TITANS, WELCOME TO YOUR NEW HOME!
SINCE WE NEVER USE THIS FLOOR, IT'S PERFECT FOR YOU, AND WE'LL BE LOCKING YOU IN HERE TO KEEP YOU OUT OF TROUBLE.
BUT IF WE EVER =SHUDDER= DUST AGAIN, WE'LL BRING ALL OF IT DOWN HERE SO YOU CAN MAKE SOME MORE FRIENDS.
INDEED. BECAUSE FRIENDS ARE THE MOST IMPORTANT THING YOU CAN HAVE. RIGHT, TEAM?
LOCK
OH, COME ON!
AH-CHOOOO!
THE END

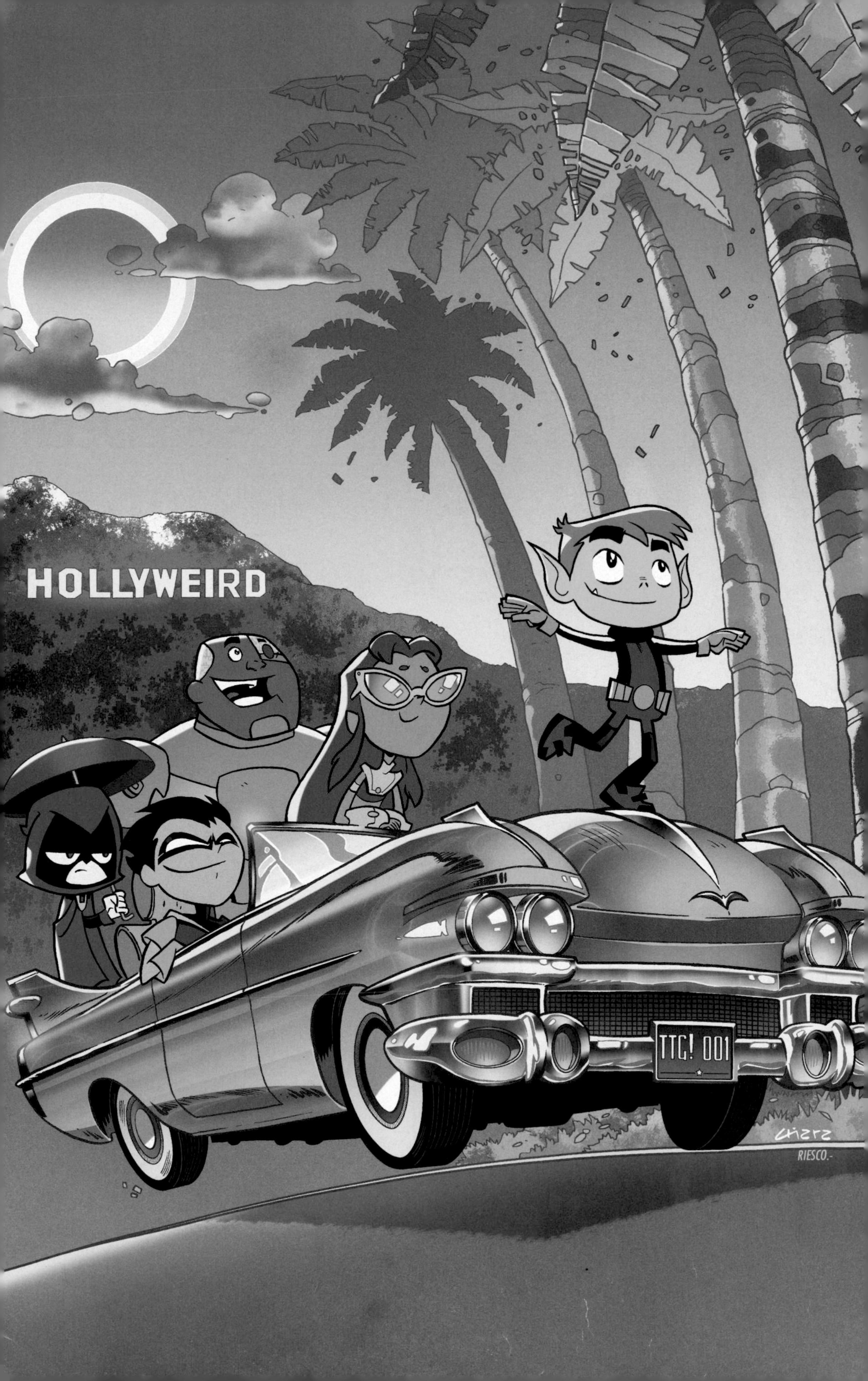
HOLLYWEIRD
TTG! 001
RIESCO.-

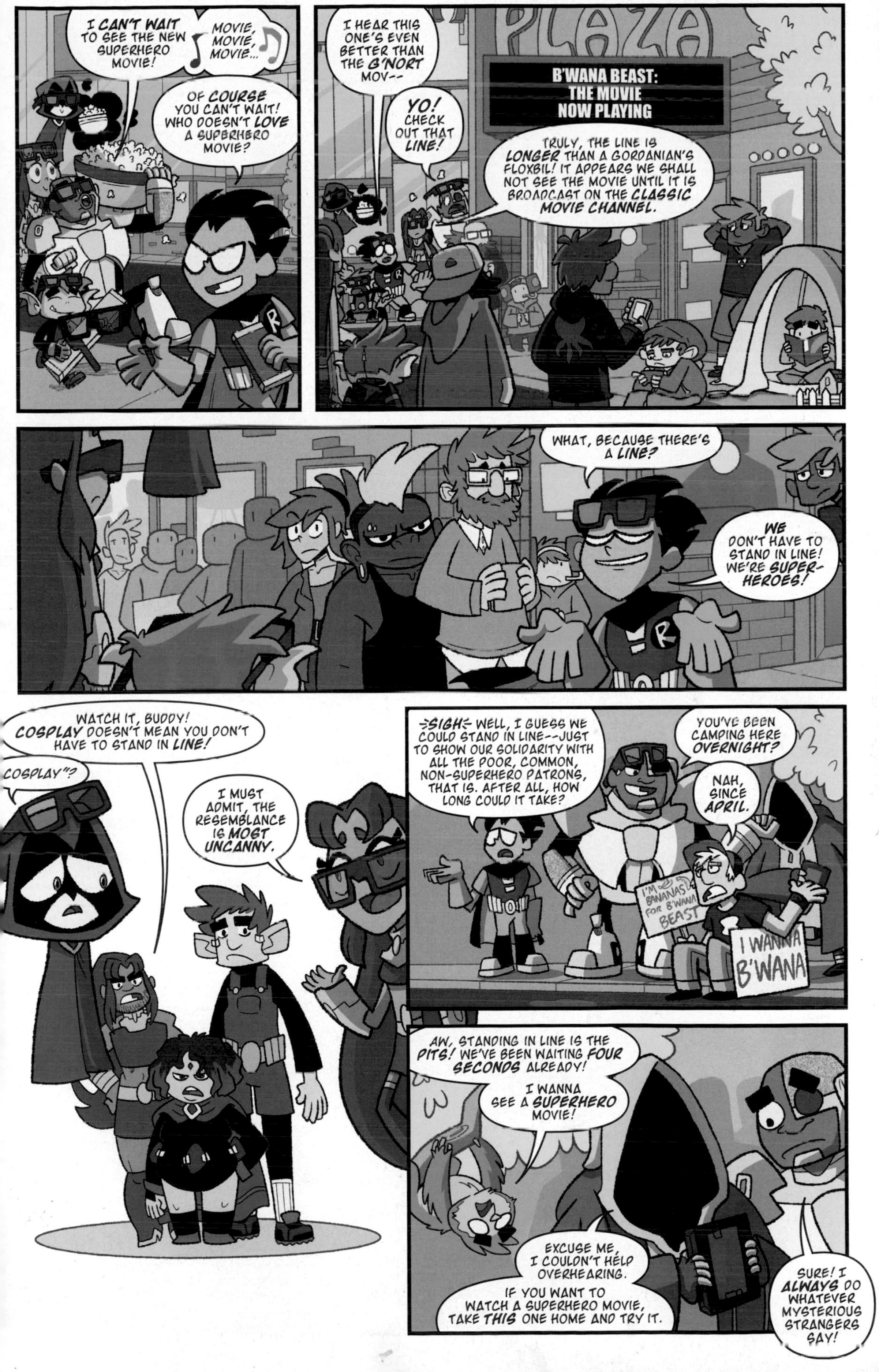
I CAN'T WAIT TO SEE THE NEW SUPERHERO MOVIE!
MOVIE, MOVIE, MOVIE...
OF COURSE YOU CAN'T WAIT! WHO DOESN'T LOVE A SUPERHERO MOVIE?
PLAZA
I HEAR THIS ONE'S EVEN BETTER THAN THE G'NORT MOV--
B'WANA BEAST: THE MOVIE NOW PLAYING
YO! CHECK OUT THAT LINE!
TRULY, THE LINE IS LONGER THAN A GORDANIAN'S FLOXBIL! IT APPEARS WE SHALL NOT SEE THE MOVIE UNTIL IT IS BROADCAST ON THE CLASSIC MOVIE CHANNEL.
WHAT, BECAUSE THERE'S A LINE?
WE DON'T HAVE TO STAND IN LINE! WE'RE SUPER-HEROES!
WATCH IT, BUDDY! COSPLAY DOESN'T MEAN YOU DON'T HAVE TO STAND IN LINE!
COSPLAY"?
I MUST ADMIT, THE RESEMBLANCE IS MOST UNCANNY.
=SIGH= WELL, I GUESS WE COULD STAND IN LINE--JUST TO SHOW OUR SOLIDARITY WITH ALL THE POOR, COMMON, NON-SUPERHERO PATRONS, THAT IS. AFTER ALL, HOW LONG COULD IT TAKE?
YOU'VE BEEN CAMPING HERE OVERNIGHT?
NAH, SINCE APRIL.
I'M BANANAS FOR B'WANA BEAST
I WANNA B'WANA
AW, STANDING IN LINE IS THE PITS! WE'VE BEEN WAITING FOUR SECONDS ALREADY!
I WANNA SEE A SUPERHERO MOVIE!
EXCUSE ME, I COULDN'T HELP OVERHEARING.
IF YOU WANT TO WATCH A SUPERHERO MOVIE, TAKE THIS ONE HOME AND TRY IT.
SURE! I ALWAYS DO WHATEVER MYSTERIOUS STRANGERS SAY!

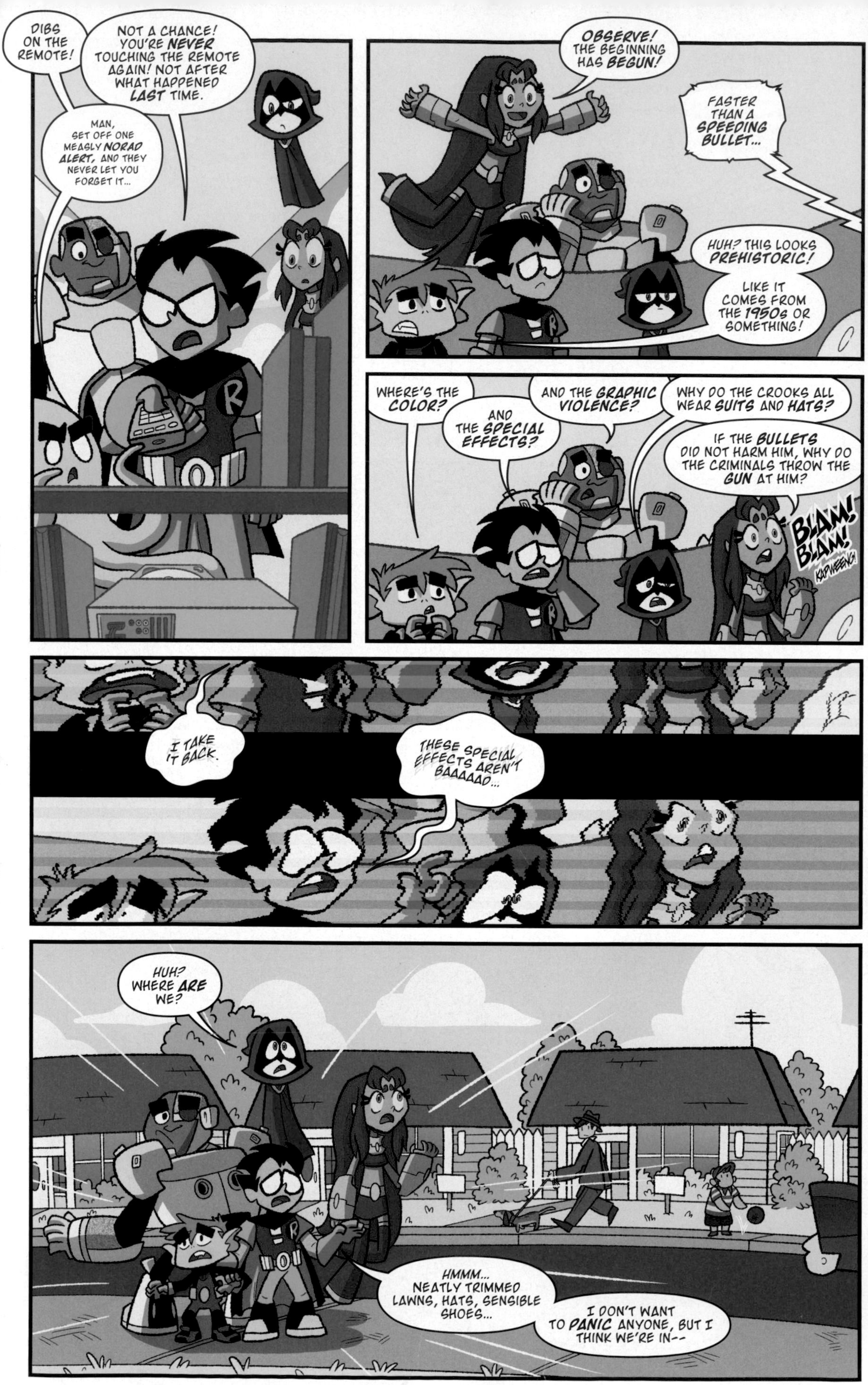
DIBS ON THE REMOTE!
NOT A CHANCE! YOU'RE NEVER TOUCHING THE REMOTE AGAIN! NOT AFTER WHAT HAPPENED LAST TIME.
MAN, SET OFF ONE MEASLY NORAD ALERT, AND THEY NEVER LET YOU FORGET IT...
OBSERVE! THE BEGINNING HAS BEGUN!
FASTER THAN A SPEEDING BULLET...
HUH? THIS LOOKS PREHISTORIC!
LIKE IT COMES FROM THE 1950s OR SOMETHING!
WHERE'S THE COLOR?
AND THE SPECIAL EFFECTS?
AND THE GRAPHIC VIOLENCE?
WHY DO THE CROOKS ALL WEAR SUITS AND HATS?
IF THE BULLETS DID NOT HARM HIM, WHY DO THE CRIMINALS THROW THE GUN AT HIM?
BLAM! BLAM!
KAPWEENG!
I TAKE IT BACK.
THESE SPECIAL EFFECTS AREN'T BAAAAAD...
HUH? WHERE ARE WE?
HMMM... NEATLY TRIMMED LAWNS, HATS, SENSIBLE SHOES...
I DON'T WANT TO PANIC ANYONE, BUT I THINK WE'RE IN--

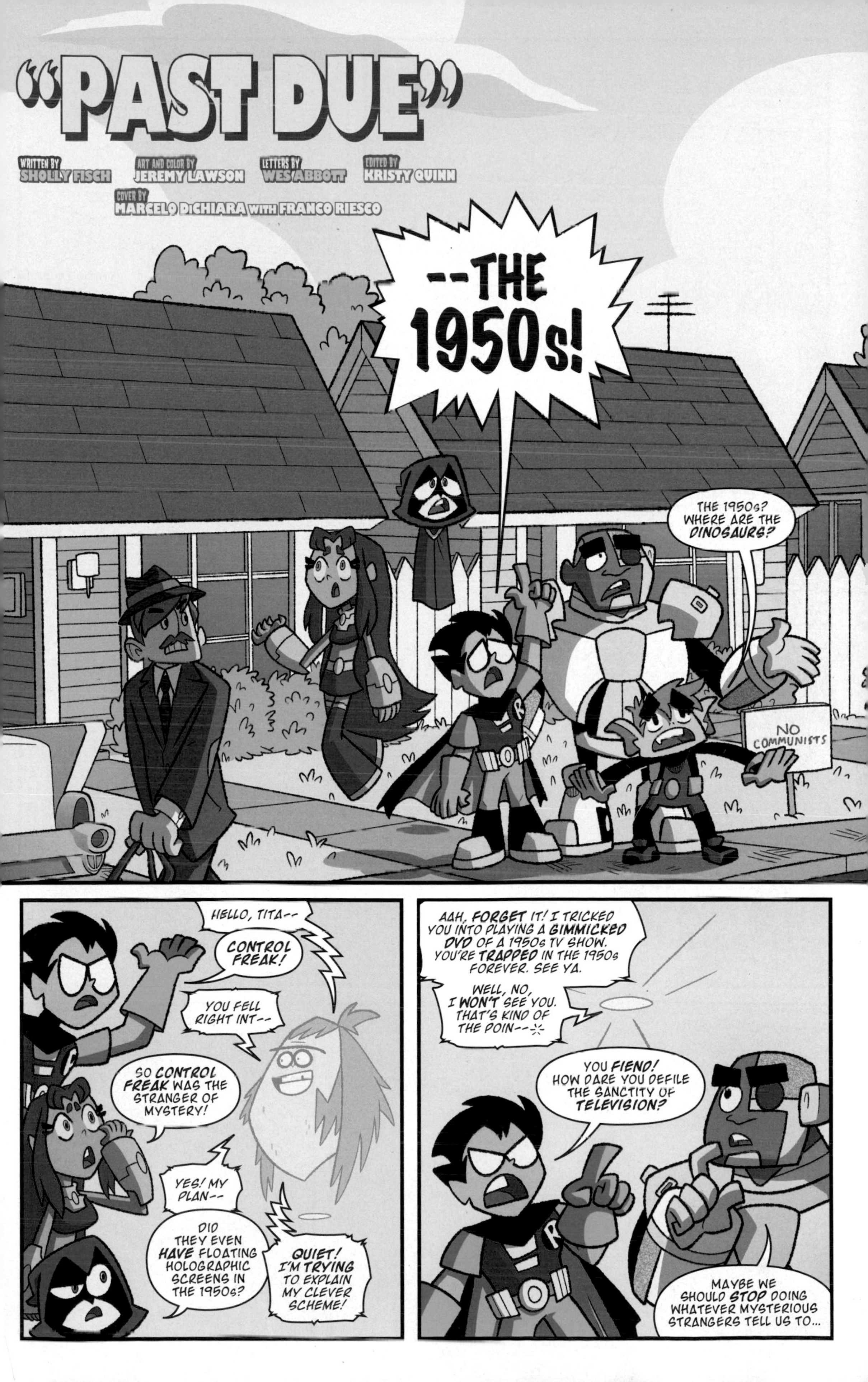
"PAST DUE"
WRITTEN BY SHOLLY FISCH
ART AND COLOR BY JEREMY LAWSON
LETTERS BY WES ABBOTT
EDITED BY KRISTY QUINN
COVER BY MARCELO DiCHIARA WITH FRANCO RIESCO
--THE 1950s!
THE 1950s? WHERE ARE THE DINOSAURS?
NO COMMUNISTS
HELLO, TITA--
CONTROL FREAK!
YOU FELL RIGHT INT--
SO CONTROL FREAK WAS THE STRANGER OF MYSTERY!
YES! MY PLAN--
DID THEY EVEN HAVE FLOATING HOLOGRAPHIC SCREENS IN THE 1950s?
QUIET! I'M TRYING TO EXPLAIN MY CLEVER SCHEME!
AAH, FORGET IT! I TRICKED YOU INTO PLAYING A GIMMICKED DVD OF A 1950s TV SHOW. YOU'RE TRAPPED IN THE 1950s FOREVER. SEE YA.
WELL, NO, I WON'T SEE YOU. THAT'S KIND OF THE POIN--
YOU FIEND! HOW DARE YOU DEFILE THE SANCTITY OF TELEVISION?
MAYBE WE SHOULD STOP DOING WHATEVER MYSTERIOUS STRANGERS TELL US TO...

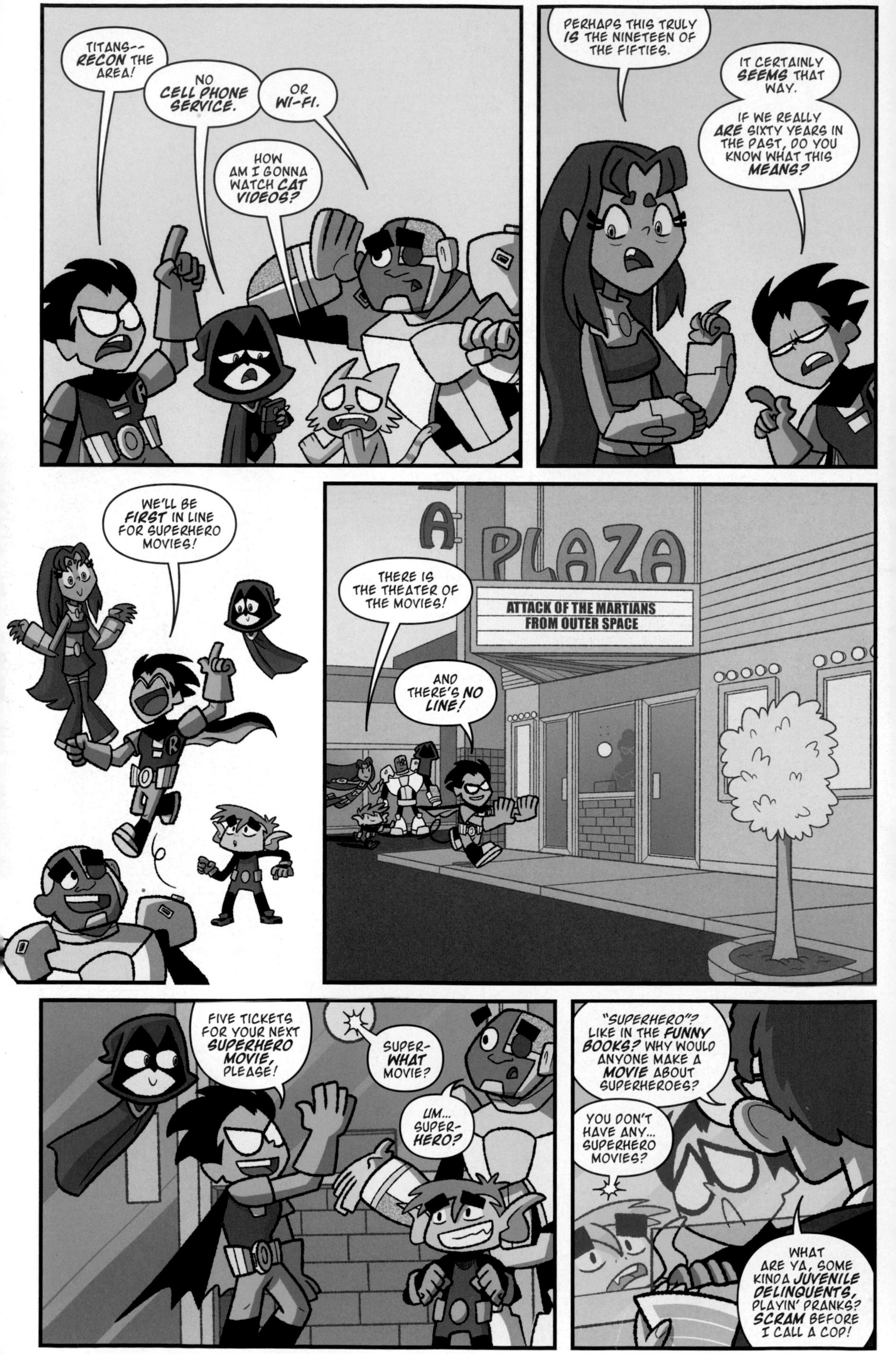
TITANS-- RECON THE AREA!
NO CELL PHONE SERVICE.
OR WI-FI.
HOW AM I GONNA WATCH CAT VIDEOS?
PERHAPS THIS TRULY IS THE NINETEEN OF THE FIFTIES.
IT CERTAINLY SEEMS THAT WAY.
IF WE REALLY ARE SIXTY YEARS IN THE PAST, DO YOU KNOW WHAT THIS MEANS?
WE'LL BE FIRST IN LINE FOR SUPERHERO MOVIES!
PLAZA
ATTACK OF THE MARTIANS FROM OUTER SPACE
THERE IS THE THEATER OF THE MOVIES!
AND THERE'S NO LINE!
FIVE TICKETS FOR YOUR NEXT SUPERHERO MOVIE, PLEASE!
SUPER-WHAT MOVIE?
UM... SUPER-HERO?
"SUPERHERO"? LIKE IN THE FUNNY BOOKS? WHY WOULD ANYONE MAKE A MOVIE ABOUT SUPERHEROES?
YOU DON'T HAVE ANY... SUPERHERO MOVIES?
WHAT ARE YA, SOME KINDA JUVENILE DELINQUENTS, PLAYIN' PRANKS? SCRAM BEFORE I CALL A COP!

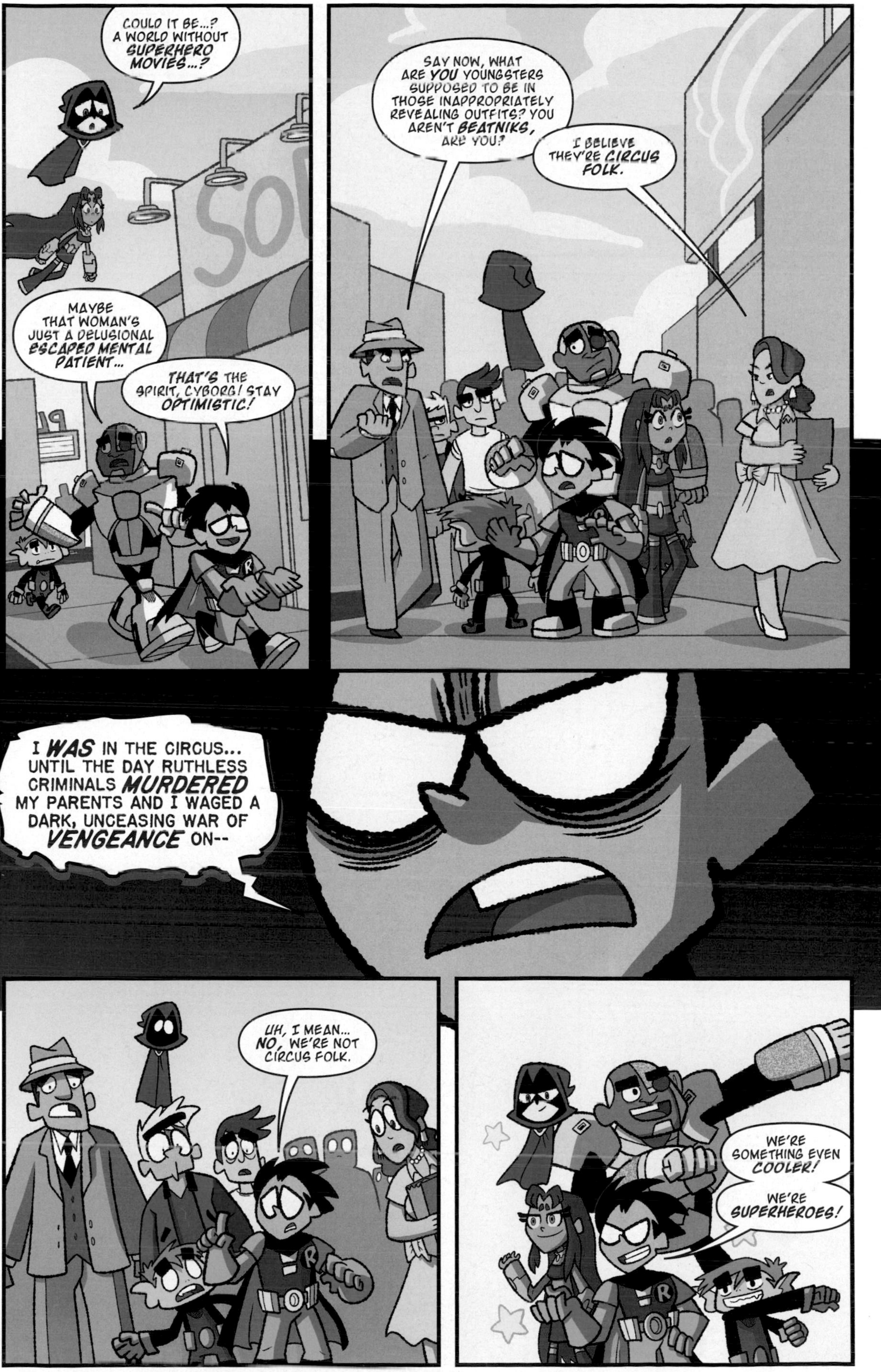
COULD IT BE...? A WORLD WITHOUT SUPERHERO MOVIES...?
MAYBE THAT WOMAN'S JUST A DELUSIONAL ESCAPED MENTAL PATIENT...
THAT'S THE SPIRIT, CYBORG! STAY OPTIMISTIC!
SAY NOW, WHAT ARE YOU YOUNGSTERS SUPPOSED TO BE IN THOSE INAPPROPRIATELY REVEALING OUTFITS? YOU AREN'T BEATNIKS, ARE YOU?
I BELIEVE THEY'RE CIRCUS FOLK.
I WAS IN THE CIRCUS... UNTIL THE DAY RUTHLESS CRIMINALS MURDERED MY PARENTS AND I WAGED A DARK, UNCEASING WAR OF VENGEANCE ON--
UH, I MEAN... NO, WE'RE NOT CIRCUS FOLK.
WE'RE SOMETHING EVEN COOLER!
WE'RE SUPERHEROES!

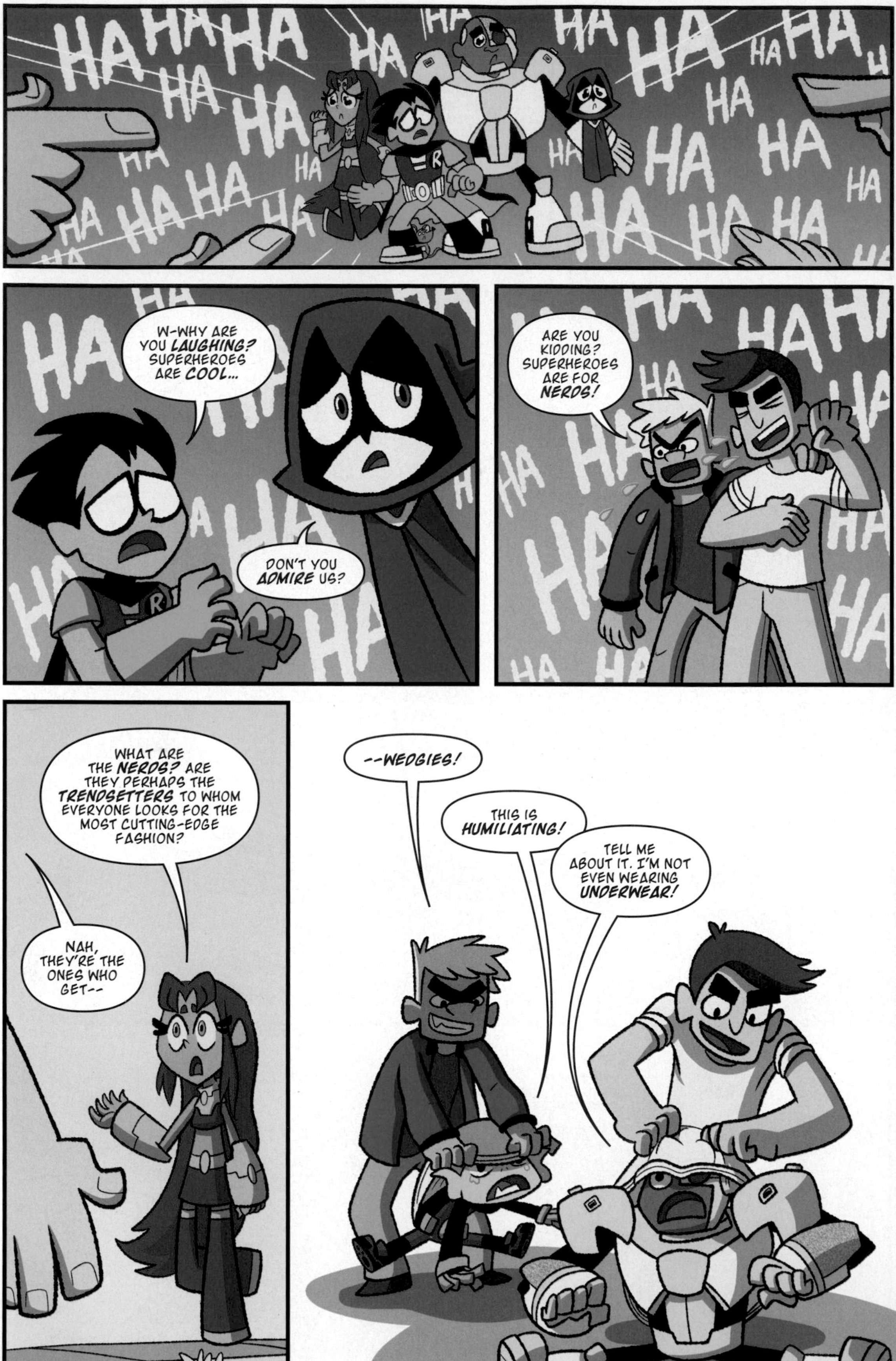
W-WHY ARE YOU *LAUGHING?* SUPERHEROES ARE *COOL*...
DON'T YOU *ADMIRE* US?
ARE YOU KIDDING? SUPERHEROES ARE FOR *NERDS!*
WHAT ARE THE *NERDS?* ARE THEY PERHAPS THE *TRENDSETTERS* TO WHOM EVERYONE LOOKS FOR THE MOST CUTTING-EDGE FASHION?
NAH, THEY'RE THE ONES WHO GET--
--*WEDGIES!*
THIS IS *HUMILIATING!*
TELL ME ABOUT IT. I'M NOT EVEN WEARING *UNDERWEAR!*

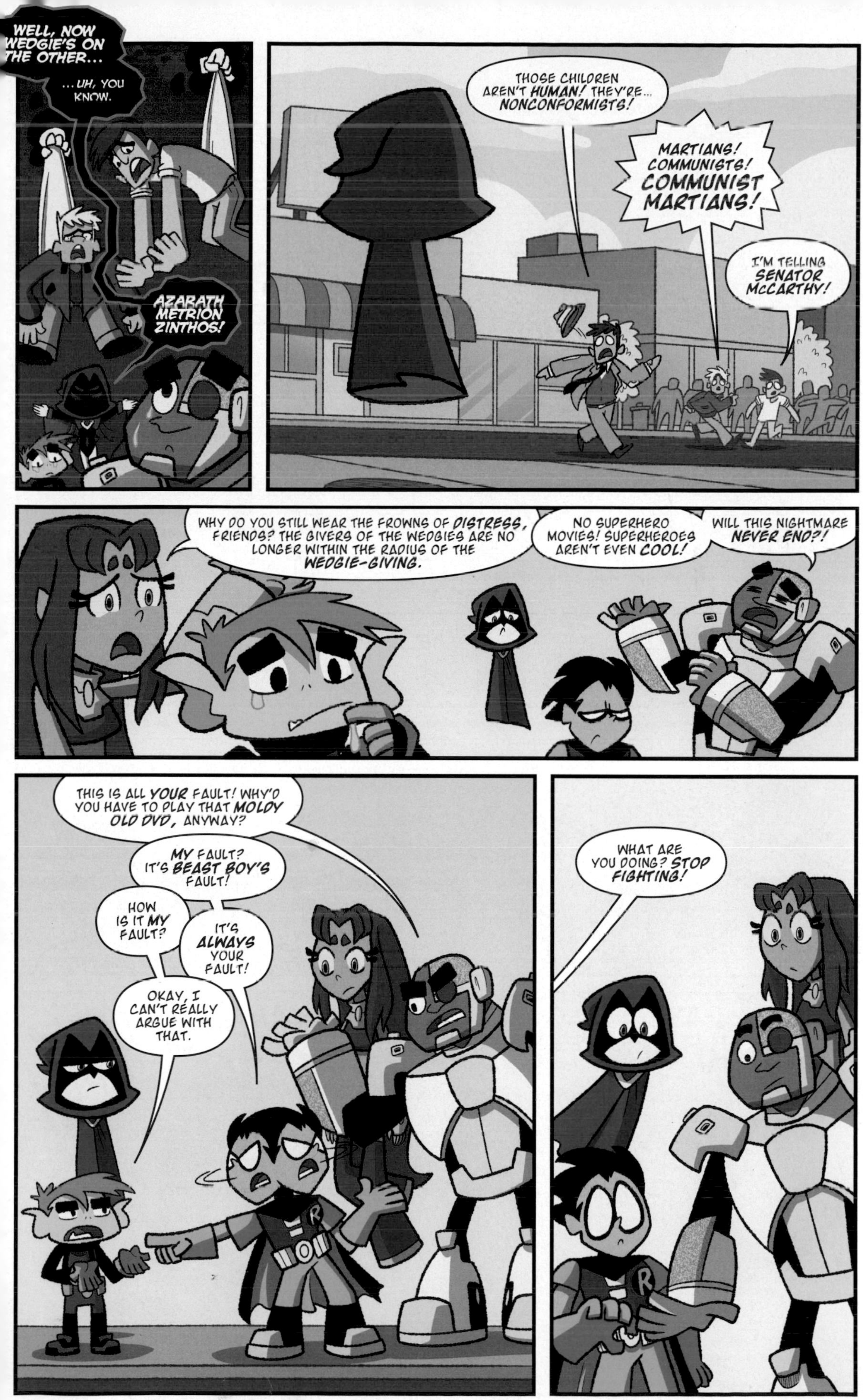
WELL, NOW WEDGIE'S ON THE OTHER...
...UH, YOU KNOW.
AZARATH METRION ZINTHOS!
THOSE CHILDREN AREN'T HUMAN! THEY'RE... NONCONFORMISTS!
MARTIANS! COMMUNISTS! COMMUNIST MARTIANS!
I'M TELLING SENATOR McCARTHY!
WHY DO YOU STILL WEAR THE FROWNS OF DISTRESS, FRIENDS? THE GIVERS OF THE WEDGIES ARE NO LONGER WITHIN THE RADIUS OF THE WEDGIE-GIVING.
NO SUPERHERO MOVIES! SUPERHEROES AREN'T EVEN COOL!
WILL THIS NIGHTMARE NEVER END?!
THIS IS ALL YOUR FAULT! WHY'D YOU HAVE TO PLAY THAT MOLDY OLD DVD, ANYWAY?
MY FAULT? IT'S BEAST BOY'S FAULT!
HOW IS IT MY FAULT?
IT'S ALWAYS YOUR FAULT!
OKAY, I CAN'T REALLY ARGUE WITH THAT.
WHAT ARE YOU DOING? STOP FIGHTING!

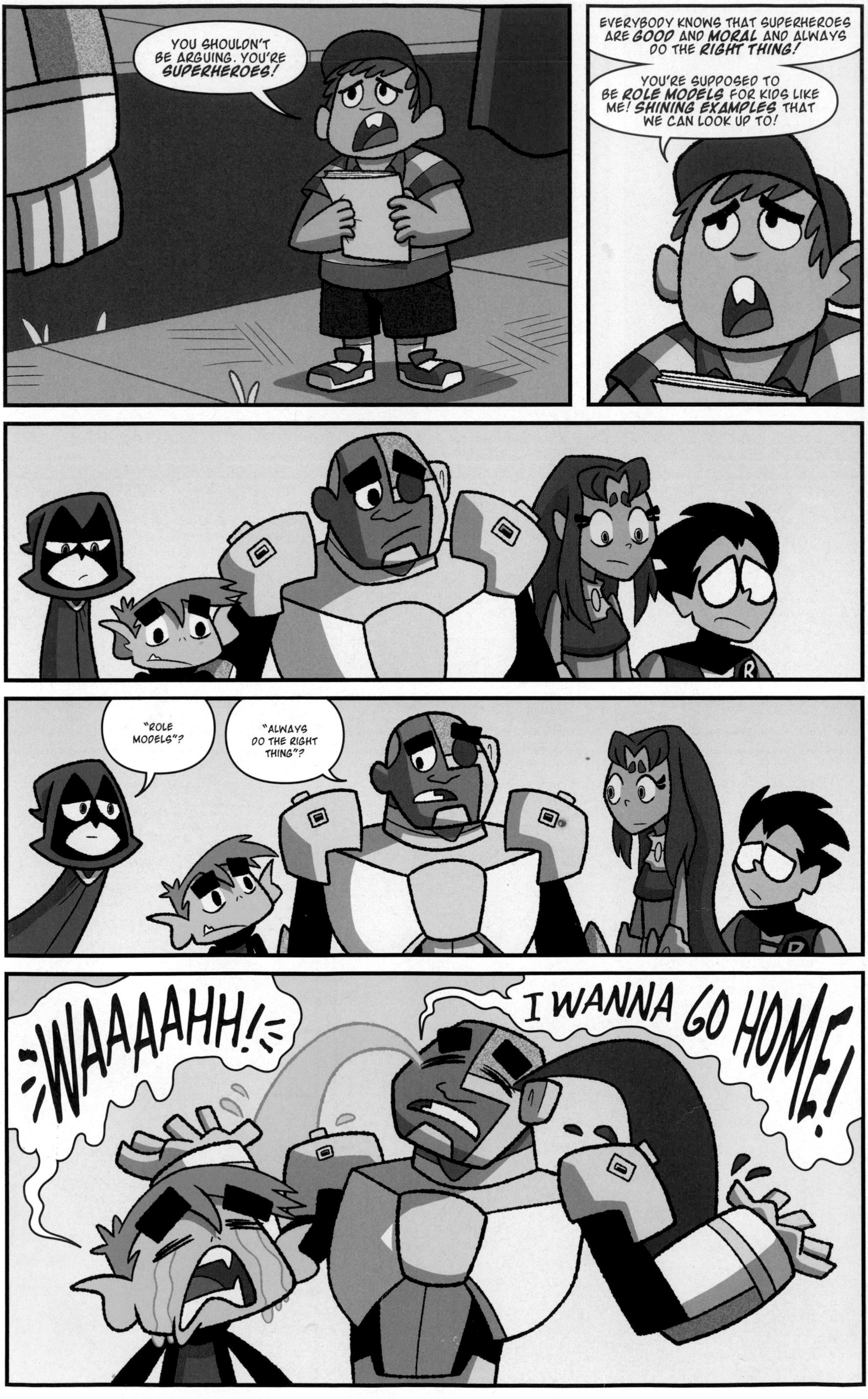
YOU SHOULDN'T BE ARGUING. YOU'RE SUPERHEROES!
EVERYBODY KNOWS THAT SUPERHEROES ARE GOOD AND MORAL AND ALWAYS DO THE RIGHT THING!
YOU'RE SUPPOSED TO BE ROLE MODELS FOR KIDS LIKE ME! SHINING EXAMPLES THAT WE CAN LOOK UP TO!
"ROLE MODELS"?
"ALWAYS DO THE RIGHT THING"?
WAAAAHH!
I WANNA GO HOME!

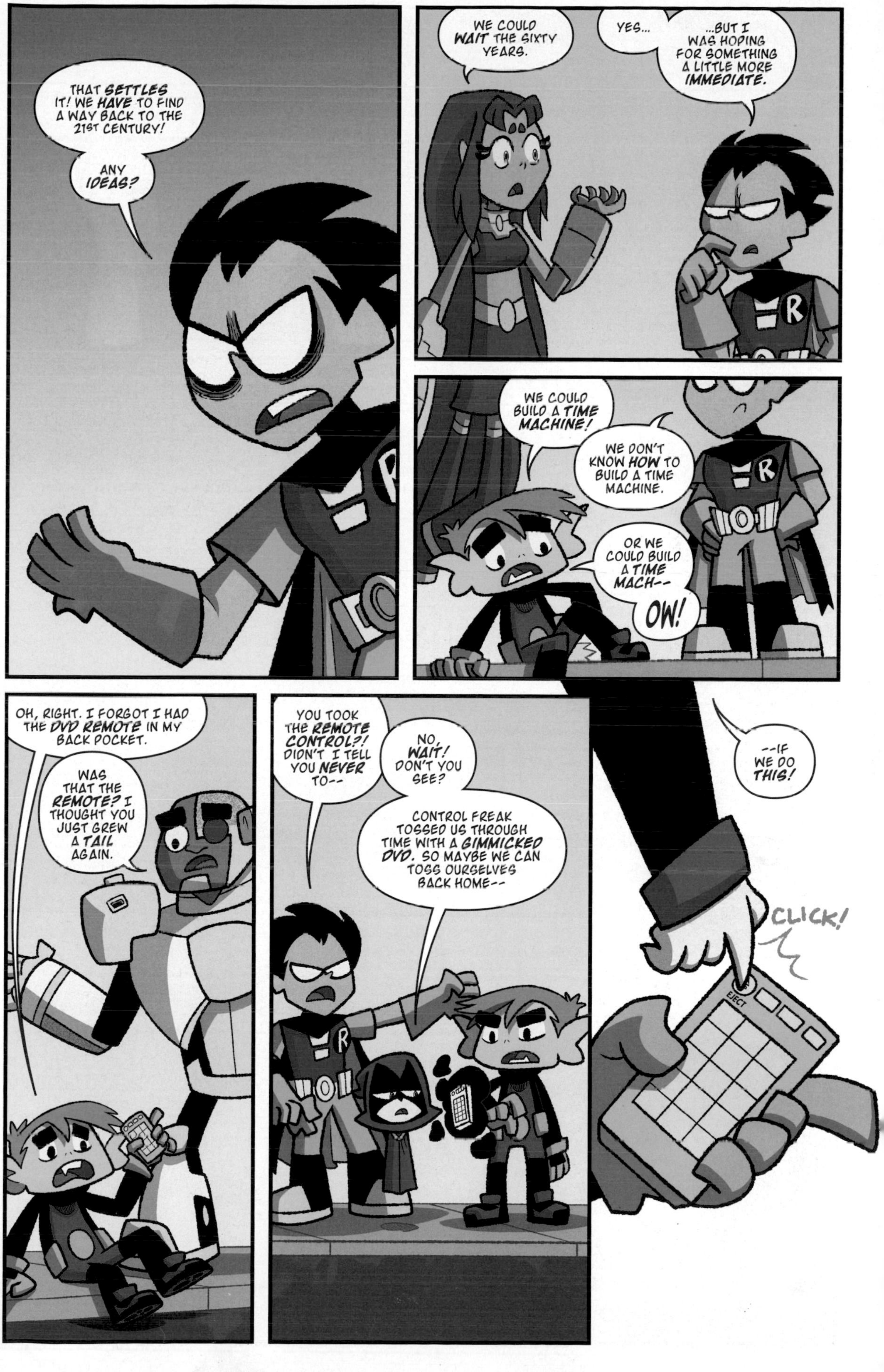

THAT SETTLES IT! WE HAVE TO FIND A WAY BACK TO THE 21ST CENTURY!
ANY IDEAS?
WE COULD WAIT THE SIXTY YEARS.
YES...
...BUT I WAS HOPING FOR SOMETHING A LITTLE MORE IMMEDIATE.
WE COULD BUILD A TIME MACHINE!
WE DON'T KNOW HOW TO BUILD A TIME MACHINE.
OR WE COULD BUILD A TIME MACH--
OW!
OH, RIGHT. I FORGOT I HAD THE DVD REMOTE IN MY BACK POCKET.
WAS THAT THE REMOTE? I THOUGHT YOU JUST GREW A TAIL AGAIN.
YOU TOOK THE REMOTE CONTROL?! DIDN'T I TELL YOU NEVER TO--
NO, WAIT! DON'T YOU SEE?
CONTROL FREAK TOSSED US THROUGH TIME WITH A GIMMICKED DVD. SO MAYBE WE CAN TOSS OURSELVES BACK HOME--
--IF WE DO THIS!
CLICK!
EJECT

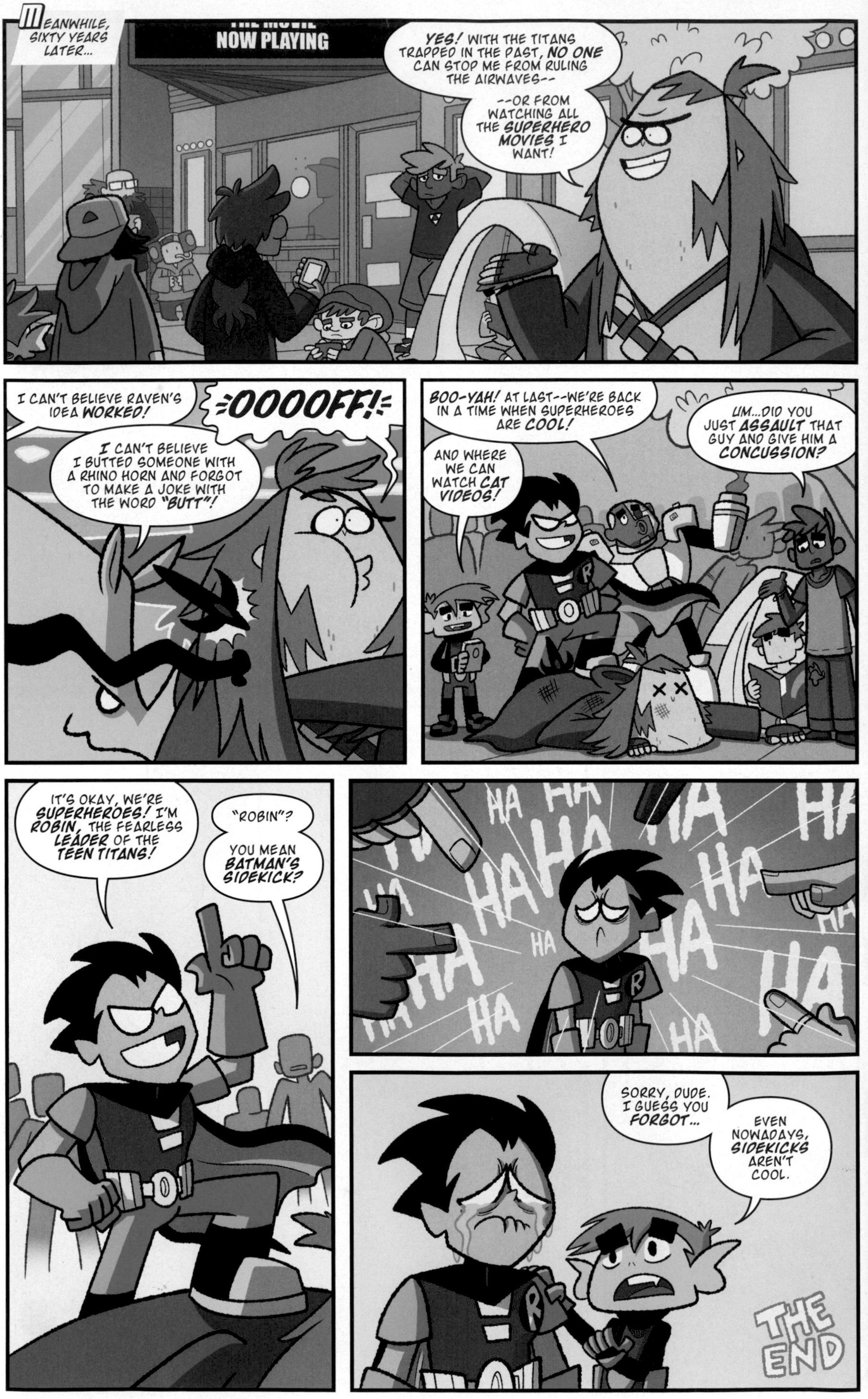
MEANWHILE, SIXTY YEARS LATER...
NOW PLAYING
YES! WITH THE TITANS TRAPPED IN THE PAST, NO ONE CAN STOP ME FROM RULING THE AIRWAVES--
--OR FROM WATCHING ALL THE SUPERHERO MOVIES I WANT!
I CAN'T BELIEVE RAVEN'S IDEA WORKED!
OOOOFF!
I CAN'T BELIEVE I BUTTED SOMEONE WITH A RHINO HORN AND FORGOT TO MAKE A JOKE WITH THE WORD "BUTT"!
BOO-YAH! AT LAST--WE'RE BACK IN A TIME WHEN SUPERHEROES ARE COOL!
AND WHERE WE CAN WATCH CAT VIDEOS!
UM...DID YOU JUST ASSAULT THAT GUY AND GIVE HIM A CONCUSSION?
IT'S OKAY, WE'RE SUPERHEROES! I'M ROBIN, THE FEARLESS LEADER OF THE TEEN TITANS!
"ROBIN"?
YOU MEAN BATMAN'S SIDEKICK?
HA HA HA HA HA HA HA HA HA HA HA HA HA
SORRY, DUDE. I GUESS YOU FORGOT...
EVEN NOWADAYS, SIDEKICKS AREN'T COOL.
THE END

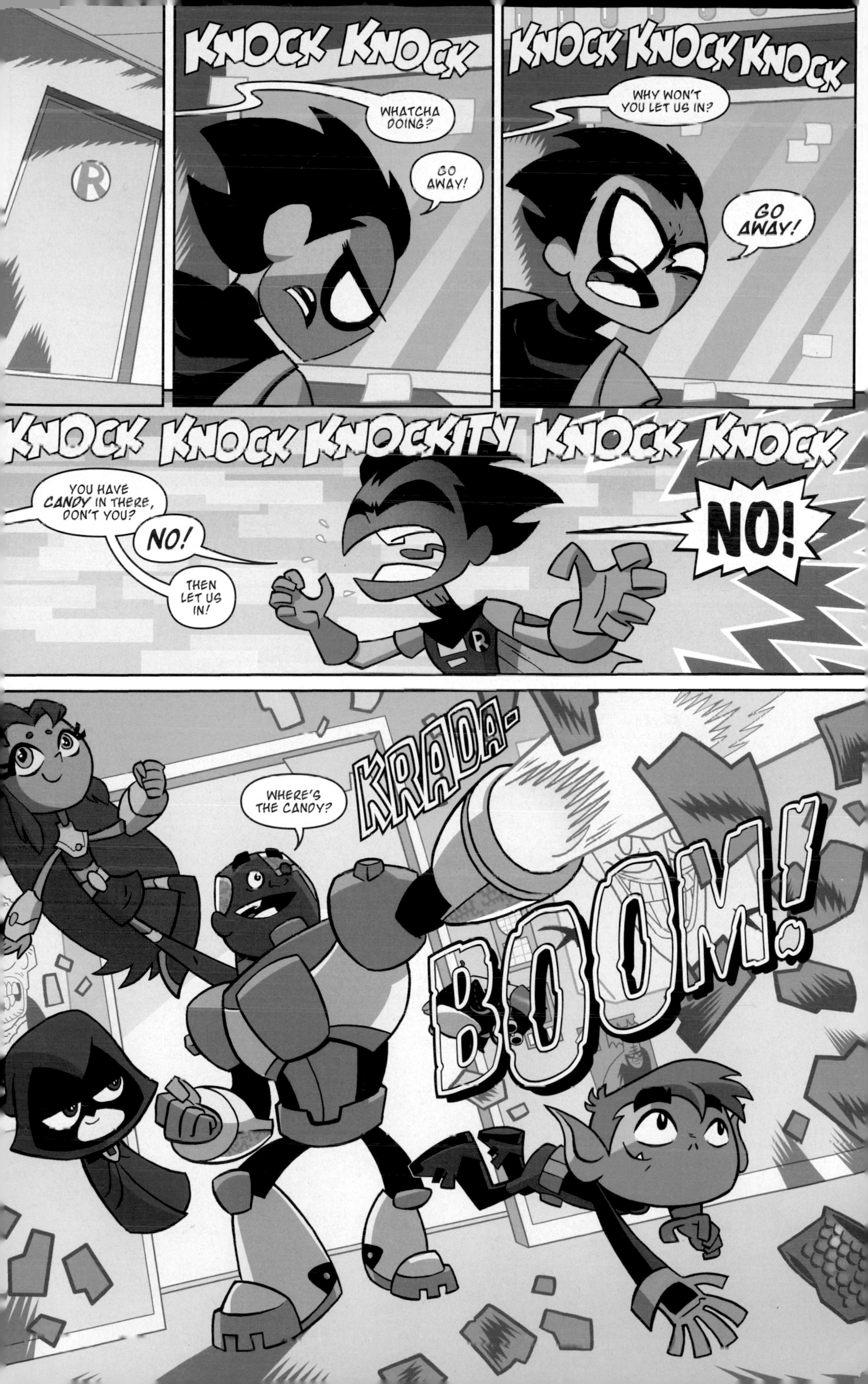
KNOCK KNOCK
WHATCHA DOING?
GO AWAY!
KNOCK KNOCK KNOCK
WHY WON'T YOU LET US IN?
GO AWAY!
KNOCK KNOCK KNOCKITY KNOCK KNOCK
YOU HAVE CANDY IN THERE, DON'T YOU?
NO!
THEN LET US IN!
NO!
WHERE'S THE CANDY?
KRADA-
BOOM!

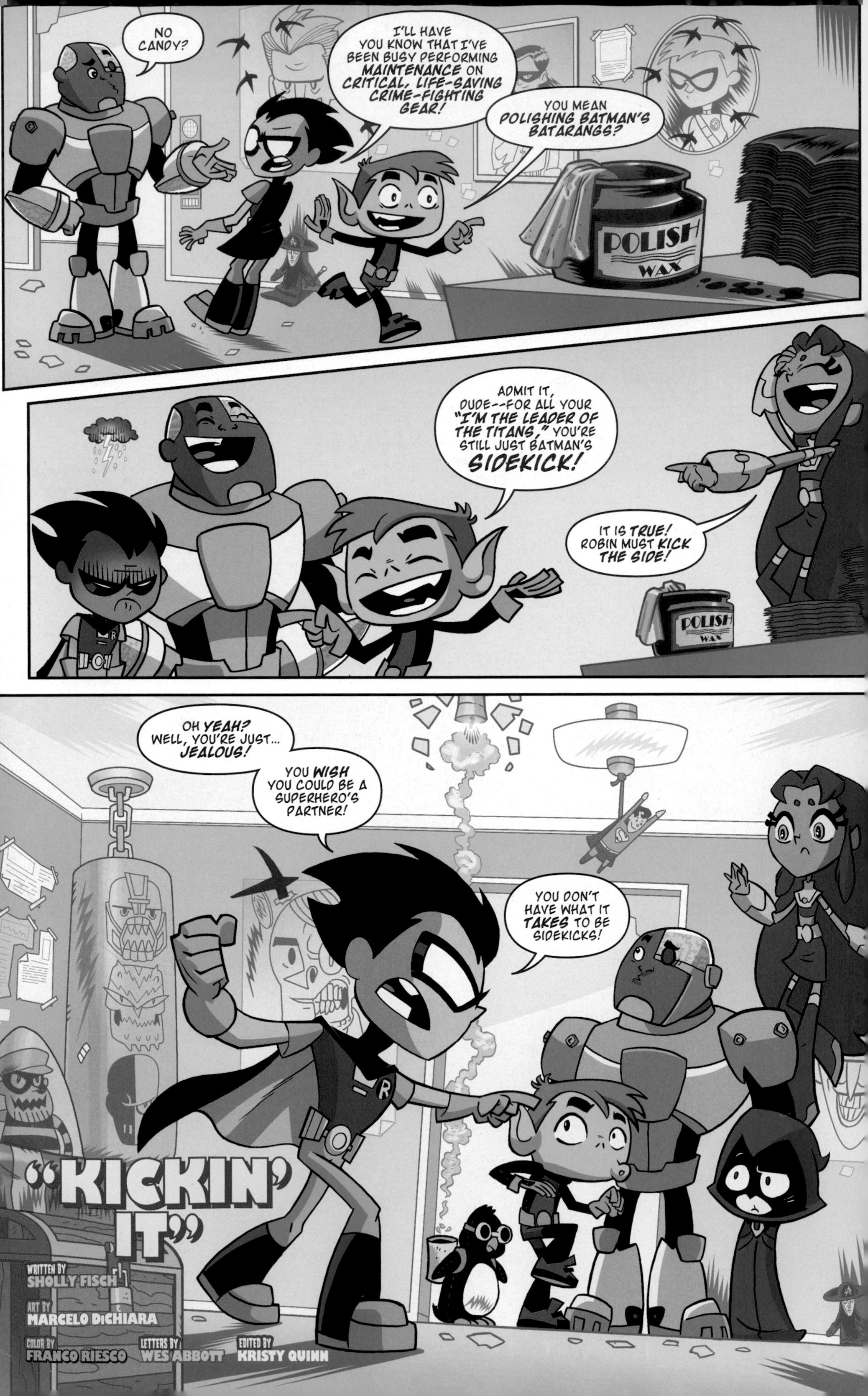
NO CANDY?
I'LL HAVE YOU KNOW THAT I'VE BEEN BUSY PERFORMING MAINTENANCE ON CRITICAL, LIFE-SAVING CRIME-FIGHTING GEAR!
YOU MEAN POLISHING BATMAN'S BATARANGS?
POLISH WAX
ADMIT IT, DUDE--FOR ALL YOUR "I'M THE LEADER OF THE TITANS," YOU'RE STILL JUST BATMAN'S SIDEKICK!
IT IS TRUE! ROBIN MUST KICK THE SIDE!
POLISH WAX
OH YEAH? WELL, YOU'RE JUST... JEALOUS!
YOU WISH YOU COULD BE A SUPERHERO'S PARTNER!
YOU DON'T HAVE WHAT IT TAKES TO BE SIDEKICKS!
"KICKIN' IT"
WRITTEN BY SHOLLY FISCH
ART BY MARCELO DICHIARA
COLOR BY FRANCO RIESCO
LETTERS BY WES ABBOTT
EDITED BY KRISTY QUINN

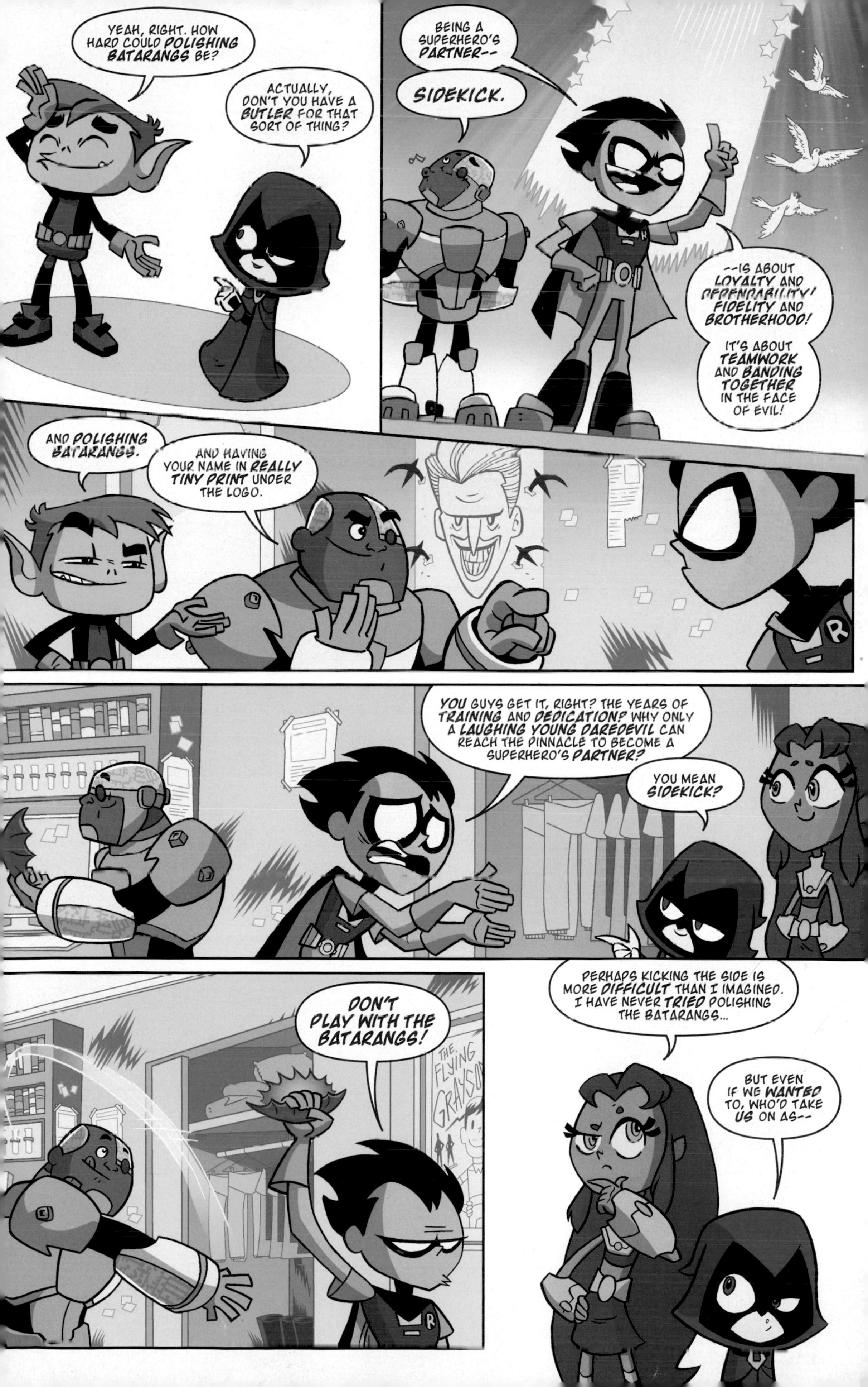
YEAH, RIGHT. HOW HARD COULD POLISHING BATARANGS BE?
ACTUALLY, DON'T YOU HAVE A BUTLER FOR THAT SORT OF THING?
BEING A SUPERHERO'S PARTNER--
SIDEKICK.
--IS ABOUT LOYALTY AND DEPENDABILITY! FIDELITY AND BROTHERHOOD!
IT'S ABOUT TEAMWORK AND BANDING TOGETHER IN THE FACE OF EVIL!
AND POLISHING BATARANGS.
AND HAVING YOUR NAME IN REALLY TINY PRINT UNDER THE LOGO.
YOU GUYS GET IT, RIGHT? THE YEARS OF TRAINING AND DEDICATION? WHY ONLY A LAUGHING YOUNG DAREDEVIL CAN REACH THE PINNACLE TO BECOME A SUPERHERO'S PARTNER?
YOU MEAN SIDEKICK?
DON'T PLAY WITH THE BATARANGS!
THE FLYING GRAYSO
PERHAPS KICKING THE SIDE IS MORE DIFFICULT THAN I IMAGINED. I HAVE NEVER TRIED POLISHING THE BATARANGS...
BUT EVEN IF WE WANTED TO, WHO'D TAKE US ON AS--

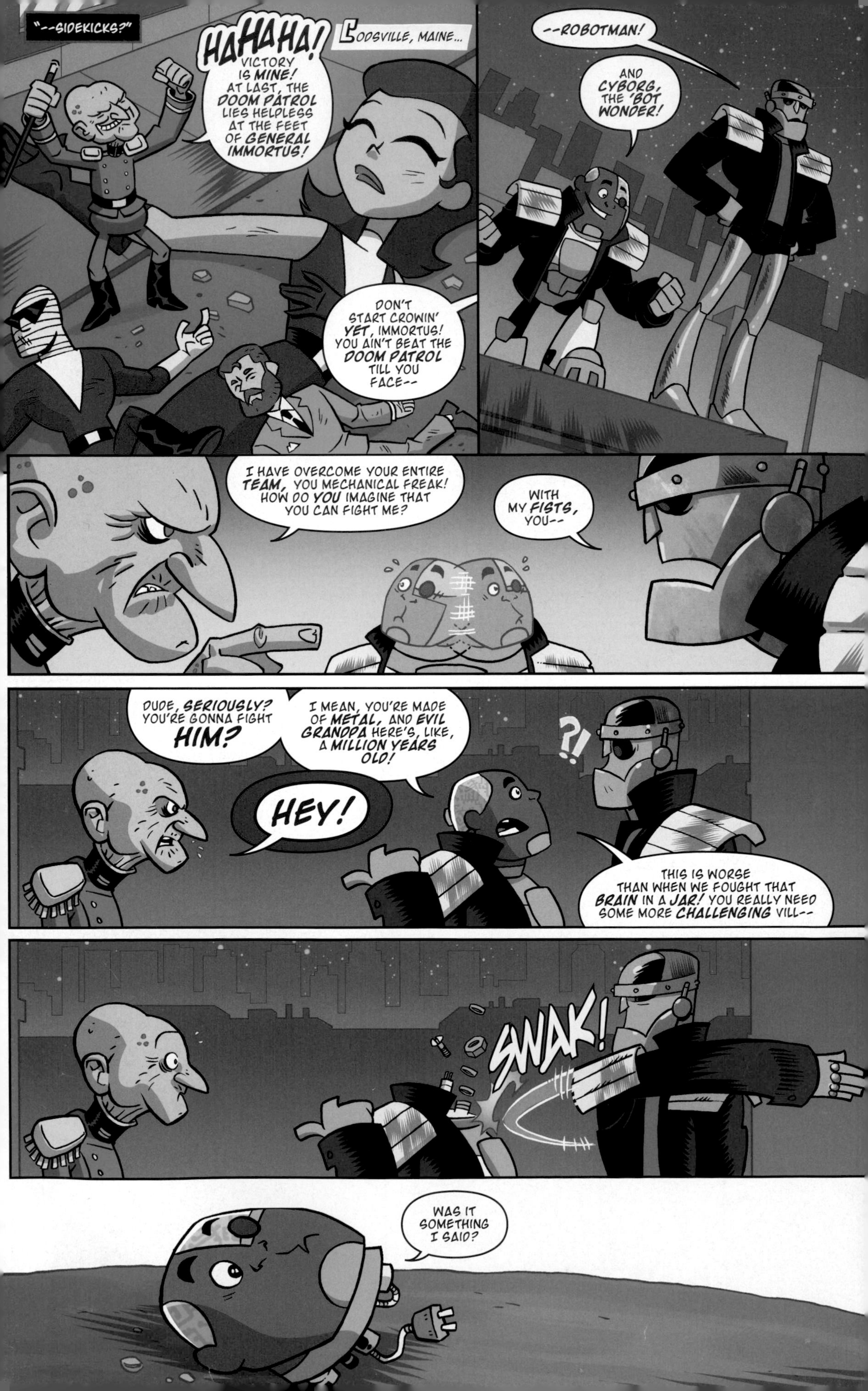
"--SIDEKICKS?"
HAHAHA!
CODSVILLE, MAINE...
VICTORY IS MINE! AT LAST, THE DOOM PATROL LIES HELPLESS AT THE FEET OF GENERAL IMMORTUS!
DON'T START CROWIN' YET, IMMORTUS! YOU AIN'T BEAT THE DOOM PATROL TILL YOU FACE--
--ROBOTMAN!
AND CYBORG, THE 'BOT WONDER!
I HAVE OVERCOME YOUR ENTIRE TEAM, YOU MECHANICAL FREAK! HOW DO YOU IMAGINE THAT YOU CAN FIGHT ME?
WITH MY FISTS, YOU--
DUDE, SERIOUSLY? YOU'RE GONNA FIGHT HIM?
I MEAN, YOU'RE MADE OF METAL, AND EVIL GRANDPA HERE'S, LIKE, A MILLION YEARS OLD!
?!
HEY!
THIS IS WORSE THAN WHEN WE FOUGHT THAT BRAIN IN A JAR! YOU REALLY NEED SOME MORE CHALLENGING VILL--
SWAK!
WAS IT SOMETHING I SAID?

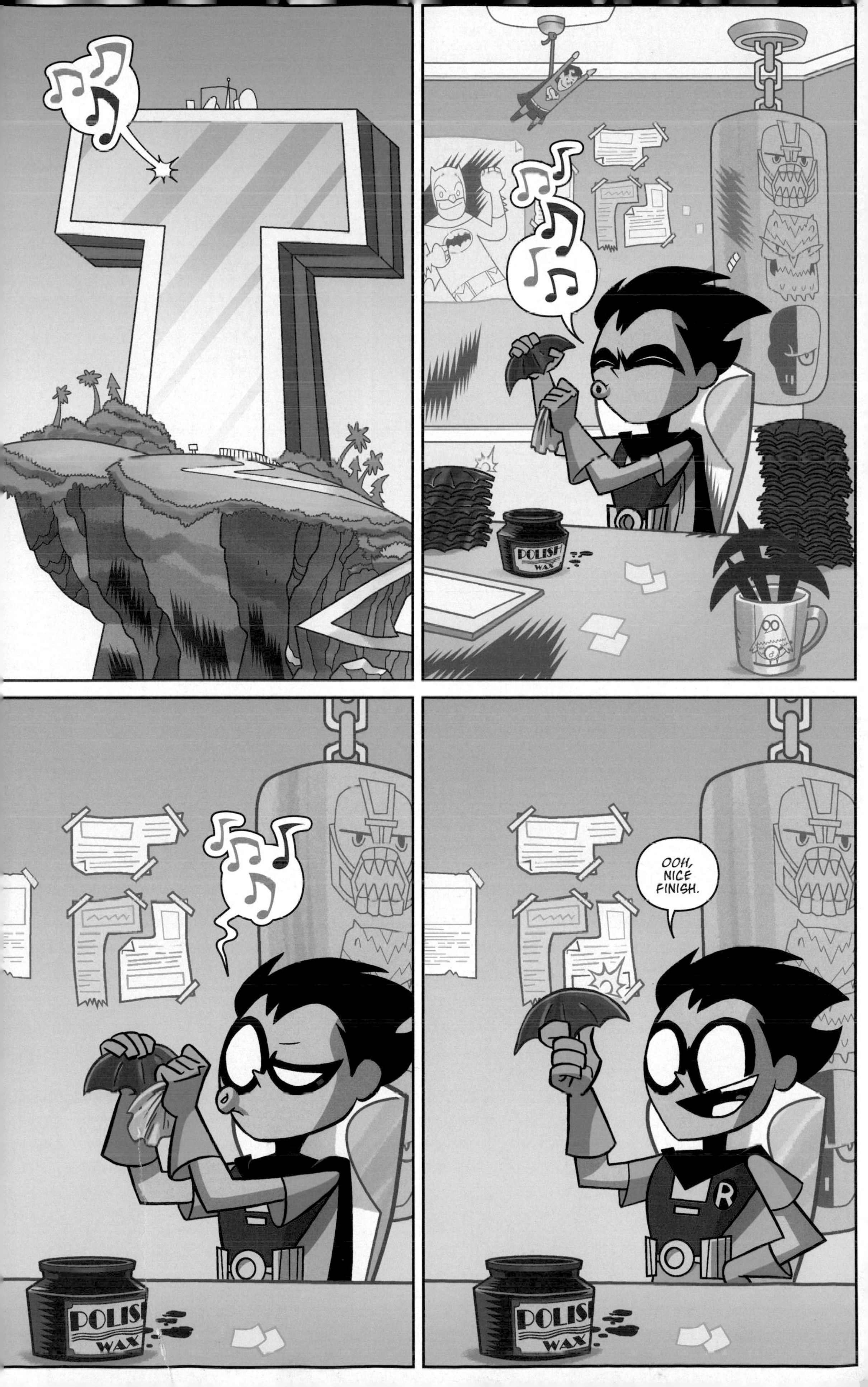
POLISH
WAX
POLIS
WAX
OOH, NICE FINISH.
POLIS
WAX

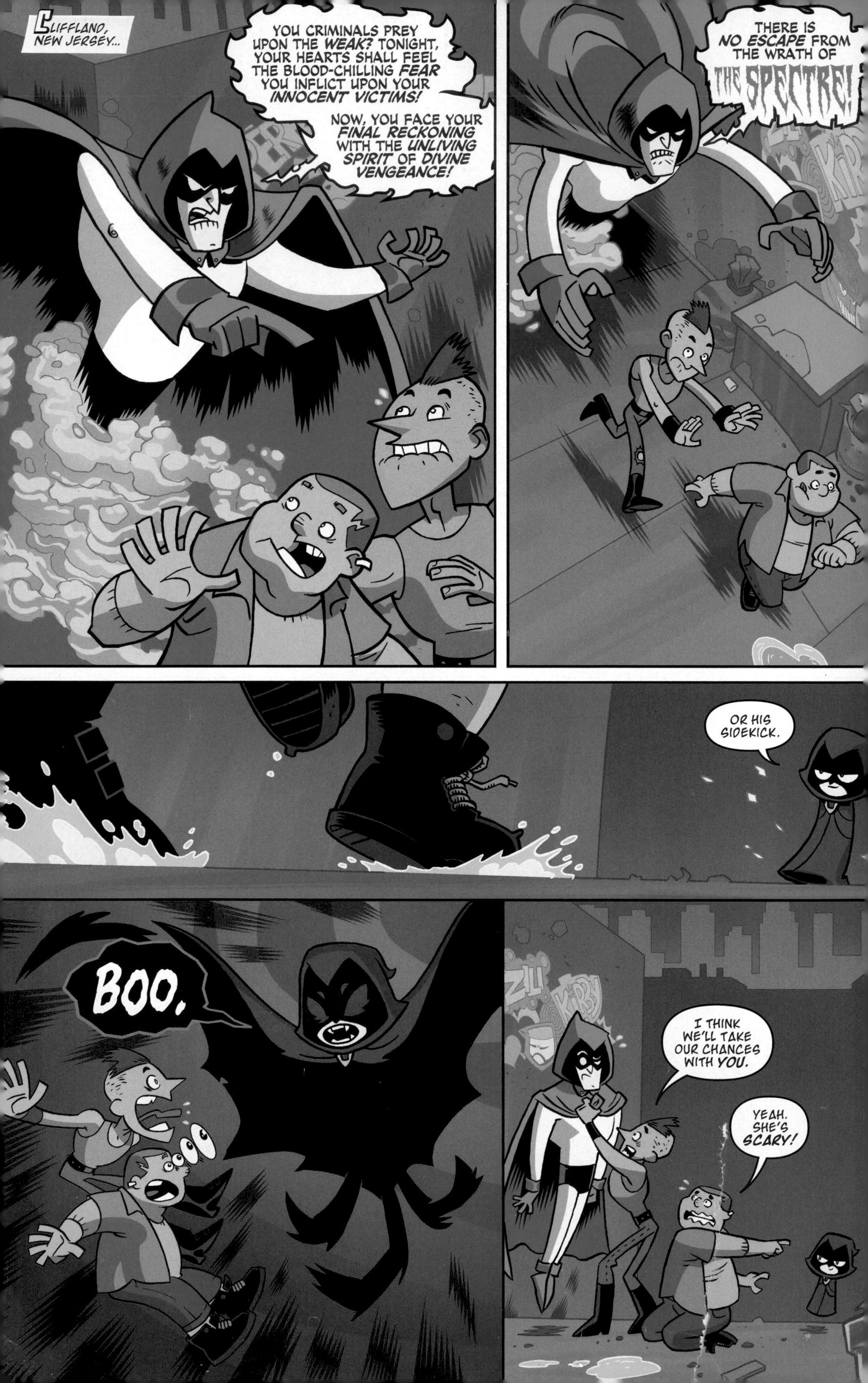
CLIFFLAND, NEW JERSEY...
YOU CRIMINALS PREY UPON THE WEAK? TONIGHT, YOUR HEARTS SHALL FEEL THE BLOOD-CHILLING FEAR YOU INFLICT UPON YOUR INNOCENT VICTIMS!
NOW, YOU FACE YOUR FINAL RECKONING WITH THE UNLIVING SPIRIT OF DIVINE VENGEANCE!
THERE IS NO ESCAPE FROM THE WRATH OF THE SPECTRE!
OR HIS SIDEKICK.
BOO.
I THINK WE'LL TAKE OUR CHANCES WITH YOU.
YEAH. SHE'S SCARY!

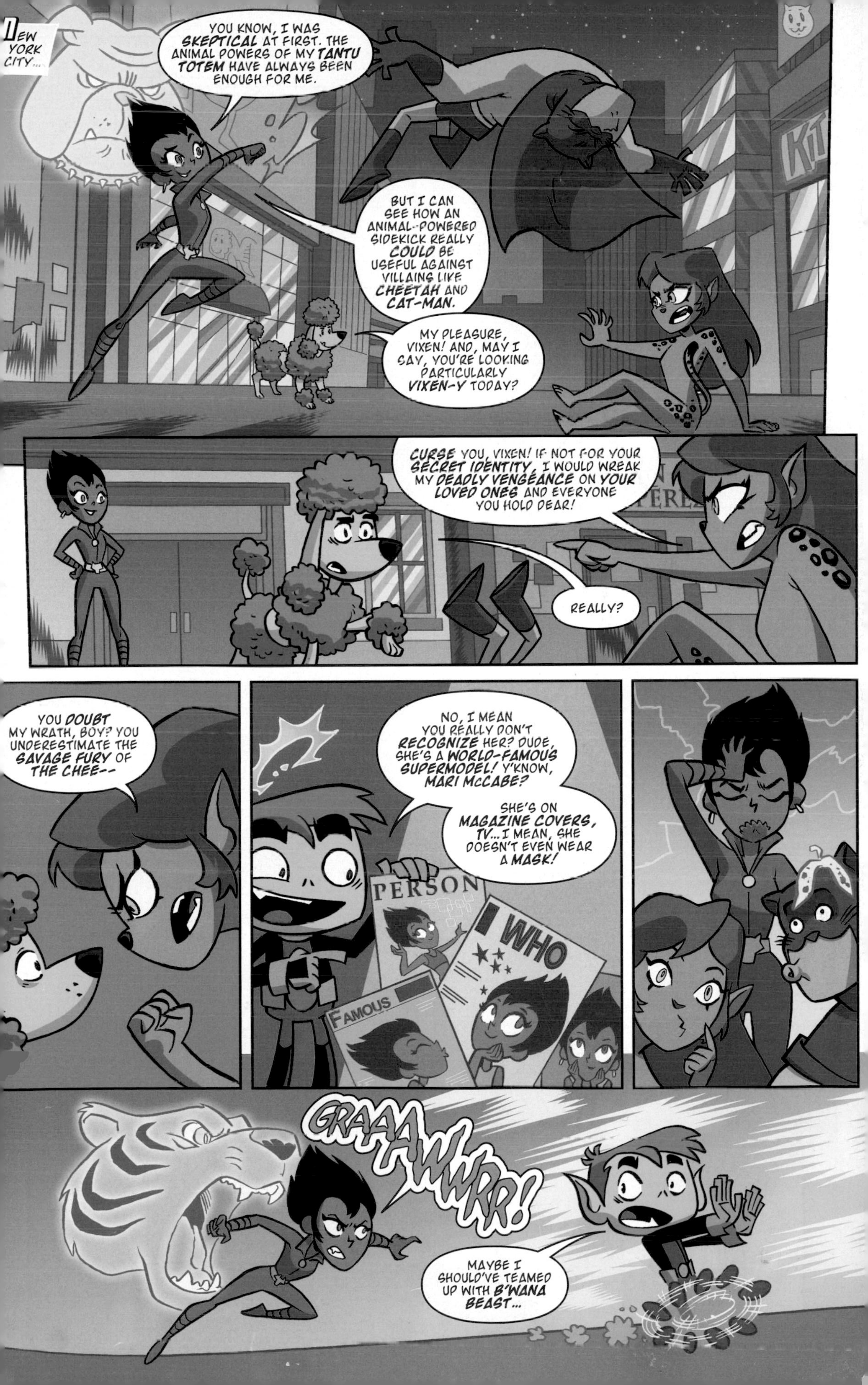
NEW YORK CITY...
YOU KNOW, I WAS SKEPTICAL AT FIRST. THE ANIMAL POWERS OF MY TANTU TOTEM HAVE ALWAYS BEEN ENOUGH FOR ME.
BUT I CAN SEE HOW AN ANIMAL-POWERED SIDEKICK REALLY COULD BE USEFUL AGAINST VILLAINS LIKE CHEETAH AND CAT-MAN.
MY PLEASURE, VIXEN! AND, MAY I SAY, YOU'RE LOOKING PARTICULARLY VIXEN-Y TODAY?
CURSE YOU, VIXEN! IF NOT FOR YOUR SECRET IDENTITY, I WOULD WREAK MY DEADLY VENGEANCE ON YOUR LOVED ONES AND EVERYONE YOU HOLD DEAR!
REALLY?
YOU DOUBT MY WRATH, BOY? YOU UNDERESTIMATE THE SAVAGE FURY OF THE CHEE--
NO, I MEAN YOU REALLY DON'T RECOGNIZE HER? DUDE, SHE'S A WORLD-FAMOUS SUPERMODEL! Y'KNOW, MARI McCABE?
SHE'S ON MAGAZINE COVERS, TV...I MEAN, SHE DOESN'T EVEN WEAR A MASK!
PERSON
WHO
FAMOUS
GRAAAWWRR!
MAYBE I SHOULD'VE TEAMED UP WITH B'WANA BEAST...

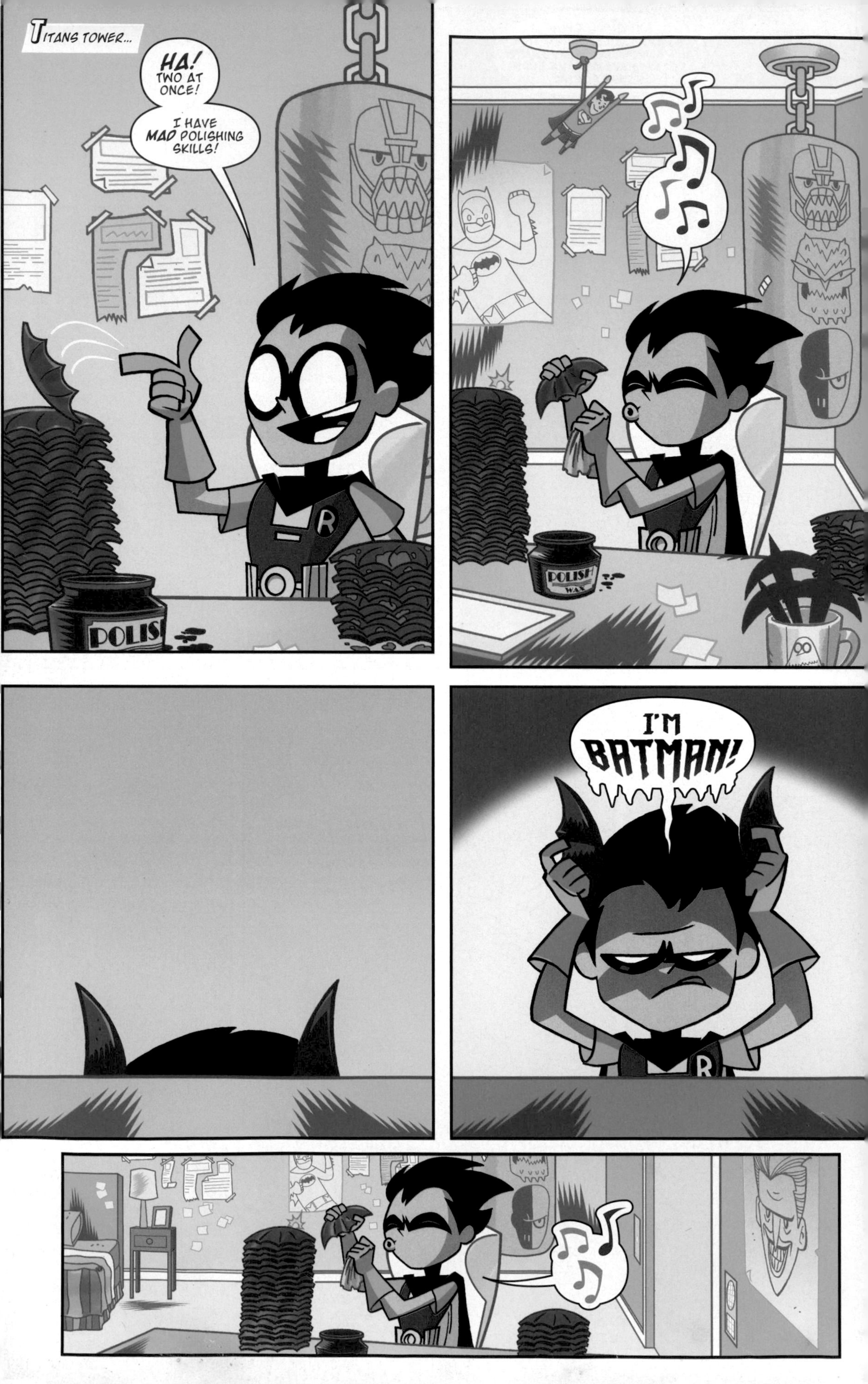
TITANS TOWER...
HA! TWO AT ONCE!
I HAVE MAD POLISHING SKILLS!
POLISH
POLISH WAX
I'M BATMAN!

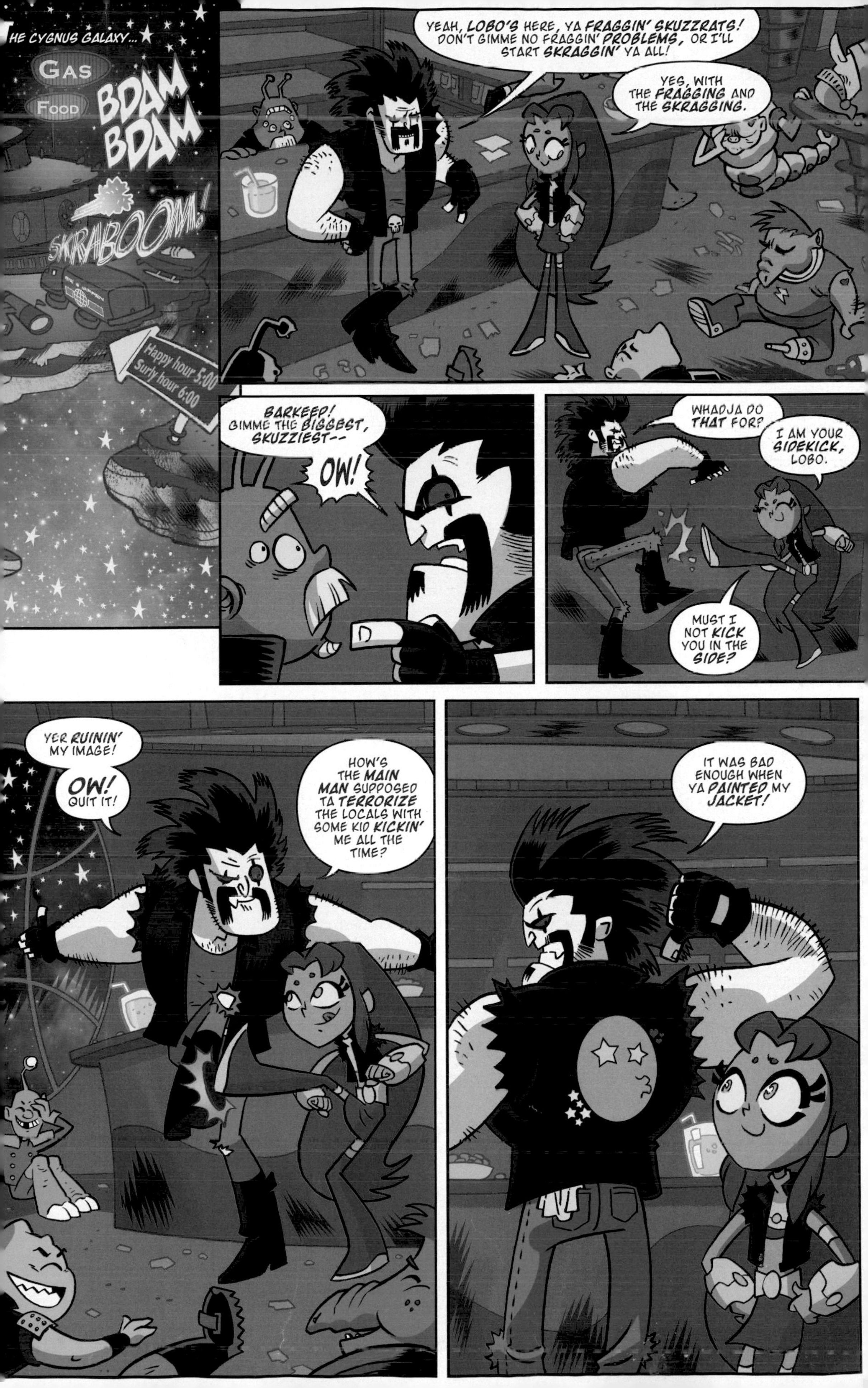
HE CYGNUS GALAXY...
GAS
FOOD
BDAM BDAM
SKRABOOM!
Happy hour 5:00
Surly hour 6:00
YEAH, LOBO'S HERE, YA FRAGGIN' SKUZZRATS! DON'T GIMME NO FRAGGIN' PROBLEMS, OR I'LL START SKRAGGIN' YA ALL!
YES, WITH THE FRAGGING AND THE SKRAGGING.
BARKEEP! GIMME THE BIGGEST, SKUZZIEST--
OW!
WHADJA DO THAT FOR?
I AM YOUR SIDEKICK, LOBO.
MUST I NOT KICK YOU IN THE SIDE?
YER RUININ' MY IMAGE!
OW! QUIT IT!
HOW'S THE MAIN MAN SUPPOSED TA TERRORIZE THE LOCALS WITH SOME KID KICKIN' ME ALL THE TIME?
IT WAS BAD ENOUGH WHEN YA PAINTED MY JACKET!

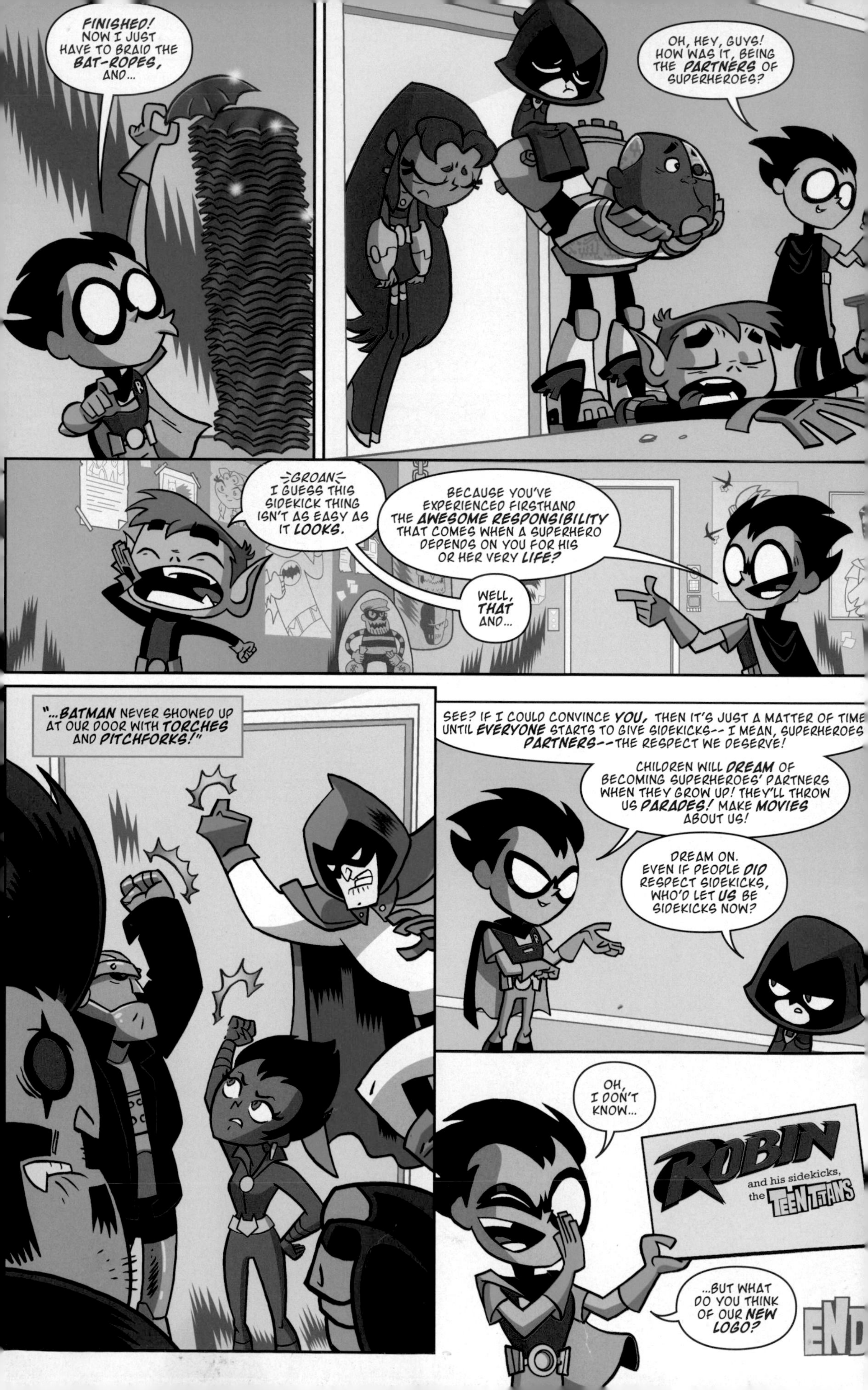
FINISHED! NOW I JUST HAVE TO BRAID THE BAT-ROPES, AND...
OH, HEY, GUYS! HOW WAS IT, BEING THE PARTNERS OF SUPERHEROES?
GROAN I GUESS THIS SIDEKICK THING ISN'T AS EASY AS IT LOOKS.
BECAUSE YOU'VE EXPERIENCED FIRSTHAND THE AWESOME RESPONSIBILITY THAT COMES WHEN A SUPERHERO DEPENDS ON YOU FOR HIS OR HER VERY LIFE?
WELL, THAT AND...
"...BATMAN NEVER SHOWED UP AT OUR DOOR WITH TORCHES AND PITCHFORKS!"
SEE? IF I COULD CONVINCE YOU, THEN IT'S JUST A MATTER OF TIME UNTIL EVERYONE STARTS TO GIVE SIDEKICKS-- I MEAN, SUPERHEROES PARTNERS--THE RESPECT WE DESERVE!
CHILDREN WILL DREAM OF BECOMING SUPERHEROES' PARTNERS WHEN THEY GROW UP! THEY'LL THROW US PARADES! MAKE MOVIES ABOUT US!
DREAM ON. EVEN IF PEOPLE DID RESPECT SIDEKICKS, WHO'D LET US BE SIDEKICKS NOW?
OH, I DON'T KNOW...
ROBIN
and his sidekicks, the TEEN TITANS
...BUT WHAT DO YOU THINK OF OUR NEW LOGO?
END

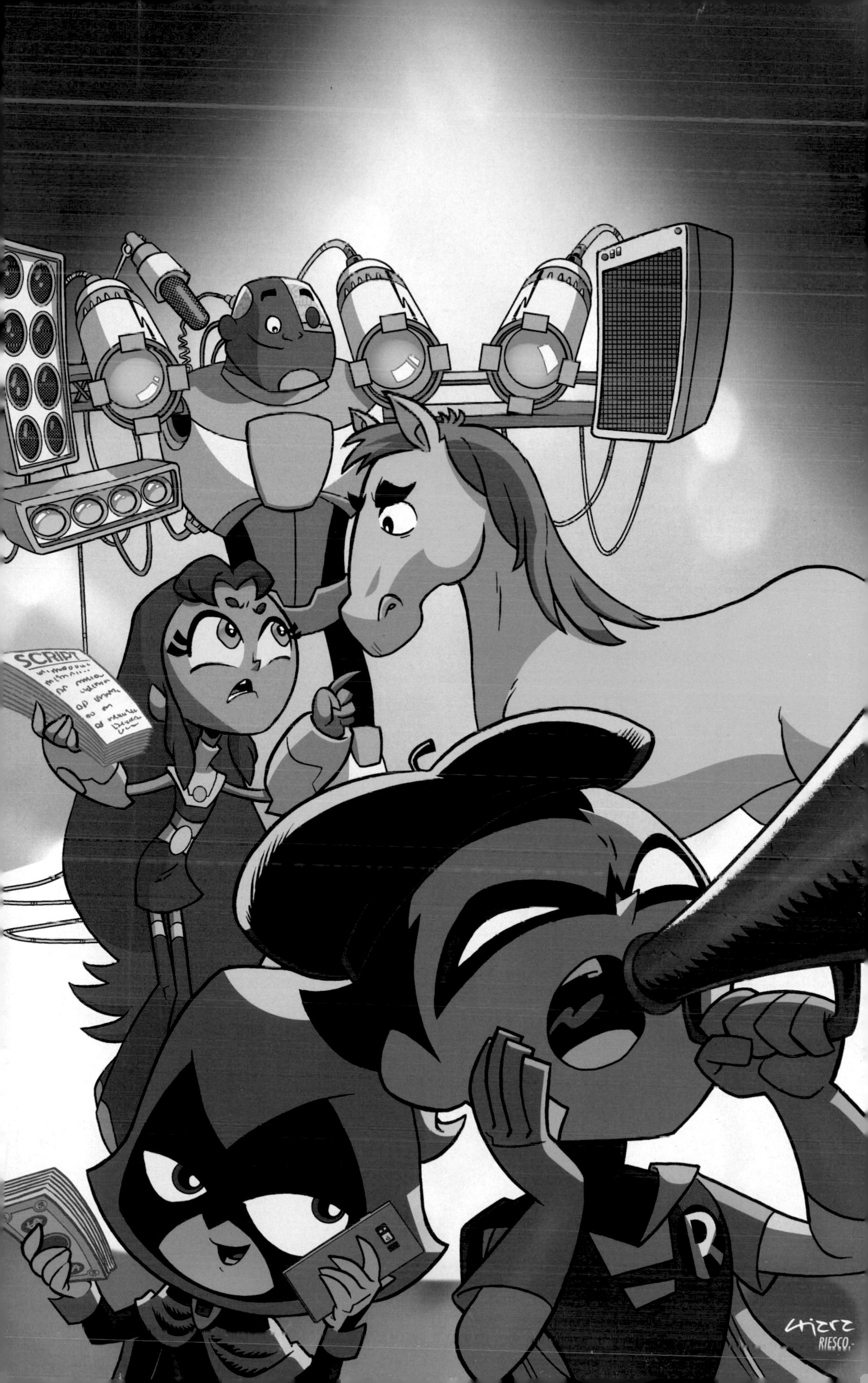
SCRIPT
RIESCO.

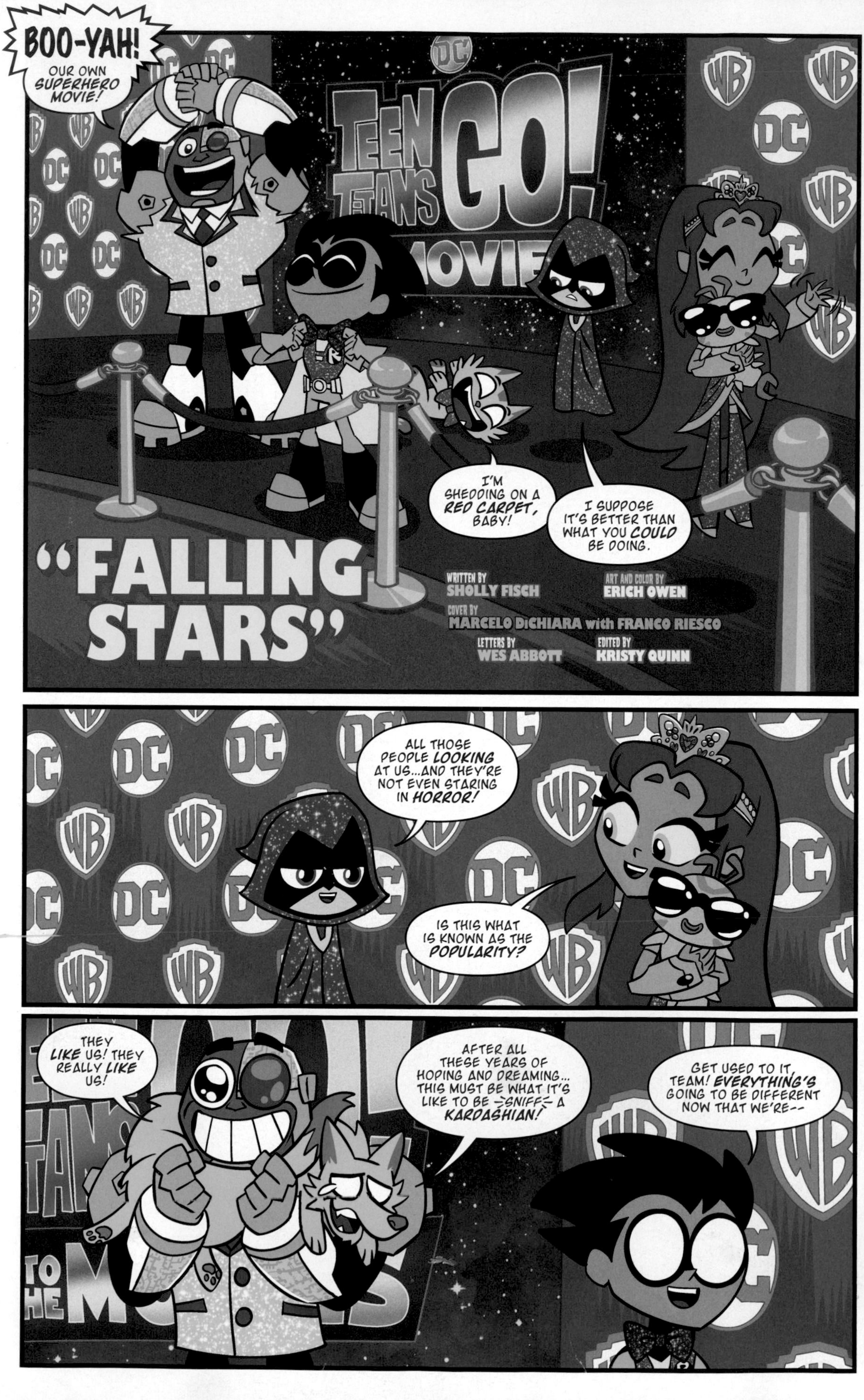
BOO-YAH! OUR OWN SUPERHERO MOVIE!
DC
TEEN TITANS GO! MOVIE
I'M SHEDDING ON A RED CARPET, BABY!
I SUPPOSE IT'S BETTER THAN WHAT YOU COULD BE DOING.
"FALLING STARS"
WRITTEN BY SHOLLY FISCH
ART AND COLOR BY ERICH OWEN
COVER BY MARCELO DiCHIARA with FRANCO RIESCO
LETTERS BY WES ABBOTT
EDITED BY KRISTY QUINN
ALL THOSE PEOPLE LOOKING AT US...AND THEY'RE NOT EVEN STARING IN HORROR!
IS THIS WHAT IS KNOWN AS THE POPULARITY?
THEY LIKE US! THEY REALLY LIKE US!
AFTER ALL THESE YEARS OF HOPING AND DREAMING... THIS MUST BE WHAT IT'S LIKE TO BE -SNIFF- A KARDASHIAN!
GET USED TO IT, TEAM! EVERYTHING'S GOING TO BE DIFFERENT NOW THAT WE'RE--

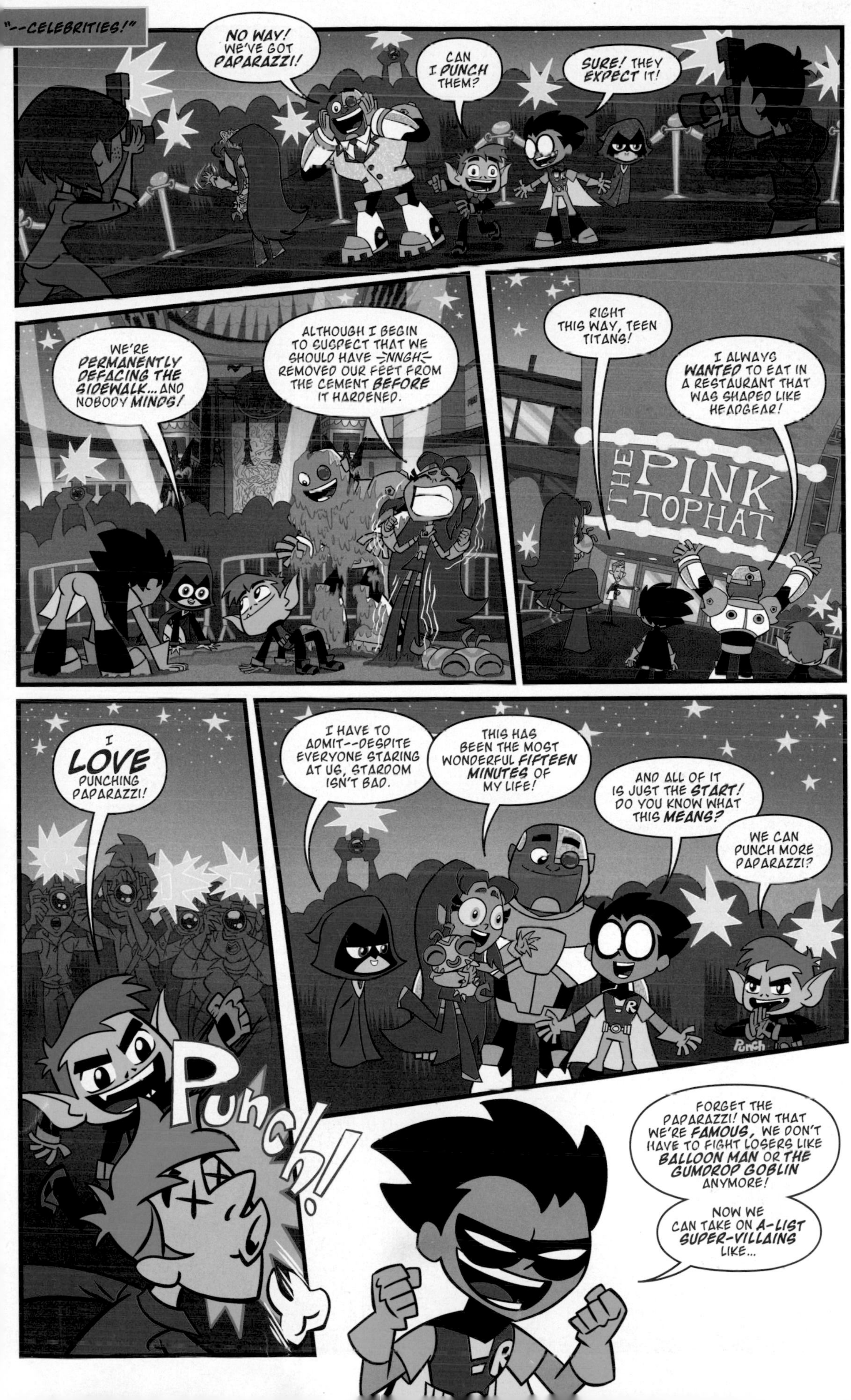
"--CELEBRITIES!"
NO WAY! WE'VE GOT PAPARAZZI!
CAN I PUNCH THEM?
SURE! THEY EXPECT IT!
WE'RE PERMANENTLY DEFACING THE SIDEWALK... AND NOBODY MINDS!
ALTHOUGH I BEGIN TO SUSPECT THAT WE SHOULD HAVE --NNGH-- REMOVED OUR FEET FROM THE CEMENT BEFORE IT HARDENED.
RIGHT THIS WAY, TEEN TITANS!
I ALWAYS WANTED TO EAT IN A RESTAURANT THAT WAS SHAPED LIKE HEADGEAR!
THE PINK TOPHAT
I LOVE PUNCHING PAPARAZZI!
PUNCH!
I HAVE TO ADMIT--DESPITE EVERYONE STARING AT US, STARDOM ISN'T BAD.
THIS HAS BEEN THE MOST WONDERFUL FIFTEEN MINUTES OF MY LIFE!
AND ALL OF IT IS JUST THE START! DO YOU KNOW WHAT THIS MEANS?
WE CAN PUNCH MORE PAPARAZZI?
PUNCH
FORGET THE PAPARAZZI! NOW THAT WE'RE FAMOUS, WE DON'T HAVE TO FIGHT LOSERS LIKE BALLOON MAN OR THE GUMDROP GOBLIN ANYMORE!
NOW WE CAN TAKE ON A-LIST SUPER-VILLAINS LIKE...

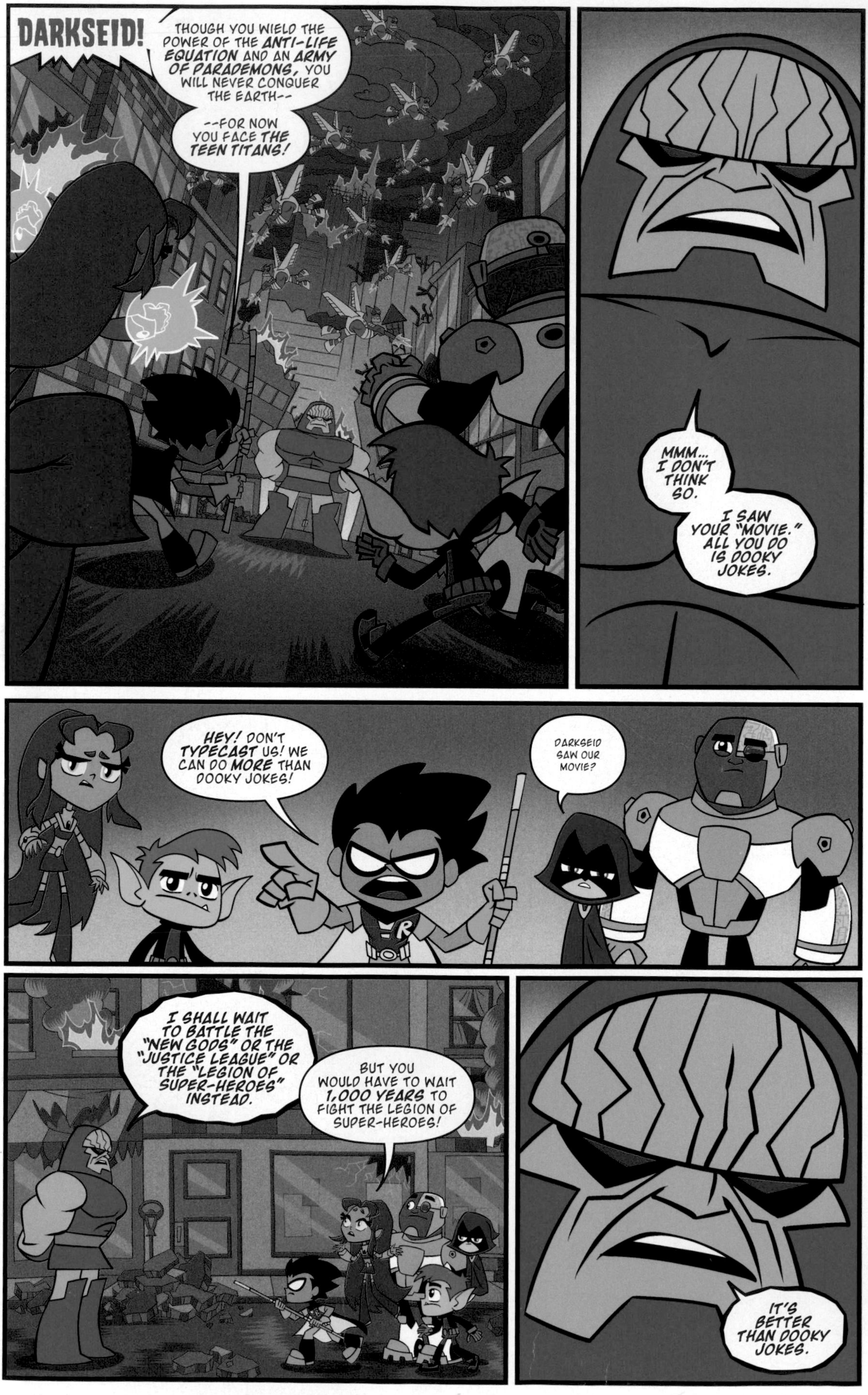
DARKSEID!
THOUGH YOU WIELD THE POWER OF THE ANTI-LIFE EQUATION AND AN ARMY OF PARADEMONS, YOU WILL NEVER CONQUER THE EARTH--
--FOR NOW YOU FACE THE TEEN TITANS!
MMM... I DON'T THINK SO.
I SAW YOUR "MOVIE." ALL YOU DO IS DOOKY JOKES.
HEY! DON'T TYPECAST US! WE CAN DO MORE THAN DOOKY JOKES!
DARKSEID SAW OUR MOVIE?
I SHALL WAIT TO BATTLE THE "NEW GODS" OR THE "JUSTICE LEAGUE" OR THE "LEGION OF SUPER-HEROES" INSTEAD.
BUT YOU WOULD HAVE TO WAIT 1,000 YEARS TO FIGHT THE LEGION OF SUPER-HEROES!
IT'S BETTER THAN DOOKY JOKES.

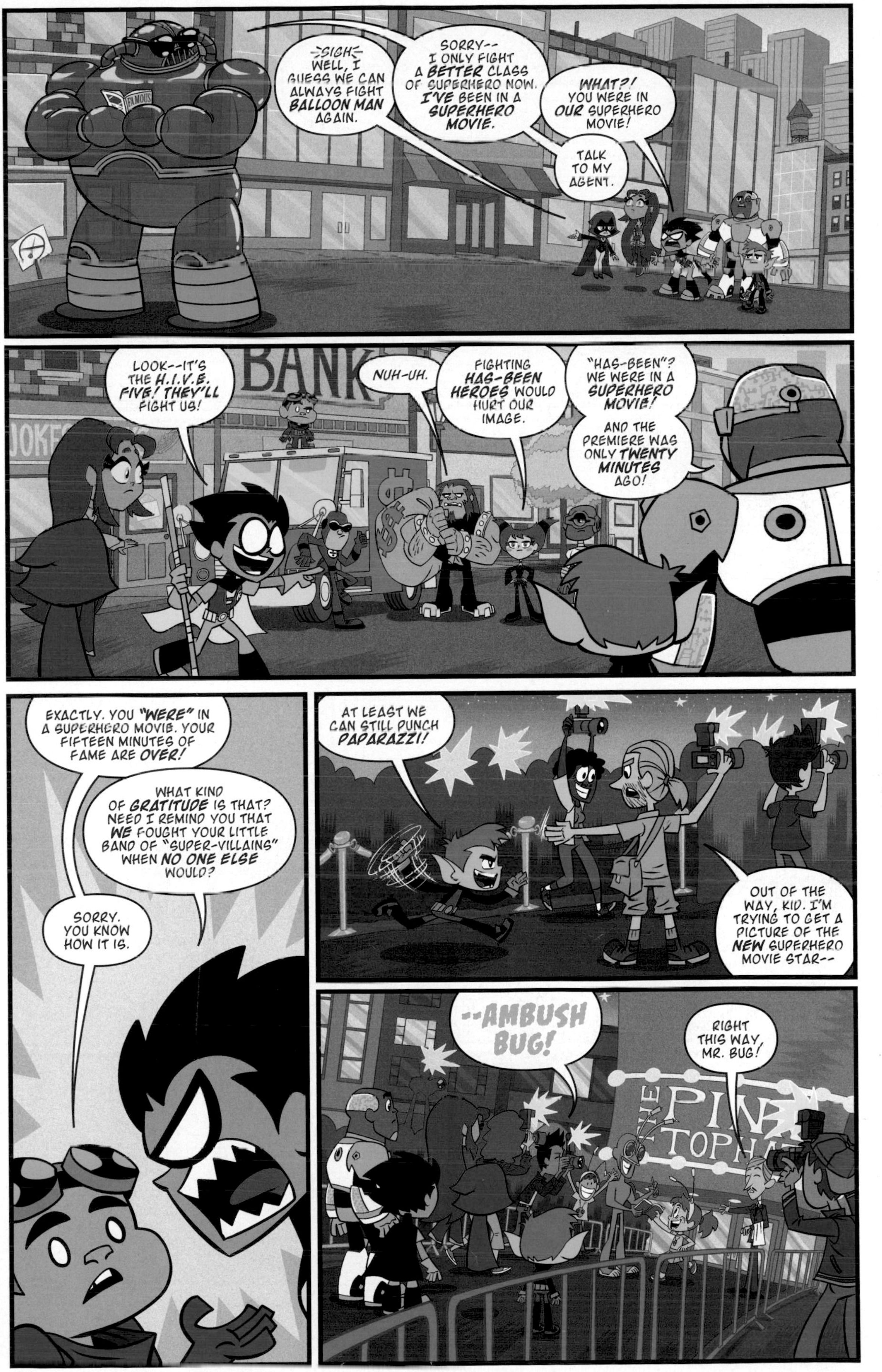

-SIGH- WELL, I GUESS WE CAN ALWAYS FIGHT BALLOON MAN AGAIN.
SORRY-- I ONLY FIGHT A BETTER CLASS OF SUPERHERO NOW. I'VE BEEN IN A SUPERHERO MOVIE.
WHAT?! YOU WERE IN OUR SUPERHERO MOVIE!
TALK TO MY AGENT.
FAMOUS
BANK
LOOK--IT'S THE H.I.V.E. FIVE! THEY'LL FIGHT US!
NUH-UH.
FIGHTING HAS-BEEN HEROES WOULD HURT OUR IMAGE.
"HAS-BEEN"? WE WERE IN A SUPERHERO MOVIE!
AND THE PREMIERE WAS ONLY TWENTY MINUTES AGO!
EXACTLY. YOU "WERE" IN A SUPERHERO MOVIE. YOUR FIFTEEN MINUTES OF FAME ARE OVER!
WHAT KIND OF GRATITUDE IS THAT? NEED I REMIND YOU THAT WE FOUGHT YOUR LITTLE BAND OF "SUPER-VILLAINS" WHEN NO ONE ELSE WOULD?
SORRY. YOU KNOW HOW IT IS.
AT LEAST WE CAN STILL PUNCH PAPARAZZI!
OUT OF THE WAY, KID. I'M TRYING TO GET A PICTURE OF THE NEW SUPERHERO MOVIE STAR--
--AMBUSH BUG!
RIGHT THIS WAY, MR. BUG!

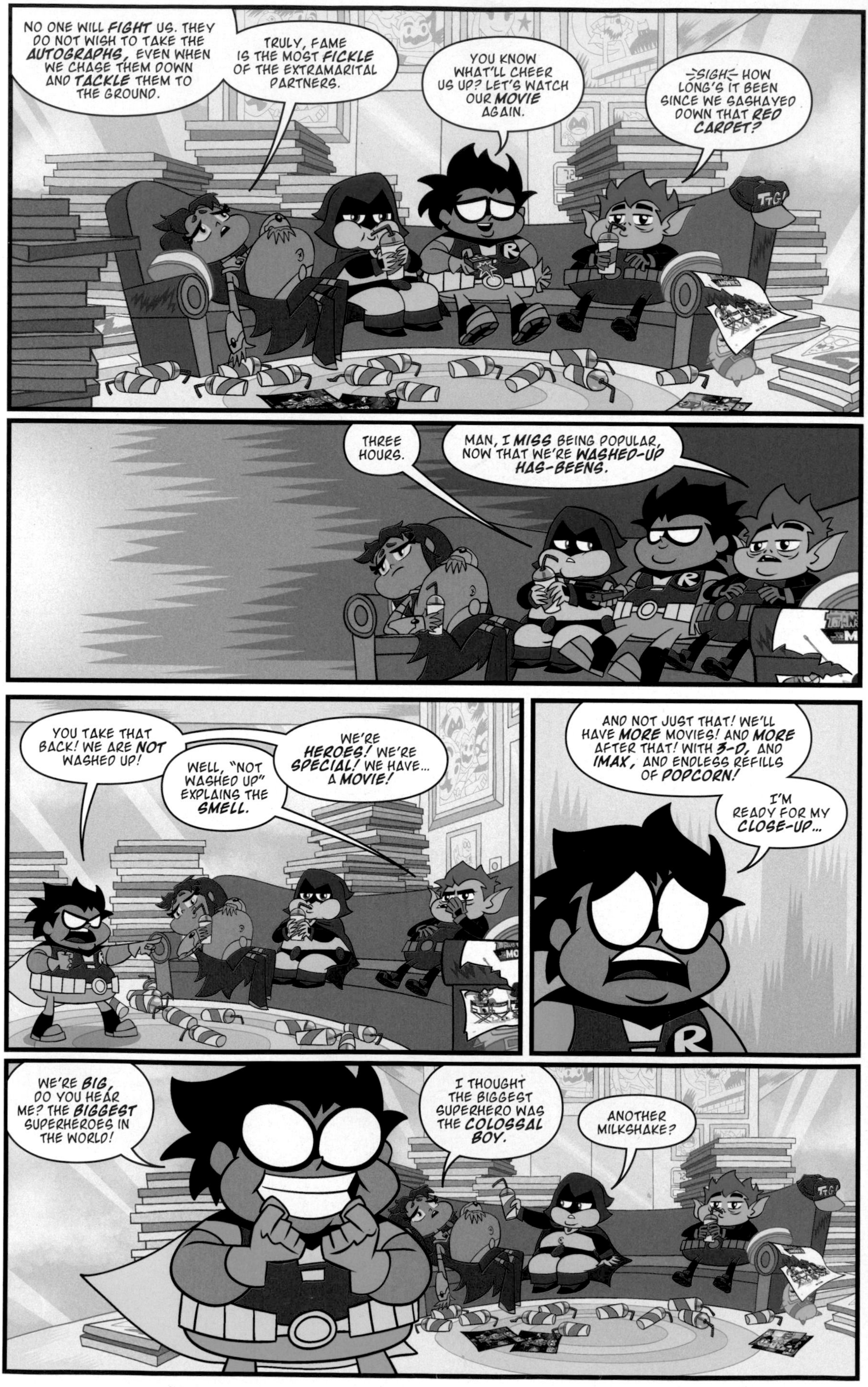
NO ONE WILL FIGHT US. THEY DO NOT WISH TO TAKE THE AUTOGRAPHS, EVEN WHEN WE CHASE THEM DOWN AND TACKLE THEM TO THE GROUND.
TRULY, FAME IS THE MOST FICKLE OF THE EXTRAMARITAL PARTNERS.
YOU KNOW WHAT'LL CHEER US UP? LET'S WATCH OUR MOVIE AGAIN.
-SIGH- HOW LONG'S IT BEEN SINCE WE SASHAYED DOWN THAT RED CARPET?
THREE HOURS.
MAN, I MISS BEING POPULAR, NOW THAT WE'RE WASHED-UP HAS-BEENS.
YOU TAKE THAT BACK! WE ARE NOT WASHED UP!
WELL, "NOT WASHED UP" EXPLAINS THE SMELL.
WE'RE HEROES! WE'RE SPECIAL! WE HAVE... A MOVIE!
AND NOT JUST THAT! WE'LL HAVE MORE MOVIES! AND MORE AFTER THAT! WITH 3-D, AND IMAX, AND ENDLESS REFILLS OF POPCORN!
I'M READY FOR MY CLOSE-UP...
WE'RE BIG, DO YOU HEAR ME? THE BIGGEST SUPERHEROES IN THE WORLD!
I THOUGHT THE BIGGEST SUPERHERO WAS THE COLOSSAL BOY.
ANOTHER MILKSHAKE?

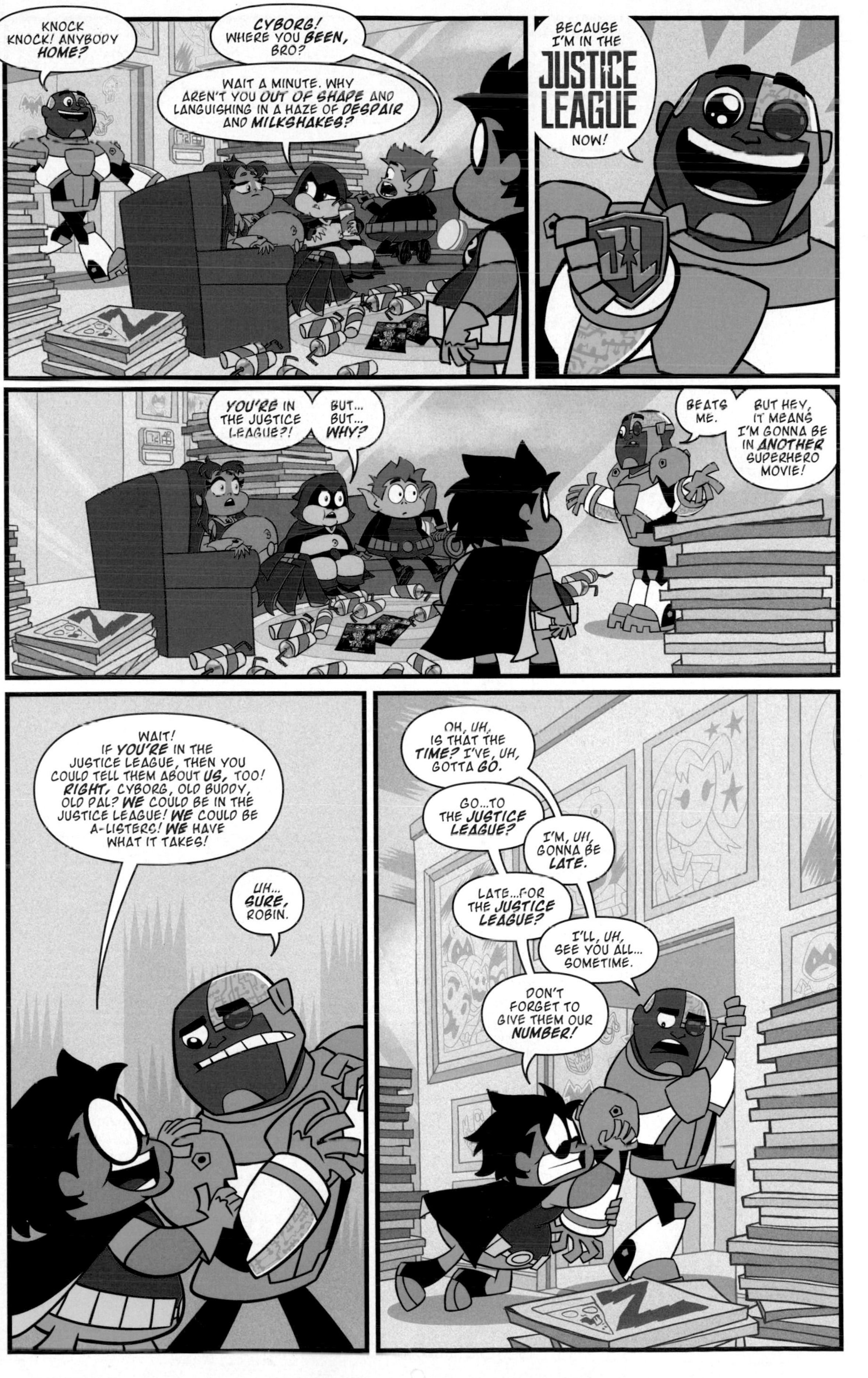
KNOCK KNOCK! ANYBODY HOME?
CYBORG! WHERE YOU BEEN, BRO?
WAIT A MINUTE. WHY AREN'T YOU OUT OF SHAPE AND LANGUISHING IN A HAZE OF DESPAIR AND MILKSHAKES?
BECAUSE I'M IN THE JUSTICE LEAGUE NOW!
YOU'RE IN THE JUSTICE LEAGUE?!
BUT... BUT... WHY?
BEATS ME.
BUT HEY, IT MEANS I'M GONNA BE IN ANOTHER SUPERHERO MOVIE!
WAIT! IF YOU'RE IN THE JUSTICE LEAGUE, THEN YOU COULD TELL THEM ABOUT US, TOO! RIGHT, CYBORG, OLD BUDDY, OLD PAL? WE COULD BE IN THE JUSTICE LEAGUE! WE COULD BE A-LISTERS! WE HAVE WHAT IT TAKES!
UH... SURE, ROBIN.
OH, UH, IS THAT THE TIME? I'VE, UH, GOTTA GO.
GO...TO THE JUSTICE LEAGUE?
I'M, UH, GONNA BE LATE.
LATE...FOR THE JUSTICE LEAGUE?
I'LL, UH, SEE YOU ALL... SOMETIME.
DON'T FORGET TO GIVE THEM OUR NUMBER!

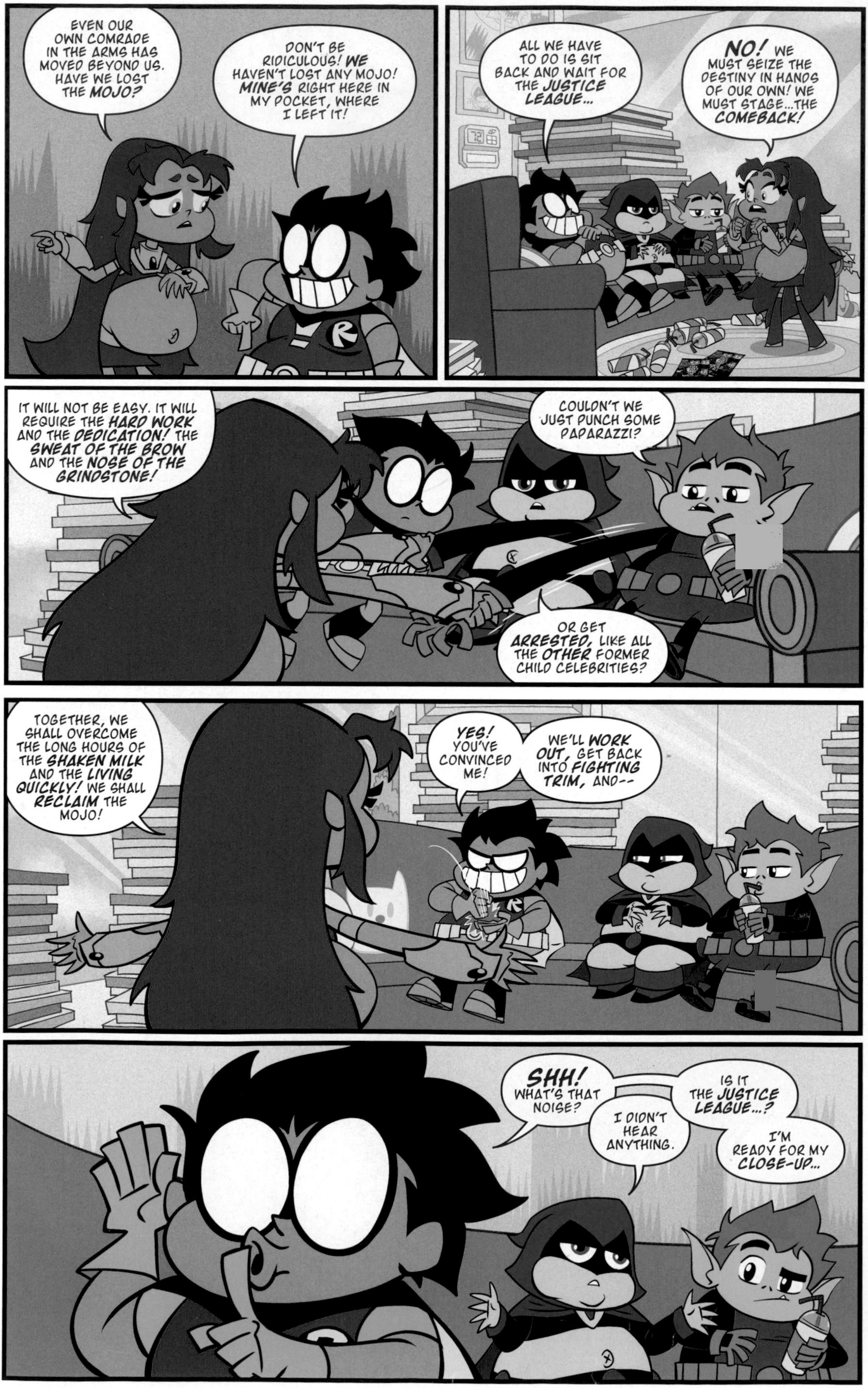
EVEN OUR OWN COMRADE IN THE ARMS HAS MOVED BEYOND US. HAVE WE LOST THE MOJO?
DON'T BE RIDICULOUS! WE HAVEN'T LOST ANY MOJO! MINE'S RIGHT HERE IN MY POCKET, WHERE I LEFT IT!
ALL WE HAVE TO DO IS SIT BACK AND WAIT FOR THE JUSTICE LEAGUE...
NO! WE MUST SEIZE THE DESTINY IN HANDS OF OUR OWN! WE MUST STAGE...THE COMEBACK!
IT WILL NOT BE EASY. IT WILL REQUIRE THE HARD WORK AND THE DEDICATION! THE SWEAT OF THE BROW AND THE NOSE OF THE GRINDSTONE!
COULDN'T WE JUST PUNCH SOME PAPARAZZI?
OR GET ARRESTED, LIKE ALL THE OTHER FORMER CHILD CELEBRITIES?
TOGETHER, WE SHALL OVERCOME THE LONG HOURS OF THE SHAKEN MILK AND THE LIVING QUICKLY! WE SHALL RECLAIM THE MOJO!
YES! YOU'VE CONVINCED ME!
WE'LL WORK OUT, GET BACK INTO FIGHTING TRIM, AND--
SHH! WHAT'S THAT NOISE?
I DIDN'T HEAR ANYTHING.
IS IT THE JUSTICE LEAGUE...?
I'M READY FOR MY CLOSE-UP...

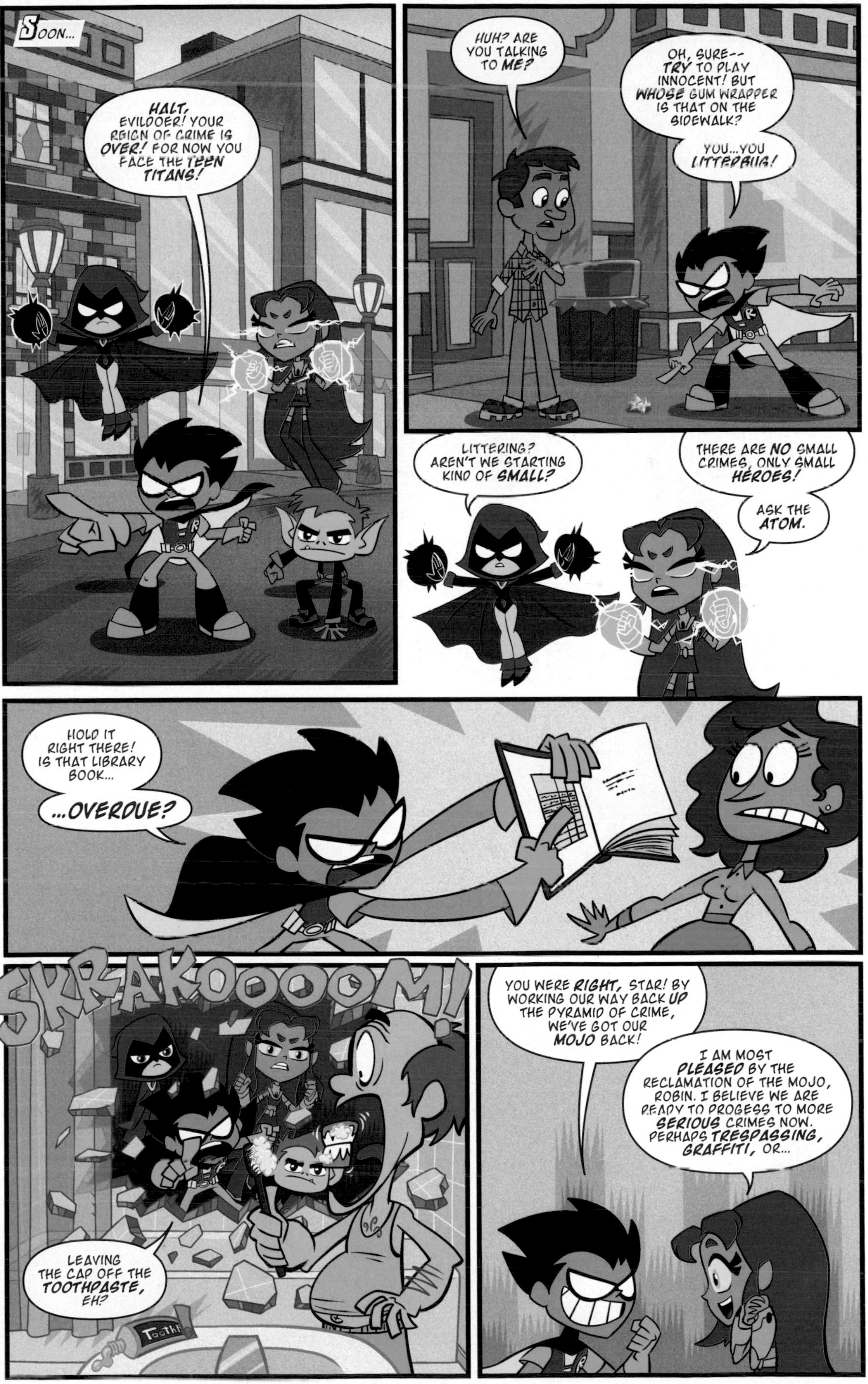
SOON...
HALT, EVILDOER! YOUR REIGN OF CRIME IS OVER! FOR NOW YOU FACE THE TEEN TITANS!
HUH? ARE YOU TALKING TO ME?
OH, SURE-- TRY TO PLAY INNOCENT! BUT WHOSE GUM WRAPPER IS THAT ON THE SIDEWALK?
YOU...YOU LITTERBUG!
LITTERING? AREN'T WE STARTING KIND OF SMALL?
THERE ARE NO SMALL CRIMES, ONLY SMALL HEROES!
ASK THE ATOM.
HOLD IT RIGHT THERE! IS THAT LIBRARY BOOK...
...OVERDUE?
SKRAKOOOOM!
LEAVING THE CAP OFF THE TOOTHPASTE, EH?
YOU WERE RIGHT, STAR! BY WORKING OUR WAY BACK UP THE PYRAMID OF CRIME, WE'VE GOT OUR MOJO BACK!
I AM MOST PLEASED BY THE RECLAMATION OF THE MOJO, ROBIN. I BELIEVE WE ARE READY TO PROGESS TO MORE SERIOUS CRIMES NOW. PERHAPS TRESPASSING, GRAFFITI, OR...

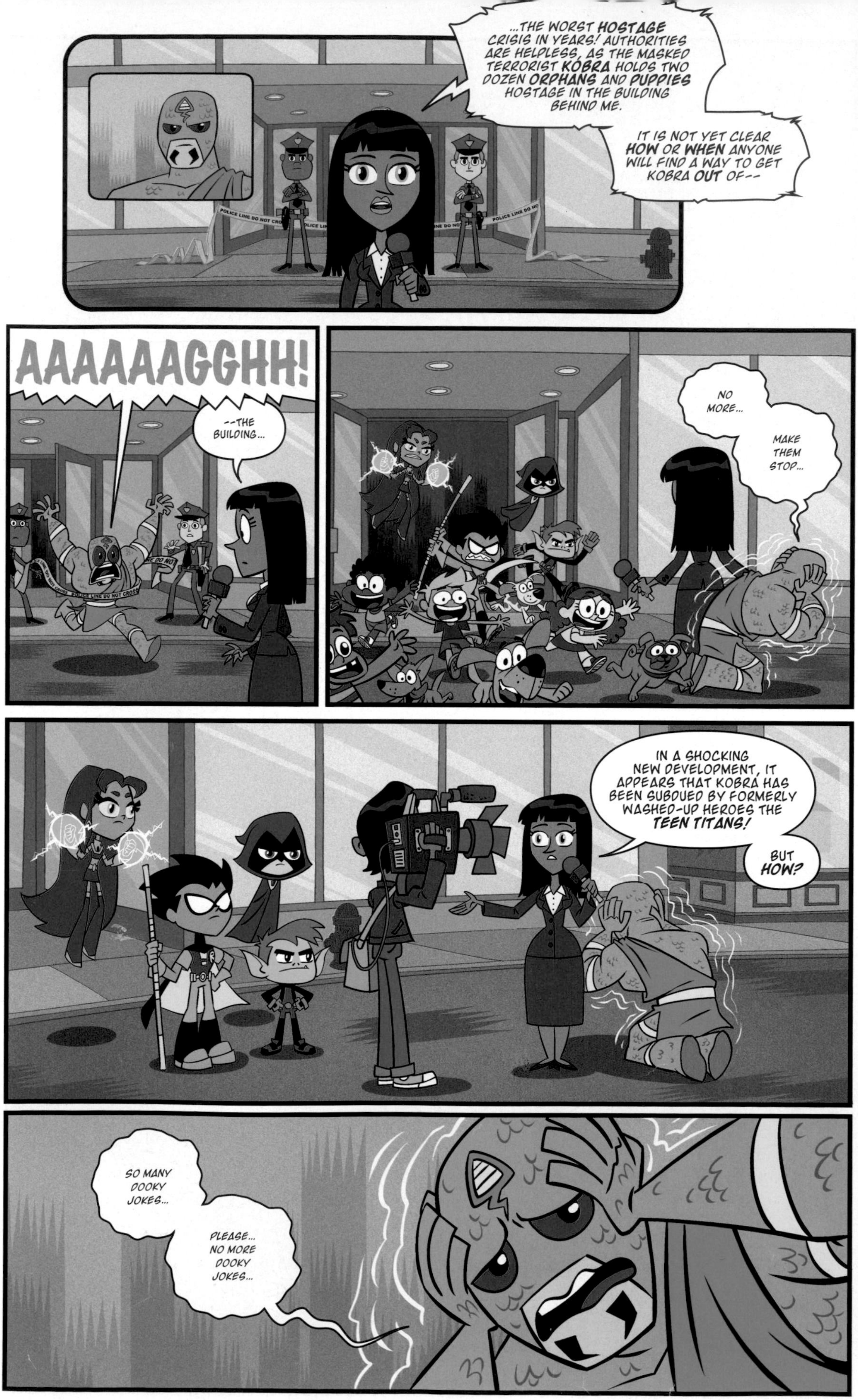

...THE WORST HOSTAGE CRISIS IN YEARS! AUTHORITIES ARE HELPLESS, AS THE MASKED TERRORIST KOBRA HOLDS TWO DOZEN ORPHANS AND PUPPIES HOSTAGE IN THE BUILDING BEHIND ME.
IT IS NOT YET CLEAR HOW OR WHEN ANYONE WILL FIND A WAY TO GET KOBRA OUT OF--
POLICE LINE DO NOT CROSS
AAAAAAGGHH!
--THE BUILDING...
NO MORE...
MAKE THEM STOP...
IN A SHOCKING NEW DEVELOPMENT, IT APPEARS THAT KOBRA HAS BEEN SUBDUED BY FORMERLY WASHED-UP HEROES THE TEEN TITANS!
BUT HOW?
SO MANY DOOKY JOKES...
PLEASE... NO MORE DOOKY JOKES...

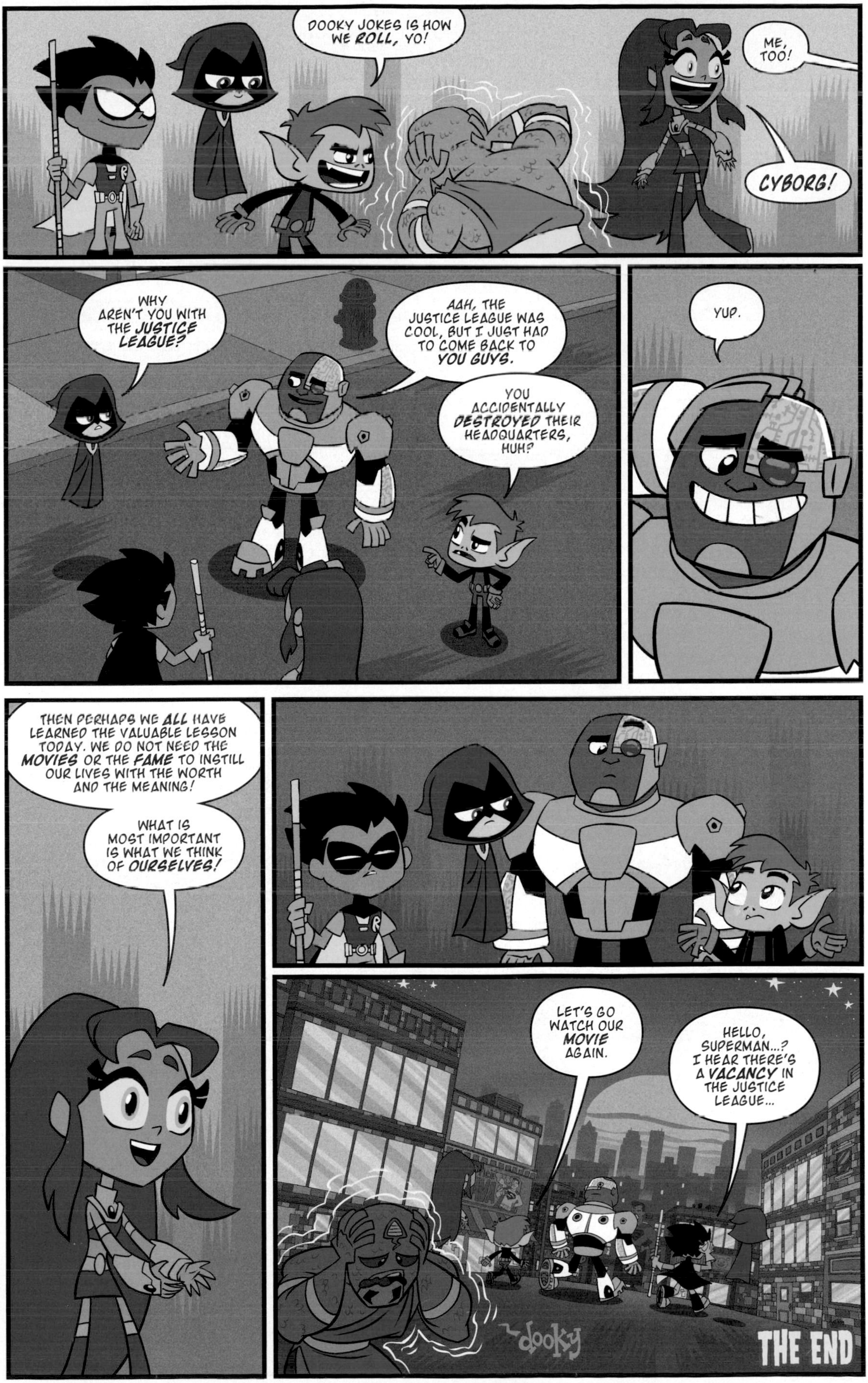
DOOKY JOKES IS HOW WE ROLL, YO!
ME, TOO!
CYBORG!
WHY AREN'T YOU WITH THE JUSTICE LEAGUE?
AAH, THE JUSTICE LEAGUE WAS COOL, BUT I JUST HAD TO COME BACK TO YOU GUYS.
YOU ACCIDENTALLY DESTROYED THEIR HEADQUARTERS, HUH?
YUP.
THEN PERHAPS WE ALL HAVE LEARNED THE VALUABLE LESSON TODAY. WE DO NOT NEED THE MOVIES OR THE FAME TO INSTILL OUR LIVES WITH THE WORTH AND THE MEANING!
WHAT IS MOST IMPORTANT IS WHAT WE THINK OF OURSELVES!
LET'S GO WATCH OUR MOVIE AGAIN.
HELLO, SUPERMAN...? I HEAR THERE'S A VACANCY IN THE JUSTICE LEAGUE...
dooky
THE END

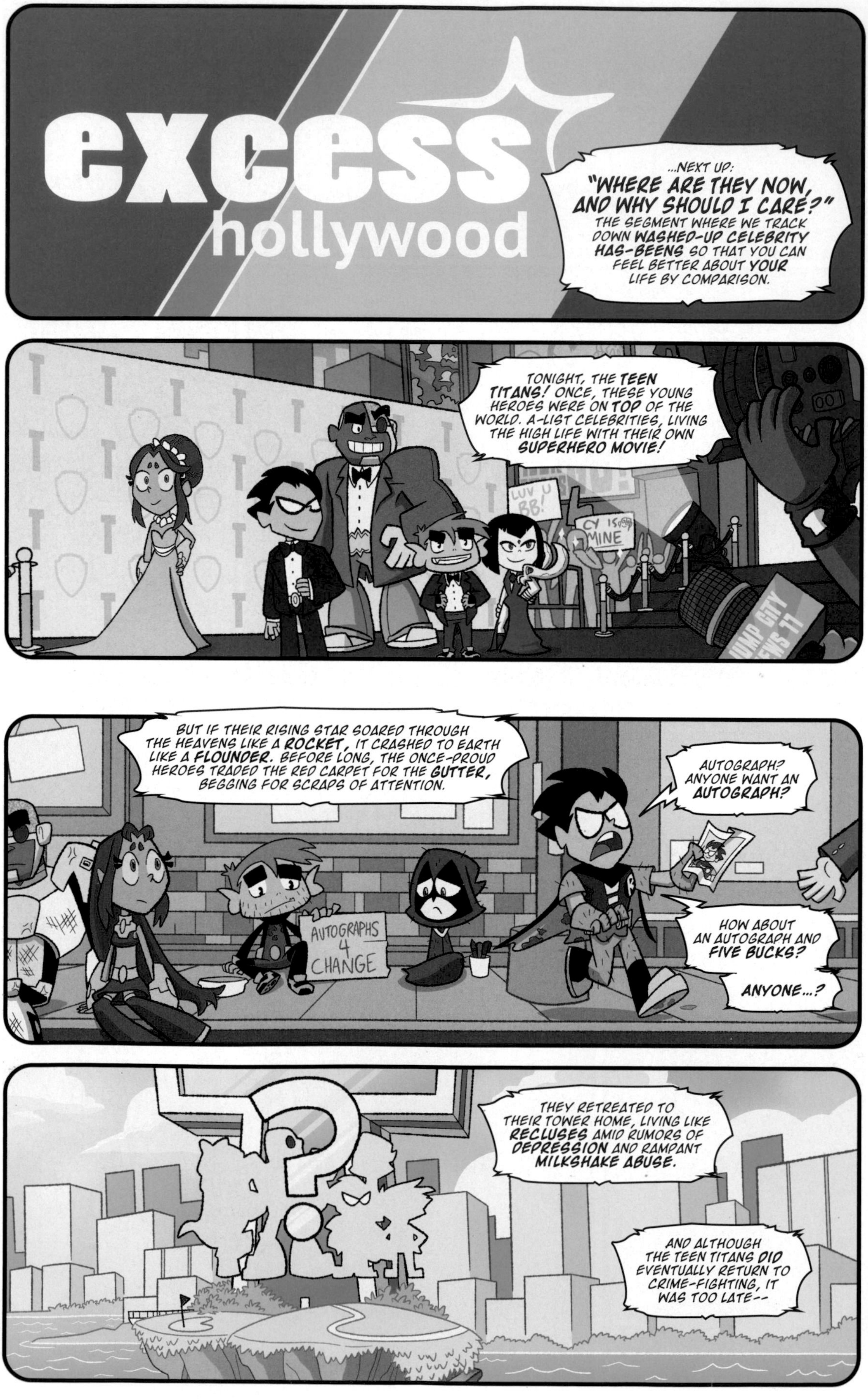
excess hollywood
...NEXT UP: "WHERE ARE THEY NOW, AND WHY SHOULD I CARE?" THE SEGMENT WHERE WE TRACK DOWN WASHED-UP CELEBRITY HAS-BEENS SO THAT YOU CAN FEEL BETTER ABOUT YOUR LIFE BY COMPARISON.
TONIGHT, THE TEEN TITANS! ONCE, THESE YOUNG HEROES WERE ON TOP OF THE WORLD. A-LIST CELEBRITIES, LIVING THE HIGH LIFE WITH THEIR OWN SUPERHERO MOVIE!
LUV U BB!
CY IS MINE
BUT IF THEIR RISING STAR SOARED THROUGH THE HEAVENS LIKE A ROCKET, IT CRASHED TO EARTH LIKE A FLOUNDER. BEFORE LONG, THE ONCE-PROUD HEROES TRADED THE RED CARPET FOR THE GUTTER, BEGGING FOR SCRAPS OF ATTENTION.
AUTOGRAPH? ANYONE WANT AN AUTOGRAPH?
AUTOGRAPHS 4 CHANGE
HOW ABOUT AN AUTOGRAPH AND FIVE BUCKS?
ANYONE...?
THEY RETREATED TO THEIR TOWER HOME, LIVING LIKE RECLUSES AMID RUMORS OF DEPRESSION AND RAMPANT MILKSHAKE ABUSE.
AND ALTHOUGH THE TEEN TITANS DID EVENTUALLY RETURN TO CRIME-FIGHTING, IT WAS TOO LATE--

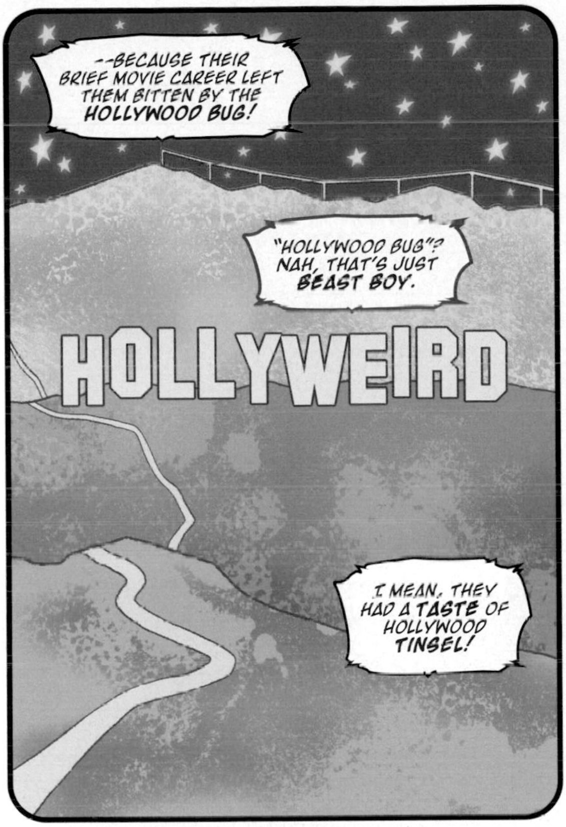
--BECAUSE THEIR BRIEF MOVIE CAREER LEFT THEM BITTEN BY THE HOLLYWOOD BUG!
"HOLLYWOOD BUG"? NAH, THAT'S JUST BEAST BOY.
HOLLYWEIRD
I MEAN, THEY HAD A TASTE OF HOLLYWOOD TINSEL!

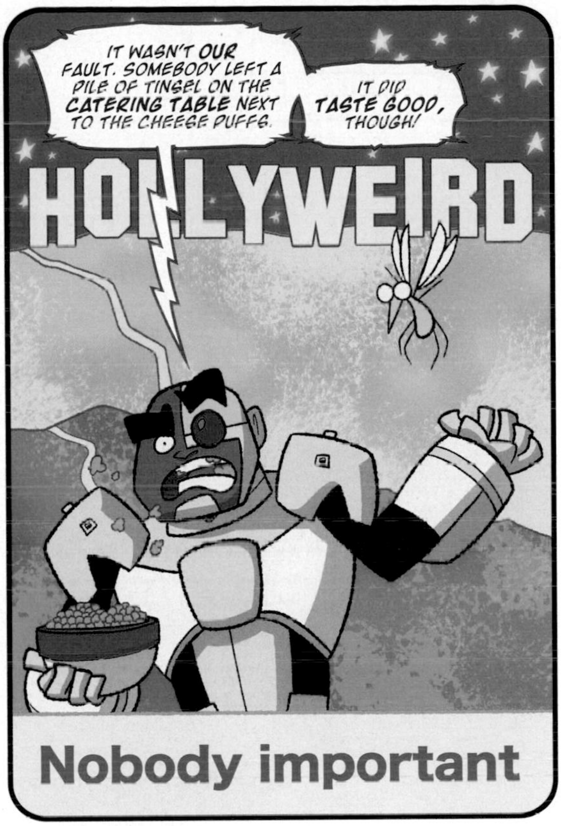
IT WASN'T OUR FAULT. SOMEBODY LEFT A PILE OF TINSEL ON THE CATERING TABLE NEXT TO THE CHEESE PUFFS.
IT DID TASTE GOOD, THOUGH!
HOLLYWEIRD
Nobody important

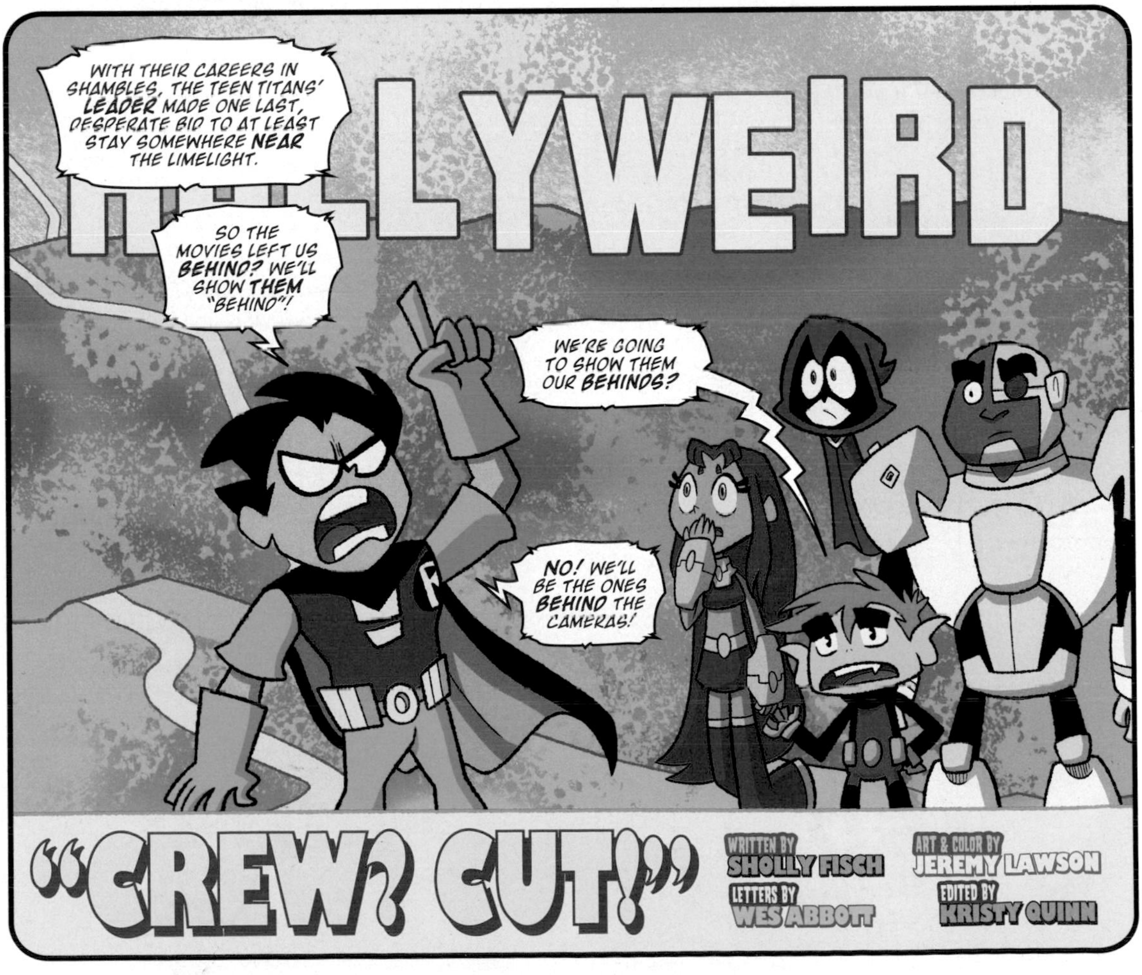
WITH THEIR CAREERS IN SHAMBLES, THE TEEN TITANS' LEADER MADE ONE LAST, DESPERATE BID TO AT LEAST STAY SOMEWHERE NEAR THE LIMELIGHT.
HOLLYWEIRD
SO THE MOVIES LEFT US BEHIND? WE'LL SHOW THEM "BEHIND"!
WE'RE GOING TO SHOW THEM OUR BEHINDS?
NO! WE'LL BE THE ONES BEHIND THE CAMERAS!
"CREW? CUT!"
WRITTEN BY SHOLLY FISCH
ART & COLOR BY JEREMY LAWSON
LETTERS BY WES ABBOTT
EDITED BY KRISTY QUINN

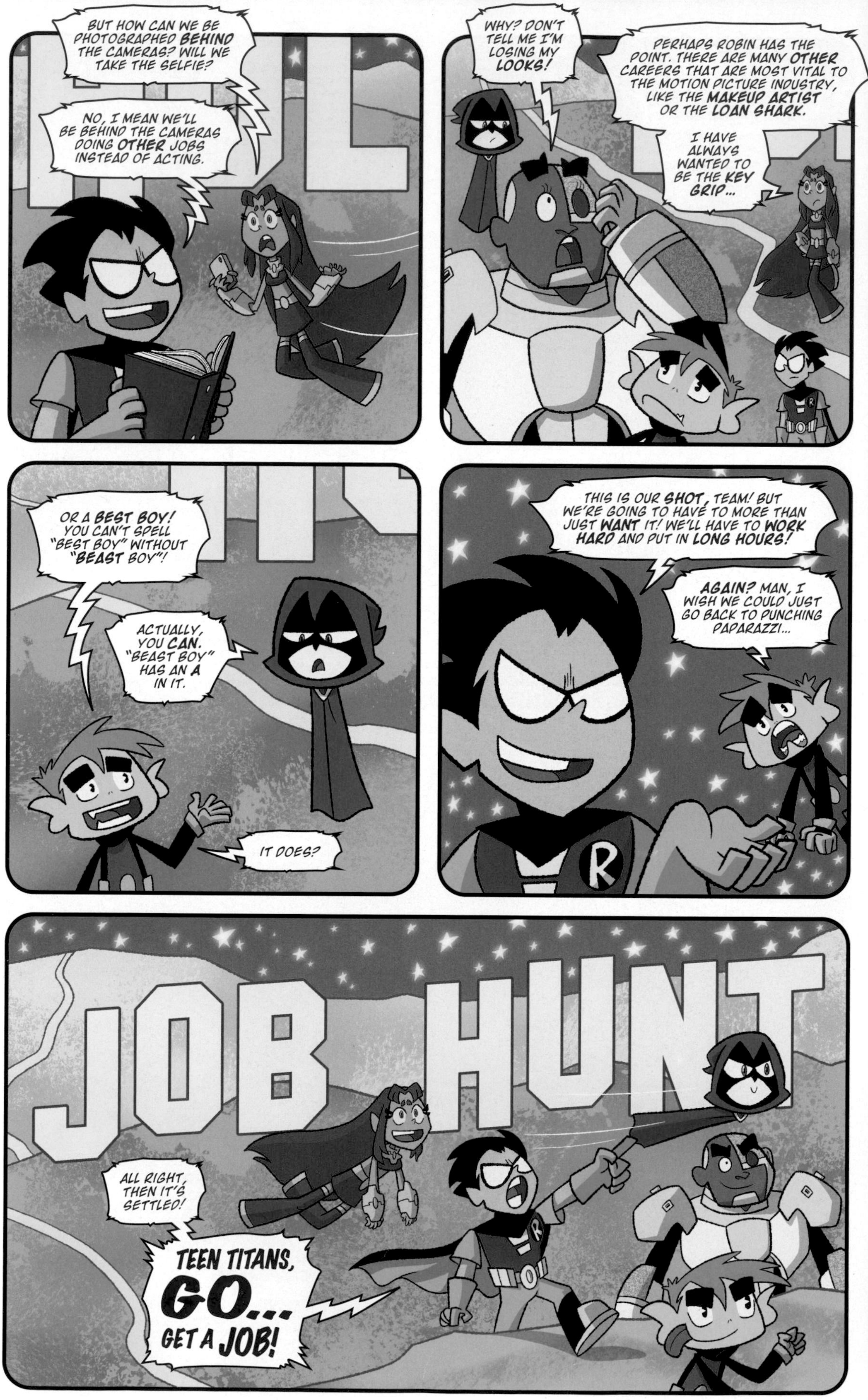
BUT HOW CAN WE BE PHOTOGRAPHED BEHIND THE CAMERAS? WILL WE TAKE THE SELFIE?
NO, I MEAN WE'LL BE BEHIND THE CAMERAS DOING OTHER JOBS INSTEAD OF ACTING.
WHY? DON'T TELL ME I'M LOSING MY LOOKS!
PERHAPS ROBIN HAS THE POINT. THERE ARE MANY OTHER CAREERS THAT ARE MOST VITAL TO THE MOTION PICTURE INDUSTRY, LIKE THE MAKEUP ARTIST OR THE LOAN SHARK.
I HAVE ALWAYS WANTED TO BE THE KEY GRIP...
OR A BEST BOY! YOU CAN'T SPELL "BEST BOY" WITHOUT "BEAST BOY"!
ACTUALLY, YOU CAN. "BEAST BOY" HAS AN A IN IT.
IT DOES?
THIS IS OUR SHOT, TEAM! BUT WE'RE GOING TO HAVE TO MORE THAN JUST WANT IT! WE'LL HAVE TO WORK HARD AND PUT IN LONG HOURS!
AGAIN? MAN, I WISH WE COULD JUST GO BACK TO PUNCHING PAPARAZZI...
JOB HUNT
ALL RIGHT, THEN IT'S SETTLED!
TEEN TITANS, GO... GET A JOB!

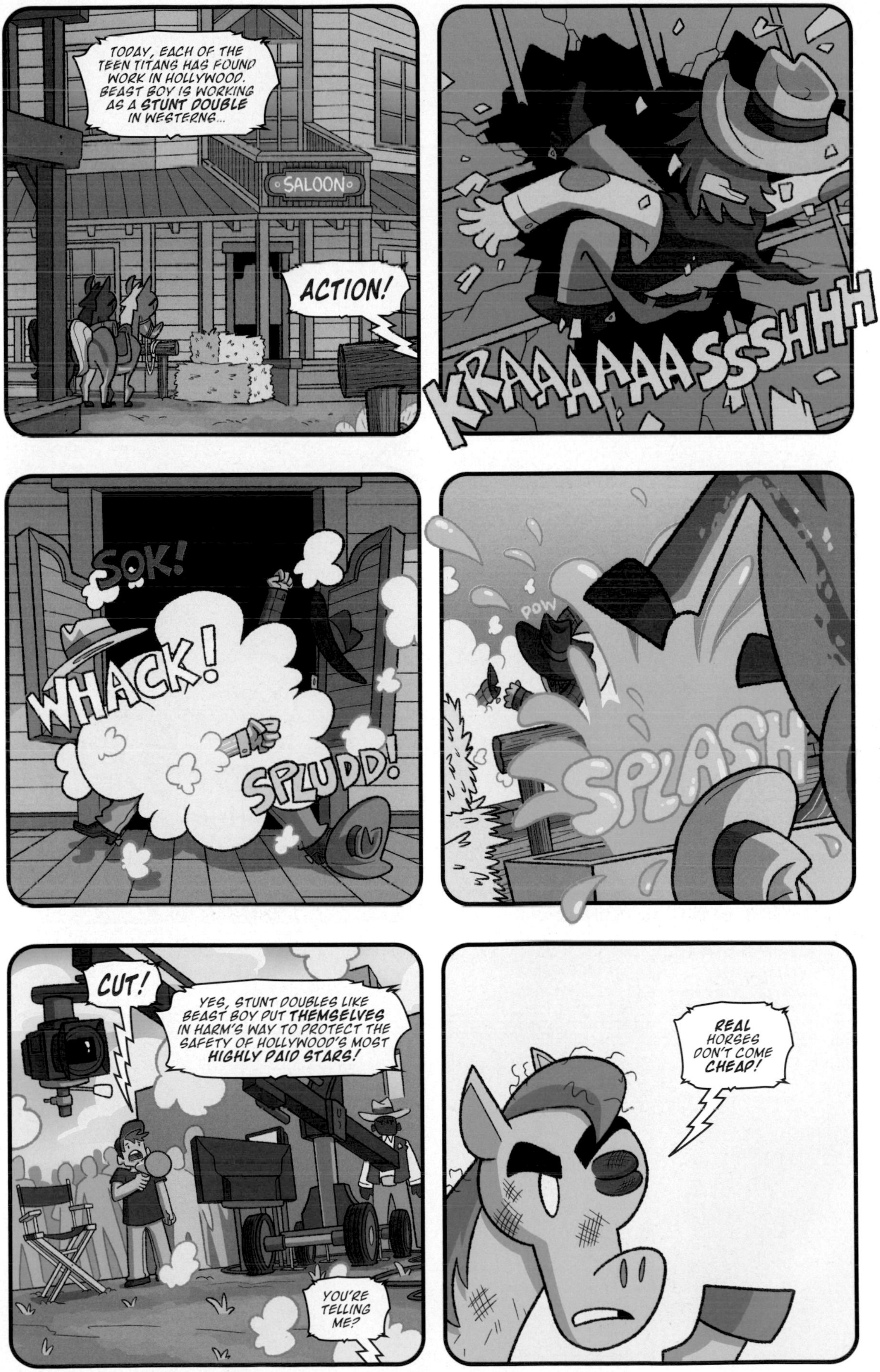
TODAY, EACH OF THE TEEN TITANS HAS FOUND WORK IN HOLLYWOOD. BEAST BOY IS WORKING AS A STUNT DOUBLE IN WESTERNS...
SALOON
ACTION!
KRAAAAAASSSHHH
SOK!
WHACK!
SPLUDD!
POW
SPLASH
CUT!
YES, STUNT DOUBLES LIKE BEAST BOY PUT THEMSELVES IN HARM'S WAY TO PROTECT THE SAFETY OF HOLLYWOOD'S MOST HIGHLY PAID STARS!
YOU'RE TELLING ME?
REAL HORSES DON'T COME CHEAP!

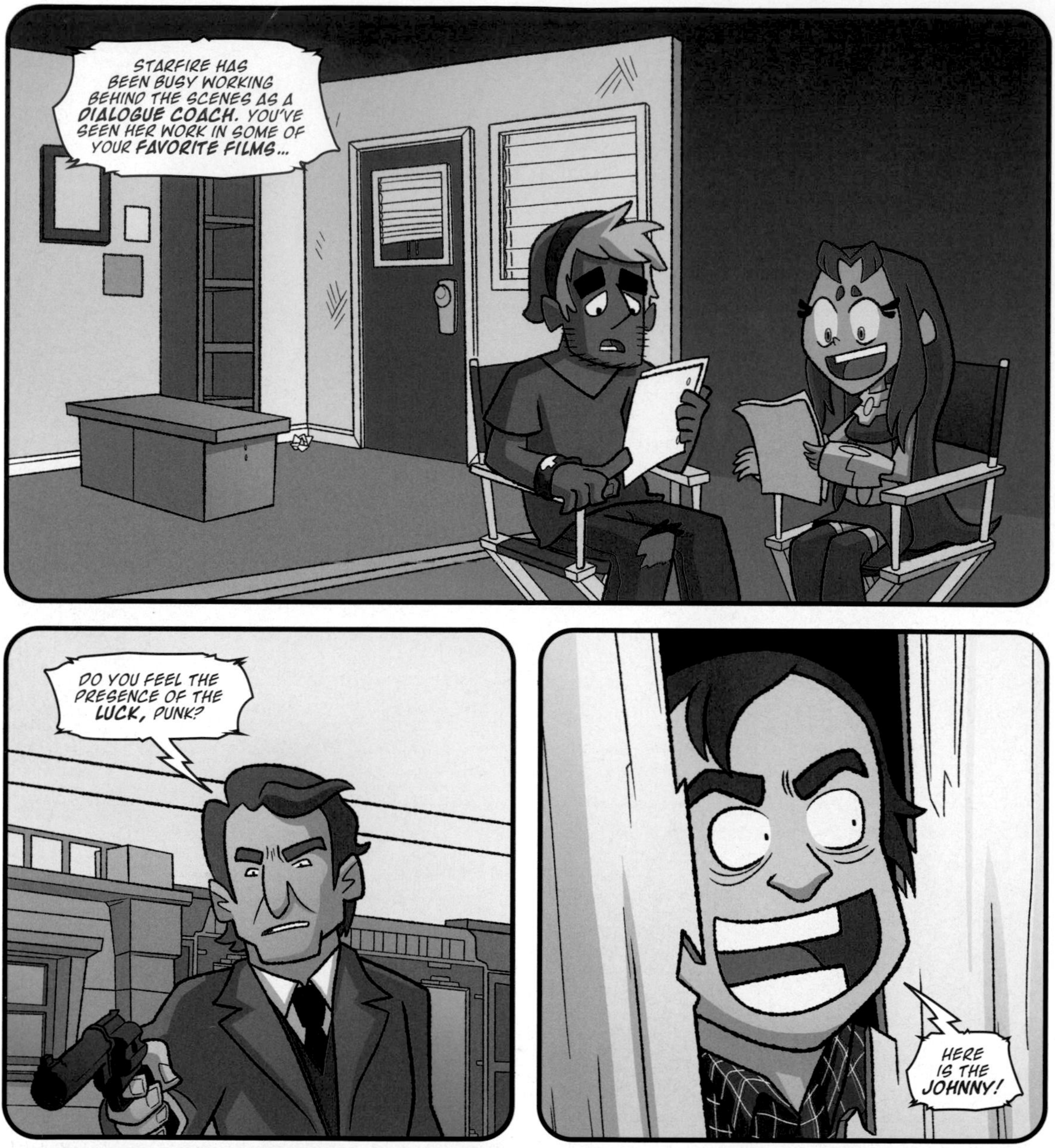
STARFIRE HAS BEEN BUSY WORKING BEHIND THE SCENES AS A DIALOGUE COACH. YOU'VE SEEN HER WORK IN SOME OF YOUR FAVORITE FILMS...
DO YOU FEEL THE PRESENCE OF THE LUCK, PUNK?
HERE IS THE JOHNNY!
YOU KNOW HOW TO WHISTLE, DON'T YOU, STEVE? YOU JUST PUT YOUR LIPS TOGETHER AND EXPEL A BLEND OF CARBON DIOXIDE AND ASSORTED TRACE GASES.
BUD OF THE ROSE...

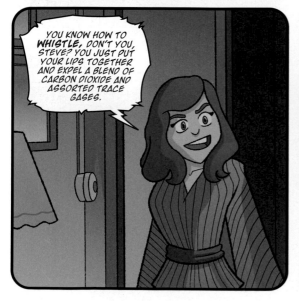

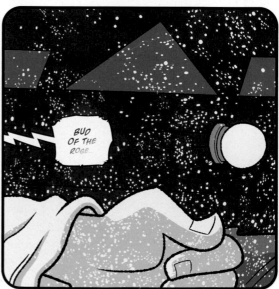

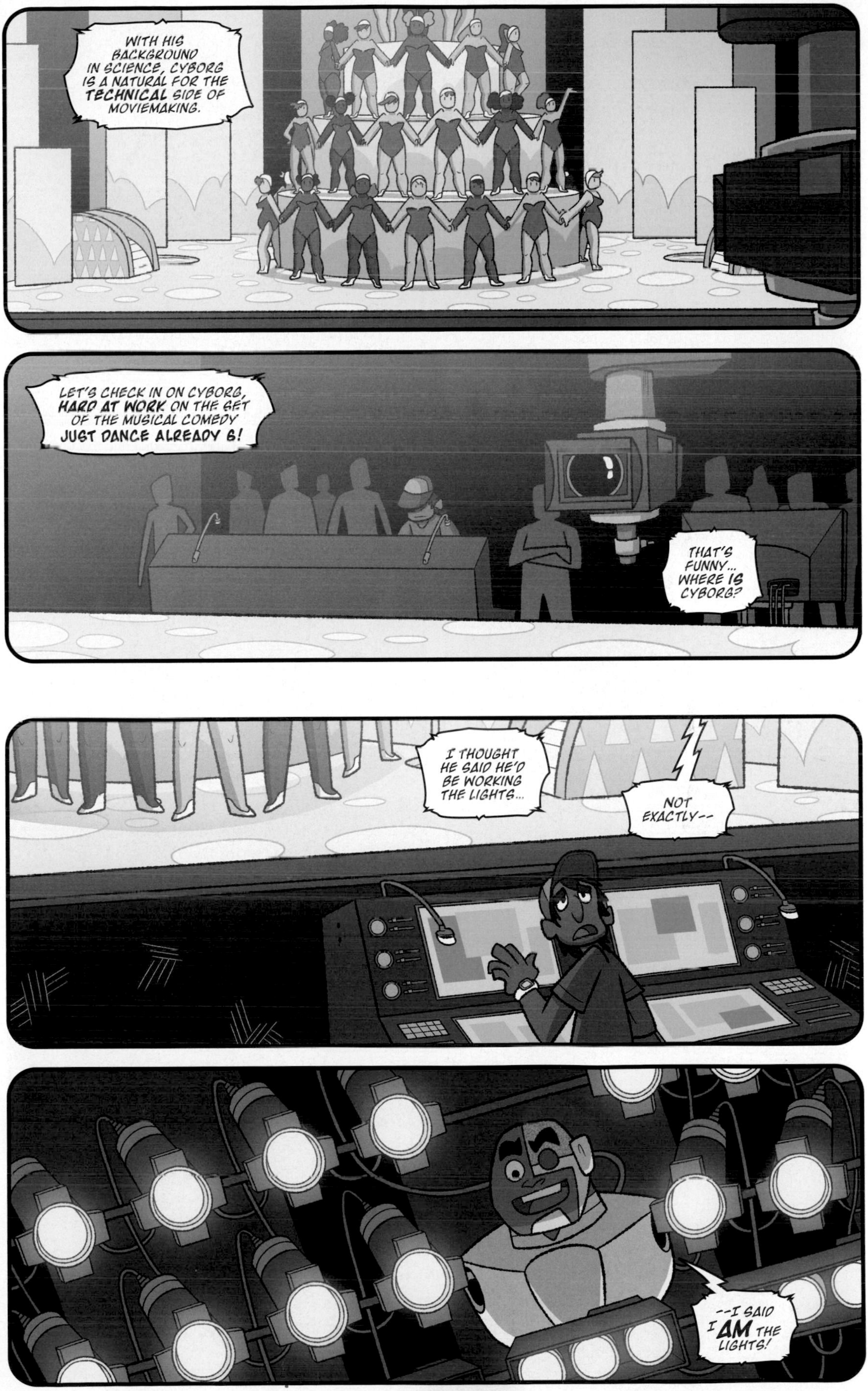

WITH HIS BACKGROUND IN SCIENCE, CYBORG IS A NATURAL FOR THE TECHNICAL SIDE OF MOVIEMAKING.
LET'S CHECK IN ON CYBORG, HARD AT WORK ON THE SET OF THE MUSICAL COMEDY JUST DANCE ALREADY 6!
THAT'S FUNNY... WHERE IS CYBORG?
I THOUGHT HE SAID HE'D BE WORKING THE LIGHTS...
NOT EXACTLY--
--I SAID I AM THE LIGHTS!

AS FOR ROBIN...

OH, I CAN EXPLAIN FOR MYSELF. I'M A HOLLYWOOD AUTEUR NOW--WRITING AND DIRECTING INDEPENDENT FILMS TO FINALLY GIVE VOICE TO MY OWN PERSONAL CREATIVE VISION!

HERE'S A SCENE FROM MY LATEST MASTERPIECE, THE FLOSS OF DESPAIR...

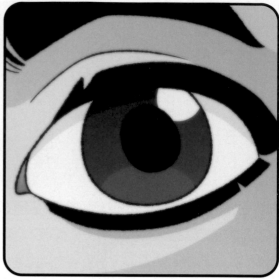

PARADE

AND THAT'S JUST A CLIP! THE WHOLE THING IS FOUR HOURS LONG! PRETTY ARTSY, HUH?

ACTUALLY, I THOUGHT IT WAS KIND OF IMPENETRABLE.

I KNOW! PERFECT, RIGHT?

SUNDANCE FILM FESTIVAL, HERE I COME!

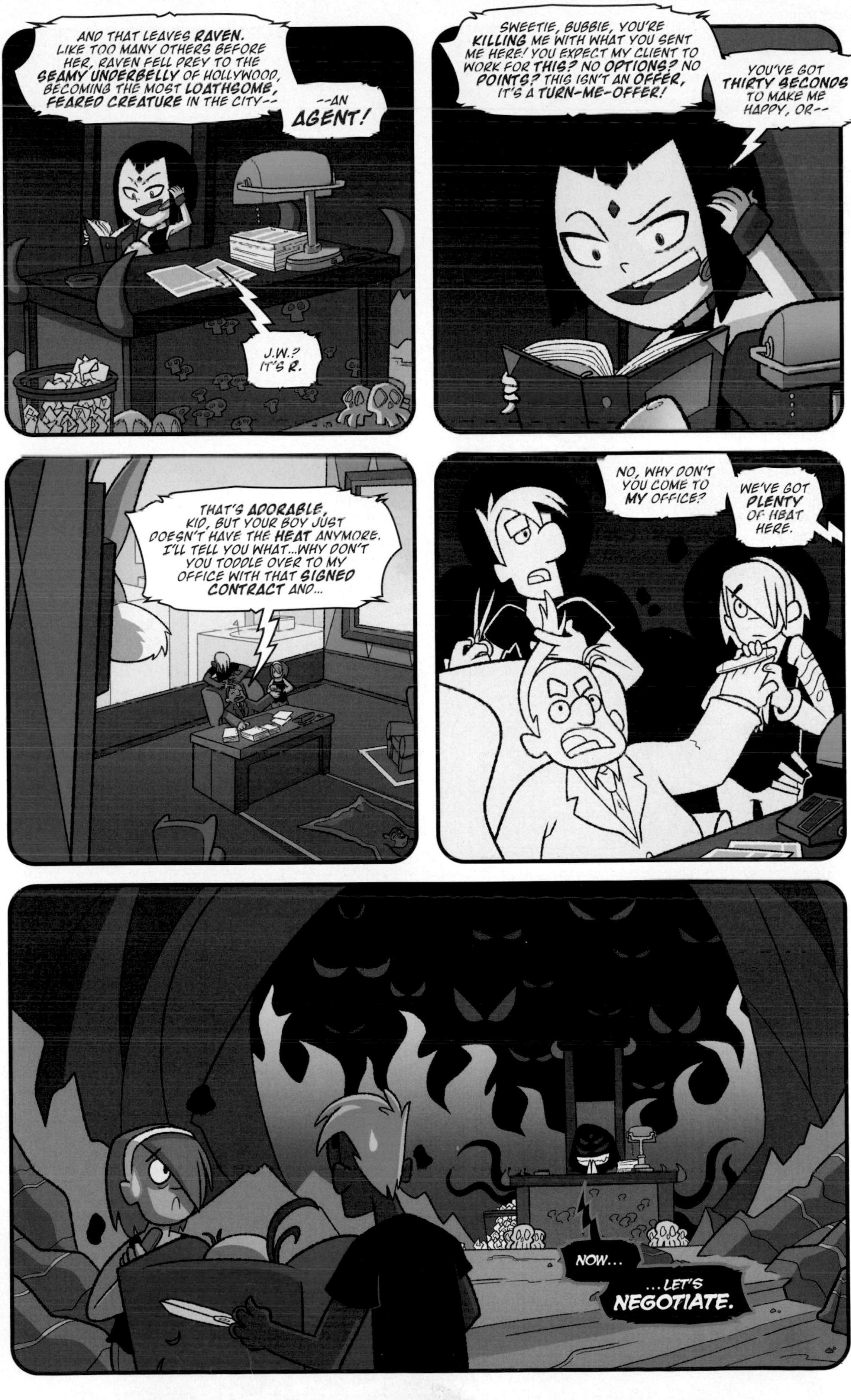
AND THAT LEAVES RAVEN. LIKE TOO MANY OTHERS BEFORE HER, RAVEN FELL PREY TO THE SEAMY UNDERBELLY OF HOLLYWOOD, BECOMING THE MOST LOATHSOME, FEARED CREATURE IN THE CITY--
--AN AGENT!
J.W.? IT'S R.
SWEETIE, BUBBIE, YOU'RE KILLING ME WITH WHAT YOU SENT ME HERE! YOU EXPECT MY CLIENT TO WORK FOR THIS? NO OPTIONS? NO POINTS? THIS ISN'T AN OFFER, IT'S A TURN-ME-OFFER!
YOU'VE GOT THIRTY SECONDS TO MAKE ME HAPPY, OR--
THAT'S ADORABLE, KID, BUT YOUR BOY JUST DOESN'T HAVE THE HEAT ANYMORE. I'LL TELL YOU WHAT...WHY DON'T YOU TODDLE OVER TO MY OFFICE WITH THAT SIGNED CONTRACT AND...
NO, WHY DON'T YOU COME TO MY OFFICE?
WE'VE GOT PLENTY OF HEAT HERE.
NOW...
...LET'S NEGOTIATE.

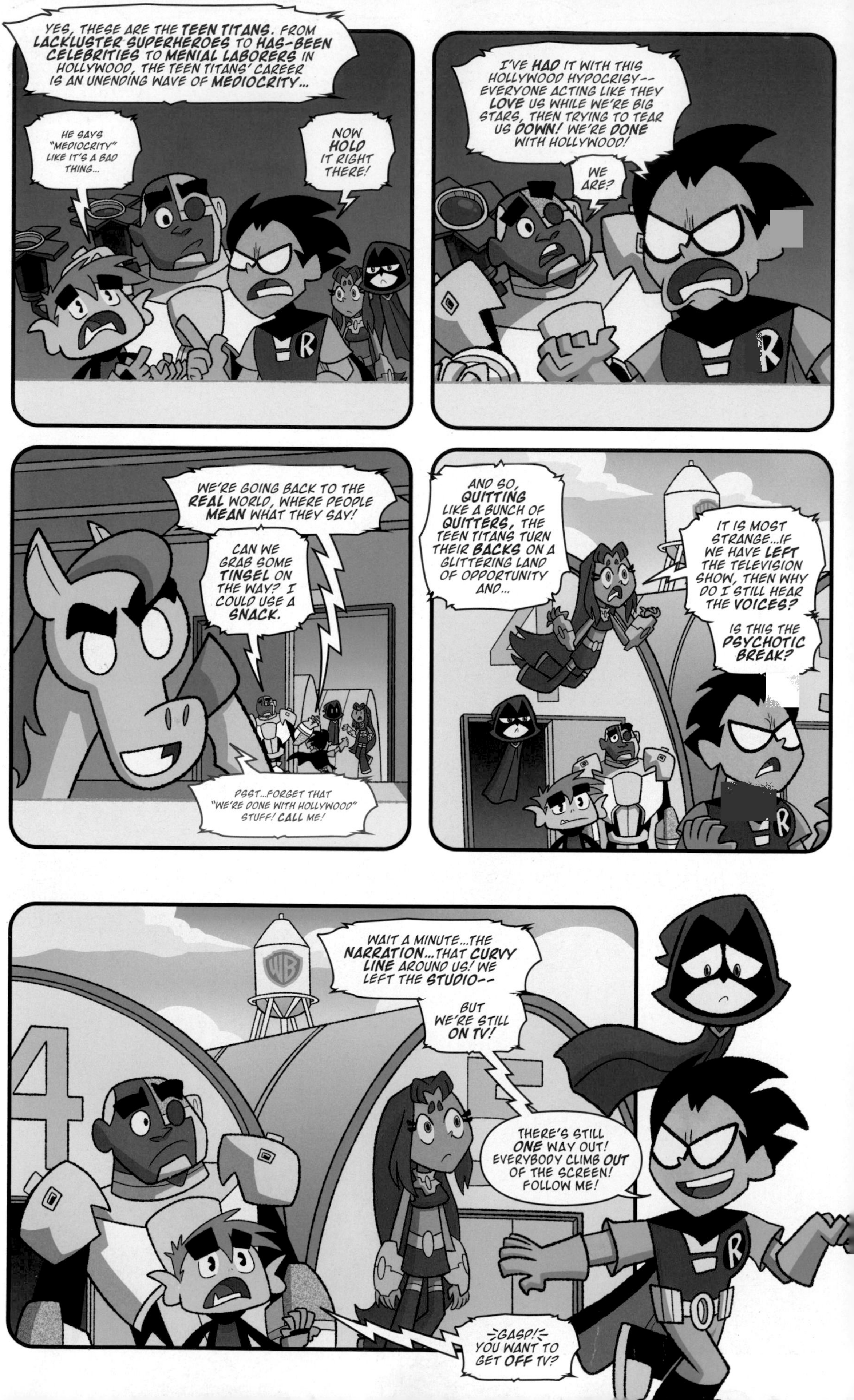

YES, THESE ARE THE TEEN TITANS. FROM LACKLUSTER SUPERHEROES TO HAS-BEEN CELEBRITIES TO MENIAL LABORERS IN HOLLYWOOD, THE TEEN TITANS' CAREER IS AN UNENDING WAVE OF MEDIOCRITY...
HE SAYS "MEDIOCRITY" LIKE IT'S A BAD THING...
NOW HOLD IT RIGHT THERE!
I'VE HAD IT WITH THIS HOLLYWOOD HYPOCRISY-- EVERYONE ACTING LIKE THEY LOVE US WHILE WE'RE BIG STARS, THEN TRYING TO TEAR US DOWN! WE'RE DONE WITH HOLLYWOOD!
WE ARE?
WE'RE GOING BACK TO THE REAL WORLD, WHERE PEOPLE MEAN WHAT THEY SAY!
CAN WE GRAB SOME TINSEL ON THE WAY? I COULD USE A SNACK.
PSST...FORGET THAT "WE'RE DONE WITH HOLLYWOOD" STUFF! CALL ME!
AND SO, QUITTING LIKE A BUNCH OF QUITTERS, THE TEEN TITANS TURN THEIR BACKS ON A GLITTERING LAND OF OPPORTUNITY AND...
IT IS MOST STRANGE...IF WE HAVE LEFT THE TELEVISION SHOW, THEN WHY DO I STILL HEAR THE VOICES?
IS THIS THE PSYCHOTIC BREAK?
WAIT A MINUTE...THE NARRATION...THAT CURVY LINE AROUND US! WE LEFT THE STUDIO--
BUT WE'RE STILL ON TV!
THERE'S STILL ONE WAY OUT! EVERYBODY CLIMB OUT OF THE SCREEN! FOLLOW ME!
=GASP!= YOU WANT TO GET OFF TV?

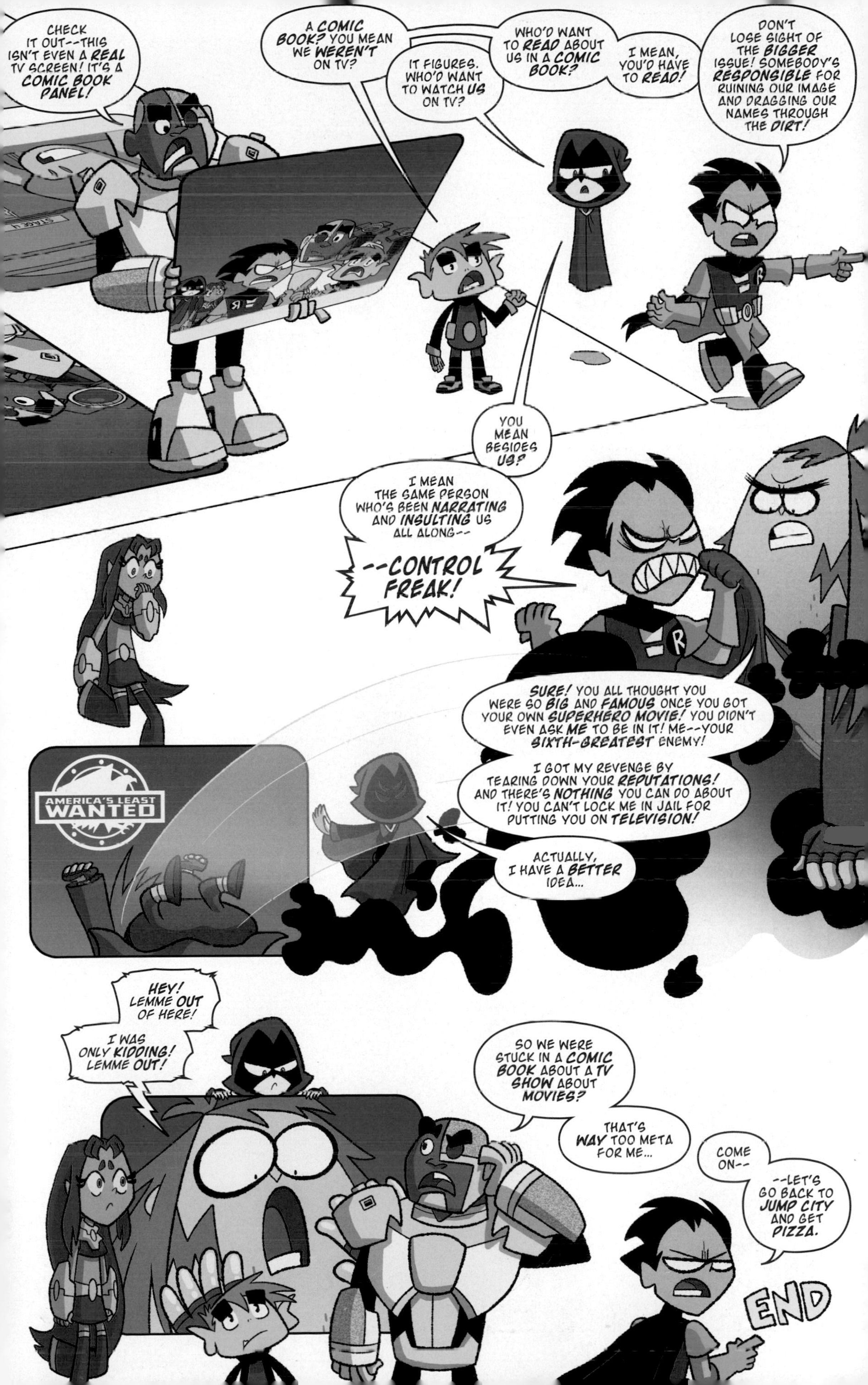
CHECK IT OUT--THIS ISN'T EVEN A REAL TV SCREEN! IT'S A COMIC BOOK PANEL!
A COMIC BOOK? YOU MEAN WE WEREN'T ON TV?
IT FIGURES. WHO'D WANT TO WATCH US ON TV?
WHO'D WANT TO READ ABOUT US IN A COMIC BOOK?
I MEAN, YOU'D HAVE TO READ!
DON'T LOSE SIGHT OF THE BIGGER ISSUE! SOMEBODY'S RESPONSIBLE FOR RUINING OUR IMAGE AND DRAGGING OUR NAMES THROUGH THE DIRT!
YOU MEAN BESIDES US?
I MEAN THE SAME PERSON WHO'S BEEN NARRATING AND INSULTING US ALL ALONG--
--CONTROL FREAK!
SURE! YOU ALL THOUGHT YOU WERE SO BIG AND FAMOUS ONCE YOU GOT YOUR OWN SUPERHERO MOVIE! YOU DIDN'T EVEN ASK ME TO BE IN IT! ME--YOUR SIXTH-GREATEST ENEMY!
I GOT MY REVENGE BY TEARING DOWN YOUR REPUTATIONS! AND THERE'S NOTHING YOU CAN DO ABOUT IT! YOU CAN'T LOCK ME IN JAIL FOR PUTTING YOU ON TELEVISION!
AMERICA'S LEAST WANTED
ACTUALLY, I HAVE A BETTER IDEA...
HEY! LEMME OUT OF HERE!
I WAS ONLY KIDDING! LEMME OUT!
SO WE WERE STUCK IN A COMIC BOOK ABOUT A TV SHOW ABOUT MOVIES?
THAT'S WAY TOO META FOR ME...
COME ON--
--LET'S GO BACK TO JUMP CITY AND GET PIZZA.
END

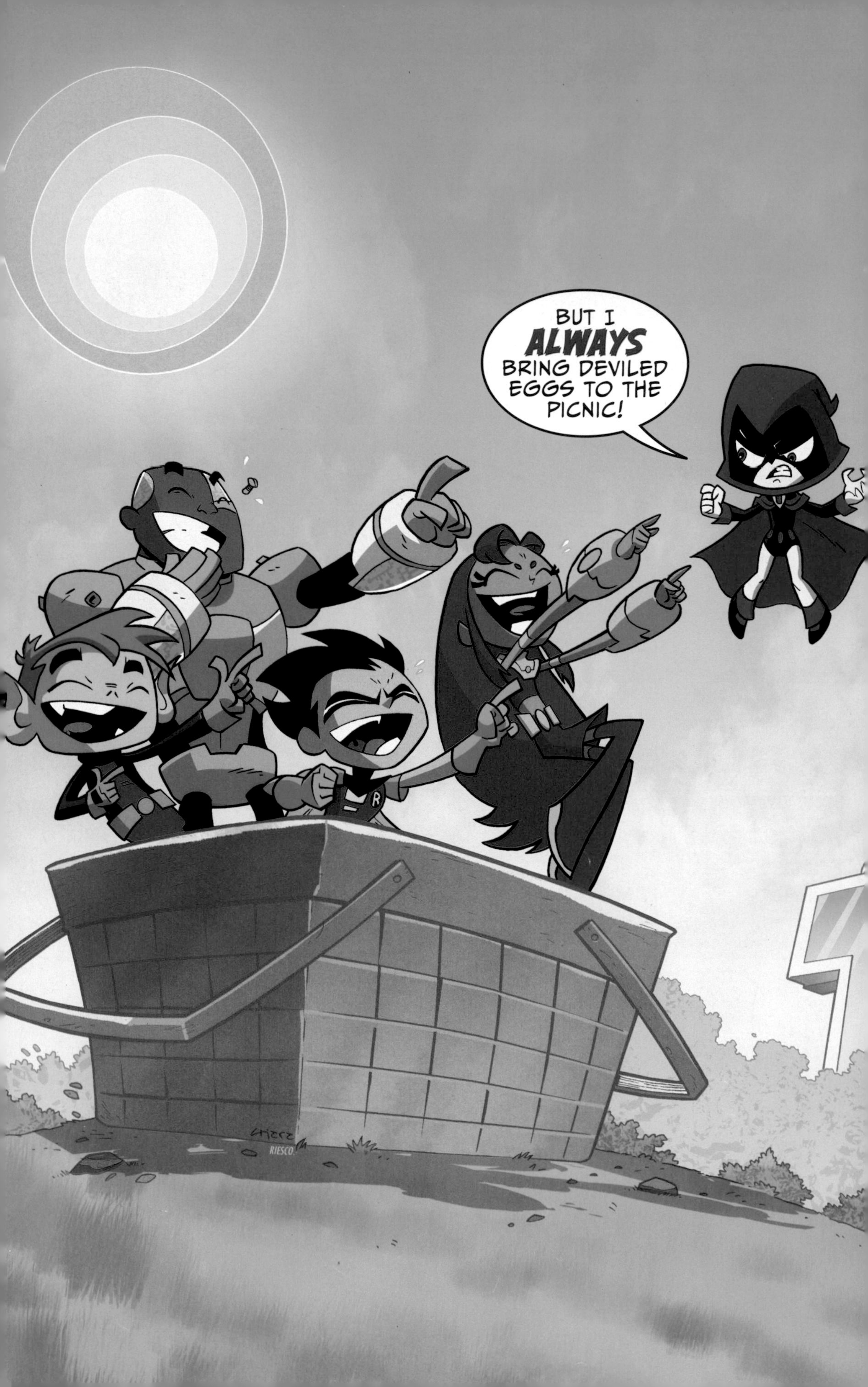
BUT I ALWAYS BRING DEVILED EGGS TO THE PICNIC!

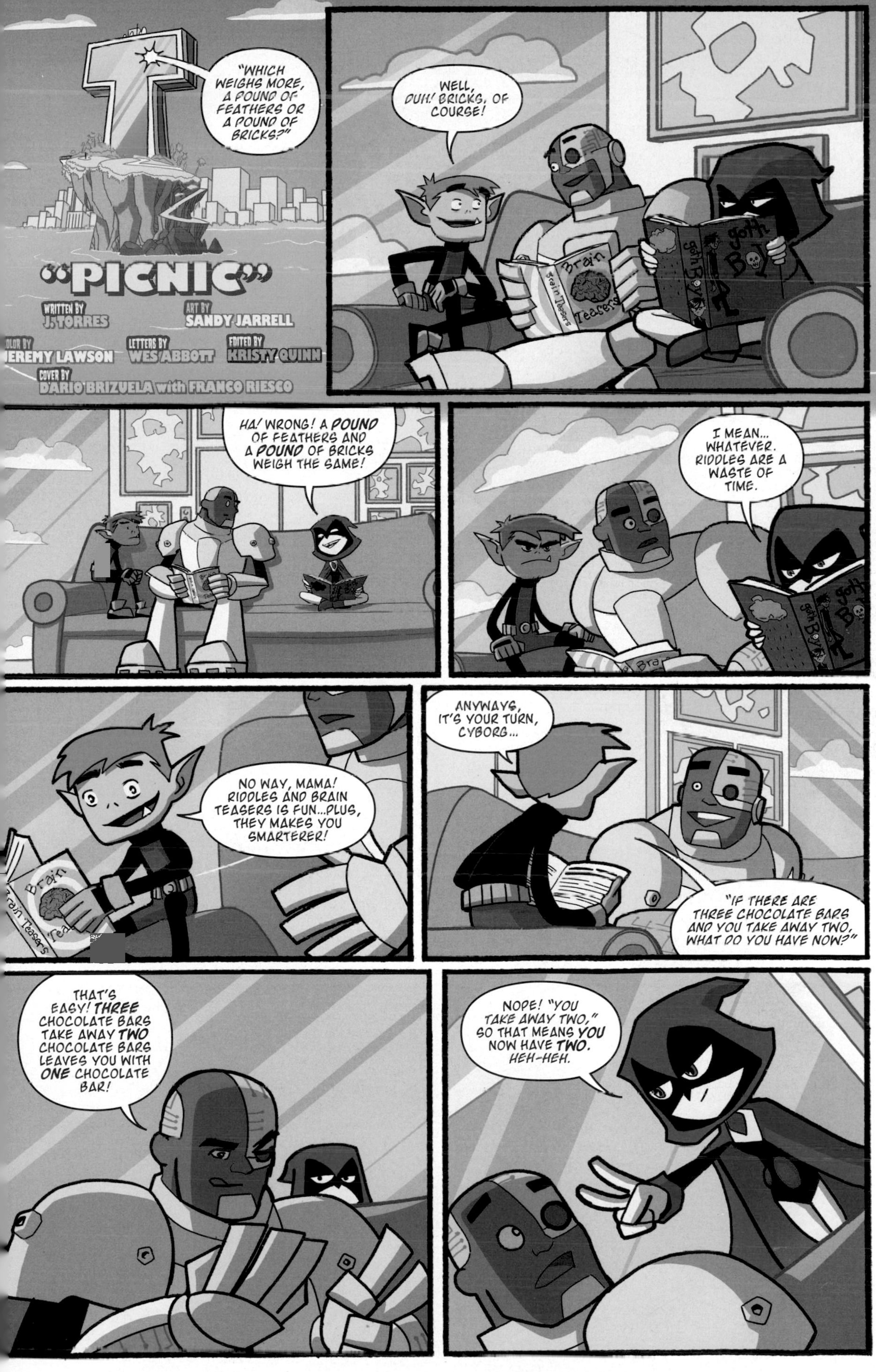

"WHICH WEIGHS MORE, A POUND OF FEATHERS OR A POUND OF BRICKS?"
"PICNIC"
WRITTEN BY J. TORRES
ART BY SANDY JARRELL
COLOR BY JEREMY LAWSON
LETTERS BY WES ABBOTT
EDITED BY KRISTY QUINN
COVER BY DARIO BRIZUELA with FRANCO RIESCO
WELL, DUH! BRICKS, OF COURSE!
HA! WRONG! A POUND OF FEATHERS AND A POUND OF BRICKS WEIGH THE SAME!
I MEAN... WHATEVER. RIDDLES ARE A WASTE OF TIME.
NO WAY, MAMA! RIDDLES AND BRAIN TEASERS IS FUN...PLUS, THEY MAKES YOU SMARTERER!
ANYWAYS, IT'S YOUR TURN, CYBORG...
"IF THERE ARE THREE CHOCOLATE BARS AND YOU TAKE AWAY TWO, WHAT DO YOU HAVE NOW?"
THAT'S EASY! THREE CHOCOLATE BARS TAKE AWAY TWO CHOCOLATE BARS LEAVES YOU WITH ONE CHOCOLATE BAR!
NOPE! "YOU TAKE AWAY TWO," SO THAT MEANS YOU NOW HAVE TWO. HEH-HEH.

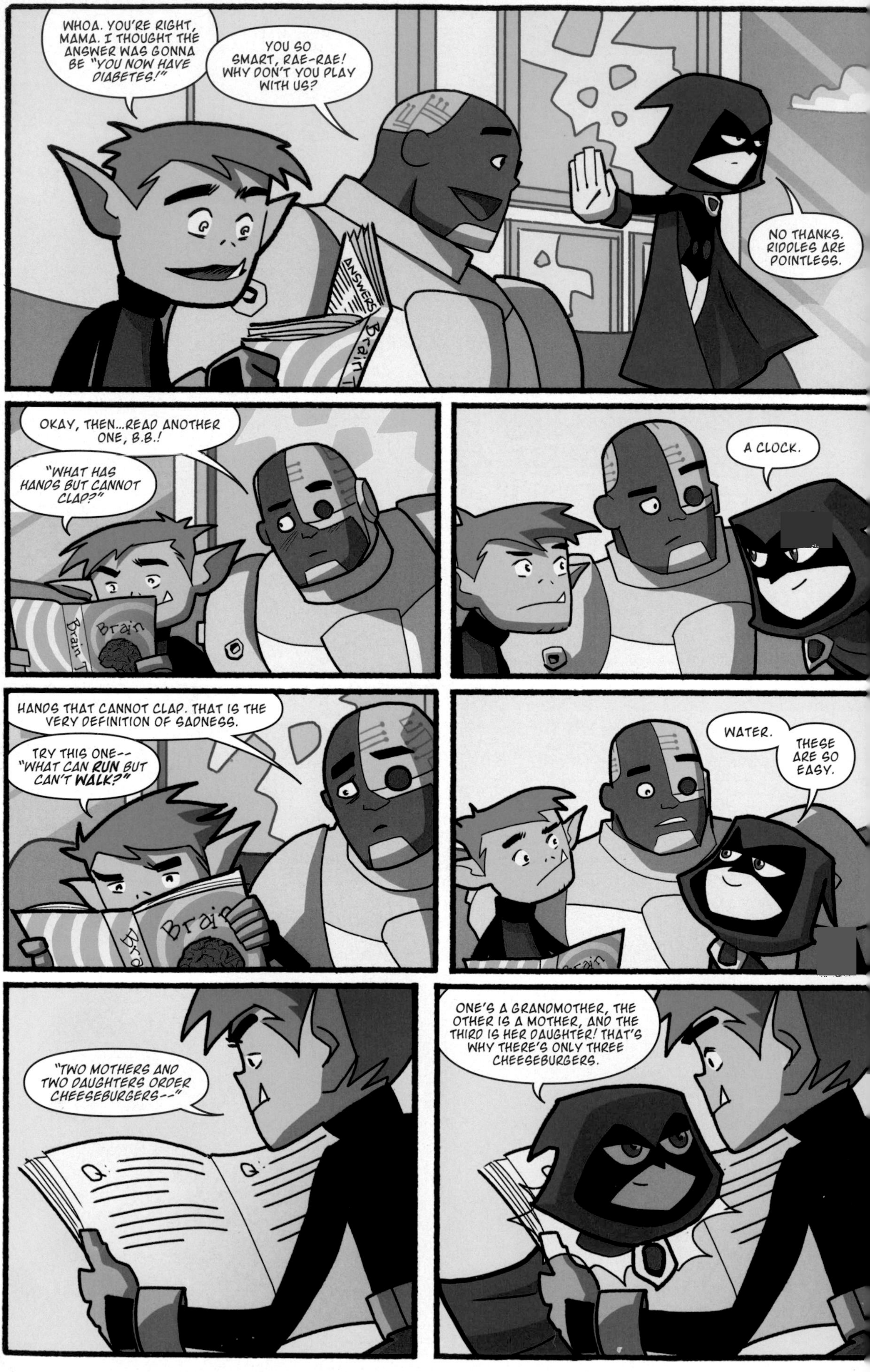
WHOA. YOU'RE RIGHT, MAMA. I THOUGHT THE ANSWER WAS GONNA BE *"YOU NOW HAVE DIABETES!"*
YOU SO SMART, RAE-RAE! WHY DON'T YOU PLAY WITH US?
NO THANKS. RIDDLES ARE POINTLESS.
OKAY, THEN...READ ANOTHER ONE, B.B.!
"WHAT HAS HANDS BUT CANNOT CLAP?"
A CLOCK.
HANDS THAT CANNOT CLAP. THAT IS THE VERY DEFINITION OF SADNESS.
TRY THIS ONE-- *"WHAT CAN **RUN** BUT CAN'T **WALK**?"*
WATER.
THESE ARE SO EASY.
"TWO MOTHERS AND TWO DAUGHTERS ORDER CHEESEBURGERS--"
ONE'S A GRANDMOTHER, THE OTHER IS A MOTHER, AND THE THIRD IS HER DAUGHTER! THAT'S WHY THERE'S ONLY THREE CHEESEBURGERS.

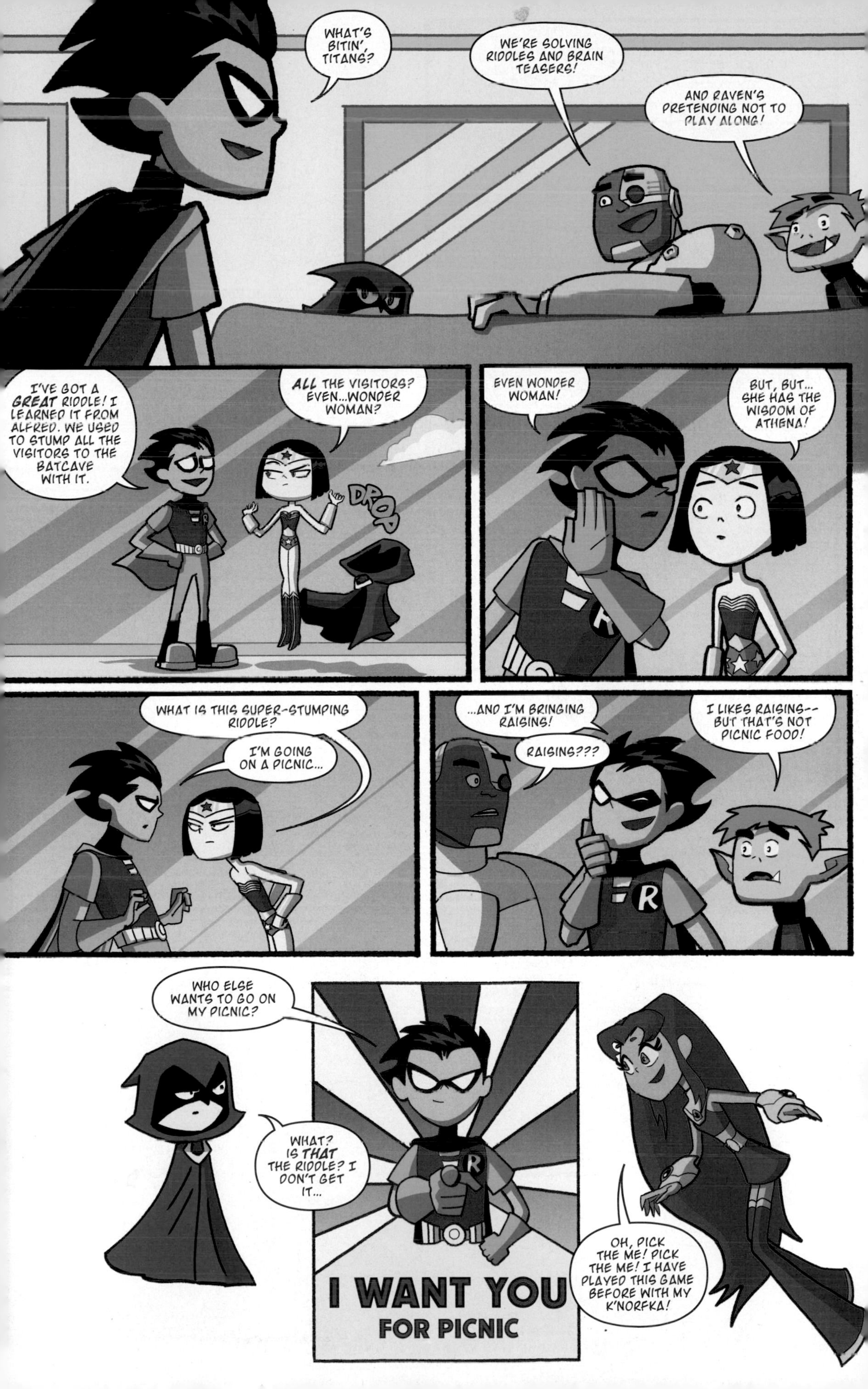
WHAT'S BITIN', TITANS?
WE'RE SOLVING RIDDLES AND BRAIN TEASERS!
AND RAVEN'S PRETENDING NOT TO PLAY ALONG!
I'VE GOT A GREAT RIDDLE! I LEARNED IT FROM ALFRED. WE USED TO STUMP ALL THE VISITORS TO THE BATCAVE WITH IT.
ALL THE VISITORS? EVEN...WONDER WOMAN?
DROP
EVEN WONDER WOMAN!
BUT, BUT... SHE HAS THE WISDOM OF ATHENA!
WHAT IS THIS SUPER-STUMPING RIDDLE?
I'M GOING ON A PICNIC...
...AND I'M BRINGING RAISINS!
RAISINS???
I LIKES RAISINS-- BUT THAT'S NOT PICNIC FOOD!
WHO ELSE WANTS TO GO ON MY PICNIC?
WHAT? IS THAT THE RIDDLE? I DON'T GET IT...
I WANT YOU FOR PICNIC
OH, PICK THE ME! PICK THE ME! I HAVE PLAYED THIS GAME BEFORE WITH MY K'NORFKA!

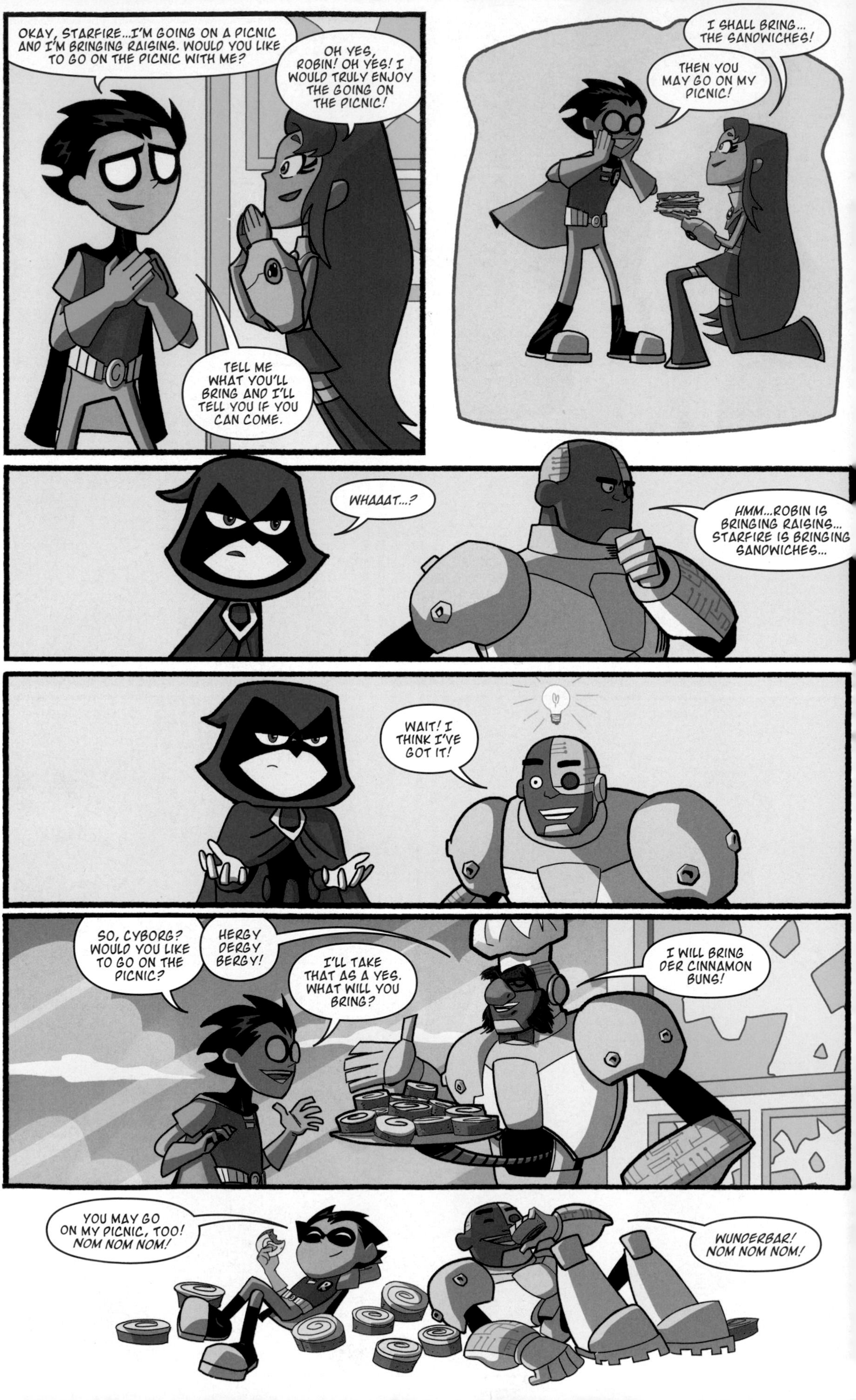

OKAY, STARFIRE...I'M GOING ON A PICNIC AND I'M BRINGING RAISINS. WOULD YOU LIKE TO GO ON THE PICNIC WITH ME?
OH YES, ROBIN! OH YES! I WOULD TRULY ENJOY THE GOING ON THE PICNIC!
TELL ME WHAT YOU'LL BRING AND I'LL TELL YOU IF YOU CAN COME.
I SHALL BRING... THE SANDWICHES!
THEN YOU MAY GO ON MY PICNIC!
WHAAAT...?
HMM...ROBIN IS BRINGING RAISINS... STARFIRE IS BRINGING SANDWICHES...
WAIT! I THINK I'VE GOT IT!
SO, CYBORG? WOULD YOU LIKE TO GO ON THE PICNIC?
HERGY DERGY BERGY!
I'LL TAKE THAT AS A YES. WHAT WILL YOU BRING?
I WILL BRING DER CINNAMON BUNS!
YOU MAY GO ON MY PICNIC, TOO! NOM NOM NOM!
WUNDERBAR! NOM NOM NOM!

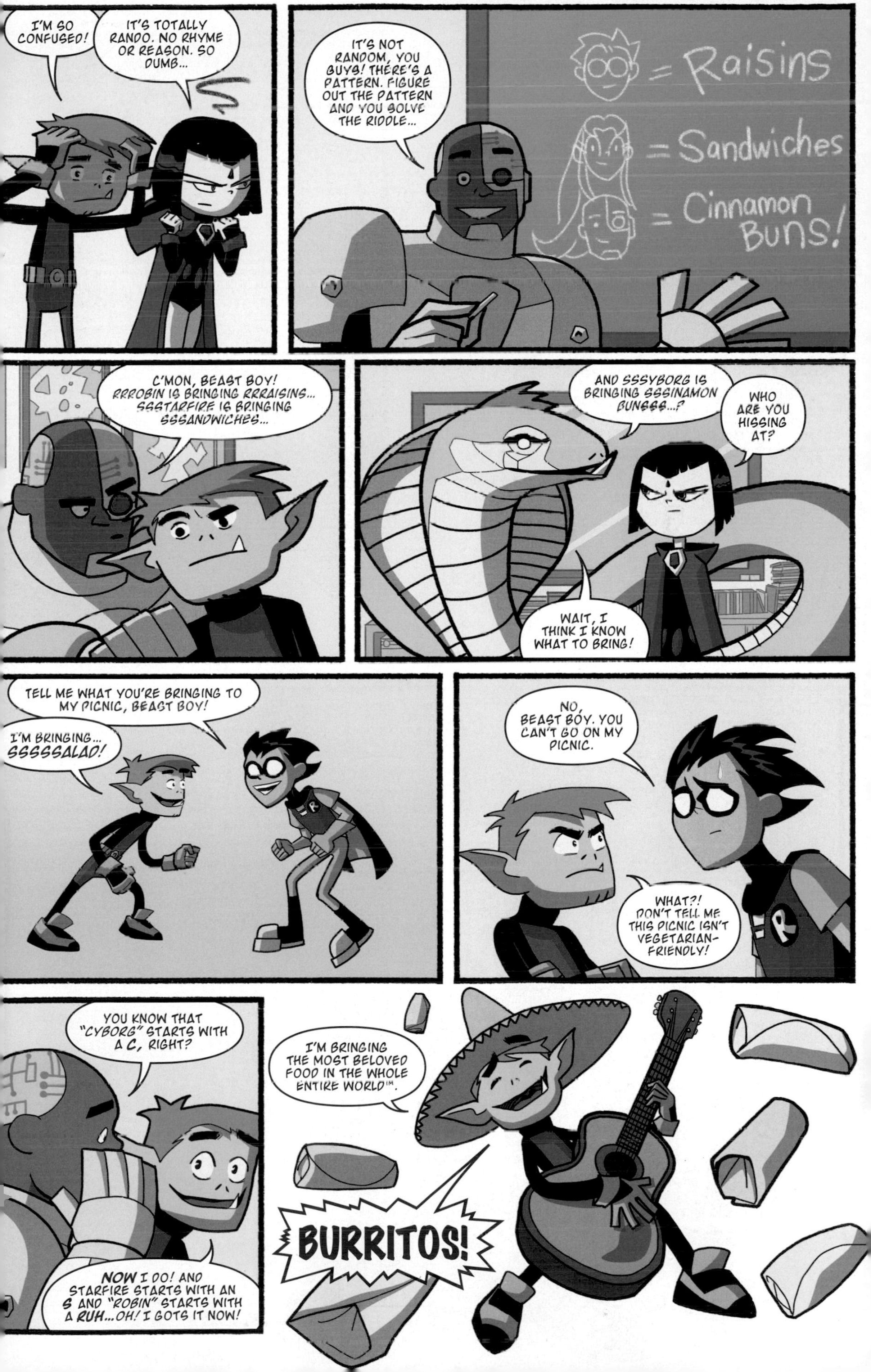
I'M SO CONFUSED!
IT'S TOTALLY RANDO. NO RHYME OR REASON. SO DUMB...
IT'S NOT RANDOM, YOU GUYS! THERE'S A PATTERN. FIGURE OUT THE PATTERN AND YOU SOLVE THE RIDDLE...
= Raisins
= Sandwiches
= Cinnamon Buns!
C'MON, BEAST BOY! RRROBIN IS BRINGING RRRAISINS... SSSTARFIRE IS BRINGING SSSANDWICHES...
AND SSSYBORG IS BRINGING SSSINAMON BUNSSS...?
WHO ARE YOU HISSING AT?
WAIT, I THINK I KNOW WHAT TO BRING!
TELL ME WHAT YOU'RE BRINGING TO MY PICNIC, BEAST BOY!
I'M BRINGING... SSSSSALAD!
NO, BEAST BOY. YOU CAN'T GO ON MY PICNIC.
WHAT?! DON'T TELL ME THIS PICNIC ISN'T VEGETARIAN-FRIENDLY!
YOU KNOW THAT "CYBORG" STARTS WITH A C, RIGHT?
NOW I DO! AND STARFIRE STARTS WITH AN S AND "ROBIN" STARTS WITH A RUH...OH! I GOTS IT NOW!
I'M BRINGING THE MOST BELOVED FOOD IN THE WHOLE ENTIRE WORLD™.
BURRITOS!

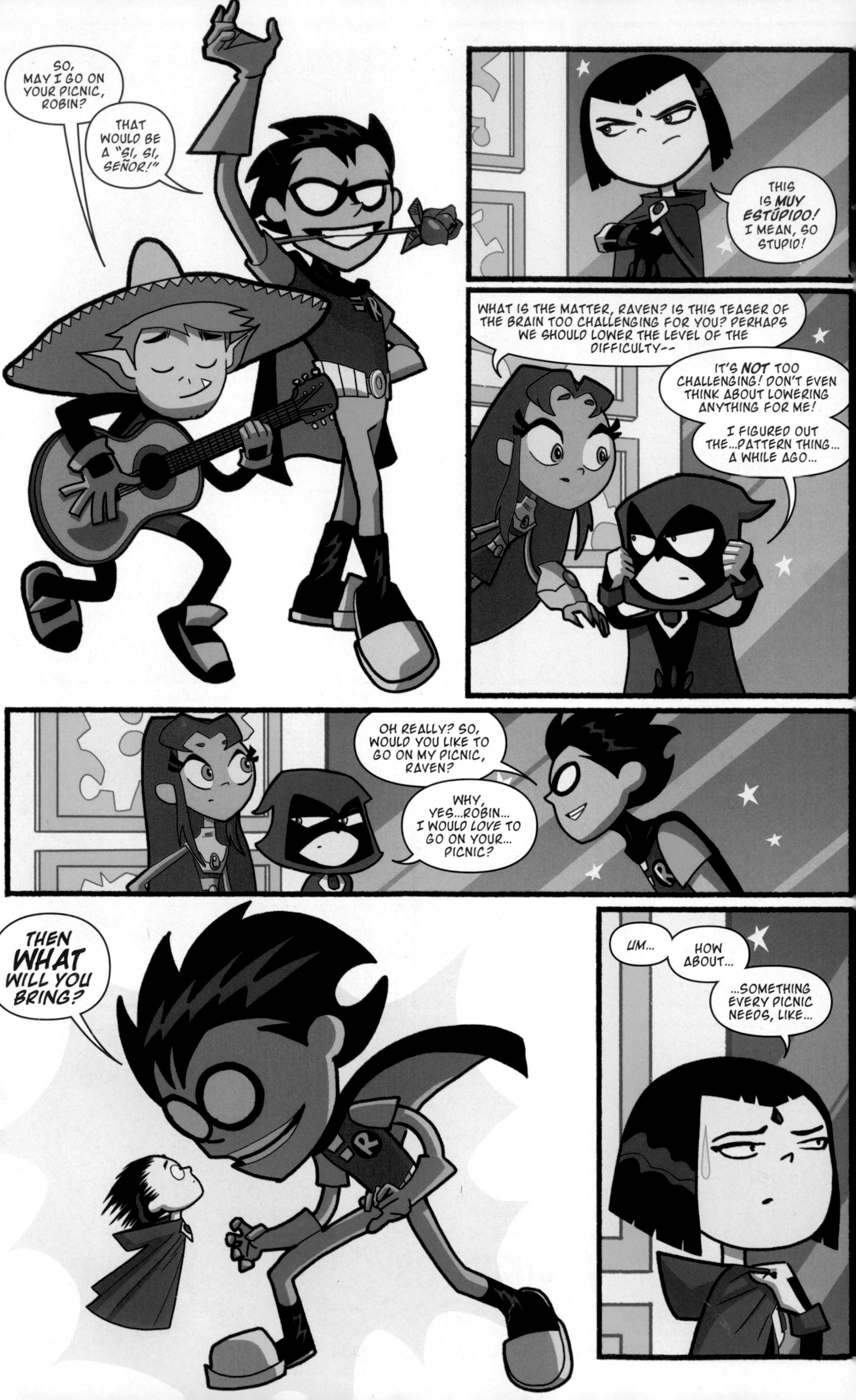
SO, MAY I GO ON YOUR PICNIC, ROBIN?
THAT WOULD BE A "SI, SI, SEÑOR!"
THIS IS MUY ESTÚPIDO! I MEAN, SO STUPID!
WHAT IS THE MATTER, RAVEN? IS THIS TEASER OF THE BRAIN TOO CHALLENGING FOR YOU? PERHAPS WE SHOULD LOWER THE LEVEL OF THE DIFFICULTY--
IT'S NOT TOO CHALLENGING! DON'T EVEN THINK ABOUT LOWERING ANYTHING FOR ME!
I FIGURED OUT THE...PATTERN THING... A WHILE AGO...
OH REALLY? SO, WOULD YOU LIKE TO GO ON MY PICNIC, RAVEN?
WHY, YES...ROBIN... I WOULD LOVE TO GO ON YOUR... PICNIC?
THEN WHAT WILL YOU BRING?
UM...
HOW ABOUT...
...SOMETHING EVERY PICNIC NEEDS, LIKE...

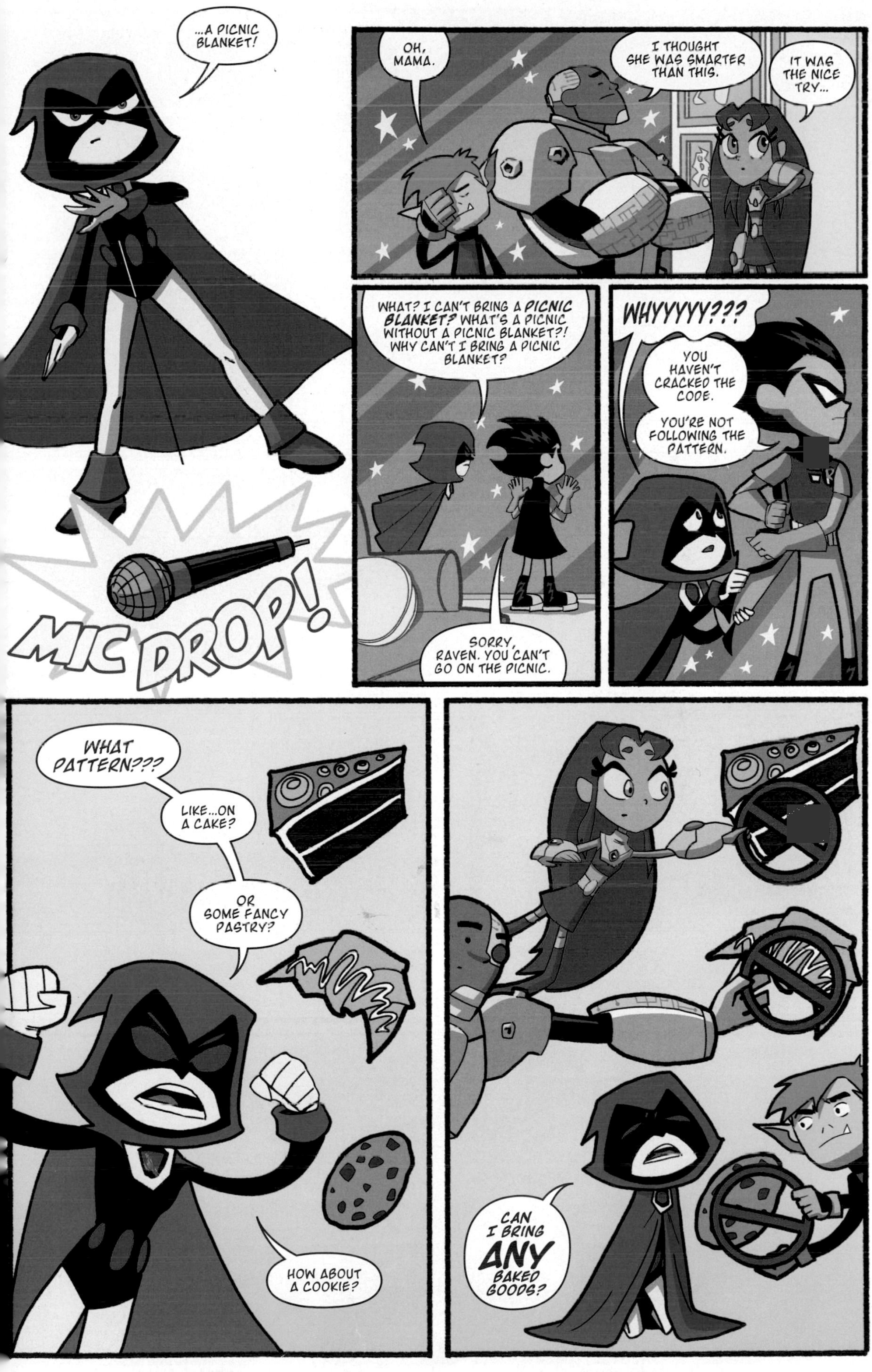
...A PICNIC BLANKET!
MIC DROP!
OH, MAMA.
I THOUGHT SHE WAS SMARTER THAN THIS.
IT WAS THE NICE TRY...
WHAT? I CAN'T BRING A PICNIC BLANKET? WHAT'S A PICNIC WITHOUT A PICNIC BLANKET?! WHY CAN'T I BRING A PICNIC BLANKET?
SORRY, RAVEN. YOU CAN'T GO ON THE PICNIC.
WHYYYYY???
YOU HAVEN'T CRACKED THE CODE.
YOU'RE NOT FOLLOWING THE PATTERN.
WHAT PATTERN???
LIKE...ON A CAKE?
OR SOME FANCY PASTRY?
HOW ABOUT A COOKIE?
CAN I BRING ANY BAKED GOODS?

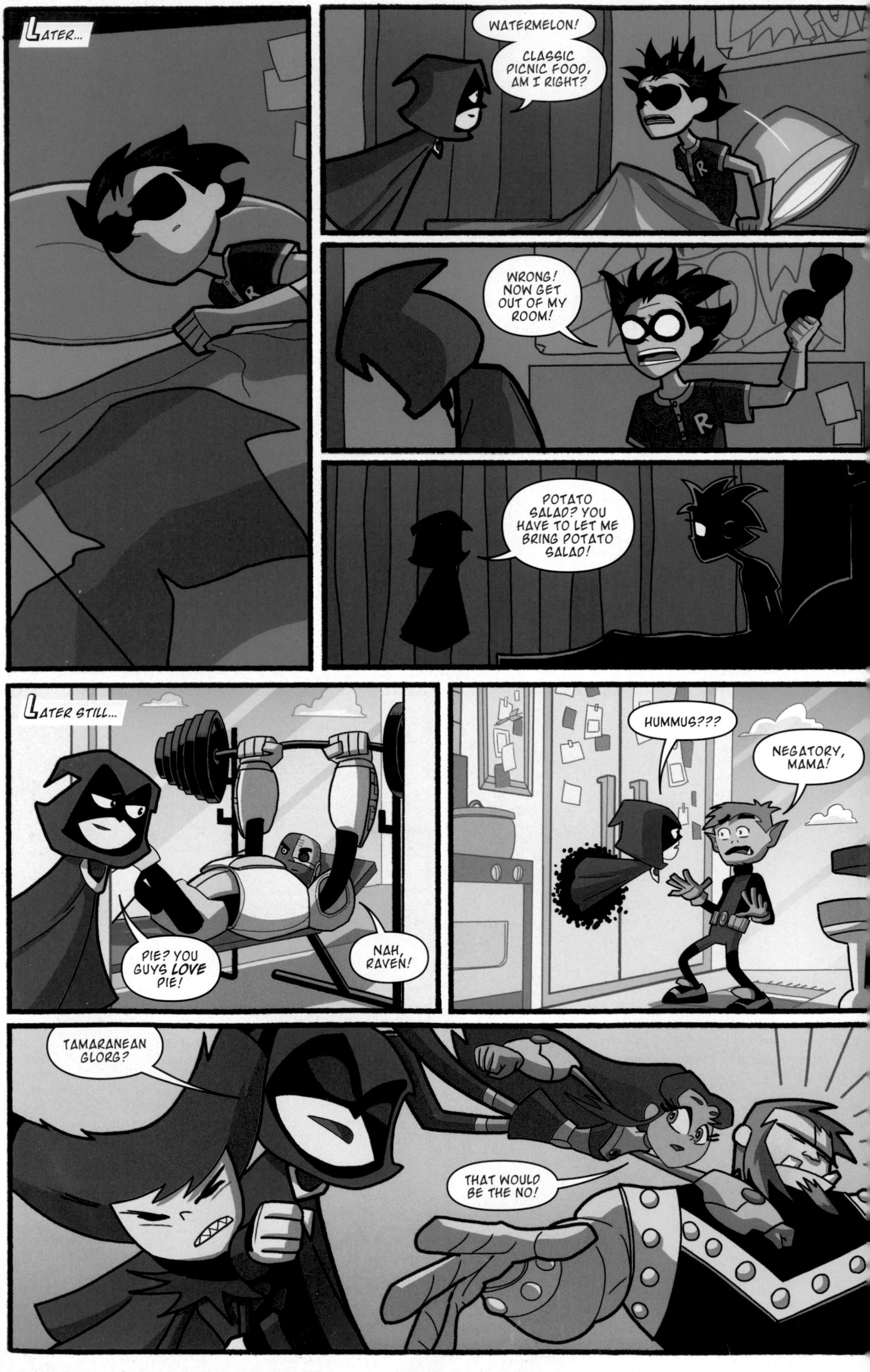
LATER...
WATERMELON!
CLASSIC PICNIC FOOD, AM I RIGHT?
WRONG! NOW GET OUT OF MY ROOM!
POTATO SALAD? YOU HAVE TO LET ME BRING POTATO SALAD!
LATER STILL...
PIE? YOU GUYS LOVE PIE!
NAH, RAVEN!
HUMMUS???
NEGATORY, MAMA!
TAMARANEAN GLORG?
THAT WOULD BE THE NO!

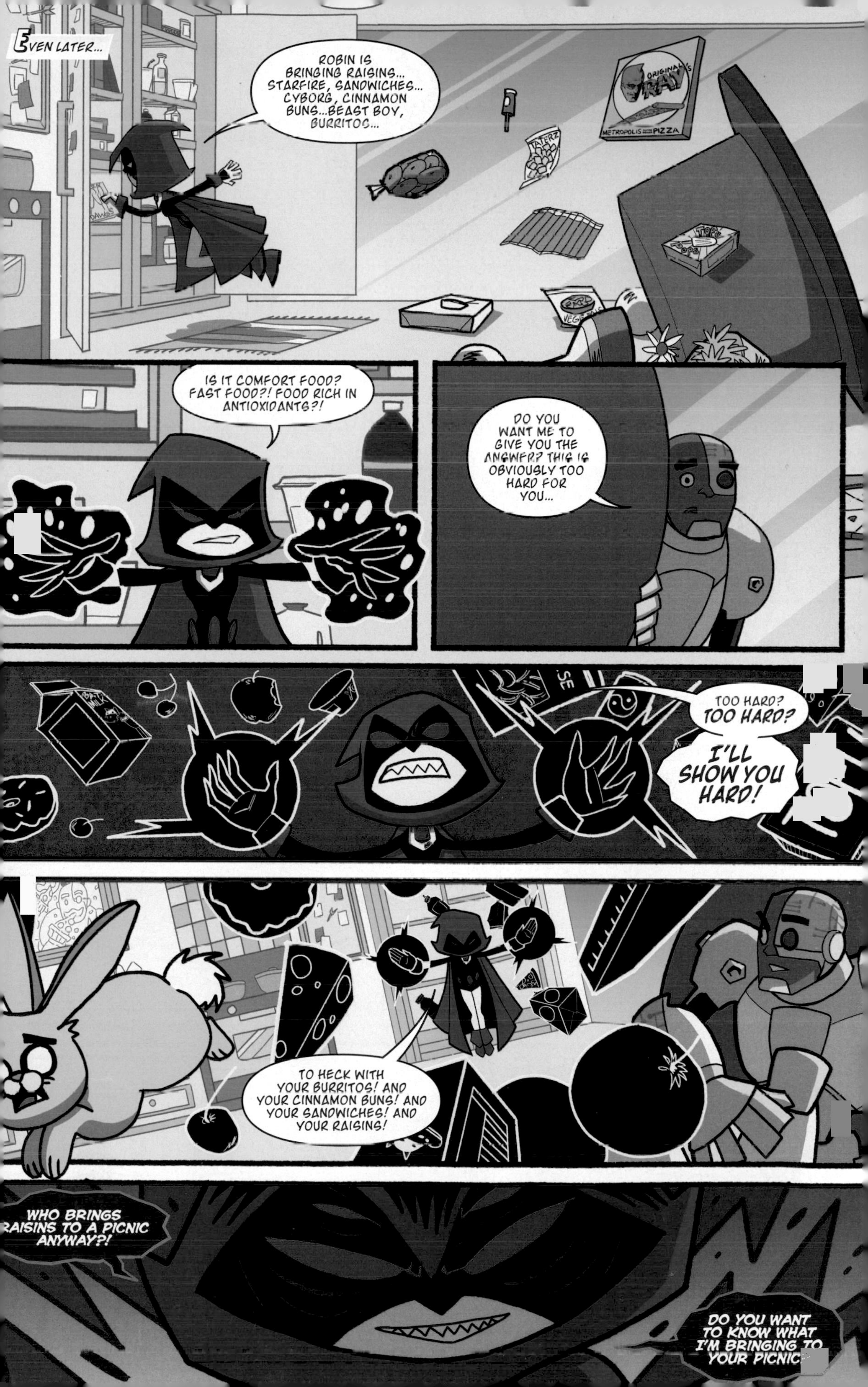
EVEN LATER...
ROBIN IS BRINGING RAISINS... STARFIRE, SANDWICHES... CYBORG, CINNAMON BUNS...BEAST BOY, BURRITOS...
METROPOLIS PIZZA
TATERZ
IS IT COMFORT FOOD? FAST FOOD?! FOOD RICH IN ANTIOXIDANTS?!
DO YOU WANT ME TO GIVE YOU THE ANSWER? THIS IS OBVIOUSLY TOO HARD FOR YOU...
TOO HARD? TOO HARD?
I'LL SHOW YOU HARD!
TO HECK WITH YOUR BURRITOS! AND YOUR CINNAMON BUNS! AND YOUR SANDWICHES! AND YOUR RAISINS!
WHO BRINGS RAISINS TO A PICNIC ANYWAY?!
DO YOU WANT TO KNOW WHAT I'M BRINGING TO YOUR PICNIC

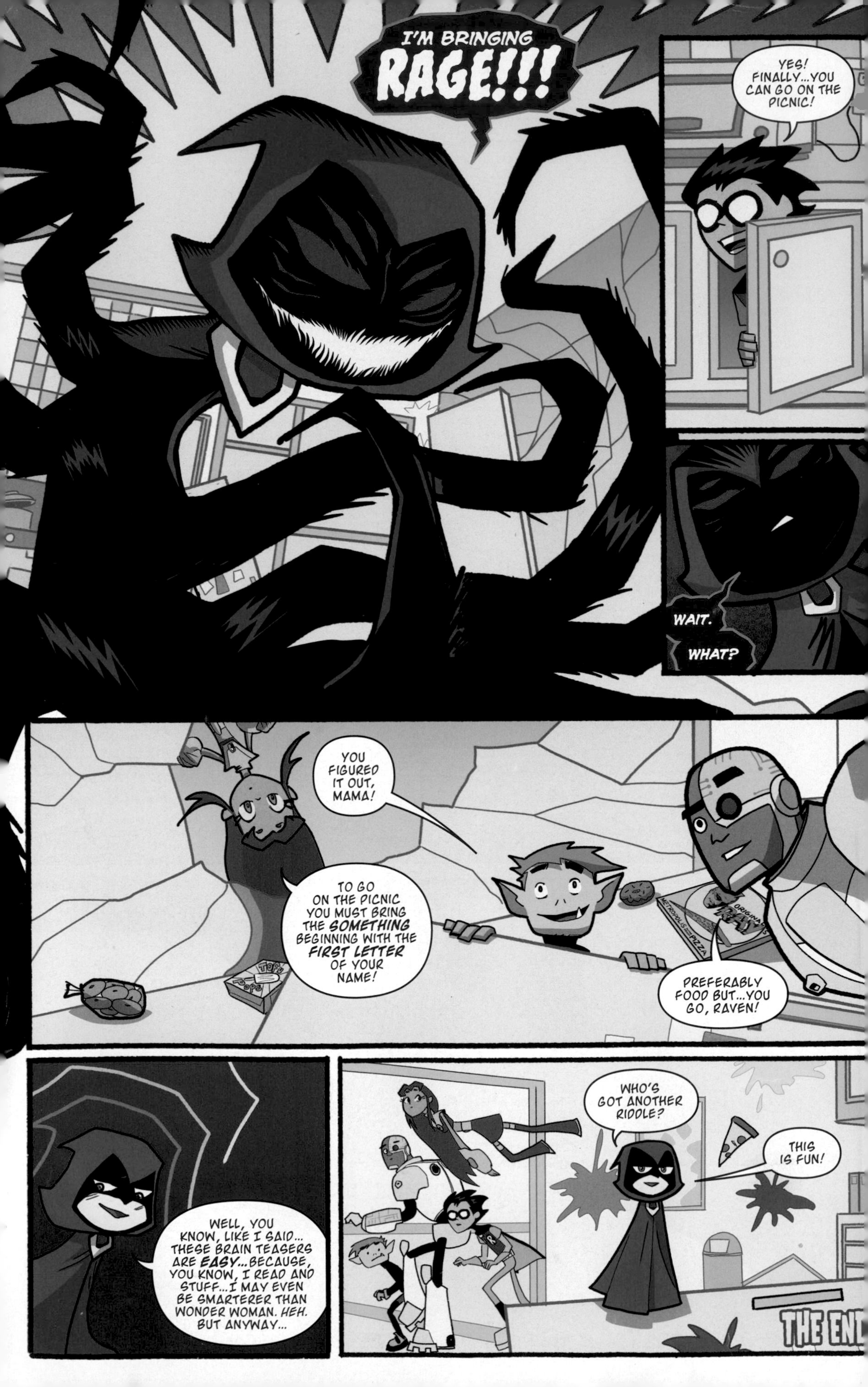
I'M BRINGING RAGE!!!
YES! FINALLY...YOU CAN GO ON THE PICNIC!
WAIT.
WHAT?
YOU FIGURED IT OUT, MAMA!
TO GO ON THE PICNIC YOU MUST BRING THE *SOMETHING* BEGINNING WITH THE *FIRST LETTER* OF YOUR NAME!
PREFERABLY FOOD BUT...YOU GO, RAVEN!
WELL, YOU KNOW, LIKE I SAID... THESE BRAIN TEASERS ARE *EASY*...BECAUSE, YOU KNOW, I READ AND STUFF...I MAY EVEN BE SMARTERER THAN WONDER WOMAN. *HEH.* BUT ANYWAY...
WHO'S GOT ANOTHER RIDDLE?
THIS IS FUN!

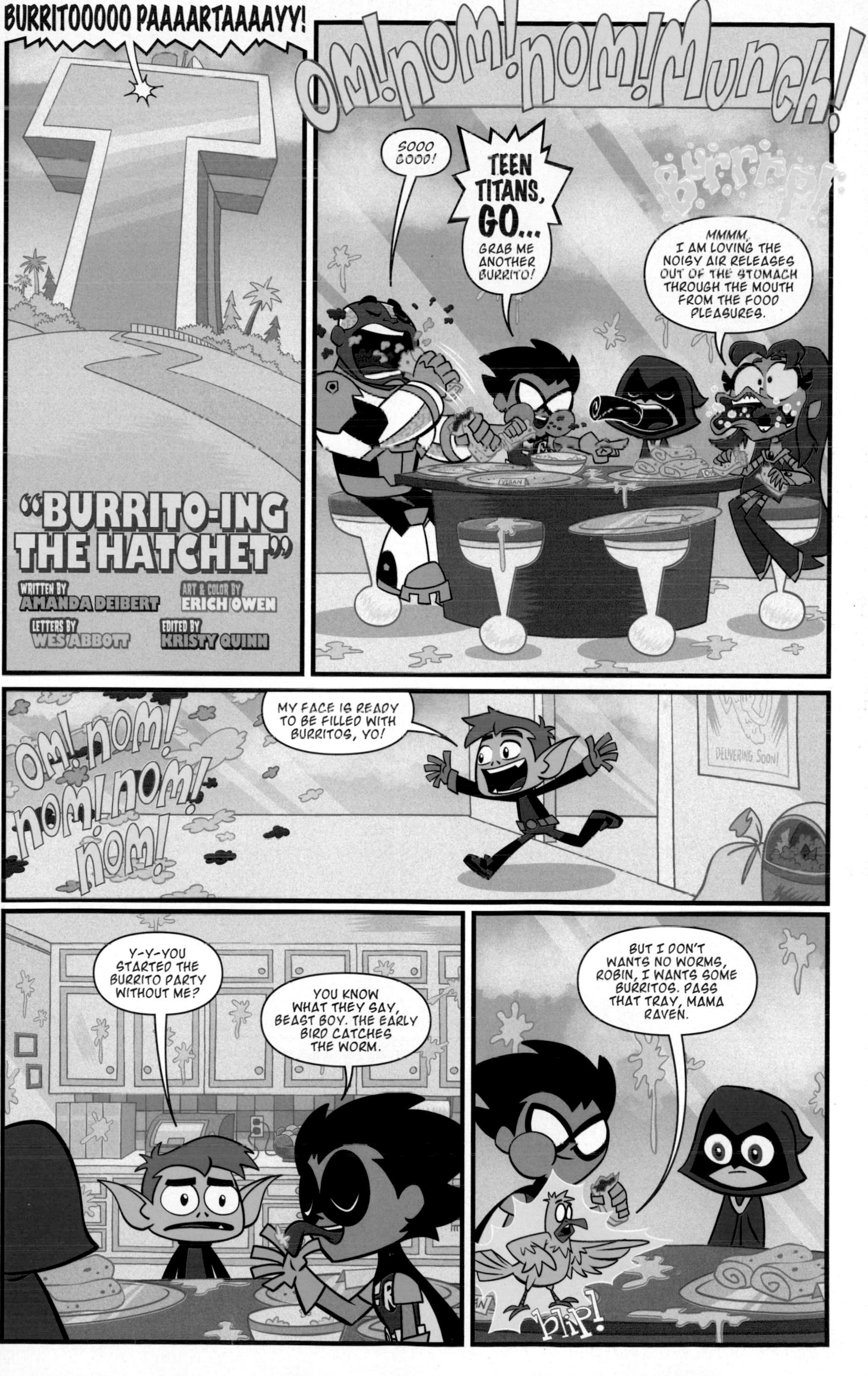
BURRITOOOOO PAAAARTAAAAYY!
"BURRITO-ING THE HATCHET"
WRITTEN BY AMANDA DEIBERT
ART & COLOR BY ERICH OWEN
LETTERS BY WES ABBOTT
EDITED BY KRISTY QUINN
OM! NOM! NOM! MUNCH!
SOOO GOOD!
TEEN TITANS, GO... GRAB ME ANOTHER BURRITO!
BURRRP!
MMMM. I AM LOVING THE NOISY AIR RELEASES OUT OF THE STOMACH THROUGH THE MOUTH FROM THE FOOD PLEASURES.
OM! NOM! NOM! NOM! NOM!
MY FACE IS READY TO BE FILLED WITH BURRITOS, YO!
DELIVERING SOON!
Y-Y-YOU STARTED THE BURRITO PARTY WITHOUT ME?
YOU KNOW WHAT THEY SAY, BEAST BOY. THE EARLY BIRD CATCHES THE WORM.
BUT I DON'T WANTS NO WORMS, ROBIN, I WANTS SOME BURRITOS. PASS THAT TRAY, MAMA RAVEN.
BLIP!

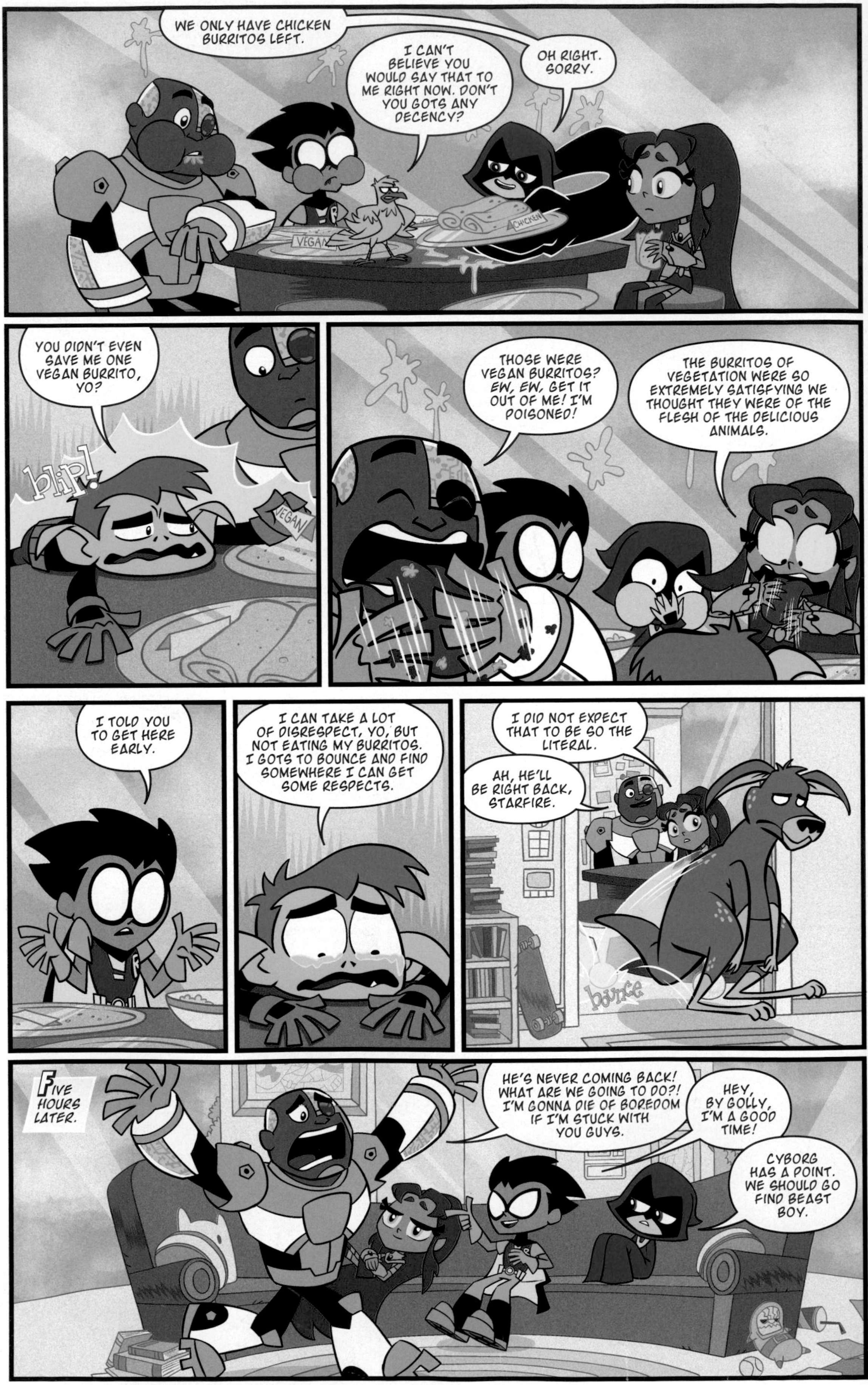

WE ONLY HAVE CHICKEN BURRITOS LEFT.
I CAN'T BELIEVE YOU WOULD SAY THAT TO ME RIGHT NOW. DON'T YOU GOTS ANY DECENCY?
OH RIGHT. SORRY.
VEGAN
CHICKEN
YOU DIDN'T EVEN SAVE ME ONE VEGAN BURRITO, YO?
blip!
VEGAN
THOSE WERE VEGAN BURRITOS? EW, EW, GET IT OUT OF ME! I'M POISONED!
THE BURRITOS OF VEGETATION WERE SO EXTREMELY SATISFYING WE THOUGHT THEY WERE OF THE FLESH OF THE DELICIOUS ANIMALS.
I TOLD YOU TO GET HERE EARLY.
I CAN TAKE A LOT OF DISRESPECT, YO, BUT NOT EATING MY BURRITOS. I GOTS TO BOUNCE AND FIND SOMEWHERE I CAN GET SOME RESPECTS.
I DID NOT EXPECT THAT TO BE SO THE LITERAL.
AH, HE'LL BE RIGHT BACK, STARFIRE.
bounce
FIVE HOURS LATER.
HE'S NEVER COMING BACK! WHAT ARE WE GOING TO DO?! I'M GONNA DIE OF BOREDOM IF I'M STUCK WITH YOU GUYS.
HEY, BY GOLLY, I'M A GOOD TIME!
CYBORG HAS A POINT. WE SHOULD GO FIND BEAST BOY.

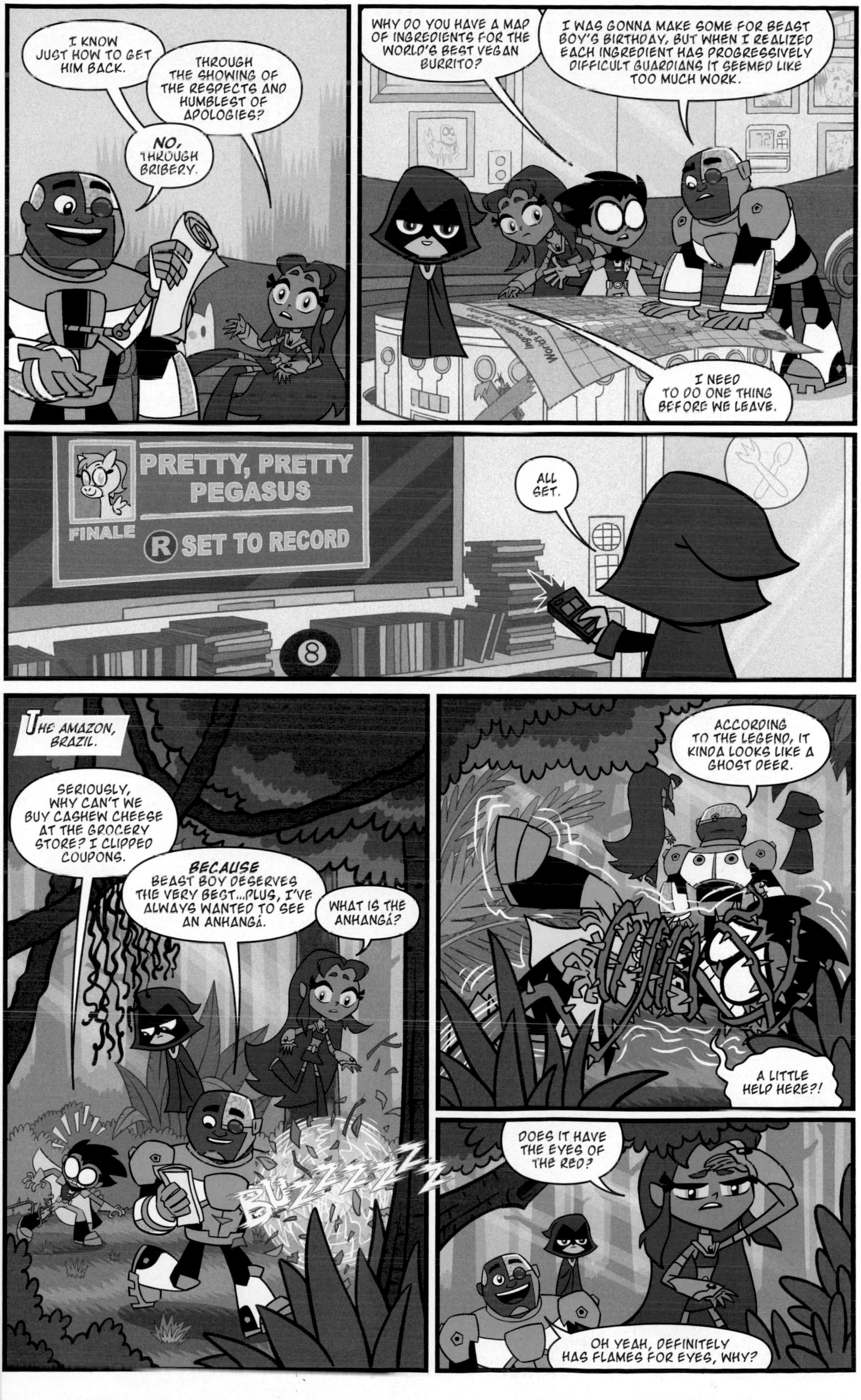

I KNOW JUST HOW TO GET HIM BACK.
THROUGH THE SHOWING OF THE RESPECTS AND HUMBLEST OF APOLOGIES?
NO, THROUGH BRIBERY.
WHY DO YOU HAVE A MAP OF INGREDIENTS FOR THE WORLD'S BEST VEGAN BURRITO?
I WAS GONNA MAKE SOME FOR BEAST BOY'S BIRTHDAY, BUT WHEN I REALIZED EACH INGREDIENT HAS PROGRESSIVELY DIFFICULT GUARDIANS IT SEEMED LIKE TOO MUCH WORK.
I NEED TO DO ONE THING BEFORE WE LEAVE.
PRETTY, PRETTY PEGASUS
FINALE
R SET TO RECORD
ALL SET.
THE AMAZON, BRAZIL.
SERIOUSLY, WHY CAN'T WE BUY CASHEW CHEESE AT THE GROCERY STORE? I CLIPPED COUPONS.
BECAUSE BEAST BOY DESERVES THE VERY BEST...PLUS, I'VE ALWAYS WANTED TO SEE AN ANHANGÁ.
WHAT IS THE ANHANGÁ?
BUZZZZZZZ
ACCORDING TO THE LEGEND, IT KINDA LOOKS LIKE A GHOST DEER.
A LITTLE HELP HERE?!
DOES IT HAVE THE EYES OF THE RED?
OH YEAH, DEFINITELY HAS FLAMES FOR EYES, WHY?

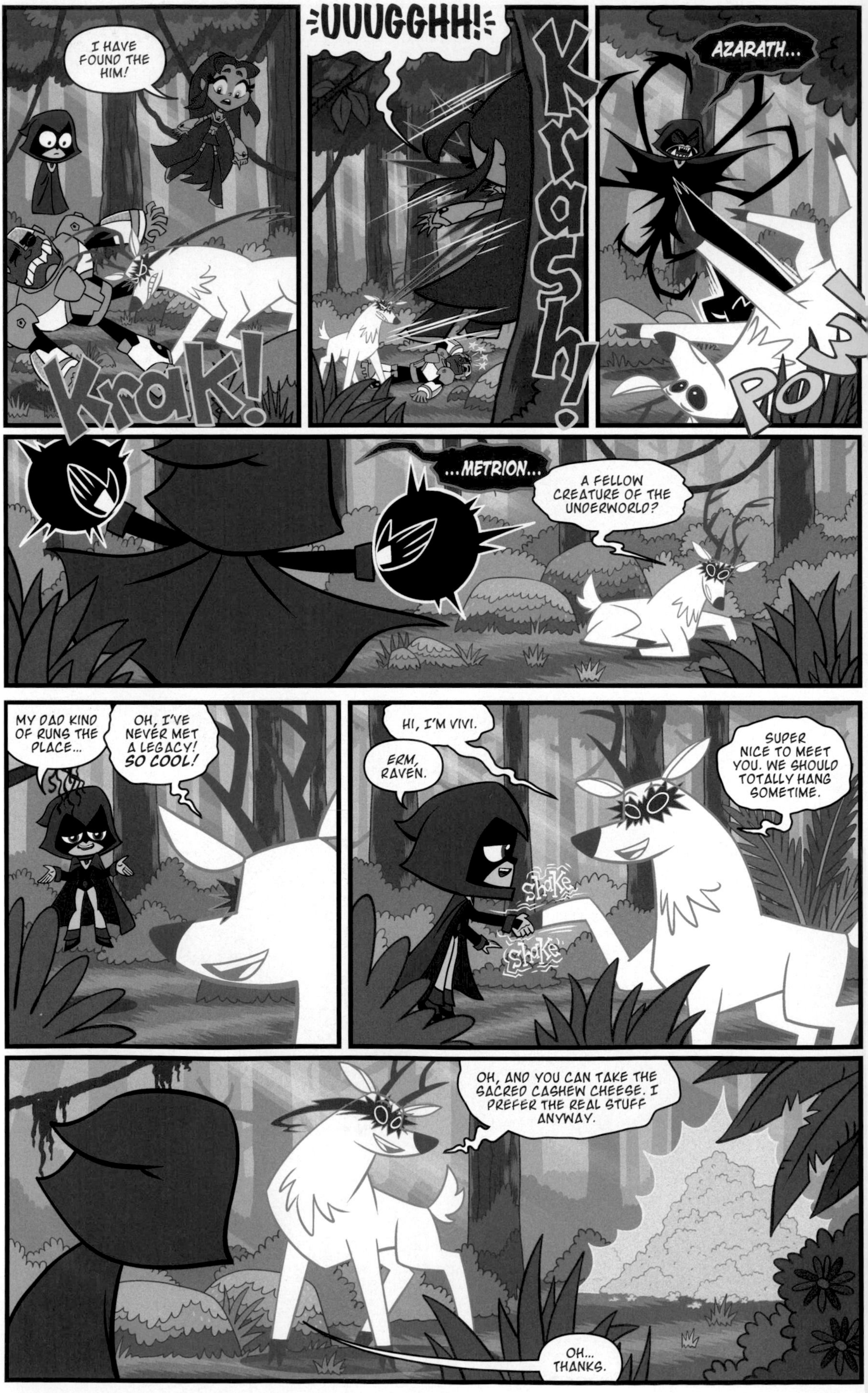
I HAVE FOUND THE HIM!
KRAK!
UUUGGHH!
KRASH!
AZARATH...
POW!
...METRION...
A FELLOW CREATURE OF THE UNDERWORLD?
MY DAD KIND OF RUNS THE PLACE...
OH, I'VE NEVER MET A LEGACY! SO COOL!
SIGH
HI, I'M VIVI.
ERM, RAVEN.
SUPER NICE TO MEET YOU. WE SHOULD TOTALLY HANG SOMETIME.
SHAKE
SHAKE
OH, AND YOU CAN TAKE THE SACRED CASHEW CHEESE. I PREFER THE REAL STUFF ANYWAY.
OH... THANKS.

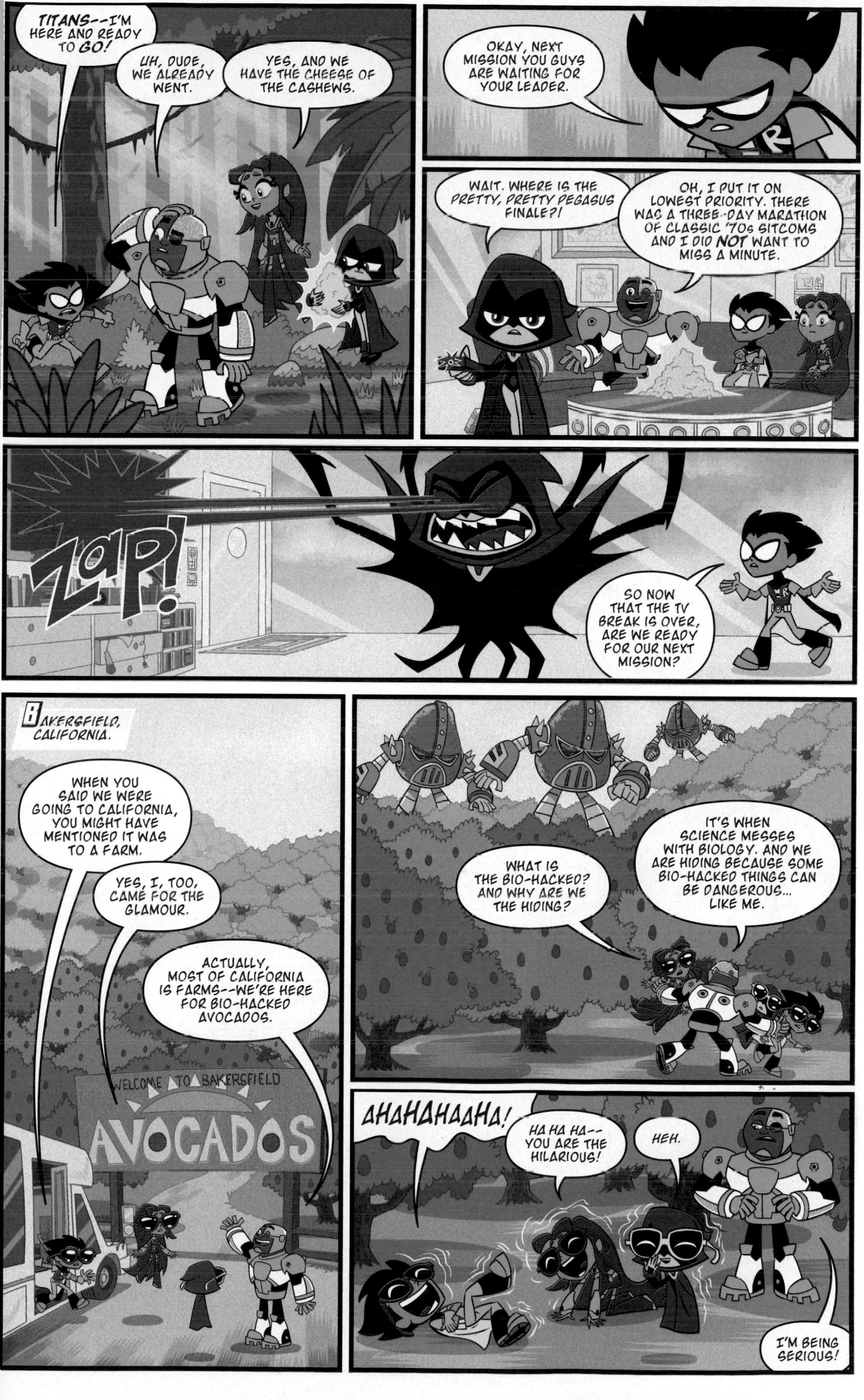
TITANS--I'M HERE AND READY TO GO!
UH, DUDE, WE ALREADY WENT.
YES, AND WE HAVE THE CHEESE OF THE CASHEWS.
OKAY, NEXT MISSION YOU GUYS ARE WAITING FOR YOUR LEADER.
WAIT. WHERE IS THE PRETTY, PRETTY PEGASUS FINALE?!
OH, I PUT IT ON LOWEST PRIORITY. THERE WAS A THREE-DAY MARATHON OF CLASSIC '70s SITCOMS AND I DID NOT WANT TO MISS A MINUTE.
ZAP!
SO NOW THAT THE TV BREAK IS OVER, ARE WE READY FOR OUR NEXT MISSION?
BAKERSFIELD, CALIFORNIA.
WHEN YOU SAID WE WERE GOING TO CALIFORNIA, YOU MIGHT HAVE MENTIONED IT WAS TO A FARM.
YES, I, TOO, CAME FOR THE GLAMOUR.
ACTUALLY, MOST OF CALIFORNIA IS FARMS--WE'RE HERE FOR BIO-HACKED AVOCADOS.
WELCOME TO BAKERSFIELD
AVOCADOS
WHAT IS THE BIO-HACKED? AND WHY ARE WE THE HIDING?
IT'S WHEN SCIENCE MESSES WITH BIOLOGY. AND WE ARE HIDING BECAUSE SOME BIO-HACKED THINGS CAN BE DANGEROUS... LIKE ME.
AHAHAHAHAAHA!
HA HA HA--YOU ARE THE HILARIOUS!
HEH.
I'M BEING SERIOUS!

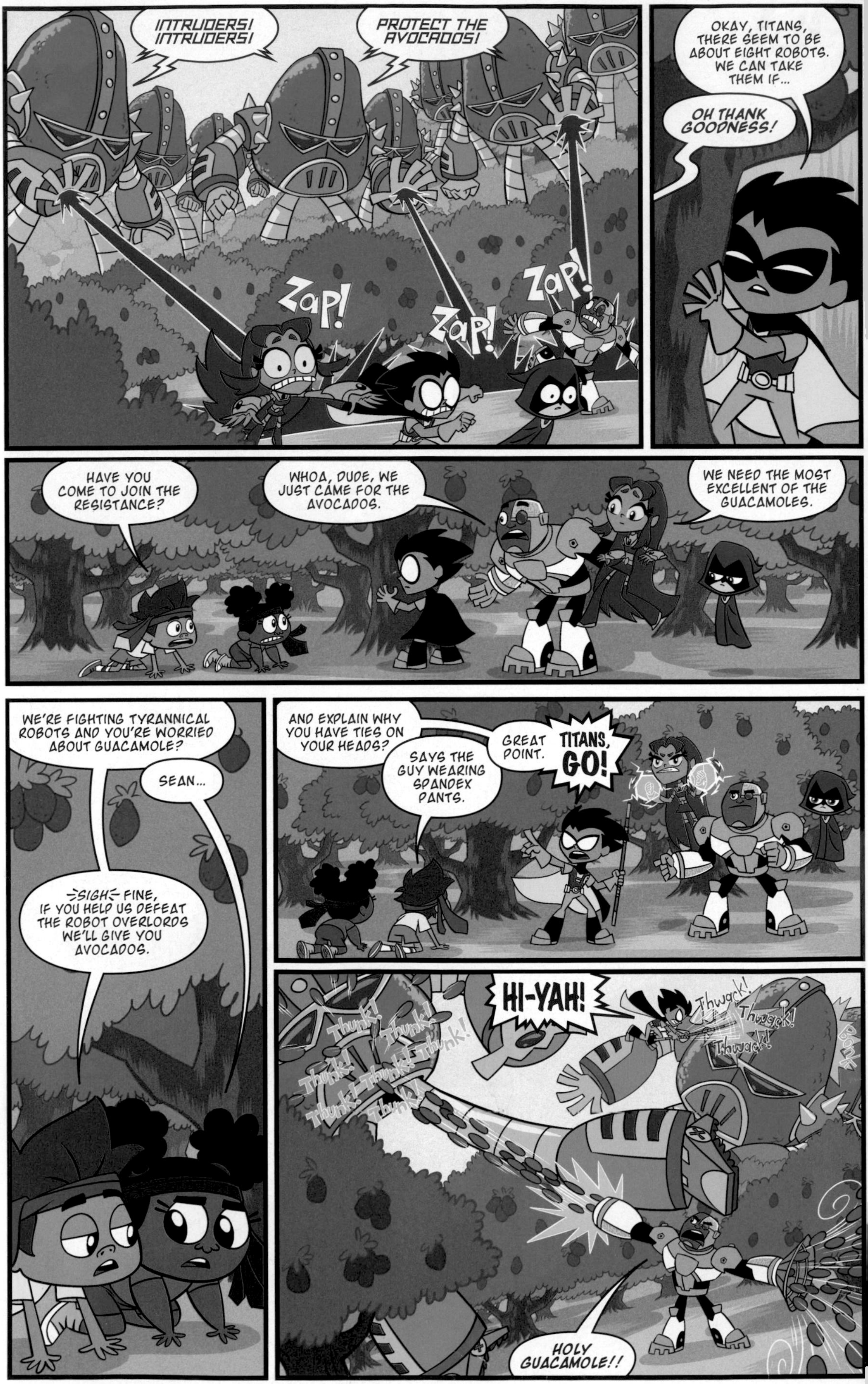

INTRUDERS! INTRUDERS!
PROTECT THE AVOCADOS!
ZAP!
ZAP!
ZAP!
OKAY, TITANS, THERE SEEM TO BE ABOUT EIGHT ROBOTS. WE CAN TAKE THEM IF...
OH THANK GOODNESS!
HAVE YOU COME TO JOIN THE RESISTANCE?
WHOA, DUDE, WE JUST CAME FOR THE AVOCADOS.
WE NEED THE MOST EXCELLENT OF THE GUACAMOLES.
WE'RE FIGHTING TYRANNICAL ROBOTS AND YOU'RE WORRIED ABOUT GUACAMOLE?
SEAN...
=SIGH= FINE, IF YOU HELP US DEFEAT THE ROBOT OVERLORDS WE'LL GIVE YOU AVOCADOS.
AND EXPLAIN WHY YOU HAVE TIES ON YOUR HEADS?
SAYS THE GUY WEARING SPANDEX PANTS.
GREAT POINT.
TITANS, GO!
HI-YAH!
Thwack! Thwack! Thwack!
Thunk! Thunk! Thunk! Thunk! Thunk! Thunk! Thunk! Thunk!
HOLY GUACAMOLE!!

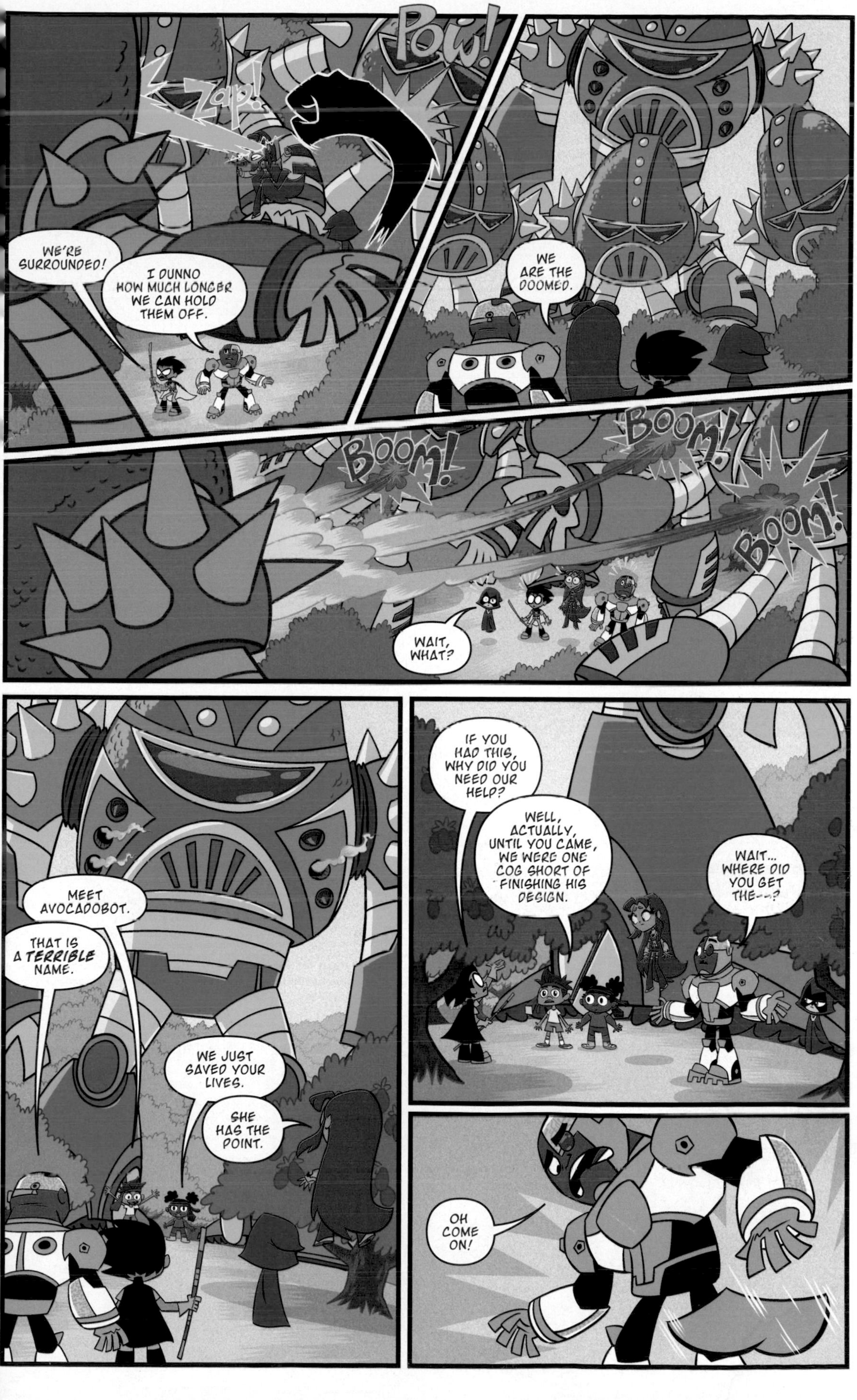
ZAP!
POW!
WE'RE SURROUNDED!
I DUNNO HOW MUCH LONGER WE CAN HOLD THEM OFF.
WE ARE THE DOOMED.
BOOM!
BOOM!
BOOM!
WAIT, WHAT?
MEET AVOCADOBOT.
THAT IS A *TERRIBLE* NAME.
WE JUST SAVED YOUR LIVES.
SHE HAS THE POINT.
IF YOU HAD THIS, WHY DID YOU NEED OUR HELP?
WELL, ACTUALLY, UNTIL YOU CAME, WE WERE ONE COG SHORT OF FINISHING HIS DESIGN.
WAIT... WHERE DID YOU GET THE--?
OH COME ON!

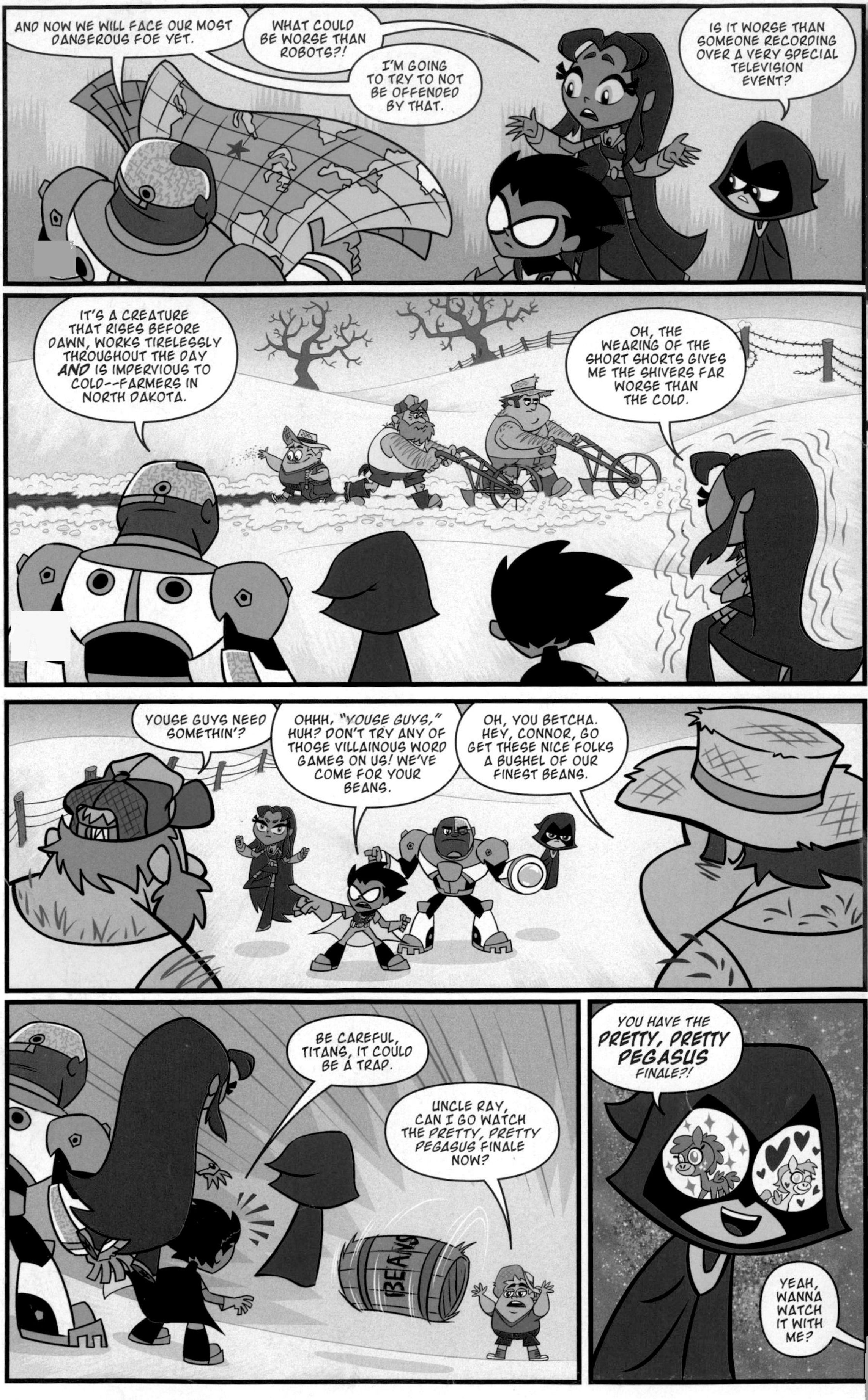
AND NOW WE WILL FACE OUR MOST DANGEROUS FOE YET.
WHAT COULD BE WORSE THAN ROBOTS?!
I'M GOING TO TRY TO NOT BE OFFENDED BY THAT.
IS IT WORSE THAN SOMEONE RECORDING OVER A VERY SPECIAL TELEVISION EVENT?
IT'S A CREATURE THAT RISES BEFORE DAWN, WORKS TIRELESSLY THROUGHOUT THE DAY AND IS IMPERVIOUS TO COLD--FARMERS IN NORTH DAKOTA.
OH, THE WEARING OF THE SHORT SHORTS GIVES ME THE SHIVERS FAR WORSE THAN THE COLD.
YOUSE GUYS NEED SOMETHIN'?
OHHH, "YOUSE GUYS," HUH? DON'T TRY ANY OF THOSE VILLAINOUS WORD GAMES ON US! WE'VE COME FOR YOUR BEANS.
OH, YOU BETCHA. HEY, CONNOR, GO GET THESE NICE FOLKS A BUSHEL OF OUR FINEST BEANS.
BE CAREFUL, TITANS, IT COULD BE A TRAP.
BEANS
UNCLE RAY, CAN I GO WATCH THE PRETTY, PRETTY PEGASUS FINALE NOW?
YOU HAVE THE PRETTY, PRETTY PEGASUS FINALE?!
YEAH, WANNA WATCH IT WITH ME?

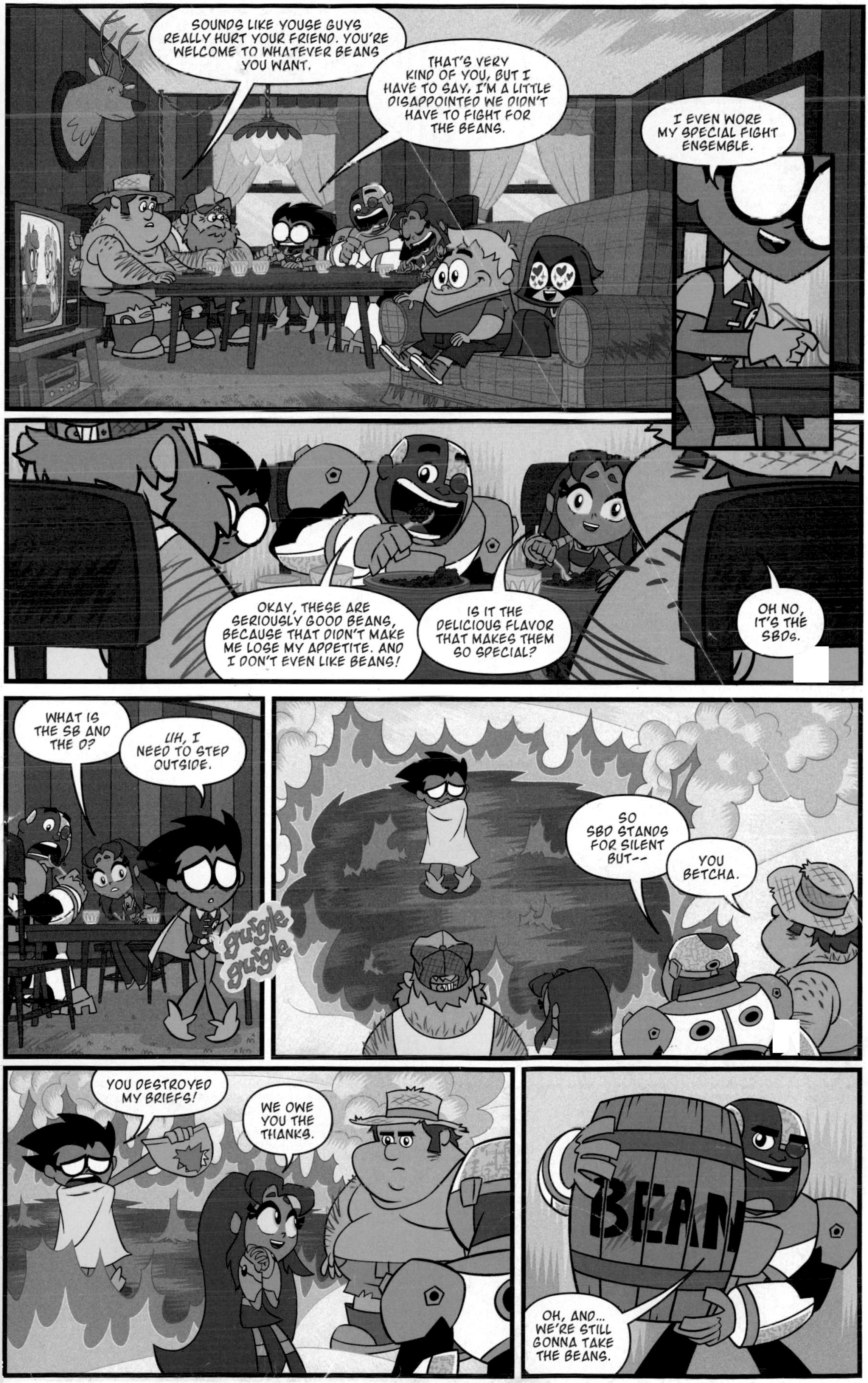
SOUNDS LIKE YOUSE GUYS REALLY HURT YOUR FRIEND. YOU'RE WELCOME TO WHATEVER BEANS YOU WANT.
THAT'S VERY KIND OF YOU, BUT I HAVE TO SAY, I'M A LITTLE DISAPPOINTED WE DIDN'T HAVE TO FIGHT FOR THE BEANS.
I EVEN WORE MY SPECIAL FIGHT ENSEMBLE.
OKAY, THESE ARE SERIOUSLY GOOD BEANS, BECAUSE THAT DIDN'T MAKE ME LOSE MY APPETITE. AND I DON'T EVEN LIKE BEANS!
IS IT THE DELICIOUS FLAVOR THAT MAKES THEM SO SPECIAL?
OH NO, IT'S THE SBDs.
WHAT IS THE SB AND THE D?
UH, I NEED TO STEP OUTSIDE.
gurgle gurgle
SO SBD STANDS FOR SILENT BUT--
YOU BETCHA.
YOU DESTROYED MY BRIEFS!
WE OWE YOU THE THANKS.
BEAN
OH, AND... WE'RE STILL GONNA TAKE THE BEANS.

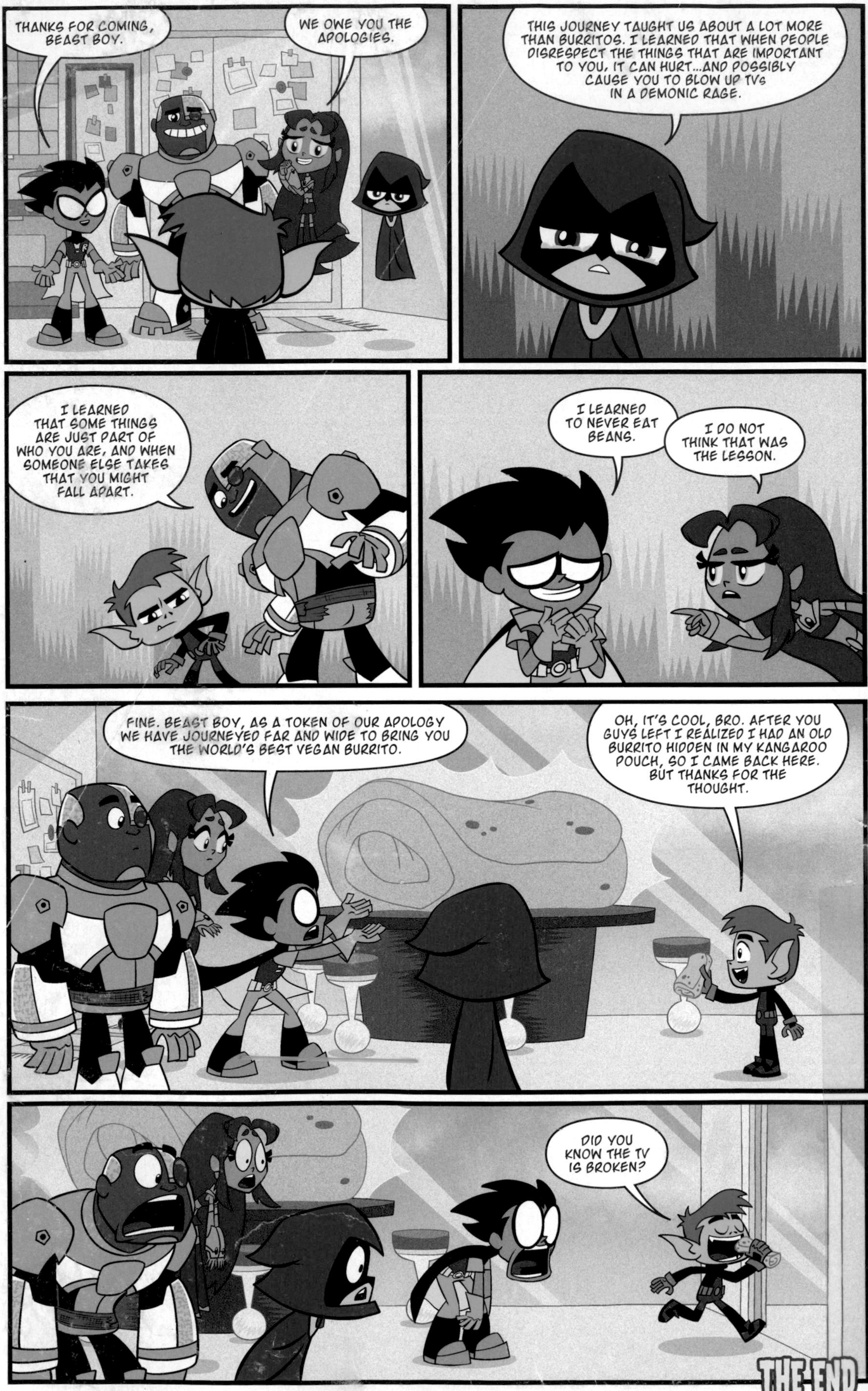
THANKS FOR COMING, BEAST BOY.
WE OWE YOU THE APOLOGIES.
THIS JOURNEY TAUGHT US ABOUT A LOT MORE THAN BURRITOS. I LEARNED THAT WHEN PEOPLE DISRESPECT THE THINGS THAT ARE IMPORTANT TO YOU, IT CAN HURT...AND POSSIBLY CAUSE YOU TO BLOW UP TVs IN A DEMONIC RAGE.
I LEARNED THAT SOME THINGS ARE JUST PART OF WHO YOU ARE, AND WHEN SOMEONE ELSE TAKES THAT YOU MIGHT FALL APART.
I LEARNED TO NEVER EAT BEANS.
I DO NOT THINK THAT WAS THE LESSON.
FINE. BEAST BOY, AS A TOKEN OF OUR APOLOGY WE HAVE JOURNEYED FAR AND WIDE TO BRING YOU THE WORLD'S BEST VEGAN BURRITO.
OH, IT'S COOL, BRO. AFTER YOU GUYS LEFT I REALIZED I HAD AN OLD BURRITO HIDDEN IN MY KANGAROO POUCH, SO I CAME BACK HERE. BUT THANKS FOR THE THOUGHT.
DID YOU KNOW THE TV IS BROKEN?
THE END